To Karen,
With love and admiration —

Mark Heinz

Shine

Mark Heinz

Livingston Press
The University of West Alabama

Copyright © 2009 Mark Heinz
All rights reserved, including electronic text
isbn 13: 978-1-60489-035-8 library binding
isbn 13: 978-1-60489-036-5 trade paper
Library of Congress Control Number 2009931604
Printed on acid-free paper.
Printed in the United States of America,
Publishers Graphics
Hardcover binding by: Heckman Bindery

Typesetting and page layout: Joe Taylor
Cover design and layout: Jennifer Brown
Cover photo of Lake UWA: Jennifer Brown
Cover and inset photo of moonshine still:
Courtesy Bureau of Alcohol, Tobacco, and Firearms (ATF) Archives
and Barbara Osteika
Proofreading: Connie James, Joe Taylor, Johnnie Scott

This is a work of fiction.
Any resemblance
to persons living or dead is coincidental.

Livingston Press is part of The University of West Alabama,
and thereby has non-profit status.
Donations are tax-deductible:
brothers and sisters, we need 'em.

first edition
6 5 4 3 2

Shine

Chance Encounter 1

The old man leant against the railing at the Nolin River Dam and gazed downward at the car-sized roils of water spewing from the spillway. Madly they dashed down the narrow stretch of river, surging and jostling like unruly thoroughbreds fresh out of the starting gate. Occasional sprays of cold water were tossed pell-mell from the maelstrom. The sound of the rampaging water was sufficiently loud to drown out normal speech. Virtually everyone who visited the dam felt compelled to lean against the railing and stare at the raging water below, yet the vast majority lingered but a moment or two. The cold spray and the persistently loud noise made longer viewings unpleasant, and the mere sight of the tumultuous water typically precipitated a sense of vertigo which quickly proceeded to the verge of nausea. Yet the little old man against the railing gazed down at the water for at least several minutes, apparently unbothered by the spray and the sound, and unaffected by the dizzying and mildly nauseating sight of the fast-moving water.

He was quite small, this little old man, just a few inches taller than five feet, and no more than one hundred and thirty pounds. His clothing was abominable, too shabby even for a homeless person, who most probably could and would receive more decent attire at any homeless shelter in the country. His boots were scuffed and worn to a point which prohibited their easy identification; they were in fact of a military type which hadn't been issued since the Vietnam War. Oversized jeans, cuffed at least six inches above his boots and lapped a similar length about his waist, were hopelessly bespattered with mud and motor oil and innumerable unnamable substances, presenting something like an artist's palette of filth and grime. Incredibly, his leather winter jacket was even more heavily soiled and stained; its extreme filthiness gave it the appearance of weightiness, as if its original mass had been doubled or trebled by countless layers of grease and grime and dirt. Atop his head, a bright red cap, embroidered in white with the single word, **MARLBORO**, was the sole article of clothing that didn't beg for multiple washings or incineration. It was, in fact, apparently new and immaculately clean.

Longish wisps of snow-white hair—in sharp contrast with the bright red cap, and a perfect match for the white embroidery—reached an inch or two below the darkly stained collar of his jacket. A snow-white beard wrapped his jawline from his ears to his chin, where it culminated in a slightly twisted point that imparted an elfish or gnomish look to his face. His basic black military-style glasses, like his boots, were relics from a bygone era.

Again, he was too shabby and dirty even for a homeless person. Further, he evinced a marked casualness and familiarity which almost certainly identified him as a member of the local citizenry. He exuded nothing that smacked of shame or self-consciousness. On the contrary, he seemed not only comfortable with himself, but rather at ease and self-confident, if not downright proud.

A fisherman, aiming to try his luck on the other side of the river, trudged up the concrete walkway toward the top of the dam where the old man leant against the railing. He saw at a glance the incredible shabbiness of the little old man, but noticed also his casual and easy demeanor. In no conceivable manner did the old man pose a threat, but the fisherman charted a course wide around him anyway, mainly to respect his privacy, and not disturb the apparent rapture induced by his prolonged gazing at the tempestuous water below. The fisherman passed by the old man at a distance of about eight feet—there was not room at the top of the dam to allow a greater berth—and thought his passage unnoticed, when suddenly and unexpectedly the old man wheeled about to face him.

"Do you think it would kill a man if he fell in there?" the old man asked, indicating the spillway with a slight toss of his head, as he closed the distance between them with a few small quick steps.

The fisherman was taken aback by the abruptness of the question, as well as by the fact that the old man's black military-style glasses contained only one lens. The old man's eyes were turquoise blue and rather soft—not at all threatening. But it was like looking at a cross-eyed person and trying to determine which eye should be engaged. The fisherman looked first at the naked eye, then at the one behind the lens, back and forth, unable to decide which should gain his favor. His confusion was complicated by the din of the roiling water; he wasn't sure if he'd heard correctly the old man's question.

"What?" asked the fisherman, repeatedly searching one blue eye, and then another.

"Do you think it would kill a man if he fell in there?" the old man repeated, practically shouting to make himself heard.

The fisherman's scrutiny settled on the old man's naked eye and found there a simple straightforwardness he felt obliged to reciprocate. He stepped somewhat past the old man and peered over the railing. As always, it made him immediately dizzy and nearly nauseous. But he forced his eyes up and down the churning river, and surveyed the scene with a determined objectivity that bordered on the scientific.

Returning to the old man's side, he shouted through the wisps of snow-white hair, directly into his ear, "If you survived the first forty or fifty feet, and it washed you downriver where it's not so rough, I think you could survive it."

A beautiful, almost womanly smile spread across the old man's face, as he nodded his head and stated emphatically, "Yeah, that's right. That's what I think, too."

Not only was the old man's smile infectious, the immediate and wholehearted agreement engendered at once a simpatico and camaraderie between the two. The fisherman returned the old man's smile. But of course the two men could not stand there on the dam structure above the spillway and smile at each other all day. The fisherman nodded curtly at the old man, as if to say 'nice to make your acquaintance,' then started again his journey around the top of the dam structure to the far side of the river.

"What are you trying to catch?" the old man asked loudly before the fisherman had quite turned away.

"Anything that bites," the fisherman replied. "Crappie mostly, I guess."

"Are you catching any?" the old man asked.

"No, not today. I haven't had a bite."

Indeed, the fisherman had fished for more than an hour on the near side of the river without as much as a nibble. He honestly didn't expect any better results on the other side of the river. But it was Sunday afternoon, and a fairly fine day for December, and he had felt an irresistible urge to escape from his wife and kids for a few hours, fish or no fish.

"You could probably catch some crappie and maybe a few bass in my lake if you wanted," the old man declared.

"Really?" the fisherman asked. Optimism engulfed him in a great heartwarming embrace. He knew there were private lakes thereabouts absolutely loaded with fish. Most property owners guarded them fiercely, allowing access only to a few friends and family members. But this seemed a fair and friendly invitation. "Where's your lake at?"

"Not far—about five miles from here," the old man said. "I'm fixin' to leave pretty soon. You can follow me home if you want."

"Sure, that'd be great—thanks," the fisherman replied warmly, scarcely able to believe his good fortune. A sudden inclination prompted him to formalize the meeting, mainly to secure and finalize the invitation.

"My name is Joe Bass," the fisherman announced. He stooped a bit to place his tackle box on the walkway, and offered his right hand.

"Joe Bass," echoed the old man, as he gripped the extended hand in his tough leathery mitt. "That's a good name for a fisherman, ain't it?"

"Yeah, that's what they tell me."

"I'm Edgar J. Johnson," the old man stated very importantly, as if announcing a visiting dignitary to the royal court. "You've heard of J. Edgar Hoover? Well, I'm Edgar J. Johnson."

"It's good to meet you, Mister Johnson."

"Just call me Edgar," the old man said.

Abruptly the introductions were concluded as the old man turned and headed down the concrete walkway toward the parking lot. Joe Bass the fisherman picked up his tackle box and followed anxiously. Initially he had hoped for little more than a few hours of fresh air and the chance to stretch his legs a bit; fishing in the river had been off for the past few weeks. But now he believed there was a very good chance he would catch some fish that afternoon, and he was eager to get started.

Edgar walked straightway across the parking lot to a rusty old wreck of a car occupied by two men. They appeared to be about Edgar's age, but not quite as shabby. The old man in the driver's seat rolled down his window and greeted Edgar by name. Edgar propped an arm against the roof of the car and assumed a position that looked fairly comfortable and indefinitely maintainable.

Joe halted about fifteen feet from the parked car and chatting men. At first he thought Edgar might call him over and make introductions, but nothing of the sort occurred. Edgar and the men in the car ignored Joe entirely as their voices droned on and on, softly and slowly and unhurriedly, yet somehow rife with an unassuming importance and an understated dignity. After ten or twelve minutes, Joe claimed an out-of-the-way spot nearby and sat down his gear. Another ten or twelve minutes dragged by; Joe found a tree stump and sat himself down.

Half an hour passed, and still there was nothing in Edgar's voice or posture to indicate an end to his conversation. Joe stood up, grabbed his fishing tackle, and mentally composed a farewell to his newly made acquaintance: *It was nice to meet you but it's getting late and I need to go home.*

At that moment the rusty old wreck of a car fired its engine, Edgar removed his hand from the roof, the driver's window went up, and the car slowly drove away. Edgar waved goodbye to the vehicle's rear end. Joe walked over to join him.

The unexpected delay had diminished considerably Joe's desire to fish at old Edgar's lake. He had half a mind to deliver the little 'nice to meet you but' farewell speech so recently prepared, while the other half still wanted to catch some fish. Joe rather expected Edgar to apologize for his dalliance, and usher him off toward his lake without further postponement. Joe stepped up close to Edgar and looked at him anxiously, waiting for the apology and quick departure.

"I'm gettin' three hundred thousand dollars in a day or two," old Edgar stated suddenly and importantly. "They're mailin' me a check."

The sudden and rather implausible declaration wasn't what Joe had expected to hear. Old Edgar looked like he hadn't seen three hundred dollars in one lump sum in his entire life. Three hundred thousand dollars? What? Who was mailing him a check? Had he and the man in the car just finalized a real estate deal or some other business transaction? No, that didn't seem right; the guy in the car looked as if he too had never seen three hundred dollars in his entire life. Joe was virtually speechless with incredulity, but managed at last to say, "Oh really?"

"Yeah, I was just tellin' my friends about it. I got a letter in the mail today. I was in the military for fourteen years. Were you ever in the military?"

"Yes, I was in the Army for three years."

"Well, I was in the military for *fourteen* years," Edgar repeated, assuming a tone of unmistakable superiority. "For fourteen years they took a little bit out of my paycheck every month and put it in a special savings account. When I got out o' the Army, that was way back in nineteen-sixty, they said they couldn't find my account, said they had a little mix-up with my social security number, so I didn't get my money."

Old Edgar paused in his story and eyeballed Joe Bass. The warmth and sweetness Edgar had displayed above the spillway had vanished entirely, replaced by what sounded like arrogance, braggadocio and mischievousness. Edgar's previously soft blue eyes now glinted like cheap glass jewelry, appearing both hard and false.

Joe had been a company clerk in the Army for three years and never had heard of an Army savings-account program. It was possible, but highly improbable, that such a program existed prior to Joe's enlistment. Further, Edgar neither looked nor acted like a man on the verge of receiving a relative fortune. Rather, he looked like a man determined to tell a lie; for what reason or reasons, Joe Bass couldn't even begin to guess.

"Yep, the Army sent me a letter," the old man persisted. "I got it today. That money in my bank account, they finally found it, and it's been earning interest since nineteen-sixty. How many years is that?"

The math was simple enough, but Joe Bass was loath to answer. He believed old Edgar was spinning a yarn, and he definitely did *not* want to get tangled up in it. What in the hell was going on here, anyway? He experienced a brief moment of the fantastic that bordered on the surreal. His mind reeled; he felt slightly dizzy, as if staring down at the water roiling from the spillway.

Old Edgar continued to stare stubbornly at Joe Bass. He wanted an answer, by God, and he would not be denied.

Joe Bass finally answered him. "That's forty-seven years, I guess."

Edgar smiled, and nodded approvingly. "That's right, forty-eight years. Forty-seven my money's been earning interest in that savings account, and now they finally found it. Can you imagine that? Forty-seven years... It comes to right at three hundred thousand dollars. It might even be a little bit more by now—I'm not sure when they mailed me that letter. But I'll be gettin' at least three hundred thousand."

Joe could no longer respond with any degree of sincerity. This raggedy old man, he figured, was at the very least delusional, if not downright crazy. "That's great," Joe stated falsely, determined to humor the old fool. "I'm glad to hear it. Good for you. I'm really happy for you. Three hundred thousand dollars, wow! That's a whole lot of money.

Good for you!"

Old Edgar's eyes suddenly softened, and his smile widened—a beautiful, almost womanly smile. He stepped very close to Joe Bass and peered at him intently with his naked eye, his head cocked slightly to one side, like a robin listening for a worm. "Three hundred thousand dollars *really is* a lot o' money, ain't it?" he asked conspiratorially, as if the two finally might share one true thing.

"Yeah, sure it is," Joe replied at once.

"Come on," said Edgar. "Follow me down to my place and let's see if you can catch some fish."

Edgar's Place   2

Edgar's car was every bit as battered, tattered and ratty as Edgar's clothing. A Pontiac sedan, about twenty years old, practically each and every body part—hood, grille, fenders, bumpers—displayed minor or major damage. A few of its old and rusty wounds had been treated with various colors of spray paint, creating a blotchy appearance that made the car look not just seriously injured, but also diseased. Its original tone had been an indeterminate shade of grey, faded now by a few decades of sunlight to the color of oblivion and nothingness. A thin but pervasive stream of oily black smoke dribbled out its tailpipe as it puttered down the road.

Joe tailed the ratty old sedan in his big red Ford truck, careful not to crowd or rush the old man, and equally careful not to lose sight of him. Mainly Joe's thoughts dwelt in the immediate future; if old Edgar's lake proved just half as fruitful as he hoped, he'd catch a good mess of fish and still make it home in time for supper. On Sundays they always went to his in-laws' house for supper; his wife had reminded him not to be late as he'd rushed out the door to go fishing. He glanced at his watch, 2:25, and noticed also the day: SUN.

Of course, it was *Sunday*. Edgar had said he'd received his letter concerning the newly discovered bank account "today," but today was Sunday, and the mail wasn't delivered on Sunday. No doubt remained; the old man had lied about the long-lost bank account and the imminent arrival of three hundred thousand dollars.

Joe figured it was probably a harmless lie; a lot of the old-timers thereabouts "told stories," as the euphemism went, as if lying was a sort of recreational pastime, or sport. All the little country stores, the barbershops, the lumberyards, the auto repair shops—any and all public places thereabouts—were likely to contain at any given time at least a few elderly and not-so elderly loiterers who whiled away countless hours telling tales, or stories, and pulling each other's legs. It was a time-honored and traditional type of entertainment that could be perceived as

Kentucky folk art.

However, Edgar's tale had not been told in a public place to a crowd of cronies accustomed to such licentiousness. Further, its content, tone and delivery were all inconsistent with the unwritten rules and traditions which unofficially governed the public telling of tales. Edgar had been both out-of-line and out-of-place, like a suited and helmeted football player tackling an unsuited and unsuspecting bystander in a church parking lot.

Again, Joe figured it was probably a harmless lie. But extreme poverty, he knew, had nudged more than a few of the local citizenry into various types of criminal chicanery. (Insurance scams were the most popular. A crummy old trailer, or crummy old house, and its contents would be insured for at least twice their actual value, and an accomplice would torch the place while the owner was many miles distant from both flames and formal accusations. Similarly, faked storm damage and staged automobile accidents were not uncommon.) Old Edgar hadn't struck Joe as a bad or immoral person; and the old man seemed far too stupid and unsophisticated to even attempt any type of scam or fraud. Still, Joe determined to be on his guard. He certainly wasn't going to loan Edgar any money in advance of his fictitious three hundred thousand dollars. Perhaps, if he got the chance, he'd ask Edgar how he had managed to receive a letter in the mail on Sunday.

Edgar and his funky old car signaled and then turned left off the state highway onto a narrow and twisting country road. Not far behind, Joe prudently noted the road sign: SYCAMORE CHURCH ROAD. About a mile farther on, Edgar again signaled left.

Looking to the left, Joe's heart leapt in his chest as he first caught sight of Edgar's lake. It was not at all a pond, but every bit a lake, at least seven or eight acres. The afternoon sun was mirrored in myriads of small ripples roused by a gentle westerly breeze. It was a beautiful sight, more radiant and alluring than any neon sign. Of course Joe had no real way of knowing what lurked beneath its glittering surface. Call it faith, or optimism, or wishful thinking; or call it stupidity, or irrationality, or presumptuousness: Joe did not merely believe the lake contained a reasonable number of fish. Rather, he was absolutely certain this was the fishing find of a lifetime—the El Dorado, Bali Hai, and Shangri-La of all fishing lakes—now just a matter of moments and yards away.

Joe hated to tear his eyes away from the beautiful sparkling lake, but he did so as he followed Edgar leftward off the narrow country road and onto a nearly indiscernible drive, but vaguely defined by two parallel rutted and potholed ribbons of dirt barely visible beneath a sea of knee-high broom grass.

Up ahead, Edgar's old mess of a car slowed to a stop and was immediately mobbed by a seething, snarling pack of dogs—at least five or six largish brutes of mixed ancestry that materialized as if by magic out of the thick broom grass. Edgar got out of his car, apparently unbothered by the dogs as they yelped and snapped and jumped, sometimes as high as his head, frenetically about him. Edgar spoke loudly to the dogs, and motioned sternly with his hands, and managed to settle them down somewhat.

Then the dogs took first notice of the new arrival, and rushed with renewed frenzy to mob Joe's big red truck. Occasionally one of the wild hounds leapt as high as Joe's window, and stared malevolently at him at eye level, at which time Joe was mighty glad his windows were up. No way would Joe emerge from the safety of his truck into that crazy pack of dogs; perhaps he wouldn't catch any fish today after all.

Calmly, unhurriedly, as if the dog pack's antics were in no way unusual or alarming, Edgar sauntered over to Joe's truck and again used a loud voice and stern motions to quiet the beasts. Still, Joe did not exit the safety of his truck until Edgar twice told him it was okay; the dogs wouldn't hurt him.

Joe put on a brave face and stepped out into the rollicking dog pack. In a few short moments the beasts had finished sniffing him from top to bottom, and finding nothing of special interest, they shortly abandoned him and returned to their presumed master, Edgar. Joe noticed the dogs seemed mainly hungry—as if they were fed irregularly, or never—and not particularly mean or vicious, as they gave Edgar a second going-over. Having satisfied themselves that neither of the men possessed any edibles, four of the beasts slunk off into the broom grass from whence they came. The remaining two stayed close by, seemingly more patient or determined, as Joe grabbed from the back of his truck his tackle box, cooler, and two fishing poles.

Edgar stalked off through the broom grass along a faint trail with the two hounds close behind, and Joe behind the dogs. They passed a rusted old camper, about ten feet long, its side profile egg-shaped, that Joe assumed to be abandoned, along with a similarly rusted refrigerator and chest-type freezer. They crossed the lake's overflow atop a small wooden bridge, about three feet wide, and cobbled together from a motley assortment of scrap lumber—two-by-fours, two-by-sixes, all the way up to two-by-twelves. Despite its rather random and haphazard components, Joe noted it seemed very sturdy. He also noted a small but appreciable rivulet of water streaming out through the overflow.

They crossed the wooden bridge onto the broad crest of the earthen dam structure, about twenty feet in width, and utterly devoid of vegetation. One side dropped off precipitously about eight feet to the water's surface. The other side dropped off just as steeply about a hundred feet to the bottom of a ravine where the overflow's rivulet assumed the character of a little creek. From atop the dam structure Joe could see every square foot of the lake and conjecture its original construction: L-shaped, both axes had been deep ravines, or gullies, that converged into a deeper and wider ravine which formed the main body of the lake.

"How old is this lake?" Joe called up to his host.

"About thirty years."

"How deep is it?"

"It's deepest here at the dam," Edgar called back over his shoulder. "It's every bit of fifty feet."

"Wow," said Joe. "I wonder why they made it so deep?" Most of the small lakes thereabouts were around eight feet deep—ten at the most.

"I didn't want me no little cow pond. I wanted me a *lake*," Edgar stated firmly, with no small pride.

"Did you build this lake?" Joe asked incredulously. It seemed a very large task for such a tiny man.

"Yep—I bought me a bulldozer and dug it myself. Took me two years... I wore out four sets of sprockets."

"That's amazing," Joe said with unfeigned admiration. "I noticed there was water in the overflow. Is it spring-fed?"

"Three of 'em. The biggest one was over there towards my camper; that one never ran dry. And sweet? That was the sweetest water in the county. I used to have my log cabin over there where that little camper is now. There's a little creek that feeds it too."

"I'm guessing this lake is... what? Seven or eight acres, maybe?"

"It's every bit of eight," Edgar confirmed.

"How much property do you have here altogether?" Joe asked.

Edgar stopped suddenly, and presented Joe with a surly and

unfriendly expression. Finally, he replied, "Fourteen acres... now." His tone of voice seriously discouraged further inquiries.

They stopped a little more than halfway down the axis of the L farthest from the road. Directly across the lake, up on a hill, a gray trailer squatted some fifty or sixty feet above the men's positions. Joe decided to risk yet one more question; it seemed perfectly harmless. "Is that your trailer up there?"

"No," said Edgar. "That belongs to my daughter, Bobbie. Now, if you want to fish, this here is as good a spot as any."

"Looks good to me," said Joe, as he set down his cooler, tackle box, and spare pole. Before casting his lure, he presented it to Edgar for approval. "This jig works good down at the river. Do you think the fish here will bite it?"

Edgar shrugged dismissively. "They're usually not too picky. Just give it a toss."

The jig arched more than half the distance to the far bank. Joe allowed a few seconds for it to sink a few feet, then began a slow and steady retrieve. Immediately the lure snagged into something heavy; Joe thought it a stump or other underwater obstruction until it veered off sharply toward the dam.

"Damn," Joe muttered under his breath. "First cast." He fought the fish silently and grimly for about five minutes. When he was satisfied the fish was played out, he heaved it up on shore—a fat, healthy three-pound largemouth bass.

At once the two dogs leapt upon the fish, growling, snarling, ravenously hungry and unwilling to share the finny feast one with the other. Joe was loath to pull the fish away lest the hook in the fish somehow become impaled in one of the dogs. With equal speed and ferocity, Edgar leapt upon the hungry hounds, grabbed both by the scruffs of their necks, and hurled them forcibly some eight or ten feet away from Joe's big bass.

"Tony, Blue, you stay back now," Edgar admonished the dogs as they angled in for another attack. To Joe he said, "If you want to keep that fish, you need to put it away quick."

Joe quickly unhooked the bass, tossed it into his cooler, and locked the handle across the cooler's lid. Edgar turned away from the dogs; immediately they rushed and inspected the cooler for any sign of weakness or ingress. Finding none, they licked the slaver from their jowls, squatted on their haunches, and waited for a fresh opportunity.

Joe's next few casts were fruitless, but soon he hooked up with another fish. He determined by the feel of it—its power seemed less than its weight—that it was most likely a crappie, and it was. As he prepared to heave it out of the lake, Edgar preemptively restrained the two dogs. Joe quickly unhooked the crappie and secured it in the cooler. The dogs no longer seemed the least bit threatening or vicious; rather, they seemed pitiable and pathetic in their hunger.

"I could give your dogs a fish to eat, if you want," Joe generously offered.

"No, no—don't do that. You could never fish here again without these dogs a-worryin' you to death. Don't you ever feed them anything, ya hear?"

"Okay," said Joe, as he resumed fishing.

A few casts later he connected with another largemouth bass, a bit smaller than the first, but still a respectable fish. Edgar kept an eye on the dogs but did not restrain them. The dogs eyed Joe's bass hungrily for a brief moment, then wheeled about and headed back down the trail.

Noses to the ground, eyes and ears alert, they zigzagged back and forth, hoping to pick up a scent or flush an animal from hiding—the hounds were in full hunting mode.

Better Acquainted   3

The afternoon temperature peaked in the mid-forties, and for a while the sun packed a radiant punch. The gentle westerly breeze died away to an occasional wistful sigh. Birdsong of cardinals and catbirds celebrated the mild and pleasant weather.

With the dogs gone, and the fish biting, and the birds singing, and the sun shining warmly, Joe Bass felt relaxed and elated and eminently satisfied. It was as if he'd waited two hours for a table at a fine restaurant, and yet another hour for his food to be served, and then finally enjoyed the very best meal of his entire life, indescribably delectable, well worth the wait. Every worry-line and wrinkle vanished from his face. Unconsciously he smiled a little smile of sublime pleasure as the fish kept coming, mostly crappie but an occasional bass, one after the other, on average every fifth or sixth cast, or five or six minutes.

Old Edgar sat himself down on a soft green tuft of moss, stuffed a chaw of tobacco into his maw, took off his cap, and scratched slowly, languorously at the bald top of his head. He didn't look as if he was scratching an itch; rather, he looked as if he enjoyed the feel of his gnarly old fingernails caressing his hairless pate. After three or four minutes of this simple self-indulgence, he replaced his cap, stretched his legs, and braced his arms behind him.

"That letter you said you got from the Army," Joe began. "The one about the three hundred thousand dollars… When did you say you got that letter?"

Joe's tone was neither inquisitional nor antagonistic. He simply wanted to clear up that small matter at the onset of what he hoped to be a very long relationship with Edgar, and more importantly, with Edgar's lake. Joe truly did not care if Edgar was a liar or not, as long as he granted him fishing privileges.

"Oh, I don't know," Edgar said dismissively. "It's been maybe a day or two I reckon." His voice trailed off into nothingness as if this was not a topic of conversation he wished to pursue.

Joe prudently dropped the matter, and changed the subject. "This sure is a beautiful lake you've got here."

"It is, ain't it?" Edgar agreed brightly, smiling.

"You said you dug it with a bulldozer. Is that what you did for a living?—heavy equipment operator?"

"No, not really. A little bit, on and off, you might say. Mostly I farmed. I used to have two hundred and twenty acres here."

"Really? What happened to it?"

Edgar spat tobacco juice as if this, too, was not a tasteful and suitable topic of conversation. He answered in a flat voice, insincere and somewhat spiteful. "I leased most of it out to a man who was supposed to raise a big tobacco crop. He had me sign some kind o' papers on the lease. Then he got real sick with sugar and died, and the people at the courthouse gave most o' my place to his family."

Edgar's explanation didn't make a lot of sense to Joe. He knew many old country people colloquially referred to diabetes as "sugar." But he couldn't begin to fathom how Edgar signing a tobacco lease could have resulted in the loss of most of his property. Edgar seemed like a man who had a lot to say, and an equally large amount to hide.

Joe caught another big fat crappie that distracted him from the issue of Edgar's lost real estate. In fact, Joe's main focus was on fishing, and not on Edgar's revelations. Conversation with Edgar was a secondary consideration, and mainly for the sake of politeness. Edgar was nice enough to let Joe catch a mess of fish from his lake. Joe reckoned he owed the old man, at the very least, some polite and friendly conversation.

"You still got your bulldozer?" Joe asked, as he tossed the crappie in his cooler.

"Nope—the feds took it."

"The feds?"

"Feds, revenuers—they claimed I used it to haul lumber out o' my woods to fire my still. They showed pictures in court of my bulldozer's tracks goin' in and out o' my woods, so they confiscated it. The bastards told me I could bid on it when it went up for auction, and there I was in prison without a dollar to my name."

"You were in prison?" Joe asked cautiously.

Joe thought it a dark and dangerous avenue to explore. But Edgar's response was unworried and unabashed; evidently he didn't mind talking about his time behind bars.

"I served a year in Marion for makin' moonshine. It's a federal crime so they put me in a federal pen. One o' my neighbors here turned me in for a reward. The feds showed up just that quick, and I had me a batch cookin' right over there in those trees, so there wasn't a whole lot I could say about it."

"You used to make moonshine?" asked Joe, bemused.

"Let me tell you what—I didn't just make moonshine. I made the best damn moonshine in the whole state of Kentucky. It was just like this here lake—when I set out to do somethin', I do it *right*, by God. I make it the very best I can make it. You can ask anybody about my shine. It wasn't just good. It was the best damn shine in the state."

Joe hooked another fine crappie. Again, his main focus was on fishing; he was listening to Edgar with one ear only, paying just enough attention to ask an occasional question, thereby keeping up his end of the conversation. Still, the very idea of old Edgar making moonshine, and serving time for it, registered with Joe more deeply than anything else the old man had said thus far. Joe thought it rather quaint and romantic.

"Where did you learn how to make moonshine?" Joe asked, as he tossed the crappie into his cooler.

"I learned right here on the farm. My dad and my granddad taught me. I started helpin' 'em make it, and I had my first drink o' shine, when I was maybe three or four years old."

"You drank moonshine when you were three?"

"Three or four, I can't remember for sure, but I wasn't no more than four. I drank it out of a two-quart Mason jar—I remember that real clear."

"Did your dad and granddad sell a lot of moonshine?"

"No, they didn't sell much at all. Sometimes they might give a pint or two to a neighbor or a friend, but mostly they made it for themselves. Ya see, things were a lot different back then. That road out there wasn't nothin' but dirt—mud, most o' the time. The state highway we came in on was gravel; they didn't pave that over till after World War Two. The closest electricity was ten miles away in Brownsville. There weren't any stores; well, there was one little bitty store up on the highway, but nobody had any money to buy anything. People had to make do on their own. We raised cows and hogs and chickens for meat, and we got our vegetables from the garden or the root cellar. When we wanted a drink o' whiskey, we made our own, and it was the best damn shine in the whole state of Kentucky."

"That was corn whiskey you made?" asked Joe.

"No, no," Edgar countered rather contemptuously. "It takes hundreds of gallons of corn squeezin's to make corn whiskey. We made our whiskey from mash. What made it so good was that we always doubled it down. That way it comes out smooth and clear. A lot o' people think they know how to make whiskey, but there wasn't nobody who made it as good as we did. You ever drink any moonshine?"

"No, I never did," Joe admitted. "But you make it sound awfully good. What exactly did you put in it?"

"Sugar, corn meal, yeast, and water—that's what makes your beer," Edgar replied authoritatively, professorially, as if he were supremely knowledgeable on the matter. "Then you cook your beer to make your whiskey."

Joe Bass was intrigued. Moonshine and moonshiners had been previously the stuff of legends, of Kentucky folklore, and not part of the real world as he knew it. Joe continued to focus mainly on his fishing, but gradually, increasingly his attention shifted away from the ceaseless procession of fish he relocated from the lake to his cooler, and towards old Edgar and his moonshine.

"Let's say I wanted to make some moonshine…" Joe prompted.

"Sounds good," Edgar interjected enthusiastically. "Let's make us a batch one o' these days. We can make it out at your place if your neighbors ain't too nosey."

"I don't know about that," Joe demurred. "But let's just say we were gonna make some. What would we need to get started?"

"A fifty-five-gallon drum is good for makin' the beer. Fifty pounds of sugar. Fifty pounds of corn meal—it can't have no salt in it; salt won't let it work right. About thirty gallons of spring water, or this here lake water would be good—city water ain't no good 'cause of all the chemicals in it. A cake o' yeast to get it started. It takes about three or four days to make your beer, dependin' on the weather. You don't want it to be too hot or too cold when you go to make your beer. Once the yeast gets to workin' the beer gets all churned up like it's a-boilin'. When it settles down and stops churnin', that's when your beer's done. It ain't good to let your beer sit around too long. Beer can go sour, especially if it's hot, so you want to cook it right away. You can't cook it too fast or too slow, and we always doubled it down. That way it was always smooth and clear."

"You said you always 'doubled it down.' What does that mean?" asked Joe.

"You run it through twice. The first time you run it through it comes out cloudy and rough; that's what you call singlings."

"What do you call it?" asked Joe, unfamiliar with the word.

"Singlings," Edgar repeated. "A lot of people call that whiskey and that's what they drink. But we always doubled it down to make it smooth and clear."

"You distilled it twice, then" said Joe.

"I reckon you could say that," said Edgar. "You ever drink any whiskey? Or are you a beer drinker?"

"I don't really drink much these days. I used to drink some when I was in the Army, and I drank some when I was in college. But nowadays I don't drink much at all."

"Why not? What's the matter with ya? When I was your age I was runnin' flat out and wide open. Are you sick or somethin'?"

Joe chuckled out loud. "No, I'm not sick. I don't know. I drank fairly often when I was in college, but after I met my wife, well, I don't know. It just wasn't something I cared about anymore."

"Your wife won't let you drink," Edgar stated rather accusingly.

"No, that's not exactly right. It's just that—"

"When I was married I always did whatever I wanted, and my wife was the happiest woman in the world. I used to make her fried chicken on Sunday mornings, and then we'd lay around in bed and kiss for hours. I was a damn good kisser. My wife was a happy woman, I'll tell you what."

"That sounds nice," Joe stated sincerely. Something hard and testy had crept into Edgar's voice and demeanor, something Joe wanted to allay if possible. "I bet your wife was a lovely person."

"You're not from around here, are you?" Edgar asked abruptly.

Now Joe truly was concerned. He'd heard that question at least a hundred times since he'd moved from Louisville to the country, and it was never asked out of idle curiosity. Always it was an accusation; the crime, Joe was not native to the region. Rather, he was an outsider, an interloper, an intruder.

"No, I'm from Louisville," Joe admitted rather wearily. And then, offering some small defense of his right to exist outside of his hometown,

"My wife is from here."

"What's her name?" Edgar asked sharply.

"Her maiden name was Logsdon."

"They's lots of Logsdons around here. What's her daddy's name?"

"Jasper—Jasper Logsdon, from Peonia. Do you know him?"

Edgar's face contorted horribly as he extricated from his mouth the chaw of tobacco he'd totally worn out. "Yeah, I know him. I know his wife, too. Gladys, ain't it? Used to be Gladys Saltsman as I recall." Edgar's voice was mainly neutral. If it denoted anything at all, it suggested he wasn't overly fond of Joe's in-laws. Further commentary was not forthcoming.

Joe was not at all surprised that Edgar knew his parents-in-law. It seemed that all the locals over fifty years old knew each other, or at least, knew of each other.

Joe tossed yet another fine crappie into his cooler, and noticed it was more than half full. He had lost count a few dozen fish ago, but reckoned he had close to thirty fish. Hefting the cooler with his right hand he guesstimated its weight at thirty pounds or more. He was looking at about twelve pounds of fillets—four big fish fries for his family of four. It was truly a fine mess of fish.

The sun had dropped low in the sky; once again the air felt chilly, almost cold. For the first time since arriving at Edgar's place, Joe looked at his watch. It displayed 4:55, exactly the time when he and his wife and kids usually left to eat supper at his in-laws' house. Definitely, it was time to leave, past time to leave. Perhaps he'd worn out his welcome already; maybe that's why Edgar had become rather testy.

Joe divided his attention between gathering his gear, and Edgar. "Mister Johnson, I really appreciate you letting me fish here in your lake, but I gotta be going now. It really is a beautiful lake, and to tell you the God's honest truth, it's the finest fishing lake I've ever seen in my life. I've had a wonderful time here this afternoon. Thank you."

"Call me Edgar," the old man corrected in a much softer voice, apparently touched by Joe's sincere gratitude. "I don't have a lot to show for my time here on earth. This here lake is about all I got left, and I'm glad to share it with you. Here, let me carry that for you."

Edgar carried Joe's tackle box. Joe had his hands full with his fishing poles and cooler heavy with fish. They walked across the earthen dam structure, and crossed back over the little wooden bridge that spanned the spillway. When they came alongside the little egg-shaped camper, Edgar paused and stated importantly, "This is where my log cabin used to be, but all I got now is this little camper."

Already late for supper, Joe was ready to leave. But he felt obliged to stop and respond to old Edgar's comments.

"What kind of log cabin was it? Did you build it yourself or…?"

"Sure I built it myself. It was twenty feet by forty, made out o' white oak logs. I picked out every tree from my woods, picked 'em out special so they'd fit just right. I worked 'em mostly with hand tools."

"That's impressive. You raised your own meat and vegetables, made your own whiskey, built your own log cabin… You were very self-sufficient, weren't you?"

"Had to be. Back in those days you had to know how to make do on your own. Nowadays people pay money for everything they need, but when I was growin' up nobody had any money to speak of, and there weren't any stores to speak of neither. We had to make do on our own."

"What happened to your log cabin?" asked Joe.

"It burnt down. Don't know what caused it. It just burnt down one night. Damn shame, too. That was a mighty fine cabin."

"That's too bad," Joe commiserated. Then, on a more upbeat note, "That's a cute little camper. Do you ever go camping with it?"

"That's where I sleep at night," Edgar replied. "I bought it from a friend of mine after my cabin burnt down. It's okay. I wish I had me some electricity run to it, but I ain't too worried about that. One of these days I'm gonna build me another log cabin right here where the old one was. Maybe you can help. Would you help me build a new cabin?" The eye behind the one remaining glass lens searched Joe's face imploringly.

"Sure I would," Joe replied at once. "I don't know much about log cabins but I'd be glad to help any way I can."

Edgar lit up like a Christmas tree. "Good!" he exclaimed heartily. "We'll build her just like the old one, twenty by forty, out o' white oak logs. And after we get 'er all built, we'll cook us up a batch o' shine to celebrate!"

Joe smiled warmly, beamed warmth and good cheer at the old man.

"You bet we will. Sounds like a plan. But I really gotta be going now."

"You come back anytime now, ya hear? You're always welcome here at my place. If I ain't around you just make yourself at home. You're always welcome."

"Oh, I'll be back for sure. Thanks again, Edgar. It really is a wonderful place you got here."

"It is, ain't it?" Edgar replied simply and soberly.

Before Joe could reply, Edgar turned about-face and marched off through the tall broom grass, back toward his beautiful sparkling lake.

Joe Bass   4

Unlike Edgar, Joe Bass was not native to south-central Kentucky, nor was he a "country" person. Joe had been born and raised about ninety miles from the Nolin River Dam in Louisville, Kentucky. The exact year of his birth was 1964: A 22-year-old black man from Louisville named Cassius Clay, soon to become Muhammad Ali, defeated Sonny Liston to become the one and only heavyweight boxing champion of the world. A colt named *Northern Dancer* won the Kentucky Derby and the Preakness, but failed to capture the "triple crown" at the Belmont Stakes. And Joseph Thomas Bass, seven pounds-three ounces, twenty-one inches long, was born in Baptist East Hospital on June 1st to William and Irene Bass.

Joe grew up in a burg, or area, of Louisville named Lyndon, in a marginally middle-class neighborhood. His dad worked on the assembly line at the Ford truck plant. His mom was mainly a housewife; however, her constant involvement with, and unflagging service to, the Catholic Church earned her the facetious title of "plainclothes nun." Joe's dad coined the epithet, and applied it quite liberally, complaining that his wife should find a way to have herself placed on the church's payroll. But she never did.

Joe was the eldest of four children. His junior siblings were all girls. Having no desire to play Barbie, or to engage in other girlish activities with his sisters—and the girls were not at all inclined towards sports or boyish pastimes—Joe spent most of his time roaming the neighborhood streets and sidewalks with his pals.

Joe managed to stay out of trouble for the most part. Occasionally he found himself rather bitterly embroiled with male adversaries, or rivals, at high school. And occasionally adolescent romances became complicated and unmanageable and hurtful. None of these rivalries or romances was very remarkable, though. Truth be told, there was little, if anything, truly remarkable about Joe Bass. For the most part Joe was, well, an "ordinary Joe." At school he earned mostly mediocre grades of

Bs and Cs, and an occasional A. For the most part he was fairly well-liked by his teachers and his peers, but not at all considered popular. He stood five feet and ten inches tall—the precise median for adult American males. He was of medium build, neither heavy nor slim, with light brown hair and dark brown eyes. Most girls at school considered him cute enough to go out with, but his looks were in no way striking or distinguished.

However, his acutely, nearly preternaturally, normal and unremarkable sojourn through high school was rudely interrupted by an incident that occurred near the conclusion of his senior year, and graduation: Joe had ducked into the restroom to take a pee between afternoon classes, when a tremendous, ear-shattering explosion blew to pieces a porcelain commode near the rear of the facility. Not knowing exactly what had happened, Joe dashed headlong from the restroom straightway into the vice-principal, who assumed Joe was responsible, and grasped and forcibly restrained him. Meanwhile a second lad, the guy who had tossed an M-80 fireworks explosive into the toilet, slipped quietly away from the scene.

Despite Joe's vigorous and repeated denials of culpability, he was suspended from school for a week. Once the hubbub had died down, the vice-principal admitted he had seen a second boy exit the restroom. When questioned, the boy's declarations of noninvolvement seemed dubious at best, but school officials had not one scrap of evidence against him, so the true culprit got off scot-free. Eventually school authorities softened their stance on the issue and informally and unofficially allowed some possibility of Joe's innocence, but nothing like an apology or acquittal came forth. When Joe graduated a few weeks later he harbored still a keen sense of having been misjudged, mistreated and wrongly maligned.

If there was any such thing as a significant emotional event in Joe's mainly mundane young life, the wrongful and undeserved suspension at the high school was it. While most seniors literally bristled with excitement at the prospect of being disgorged into the larger world, Joe was hesitant, doubtful, mistrusting, and bitter. His parents did all they could to assuage his anxieties and smooth things over—they had believed him innocent all along—but his parents' love and support could not and did not compensate for the egregious loss of status among his peers at school.

Joe never had been scholarly. That, plus the wrongful suspension, formed the basis of his decision to forego college, at least for the time being. He took a job working thirty to forty hours a week at a Kroger store while his dad tried to push through his application at the Ford plant.

A year passed, during which Joe became increasingly dissatisfied with his life. His job at the Kroger store was a job and nothing more—low pay and little job satisfaction. He felt suddenly too old to be living at home with his parents and little sisters, but lacked the wherewithal to make it on his own. He dated occasionally, but nothing serious ensued. Overall he felt frustrated and wanting and anxious.

Like many young men who don't quite know what to do with themselves, Joe landed himself in the military, in the Army. There Joe discovered harsh and unfair disciplinarians who by comparison made his malefactors at the high school look like guardian angels. He also discovered there were far worse things in life than a boring job in a grocery store—like working sixty to seventy hours a week in the Army for less than two dollars an hour.

Joe developed a taste for alcohol while stationed at Fort Bragg, North Carolina. By no means was he a hardcore drinker, but a few beers or a few whiskey cocktails, he found, provided affordable and immediate relief from the unholy combination of stress and boredom that typified daily existence in the peacetime Army. Occasionally, he and a few of his fellow soldiers became stinking, puking, falling-down drunk. Usually though, Joe drank just enough to make himself feel good, and to hurry along the time he had to serve before his discharge from the Army.

Also to help pass the time, Joe attended a few college classes while stationed at Fort Bragg. The Army paid for everything but his books. He enjoyed and appreciated the respect and attention of his professors and teachers who treated him like a sentient and worthwhile human being, much unlike his teachers at high school who had treated him like an overgrown and possibly malicious child, and very much unlike his Army superiors and instructors who had treated him like a servant or slave.

Upon his honorable discharge in 1986, Joe immediately enrolled at Western Kentucky University, an affordable and modest state college in Bowling Green. University was like ascending into heaven after three years of purgatory in the Army. He rented a two-bedroom apartment with three other guys. The lack of privacy and beery weekends were somewhat reminiscent of barracks life, but the absence of supervision and discipline and regimentation created a much more enjoyable atmosphere. Every day upon awaking he relished the fact he did not have to fall out for company formation, and undergo an hour of physical training, and then pick up trash and cigarette butts in the common areas, all before reporting to work in company headquarters. He would've been perfectly happy at university save for the nagging, guilty feeling that he should've been there sooner. But, had it not been for his tortuous years in the Army, university life would not have seemed nearly as sweet.

Joe met his wife, Jolene, at Western Kentucky University, where both majored in public relations. Joe did not pick her out; she picked Joe. Never did she voice or indicate any specific reasons why she picked him, yet from the very onset of their relationship she acted as if Joe were the greatest catch in the entire school, and she was fortunate indeed to land him before any other woman got her hooks in him. Jolene didn't drink and she discouraged Joe from imbibing. Joe was so busy falling in love and being in love with Jolene, he scarcely noticed his transition into sobriety.

Joe and Jolene were nonpracticing Catholics. Mainly to appease Jolene's devoutly Catholic parents, and Joe's very Catholic mother, they married in a Catholic church near Jolene's parents' home in Peonia, in south-central Kentucky, immediately after graduation.

They began married life in Louisville in 1990, a time of economic recession, especially for Louisville, which recently had been claimed by the geo-economic area called the "rust belt." (Old and established manufacturing companies moved farther south to what was called the "sun belt." New industries, especially technology companies, tended to situate themselves in Lexington.)

Neither Joe nor Jolene was able to find work in public relations. Joe took a full-time job at a Louisville Kroger store. Jolene worked at a florist's shop. In 1991 she became pregnant. The smell of flowers then made her nauseous, so she quit her job. They struggled mightily to get by on Joe's grocery-story salary. Jolene missed and wanted her family, especially her mom. Their first child, a boy, was born in Louisville, in Baptist East Hospital, in 1992. A month later they moved from their Louisville apartment to Jolene's parents' house in Peonia.

They bought a modest three-bedroom home less than a mile from Jolene's parents after Joe found work at a local company that manufactured air compressors. He began on the assembly line, but within a year found a more suitable position: part secretary and part PR man, he did everything from drafting business letters to improving community relations.

A second child, a girl, was born in 1993. Joe and Jolene were thoroughly satisfied. While dating at Western Kentucky University, they'd decided they wanted a small family, a boy and a girl, preferably in that order, and that's exactly what they got. Jolene went on the pill, and then went to work the following year for the county government as Director of Tourism. The pay was modest, and while she was officially the "director," there was no one to direct; she was the sole person in the county's tourism department. Still she liked the job; essentially she was her own boss, with the freedom and flexibility to set her own agenda and schedule. Typically she spent half her workdays at her office in town and the other half at home on her computer. Her mom, less than a mile away, was only too happy to help out with the children, her first and only grandkids.

The children grew up to become hardworking and well-behaved students who thrived at the local schools. Joe and Jolene settled into their jobs, and took pride in their work and their children and their lives as a whole. Although they never went to church, they frequently gave thanks for their happy and healthy children, and also for their jobs, which were really quite good in that particular rural area where employment opportunities were extremely limited.

The only thing Joe Bass found lacking in his otherwise ideal and idyllic life was the area's lack of entertainment. The nearest movie theaters and the nearest decent restaurants were forty miles away—northeast to Elizabethtown, or southwest to Bowling Green. When Joe and Jolene wanted dinner and a movie, usually they drove to Bowling Green and revisited their old college stomping grounds. Yet Joe often found their trips to Bowling Green less than satisfying. With a population of about forty thousand, Bowling Green was by no means a burgeoning metropolis, and Elizabethtown was even smaller.

There was, however, entertainment to be found closer to home in the region's many fine outdoor recreation areas, to include Rough River Lake, Nolin River Lake, and the Nolin River below the Nolin River Dam. Joe Bass was too softhearted to hunt birds or mammals, but he always had liked to fish. Joe's dad often worked long hours at the Ford plant and had little time to spend with his son, but occasionally he had found time to take Joe fishing. Some of Joe's fondest memories were of fishing in his youth with his dad.

Joe enjoyed TV shows and movies—they subscribed to premium satellite television service—but sometimes he was possessed by something like a "call of the wild" that propelled him up and off the sofa, away from the TV, away from his beloved wife and kids, out the door, into his truck, and off to the lake or the river to fish.

Cautionary In-laws   5

Joe Bass cruised homeward in his big red Ford truck, thoroughly pleased and satisfied. No way could he make it to his in-laws' house in time for supper, so he took his time and savored the sweetness of his eminently successful fishing expedition. He knew guys at work and elsewhere who would sell their souls for access to a lake like Edgar's, and old Edgar had told him to come back anytime, and make himself at home. It might seem strange or unseemly to a non-fisherman, but Joe ranked his encounter with Edgar, and subsequent invitation to fish, right up there with other major events in his life: his discharge from the Army, meeting and marrying his wife, graduating from college, the births of his children, and landing his current job. He was really that impressed with Edgar's lake.

He wasn't entirely sure what to make of old Edgar, though. Edgar had oscillated from kindly and generous grandfatherly type to cantankerous old coot, back and forth, with no apparent reason for the sudden shifts in attitude. Joe figured that was simply due to Edgar's age; Edgar was old, and old people were likely to act irrationally, even meanly, at times. Still, that story about the three hundred thousand dollars simply was not true. Ditto for Edgar's explanation of how he'd lost his land through a tobacco lease.

Edgar making moonshine and serving a year in a federal penitentiary didn't worry Joe in the least; he thought it rather quaint and romantic. Nor did Joe care one whit about Edgar's raggedy, filthy appearance, or about his one-lens glasses, which made him ponder the old question: Is the glass half empty or half full? (It also made him think of a joke: A guy from Indiana picks up a hitchhiker in rural Kentucky who only has one shoe. 'What happened?' the driver asks. 'Did you lose a shoe?' 'No,' replied the hitchhiker. 'I found one.')

And why did Edgar sleep at nights in that tiny little camper, with no electricity or plumbing, and not in his daughter's trailer? A few other minor issues gnawed at the edges of Joe's consciousness, but mainly he ignored them. Mostly he thought about all the fish he'd caught, and all the fish he would catch at Edgar's place in the days and years to come, and he was thoroughly pleased and satisfied.

Daylight savings time, and a few days away from the winter solstice, it was nearly dark when Joe parked behind his wife's Jeep Grand Cherokee in her parents' driveway. Joe wasn't worried about the fish in his cooler. With the sun below the horizon, the temperature was dropping quickly; it was as good as having the fish in a refrigerator.

Joe entered through the front door without knocking. Heady food aromas and the sounds of dishes being gathered and stacked greeted him inside. In the dining room, his father-in-law Jasper Logsdon sat in his customary head-of-the-table chair, nibbling intently at the few scraps of fried chicken that his grandkids had left on the bones. Joe's wife gathered up dirty plates and glasses and silverware, carried them to the adjoining kitchen, and placed them near the sink where her mother was just beginning to wash dishes.

"Sorry I'm late," Joe said gaily, with no genuine regret or remorse, as he claimed his usual spot on the right hand of his father-in-law.

"Another two minutes and there would be no food for you," Jolene scolded mildly as she positioned on the table in front of him a platter bearing a few pieces of fried chicken, a bowl of mashed potatoes, a tureen of gravy, a bowl of green beans, and a tossed salad.

The chilly fresh air and the excitement of catching a big mess of fish had given Joe a Herculean appetite. He hurriedly filled his plate and started eating.

"So, did you catch any fish this afternoon?" Jasper asked genially.

Joe quickly chewed and swallowed, eager to share his phenomenal success story. "You wouldn't believe the fish I caught," said Joe. "I got about thirty pounds of crappie and bass out in my cooler. I'll show you as soon as I finish eating."

"Really? Where'd you catch 'em? The lake or the river?"

"A *private* lake," Joe stated importantly. "And I swear to God, it's absolutely the best fishing lake I've ever seen in my life. It's chockfull of bass and crappie—I caught a fish damn near every other cast."

Jolene shot Joe an admonishing look—she didn't appreciate him swearing and cursing in her parents' house—that he missed entirely. Bad language, especially at the table, could launch Jolene's mother into a Sunday sermon exhorting the many benefits of church membership and attendance, and denouncing the lack of same. *What kind of people are your children going to be when they grow up? What kind of example are you setting for them? Are they receiving any type of religious training at all? At the very least you need to have them baptized.* And so on. Similar sermons precipitated by Joe's careless irreverence had ruined at least a few otherwise peaceful Sunday evenings in the past.

"Is that right? Where is this lake?" asked Jasper.

"It's about a mile off the highway on Sycamore Church Road," Joe replied around a mouthful of mashed potatoes and gravy.

"Do you know who owns it?" Jasper inquired further.

"Yep—the guy's name is Edgar J. Johnson. Do you know him? He said he knows who you are."

Most of the color drained from Jasper's usually ruddy complexion. Jolene's mother turned completely around from the kitchen sink and fired a baleful look at her husband; from a distance of about twenty feet it slapped him like a heavy fist. Then she turned to her daughter and whispered urgently, madly in her ear.

Joe was so focused on his food—he was really quite famished—that he missed entirely his father-in-law's blanching and his mother-in-law's dreadful looks and whisperings.

"Edgar J. Johnson," Jasper repeated portentously. "Where did you meet him at?"

"Down at the river. At the dam. He asked if I was catching anything, and I told him No, and he was nice enough to invite me out to his place to fish—the prettiest little lake I've ever seen in my life."

"Yeah, he's got a nice lake, I won't deny that," said Jasper. "But I think you'd be better off if you steered clear of Edgar Johnson. Trust me on this one, Joe—that's one man you don't want to get mixed up with."

Joe felt suddenly indignant. If Jolene's parents wanted to go to church every week and pray and sing hymns and whatnot, that was their business. And Joe could and would tolerate an occasional sermon. But he wasn't about to let his in-laws tell him who he should and should not associate with.

"Why not? What's wrong with Edgar?" Joe asked defiantly. "I know he spent a year in prison for making moonshine, but I don't think that makes him a bad person. Back in those days there weren't any stores to speak of, and nobody had any money, so when people wanted whiskey they had to make their own."

"I think you're referring to a more distant period of American history," Jasper remarked patiently. "As I recall, Edgar went to prison for making moonshine around twenty, twenty-five years ago—back in the early eighties I guess it was. Gladys, do you remember when Edgar Johnson went to prison for making shine?"

"It was nineteen eighty-five," Gladys answered firmly, loudly, without turning from the sink. "The same year Jolene graduated from high school."

Joe was nonplused by the relative recentness of Edgar's incarceration. Somehow he'd imagined it happening much further in the past. "Well, whatever," he commented lamely. "I still don't think it's that big a deal."

"Making moonshine isn't the half of it—there's a lot more to it than that," said Jasper. "I could spend the rest of the evening telling you about Edgar Johnson's evil ways. Trust me on this one, Joe—that's one man you don't want to get yourself mixed up with."

"What gives you the right to call anybody evil?" Joe asked querulously. "He's just a poor old man, that's all. I fished in his lake a few hours, and we talked some. What's the harm in that? I suppose you think we should've been warming a church pew with all you wonderful Christians. Well, just because somebody doesn't go to church doesn't make them a bad person, not in my book. Show me in the Bible where it says people have to go to church every week and not only will I go, I'll take my family with me."

"Are you finished?" Jolene demanded loudly, angrily, from just across the table. She looked as if she wanted to lean across the table and smack him.

"As a matter of fact, I am," Joe declared petulantly. "I've lost my appetite."

"Fine," said Jolene, firing daggers from her eyes. "Then I'll take your plate and put away the food now. And you, Joe Bass, you can go clean your fish or soak your head or whatever it is you need to do."

Joe started up from his chair, then something inside him collapsed, and he slumped back down into his seat. "Listen, I don't mean to make a scene here, really. It's just that I had a really good time fishing at Edgar's place today, and then I come here, and you all start running Edgar into the ground like he's some big bad criminal, and Jesus, I don't know. He's just a poor little old man, but you act like he's the devil or something."

"I thought you were gonna go clean your fish," Jolene said, deferring the subject of Edgar's character.

"I want to see those fish," Jasper declared helpfully. "Joe, are you sure you got enough to eat?"

"Yeah, I'm fine," said Joe. He didn't have much of a temper, really—Jolene could get madder than him any day of the week and twice on Sunday—and the little temper he did have always expended itself quickly. He was still somewhat hungry, though. "Just let me say Hi and Bye to the kids."

Joe found his son and daughter watching TV in the living room and gave them hugs and told them he'd see them when they got home. He knew better than to tell them about his fish; both his children were addicted to videogames; neither was the least bit interested in fish or fishing.

Outside, Joe grabbed the cooler from his truck and placed it on the porch, under the porch light, where Jasper could get a good look at his fish. He still smarted slightly from the acerbic episode in the dining room. But his peevishness transformed into pure unadulterated pride as he showed off his catch to his father-in-law.

"Wow!" said Jasper. "That really is a fine mess of fish."

"I told you," said Joe. "That's the best fishing lake I've ever seen in my life."

"Oh, I don't doubt that a bit, Joe. And I won't say another word about Edgar Johnson if you don't want me to." Jasper's voice was unnaturally pleasant, somewhat sing-songy. "It's just that, well, I've lived here all my life, and I've heard stories about Edgar ever since I was little, and, well, he's not the sort of man you want to get involved with, that's all. Now then, I won't say another word about it if you don't want me to."

"Sounds good to me," Joe replied pleasantly. "I'm heading home now. I got a lot of fish to clean. Goodnight."

"Goodnight, Joe," said Jasper.

The front door closed, the porch light went out, and Joe went home to clean his fish.

Nobody Home   6

    The holiday season for the Bass family came wrapped in a traditional patchwork of anticipation and anxiety, joy and jitters, relaxation and responsibility. Jolene prudently performed nearly all their Christmas shopping during the weekend after Thanksgiving. Still it seemed there was always something else she needed to buy, right up until the night before Christmas, when she finally managed to find that last, perfect gift.

    Joe shopped only for Jolene, which was simple enough. Much more difficult was getting together again with his family in Louisville—his parents, and his three younger sisters and their families. The logistics of their annual holiday get-togethers were not problematic. The difficulty resided in the fact that Joe saw his in-laws at least four or five times a week and his own family rarely more than twice a year. Thus he always felt rather guilty, at least initially, as if he'd betrayed his own blood. Eventually he always managed to overcome his guilt, and reestablish warm and loving bonds with his parents and sisters. Always it seemed like some kind of Christmas miracle straight from a hokey holiday movie. Always he was glad when it was over, and he could rest assured of his parents' and sisters' love and support for yet another year.

    Right after the holidays, just when people began to think it never would get cold, old man winter arrived like a scorned and bitter lover determined to regain the attention of a forgetful old flame. The Bass children missed eleven days of school in January due to ice and snow. There were a few days when Joe and Jolene couldn't travel the twelve and ten miles respectively to their jobs near and in town.

    In mid-February temperatures moderated. By the end of February there were a few days of false spring when daytime temps topped out near seventy degrees. Daffodils bravely raised their yellow heads above the chilly earth, and rumors spread that the crappie were biting in Nolin Lake.

    With the professional football season over, and no good movies on

Shine

TV, there wasn't much to keep Joe on the sofa, especially on a Sunday afternoon that felt more like May than February. The last of the fish from Edgar's lake had been consumed a few weeks earlier. Two months had passed since last he'd wet a line; Joe was more than ready to go fishing again.

Two months had diminished appreciably his memory of fishing at Edgar's place. Further, on a fundamentally unconscious level, his father-in-law's cautionary admonitions had dulled his desire to revisit Edgar and his lake. Definitely, Joe did not think that Edgar's place was permanently off limits. Indeed, some small germ of prophesy told him he most certainly would fish there again someday. But Joe's father-in-law did not approve of Edgar, and his mother-in-law did not approve of Edgar, and his wife did not approve of Edgar. Thus the path of least resistance, or more exactly, the path of least disapproval from his in-laws and wife, led him not to Edgar's lake, but to Nolin Lake.

Joe had caught hundreds of good fish from Nolin Lake in the past. During the spring spawning runs, fish were sometimes as abundant and available in Nolin as they had been at Edgar's. Unfortunately, such was not the case on this particular February afternoon. A few days of unseasonably warm temperatures had warmed the water in the lake hardly at all; it was nowhere near warm enough to trigger the feeding frenzy that accompanied the fishes' spawning activities. Joe fished his most trustworthy lures in all his favorite spots, but a few hours of determined angling yielded just two mediocre crappie.

Like any good fisherman, Joe could be patient when circumstances demanded patience. But this was not a case of waiting for the bite to start, or finding just the right lure, or the right spot. Joe immersed his hand into the cold, muddy lake and found it literally like ice water. He was rather surprised, and proud of the fact, that he'd been able to catch any fish at all. Still, one fish per hour of fishing was not enough to keep him entertained. Reluctantly, resignedly, Joe decided to call it quits.

Joe headed home in his big red Ford truck, his window down. Warm fragrant air poured into the cab, infecting him with spring fever; he felt giddy and anxious and headstrong. The two fish he'd caught in the lake had piqued his hunter-forager instinct, but had satisfied it not at all. Joe was desirous of more prey.

He briefly considered fishing in the Nolin River, but he knew from experience it typically yielded little this early in the year. Then he remembered Edgar's open invitation, and he knew immediately, without even thinking about it, he was going to Edgar's place again.

A twinge of guilt pricked momentarily at the area of his consciousness that housed his marriage vows and his respect for his in-laws. Joe dismissed it at once. He was forty-four years old, a fully grown man, and nobody was going to tell him where he should and should not fish. However, in the interest of maintaining a happy and harmonious household, Joe decided that if he caught fish at Edgar's, he could and would honestly tell his wife and in-laws he'd caught his fish in Nolin Lake, while declining to tell them exactly which two fish he'd caught there. There was no need whatsoever to tell them he'd been fishing at Edgar's.

Joe tracked the twin ruts in the broom grass to the end of Edgar's drive, such as it was, and parked about ten feet behind Edgar's old car. As soon as he keyed off the ignition, his truck was besieged by a seething, snarling pack of dogs, at least seven or eight animals, a few more than he'd seen his last visit. They bounced off the doors, fenders, hood and windows with such alarming force it was like sitting inside a big metal drum—BOOM, BOOM, BOOM—a drum that marked time to a nightmarish cacophony of barks and howls, yips and yowls. Joe felt panicked, worried not so much for his personal safety, but for the well-being of his vehicle; the dogs' assault was so fierce, it looked and sounded as if they were inflicting real physical damage to his truck.

Joe honked his horn three times, hoping to scare away the dogs, or summon Edgar to his rescue, or both. The dogs, seemingly incensed by the harsh noise, intensified their assault on Joe's truck. There was no sign of Edgar. Joe sounded his horn again, one long continuous blast lasting at least ten seconds. Finally, the crazed beasts ceased their attack and for a few blessedly silent moments looked dazed and confused.

But just as Joe was beginning to congratulate himself for some small victory, one of the dogs, a huge black beast Joe didn't remember from his previous visit, barked loudly and leapt again at his truck. Immediately the rest of the pack rejoined the attack, seemingly more furious than ever.

Having seven or eight large and savage dogs barking uproariously and hurling themselves like canine kamikazes at his truck was not something that became easier or less disturbing with time. On the contrary, Joe's panic increased with each passing second. Desperately he leaned on the horn again, and again gained a short reprieve. Again he looked around for Edgar, but saw only the crazed faces of the devilish hounds as they repeatedly leapt at his truck.

Enough was enough. Joe fired his engine, put his truck in reverse, and backed around in the broom grass. He rather hoped at least one of the beasts would be stupid enough to position itself under one of his wheels, but that didn't happen. The dogs continued to attack Joe's truck as it hurried down the drive, and for at least a few hundred feet down Sycamore Church Road.

In his driveway at home, Joe closely inspected his truck for damage. At least a dozen small and not-so-small scratches showed on the driver-side door, with a few more on the hood, left fender, and passenger-side door. Joe couldn't tell if they were made by tooth or claw, and he really didn't care; either way, the damage was done. Adding insult to injury, streaks of slaver smeared both windows and to a lesser extent the windshield; the driver-side window was practically slathered over completely with the foul viscous slime.

Joe claimed the garden hose from its winter storage in the garage, attached it to the spigot near his driveway, and sprayed off the offensive dog slaver. First chance he got, he'd buy a can of matching red Ford spray paint and touch up the scratches.

Gary Woodbine   7

Gary Woodbine was a large, beefy fellow. His hair, to include his closely cropped beard, was a tawny reddish color just one shade lighter than his Hereford cattle. His eyes were a deep chocolate brown, exactly like his livestock. He stood a few inches over six feet tall, and weighed in at well over two hundred pounds—a big bull of a man. And yet despite his bulk, he was not in any way formidable or imposing. Indeed, his movements, his facial features, his overall demeanor, were remarkably and unmistakably bovine—placid, docile, and dull, as if long years of association with his cattle had imbued him with his animals' characteristics. He was no more fearsome than any of the herbivores that grazed on his two hundred acres of pastureland.

Woodbine was a proud man, as proud as his understanding of Christianity allowed him to be. By local standards, he was very well-off. He worked in Bowling Green as manager of the parts department at a farm equipment dealership, and earned additional monies from his thriving cattle enterprise. The stately farmhouse that he shared with his wife—their two sons were grown and gone—was undeniably the grandest structure along Sycamore Church Road and for many miles around. He was proud of his wife, who held a respectable position of authority in the county courthouse that further increased their temporal wealth. He was proud of his two sons who had grown into fine God-fearing men with good families and jobs and farms and houses not unlike his own.

He was enormously proud of his healthy herd of cattle; whenever he felt the slightest doubt or misgiving regarding his role and purpose in life, he need only gaze upon his fat, sleek animals, and he was immediately and totally reassured of his own self-worth and the orderliness of the universe: God was in His heaven and the king was on his throne.

Woodbine was also proud of his deaconship in his church, a position he had held for more than a decade. As a deacon, he and the other deacons—there were twelve in all, presumably representing the twelve apostles—assisted the pastor in making decisions pertaining to the church and its affairs. It wasn't always easy.

Recently a grieving and impoverished widow had appealed to them for a few thousand dollars to provide a Christian burial for her deceased husband. Neither the woman nor her dead husband nor any of their children were church members, so the majority of the deacons and the pastor decided to deny her the money. Surely, they argued, even the best of shepherds were not responsible for those outside the flock. Woodbine was not so sure. He took to heart the parables extolling the merits of the good shepherd and the good steward, and felt their Christian duties extended beyond the limits of their immediate flock. Their church was flush with money just then, and he truly wanted to help the poor old woman. But Woodbine was voted down.

Regardless of the business at hand, when Woodbine sat in committee with the deacons and the pastor, he always felt that he was helping to oversee God's affairs here on earth, and he considered that to be no small thing.

Woodbine did not claim to be a perfect Christian, but in a few regards at least he exemplified the Christian ideal. He was definitely slow to anger. Bucolic by nature, he was no more given to anger or rashness than his cattle; his innate personality jibed perfectly with his Christian ideals, and vice versa.

Woodbine believed wholeheartedly in the Lord's commandment that he should love his neighbors as himself. His simple and unsophisticated nature denied him the ability to obfuscate the scripture's intent and meaning. This commandment appeared as an unqualified imperative in the Gospel of Matthew, and try as he might, Woodbine saw no way to circumvent its stark absoluteness, although a few of his neighbors sorely tested his faith.

Those neighbors were Edgar J. Johnson and his daughter, Bobbie. Twenty-odd years ago Woodbine had purchased most of the Johnson farm, and for twenty-odd years, a low-grade and one-sided feud (if a feud can be one-sided), had simmered between the Woodbines and the Johnsons—namely, Edgar and his daughter. The ongoing animosity had been initiated and was perpetuated entirely by the latter two persons.

Woodbine understood, at least to some extent, Edgar Johnson's resentment. Virtually everyone in the county knew the generalities, if not the specifics, of Edgar's hard-luck story, and Woodbine was not unsympathetic. Always he had seized the smallest opportunities to demonstrate his goodwill and neighborly love toward Edgar Johnson, always being careful not to appear condescending or triumphant. And always Edgar had responded with naked malice and contempt. Woodbine rarely had found opportunities to demonstrate kindness towards the daughter, Bobbie, but certainly he never had treated her unkindly. Apparently, her malice and contempt were generated solely from her allegiance to her father.

Woodbine's simple and pastoral nature was ill-equipped to cope with anything like the quandary and conundrum that ensued as a result of his fruitless attempts to love his neighbors, who invariably responded with hatred. Yet he was not naïve enough to think that living a Christian life was supposed to be simple or easy. Indeed, he knew from the scriptures that "charity suffereth long," and so he suffered many long years, enduring many injuries and injustices both small and not-so-small—all because he had purchased the property that once had belonged to Edgar J. Johnson.

At times Woodbine had found the Johnsons' animosity nearly intolerable. Twice he had offered to buy Edgar Johnson's fourteen acres for much more than they were worth. Eight acres of Edgar's land were occupied by a lake, for which Woodbine had no use—he didn't fish, and he already had sufficient water sources for his cattle; and the other six acres were mainly too rough to serve as pasture. Woodbine had tendered the offers in the hopes that Edgar Johnson would take the money and move elsewhere, leaving him to finally live in peace. Twice his offers had been vehemently rejected, accompanied by the direst threats and badmouthings. Woodbine had no choice but to continue to suffereth long.

Aside from his Christian philosophy, there was another reason why Woodbine continued to suffereth long at the hands of his spiteful neighbors. Edgar Johnson's sister, Florence Goody, was a member of his church. Flo Goody was a fine Christian woman, and she looked up to Woodbine as a church deacon, and as a good neighbor and friend. For her sake, as well as for the sake of his immortal soul, Woodbine felt obliged to weather the occasional storm visited upon him by the mean-spirited Johnsons.

Still, his charity and patience were not without limits. Two of his spring calves had been savaged within the past month. Both he and his wife had been at work when the attacks occurred, and there hadn't been enough of their remains to determine with certainty the causes of their deaths. But Woodbine was all but certain that the Johnsons' pack of dogs had killed them, and eaten them. His cattle were insured; he could have been compensated with a hundred and fifty dollars per calf, had he filed claims with his insurance company. But his insurance company would not honor his claims without a police report, and Woodbine didn't report the savageries to the police because he didn't want to create additional problems with Edgar Johnson and his daughter.

After finding the second calf dead, Woodbine had confronted Edgar's daughter, Bobbie, with his suspicion that her dogs were responsible. She bristled with unbridled hostility at his assertions, telling him that he couldn't prove anything—for all he knew, it might've been coyotes or somebody else's dogs—and shrieking all sorts of threats and obscenities. Woodbine replied calmly, as calmly as circumstances permitted, that he had the right and the obligation to protect his livestock, and politely asked Bobbie to please try to keep her dogs away from his cattle. Bobbie had responded with one final and especially foul tirade, and then slammed the trailer door.

Like many if not most rural folk, Woodbine was largely a creature of habit. On Saturday mornings, he drove his wife to Brownsville where they shopped for whatever groceries and sundries they needed to sustain them for the following week. On this particular Saturday morning, he and his wife were delighted to find country hams on sale. They purchased two large country hams, one for themselves, and one for the grieving widow recently denied funds by his church.

The widow smiled weakly as she accepted Woodbine's offering, but displayed no real gratitude. Her deceased husband had been cremated a week earlier, and a ham would not allow her husband to rise up whole again at the final resurrection. Woodbine wanted to tell her that he personally had wanted to grant the funds, but he didn't. Instead he offered his heartfelt condolences, and told her to contact him personally if there was ever anything else he could do for her.

A bittersweet feeling of failure and accomplishment accompanied Woodbine as he drove away from the widow's house, heading for home. He had tried—God knows he had tried—and that was all that any man could be expected to do. Satisfied that he had at least made some small effort to comfort the grieving widow and fulfill his Christian duties, his thoughts turned away from the widow and her problems, and toward the ham he planned to have for lunch.

His hunger grew from a mental desire to a physical craving as he turned onto Sycamore Church Road. His stomach rumbled so loudly his wife heard it, and smiled; she had her mouth set for ham as well. But as they neared their stately farmhouse, all thoughts of a quiet and tasty lunch evaporated. His worst suspicions were confirmed. There, in the pasture less than a hundred yards from his house, the Johnson dogs were attacking one of his spring calves. One dog held a death grip on a hind leg, another had hold of a foreleg, and yet another, a huge black beast, had fastened its steely jaws on the calf's snout, while the rest of the pack worried the hapless young animal from all directions. Woodbine watched in helpless horror as the calf went down; the ravenous dogs were upon it in an instant, lunging and snapping at the calf's soft underbelly, then jerking backwards with powerful convulsive motions—they were literally ripping its guts out.

Woodbine's bucolic nature was not conducive to swift and forceful action, but he responded to the horrific scene as if one of his grandchildren was being murdered. He stomped on the gas pedal, and then stomped on the brake to negotiate the turn into his driveway. He stomped the gas pedal again, and steered off his driveway, through his front yard, and then slid to a halt less than five feet from his front porch.

Without a thought or a word for his wife, he hurried from his truck to the front door, the appropriate key in hand and aimed unerringly at the door lock. He unlocked the door, flung it open, and raced inside, all in one continuous blur of activity. Less than thirty seconds later he charged from the house, the wrath of God upon his face, and a shotgun in his hands. Straightway he ran to the gate nearest the scene of carnage, where his rampage was halted by a lock and chain. The dogs, oblivious to his arrival, were just now locating and devouring the calf's tender innards, the heart and liver and lungs. Woodbine raised the shotgun to his shoulder and fired.

At a range of about eighty yards, the rabbit-shot from his improved-cylinder 12-gauge shotgun was mainly ineffective; a few of the tiny pellets struck a few of the dogs, but caused no serious injury. The booming blast, however, brought an immediate halt to the dogs' grisly feast. Bloody heads emerged from the calf's gaping stomach cavity, and stared stupidly, uncomprehendingly, in Woodbine's direction. Woodbine quickly pumped another shell into the chamber and fired again at the beasts. Immediately the dogs, all save one, bounded off in the opposite direction, appearing as a single swirling object as they ran closely together, the outermost animals continually seeking to gain safety within the center of the pack. They continued straightway for nearly a quarter mile, until they reached the far edge of the pasture, where they began a wide, sweeping turn toward the Johnsons' place. The one remaining beast, the big black dog, not only held its ground, it took a few steps in Woodbine's direction, as if to defend its kill, or get a better look at his adversary, or both.

Temporarily mindless of his bulk and his age, both of which prohibited him from readily climbing over the gate, Woodbine placed one booted foot on the gate's bottom rail; it sagged several inches beneath his weight, and only then did he remember it had been many years since he'd been able to climb over a gate. Never taking his eyes off the big black dog, he leaned the shotgun against a fence post, fished his keys from his pocket, clicked open the padlock securing the gate, returned the keys to his pocket, pushed the gate open, and retrieved his shotgun.

He chambered one of the shotgun's three remaining shells and strode forth to meet the ruthless butcher of his cattle, walking slowly, steadily, his shotgun at the ready. Caution was one reason for his moderate pace; another was his desire that the dog not run off before he was within effective range—thirty yards or less for that particular gun and ammunition. As the distance between them shortened—seventy yards, sixty, fifty, forty—the dog showed not the slightest intention of running away. Rather, it exhibited with every jet-black hair on its body sheer maliciousness and dire threat. When the distance was narrowed to about thirty yards, its ears folded back on its head and its hackles rose in a sharp crest from the nape of its neck to the base of its tail; a low, grumbling growl rumbled across the pasture.

Woodbine took three more steps, closing to within twenty yards. The grumbling growl became a nerve-shattering bark, almost a roar, and in that same moment the beast suddenly charged. Woodbine pulled the trigger; the shotgun boomed. The dog's forward progress became instantly vertical, as it leaped straight up into the air, its body and head and limbs flailing fitfully, contorting wildly in every possible direction, while it howled in desperate agony. By the time it hit the ground, Woodbine had chambered another shell. He fired again, quickly chambered his final shell, and continued walking forward.

Penetrated by dozens of small lead pellets, more than a few of which had struck vital organs, the dog was all but dead. As Woodbine stepped to within a few feet of his fallen foe, the dog's chest swelled hugely with one final breath of air, which was shortly released in a lengthy ragged sigh, and then it was totally motionless, finally dead. Woodbine aimed directly at its head and discharged his final round.

Unaccustomed to violence of any sort, Woodbine was severely shaken. He exhaled a lengthy ragged sigh, not unlike the dying dog's, and headed back to his house. Adrenaline coursed through his substantial frame like a powerful drug; not a drinking man, he was higher than ever he'd been in his life. He felt like he could kill a grizzly bear with his bare hands, and maybe he could have, though he had no desire to kill anything just then, or ever again.

As he came closer to his house, his wife stepped down off the front porch and started walking towards him. The mere sight of his wife at once returned him to a more typical and ordinary frame of mind. The adrenaline that had powered him like high-octane racing fuel drained suddenly from his body, as if somebody somewhere had pulled a very large plug. Immediately he felt weak and sick and worried.

"I had to do it," he told his wife, as she ushered him up onto the porch. "I just had to do it." He leaned the still warm and smoky shotgun against the porch railing, and collapsed in a heap into a chair.

"Of course you did," his wife agreed sympathetically. "I wish you would've killed 'em all."

"That big black one, he was the worst of the bunch—he's sure enough dead. I hate it though. I hate I had to do it."

"Well, what's done is done," said the wife. "The police are on their way over here right now. Maybe we'll be able to put an end to this business once and for all."

"You called the police?"

"Why sure I did. I thought they might try to kill you, as vicious as they are. Something has to be done about those animals. Once they've tasted blood, there won't be any end to it unless we put an end to it. We weren't sure before if it was the Johnsons' dogs are not, but we're sure enough sure now. Every single one of 'em needs to be put down, or at least locked up somewhere."

"I don't know," said Woodbine. "Let me think about it."

"I don't know what there is to think about," his wife said angrily. "That's the third calf in a month. That's almost five hundred dollars they've cost us already, a lot more if you figure what those calves would've brought us once they were all growed up."

"Just let me think about it a minute, okay?"

"You can think about it all you want," his wife replied smartly. "I need to fetch our groceries into the house."

"I'll help," said Woodbine, making a small effort to rise.

"I can manage just fine. You just sit there and think about why you want to let those animals kill our livestock."

Gertrude Woodbine—everybody called her Gertie—was much unlike her husband both physically and temperamentally. She was rather tall for a woman, about five-feet-ten, and lean and wiry, with features as sharp as a hatchet. Her personality was energetic and vivacious; near her desk in her office hung a placard bearing the motto: "Never put off till tomorrow what you can do right this minute." Still, her understanding of Christianity caused her to defer to her husband's judgment in most matters. And their happy marriage and wholesome family and ever-increasing prosperity stood as constant reminders that her husband's judgments, though sometimes contrary to her own, were not without merit.

By the time Gertie had finished toting their groceries into the house, her ire had diminished considerably. She came out of the house with a large, icy glass of Royal Crown Cola and presented it to her husband. He accepted it silently, and drank, as a county police cruiser pulled into the drive; its lights were flashing but the siren was mute.

Woodbine knew all the deputies in the county sheriff's department. He had grown up around most of them, and had gone to school with more than a few. He immediately recognized the deputy sheriff who emerged from the cruiser, as did Gertie, who routinely came into contact with all the deputy sheriffs through her job in the courthouse.

"Good morning, Tom," Woodbine hailed the officer, who limped slowly towards the porch.

About ten years earlier, Tom Stinnett had managed somehow to shoot himself in the foot. He was yet to live it down, not because his fellow officers and the folks thereabouts were especially mean or spiteful; his limp served as a constant and permanent reminder of his accidental misfire.

"Gary, Gertie," the officer replied curtly as he stepped up onto the porch, favoring his right foot with every step. "What's the problem?"

Woodbine's wife answered quickly for them both. "The problem is that vicious pack of dogs that the Johnsons keep over there. They've killed three of our spring calves already this past month. We just got home from the grocery store and there they were," she pointed with her hand, "right over there in that pasture, rippin' a little calf to shreds."

The officer stared in the direction she pointed, but saw nothing save a few dark shapes lying motionless in the pasture. "Where are they now?" he asked.

"They've all run back home 'cept for one of 'em," Gertie replied excitedly. "That big black devil, he ain't gonna cause no more problems—Gary seen to that."

The officer glanced at the shotgun, and then said to Gary, "We'd better go have a look."

Woodbine hauled his massive frame up and out of the chair, and led the deputy out to the pasture where the dog and the calf lay dead. Gertie stayed behind on the porch.

"You sure enough blew him all to hell," the deputy commented, staring at the dog. "It's too bad about your calf. Your wife said this is the third one in a month…?"

"Well, yeah, we've had three calves killed this past month, but I can't say for sure about the other two. We were both at work when the other two were killed."

"Did you call 'em in?"

"No, Tom, I didn't. I didn't want to start a fuss till I knew for sure what was going on."

"Well, now you know. It was the Johnsons' dogs, right?" The officer started scribbling on his official report pad.

"I know about this here calf," said Gary. "I can't say for sure about the other two."

"Well, Gary, I'll tell you what I can do. I can write in my report here that you lost three calves—that way you can collect all the insurance money you got comin' to you. And I'll send animal control over to the Johnson place this afternoon to round up the rest of those dogs. If you want to press charges against the Johnsons, we can do that too. As a matter of fact, I got a warrant in my car right now for Bobbie—failure to appear in court for a traffic violation. I was gonna give her a few more days to maybe scrape some money together before I served it. But now, well, I might as well serve it today, and if you want I'll lay this on her, too."

"No—no Tom. I don't want to press any charges. To tell you the truth, I'd rather you not write any of this down in your report."

The deputy looked at Woodbine as if he'd just fallen off the turnip truck. "What about your insurance money?" he asked.

"I'm not too worried about that, Tom. That big black devil, he was the worst of the bunch. I don't think we'll have any more problems around here with him out o' the way. I'd just as soon let bygones be bygones."

"That's mighty nice of you," the deputy stated dryly. "But since your wife called it in, and I'm standin' right here at the scene of a crime, I gotta write a report on it."

"Okay then—just say that I killed a dog that was worryin' my cattle, but don't write nothin' about the calf bein' killed."

"Gary, I can't do that. That calf is dead just as sure as I'm standin' here. I gotta put it down in my report."

"Well, I'm not gonna tell you how to do your job, but do me a favor if you can. Don't say anything to animal control till after I've had a chance to talk with the Johnsons. If they give me their word that they'll keep their dogs under control, I'd just as soon let this whole thing blow over. I'll call you and let you know something after I've talked with the Johnsons."

"I think you'll be wasting your time, Gary, but if that's the way you want it..."

"It is," said Woodbine. "I'll keep a close eye on my cattle the rest of the weekend. If those dogs show up again I'll give you a call. I'll try to talk with the Johnsons this afternoon and I'll let you know what happens. Thanks for comin' out."

"Okay, Gary," the officer replied. He seemed disappointed that immediate and forceful actions were not required. "You just let me know which way you want to go with this."

"I'll do it," said Woodbine. "I appreciate your time."

No Peace   8

Tom Stinnett declined Mrs. Woodbine's offer of a glass of cold soda; it was lunchtime, and he had his mouth set for a hot roast beef sandwich at Tina's restaurant. Gary Woodbine and his wife stood on the front porch and watched the cruiser drive off.

"When are they gonna send somebody over there to take care of those dogs?" asked Gertie.

"I don't know," said Gary. "I told Tom I wanted to talk to the Johnsons first."

"You what? What's there to talk about? We seen those dogs a-killin' our calf. It's a sure thing they killed those other two. There's nothin' to talk about."

"You're probably right," said Gary. "But I gotta try. Maybe Edgar's sister, Flo, can talk some sense into 'em. I think I'll give her a call."

Gary found Flo's number in the little church directory he kept near the phone in the hallway. She sounded very happy to hear from Gary, until he explained the reason for his call.

"You say you tried talkin' to Bobbie about it last week?" asked Flo. "What did she say?"

"Well, at that time I wasn't sure if it was their dogs or not. She told me I couldn't prove nothin', and she cussed me out some. I'm not worried about the cussin', but they need to start keepin' their dogs away from my cattle or else I'll have to turn it over to the law and let them handle it."

"I'd like to help you, Gary, I truly would. But once Edgar and Bobbie have their minds set against you, there ain't no makin' peace with those two. They've had their minds set against me for I don't know how many years. Bobbie's cussed me out more times than I care to recall—the mouth on that girl is shameful. I can't do nothin' with 'em—her or Edgar either one. If I tried talkin' to 'em, it'd probably just make 'em that much madder and meaner."

"Well, how about you just go over there with me? I'll do all the talkin'. Maybe they won't be so ornery if I got you with me."

Flo was temporarily silent as she mulled it over. Finally she said, "No, I'd better not. I'd be happy to go if I thought it'd do any good, but it won't. I'm sorry, but I know how they are, and I know I can't do you no good. I'm sorry."

"Well, thanks anyway," said Gary. "I'll see you in church tomorrow."

"We'll be there," Flo said brightly. "Goodbye."

Woodbine's wife had been listening nearby. "See?—there ain't nobody can talk sense to the Johnsons. Old Edgar has pickled his brain with moonshine and that useless daughter of his is all whacked out on drugs. You ought to have Tom call animal control and be done with it. They've ruined enough of our Saturday already."

"Well, I gotta try anyway," said Gary. "Least I can do is haul that dead animal over there so they can bury it. I'll be home in an hour or so."

Gertie was furiously indignant, but said nothing.

Gary tossed a shovel and an old burlap sack into the back of his truck and drove out into his pasture. With the shovel he nudged and coaxed the bloody dog corpse into the sack, heaved it up and into the back of his truck, and then drove next door to the Johnsons' place. He parked in front of Bobbie's old gray trailer and honked his horn. There was no response. About a minute later he honked again, but still there was no sign of life at the trailer.

Finally, resignedly, Gary climbed out of his truck and started toward the trailer's front door. He had taken but a few steps when the door suddenly swung open. Bobbie stood framed in the doorway, clad in nothing save a white terrycloth bathrobe. Her bleached-blonde hair stood out at impossible angles, giving her a wild and ferocious appearance. She scowled wickedly at her uninvited guest.

"What do you want?" she challenged angrily.

"Good morning," Gary replied, stopping in his tracks. "Is your dad around?"

"No, he ain't."

"Well, I'm afraid I've got some bad news for you, Bobbie."

Bobbie said nothing, but glared malevolently.

"My wife and I just got home from the grocery store a little while ago and found your dogs killin' one of our calves. Most of your dogs ran off pretty quick, but I had to shoot one of 'em—that big black dog. I'm sorry, but I had to do it."

Bobbie did not speak.

"I got him here in the back of my truck," Woodbine continued. "I thought maybe you might want to bury him."

From a distance of about twenty feet, Woodbine saw her face mottle darkly with apoplectic rage. Still she did not speak.

"If you ain't up to it," said Gary, "I guess I can take him back home and bury him for you. I suppose I could do that much for you, if that would help."

Bobbie was silent.

"That was the third calf we've lost in the past month," said Gary. "We can't afford to lose any more. It looked like that big black dog was the worst of the bunch. I'm hopin' the rest of your dogs won't cause any more problems, but I'd like you to start keepin' an eye on 'em. If you'll give me your word that you'll try to keep your animals away from my cattle, then I won't…"

Bobbie took a step backwards and violently slammed the door. Woodbine simply stood there for a minute or so, hoping she might reconsider her rash behavior and make some attempt to rectify the situation. But she did not.

A wave of anger passed briefly over Woodbine. He considered dumping the dog corpse there in her front yard, and driving off. But his anger quickly passed. He climbed back in his truck and drove home.

An hour and a half later, the dog corpse and the little dead calf had been buried in a rough patch of ground at the rear of Woodbine's property, a shallow grave protected mainly by a pile of largish rocks, and Woodbine was finally sitting down to a lunch of country ham and black-eyed peas and cornbread.

"As soon as you finish eating," said Gertie, "you need to call Tom and tell him you couldn't do any good with the Johnsons. Then one of you needs to get animal control over there to do something with those dogs."

"Not just yet," said Woodbine. "Let's just keep this under our hats for another day or two."

"I know you're tryin' to do the right thing, Gary," said Mrs. Woodbine. "But I still say you ought to let the law handle it. Nothin' good is gonna come from this. Some people don't know the meaning of good. Some people are just plain ornery."

"Maybe," said Woodbine. "But I think everybody at least deserves a chance."

"There ain't no *maybe* to it. Those dogs might be over here again anytime now, and there's no tellin' what the Johnsons might do, now that they know you killed one o' their animals. There's gonna be more trouble for sure—I just know it."

Somehow, Woodbine knew it too. His stomach suddenly flip-flopped and his appetite was gone. He wanted to finish what was left on his plate, but the ham and black-eyed peas now tasted way too salty, and he couldn't continue.

"Now look," said Gertie. "First they ruin our morning and now they've ruined your lunch. I don't see why you want to just sit around like a bump on a log and let them ruin the rest of our weekend. There'll be no peace around here till those dogs are destroyed or locked up somewhere, and the law has settled up with the Johnsons."

"Maybe," Woodbine allowed. "But I still want to talk with Edgar. We'll let things die down a little bit, then I'll go over there tomorrow and try to talk with the old man."

"You might as well try talkin' to a fence post," said Gertie. "You know what Edgar's like. As mean as his daughter is, well, she gets it from him."

"Old Edgar's had a rough life," Woodbine countered halfheartedly. "I think he deserves a chance to do the right thing, at least. We'll see how it goes tomorrow. If Edgar won't do anything about the dogs, then we'll have to let the law handle it."

Gertie sawed determinedly at her slab of country ham. "I don't care what the Johnsons do. They're not gonna ruin *my* lunch."

"That's good," said Woodbine. "I'm glad."

He sat placidly at the table and kept his wife company until she finished her lunch. Then he walked out to the front porch and comfortably situated himself in a chair that afforded a panoramic view of his pasture and his herd. His fat, sleek cattle grazed calmly, steadily, on the bright green spring grass, apparently mindless of the morning's slaughter.

Oh, that Man might possess such short memories and calm natures, thought Woodbine.

Bobbie Day   9

Bobbie Day, born Roberta June Johnson, was fast asleep when she heard a horn honk outside her old gray trailer. She figured it was probably the police. About a month earlier she had been ticketed for driving without insurance. She had been scheduled to appear in court earlier that week but had declined to do so because she didn't have any money to pay a fine, and she didn't want to go to jail. With two daughters at home, a teenager and a four-year-old, jail was not an option. And, daughters or no daughters, she'd been locked up a few times in the past and did not want to return.

Bobbie had been hoping upon hope, as only the truly poor and desperate can hope, that somehow some money would come her way and she'd be able to pay her fine before the police came after her for failing to appear in court. She had spent ten of her last twenty dollars on five 2-dollar scratch-off lottery tickets, one of which paid five bucks. For a moment or two she had dared to hope her luck had turned, and bought five more two-dollar tickets, all of which were losers. But as soon as she'd left the store, she somehow hoped again that somehow some money would come her way, and soon.

It was Saturday, and she was expecting a visit that afternoon from a guy she'd dated on and off for years, Johnny Dollar, from Louisville. Johnny had a fairly good job at General Electric. Bobbie planned to be extra nice to him that evening, and obtain a "loan" of maybe a hundred dollars, maybe even more, with which she would pay her fine.

As soon as the horn woke her up, Bobbie glanced at the clock and saw it was only half past noon. Johnny Dollar wasn't supposed to arrive until four or five that afternoon, and he never honked his horn; he always knocked on the trailer door. So she figured it was probably the police.

Bobbie crawled from her bed and peeked gingerly past the edge of the window curtain, just as the horn honked a second time. Immediately she recognized the truck and person of her neighbor, Gary Woodbine. And immediately she was furious. Damn it!—didn't she have enough troubles just then without him showing up? Probably he wanted to fuss at her some more about her dogs bothering his stupid cows. Well, he could go to hell for all she cared, and he could take his stupid cows with him. She was going back to bed.

Then something clicked in her brain—a little caution light flashed—as she recalled the facts that Woodbine's wife worked at the courthouse, and that both the Woodbines were chummy with the local police force. She decided to open the door and hear him out.

Just as she'd thought, Woodbine was there to fuss about her dogs. She hardly could stand to look at Woodbine—he was so big and sleek and evidently prosperous—much less pay any attention to him. Then something clicked in her brain again—it was the ON switch for fury and rage—when Woodbine told her he had one of their dogs, dead, in the back of his truck, and suggested she bury it. Damn Gary Woodbine! He had killed one of their dogs and he expected her to bury it? Speechless with fury and rage, she slammed shut the trailer door with all her might.

Bobbie was only four when her mother was killed in an automobile accident. Her dad, Edgar Johnson, had blamed himself for his wife's death and started drinking beyond the point of excess; he drank with totally reckless and self-destructive abandon. He was jailed frequently for alcohol-related offenses, and Bobbie was sent to live with her Aunt Flo for a few years, until Edgar finally straightened out somewhat.

Bobbie was only fifteen when her dad introduced her to her former husband, Jimmy Day. He was thirty, exactly twice her age, when they met and married. Jimmy was a drug dealer, both pot and cocaine, and the couple overindulged for years on the bounty of his drug dealings. Eventually Bobbie became pregnant. Jimmy Day was hopelessly and chronically addicted to drugs and alcohol, and far too wild and crazy to cope with the responsibilities of fatherhood. Bobbie and Jimmy fought bitterly and violently throughout her pregnancy and after the birth of their daughter, Blossom. After an especially violent episode—Jimmy ran over her with his car—she divorced him. Jimmy Day died of an overdose about a year later.

During rare moments of lucidity, Bobbie realized the awfulness of her upbringing and who was mainly responsible for it. But Bobbie never felt hatred towards her father. When her dad was not around, a mild contempt for him simmered just below the surface. But whenever she was with her dad, she felt nothing but love and devotion.

Her decidedly less than stellar childhood, followed by her awful marriage, had created a deep ambivalence towards the male of the species. Sometimes that ambivalence became manifest at or near the loving end of the spectrum, at which times she was wildly passionate and crazily romantic. At other times it became manifest at the hateful end of the spectrum, at which times her meanness and spitefulness knew no boundaries.

Her crazy sense of romanticism, molded around her steadfast devotion to her father, caused her to love the very type of men who were largely responsible for her problems—men like her dad and ex-husband. Conversely, she hated men who were respectable figures of authority, especially men who were sober and proud and well-off. At the top of that list stood Woodbine, with his big fancy house and his new truck and his stuck-up wife with her courthouse job and, most important, his 200-acre farm—land that Bobbie knew had belonged to her father during relatively better days, long ago.

Though Bobbie never felt hatred towards her father, she frequently felt enormously hateful towards other men. She hated Woodbine so fiercely at that moment, it almost felt *good*; it was damn near like a drug, energizing and electrifying like good cocaine. God damn Gary Woodbine! He had so much, and she had so little; it just wasn't fair. Just one of Woodbine's cattle was worth enough money to pay her court fine, and to enable her and her girls to live like decent human beings for a month. And Woodbine had a few hundred cattle, at least. And they were all growing fat and sleek on the fine pastureland that once had belonged to her dad, and that someday would've belonged to her. It just wasn't fair. And she was supposed to give a damn that their dogs had been bothering his cattle? They weren't even their dogs, not really. Tony and Blue rightfully belonged to Edgar, but the others were strays they didn't rightly claim, and very rarely fed. So what if they killed a calf? Woodbine had hundreds of animals, worth thousands of dollars. And she had just five lousy bucks in her purse.

Bobbie's last name, Day, was an absolute misnomer; Bobbie was a creature of the night. Typically she stayed up until four or five in the morning, watching videotapes of corny, romantic movies with her teenaged daughter, drinking Cokes and smoking cigarettes. Occasionally, when they could afford it, or when they were visited by well-provisioned guests, beer and pot replaced the soda pop and cigarettes. Bobbie and her daughters rarely arose before one or two in the afternoon. The mere fact of Woodbine's "early" arrival would have been enough to set her off in a rage. Coupled with his suggestion that she bury one of their dogs, *a dog that he had shot and killed*, her rage was virtually boundless.

Her terrible rage waned considerably, though, replaced by a blessed relief, as she became increasingly thankful that it had been Woodbine, and not the cops, who had so rudely awakened her. Johnny Dollar was due to arrive in a few hours, and she felt reasonably confident she could sweet-talk him into "loaning" her the hundred bucks she needed to pay the court.

She ate a bowl of cornflakes, and then went to the bathroom to prepare for Johnny Dollar. With a stiff hairbrush she eventually managed to subdue her wild tangles of bleached-blonde hair. Then she spent an hour in the bathtub, soaking in a scented solution, shampooing her hair, and shaving her legs and armpits. Out of the tub, she arranged her hair into a fairly attractive coiffure with a hairbrush and blow dryer, and then went to work with her makeup.

Bobbie, like her father, was a small person, nearly petite; she would have been definitively petite save for the influence of her mother's genes; her mother had been an average-sized person. In her youth Bobbie had been undeniably pretty—the prettiest girl in the county, some folks said—but she was a few years past forty now, and more than half of those years had been spent in hard and even riotous living, and had taken a toll on her looks. Still, she was not unattractive.

Frequent trips to a tanning salon, necessitated by her nocturnal habits, colored her skin a jaundiced and ocherous shade of brown which appeared both uneven and unnatural; yellowy orangey, it was distinctly different from the more pure shade of brown reflected in a natural suntan. Still, it was better than the preternaturally pale appearance she exhibited when circumstances or dire poverty kept her from the tanning bed. Her eyes were not a brilliant turquoise blue like her dad's, but more of a dullish blue-grey (again the result of her mother's genetic influence), that she brightened with livid, nearly garish, blue eye shadow.

Bobbie considered her worse feature to be her mouth, and especially her teeth, a few of which were conspicuously missing. Also, she thought her lips were too thin— "chicken lips," she called them. She overcame the former deficiency by always, or nearly always, smiling with her mouth mainly closed; she hated it when she occasionally forgot and smiled more naturally, revealing dark gaps where teeth were missing. The latter imperfection, her chicken lips, was remedied with the discreet application of lipstick—just enough to impart a fuller and healthier shape and appearance.

It took some doing, but after bathing and shaving and primping and preening for almost two hours, Bobbie Day was a fairly attractive sight to behold. As she admired in the mirror the results of her labors, her oldest daughter, Blossom, entered the bathroom.

"How do I look?" Bobbie asked her daughter, beaming.

"You look okay," said Blossom. Even without makeup, Blossom was much prettier than her mother, and she knew it, and she would not give her mom any compliments she didn't rightly deserve. "What's up with all the war paint?"

"Johnny Dollar's coming here this afternoon, remember? I told you that yesterday. I want you to look nice, too."

"Yeah, yeah, sure—God, can't I pee first?"

"You can pee all you want, but then I want you to take a bath and make yourself pretty. And don't take all day doin' it. You need to give Cricket a bath and get her dressed, too."

"God, why do I always have to take care of Cricket?" Blossom complained. "You're her mother, not me."

Bobbie shot Blossom a look that would have stopped a stampeding elephant in its tracks. Blossom knew from sorry experience her mother's mean look could be followed shortly by a fist, or two, to her face. Blossom stared down at the worn-out vinyl between her bare feet, and said nothing.

Johnny Dollar showed up around four with a case of beer, a few joints, and a "special surprise" he was saving for later. He and Bobbie sat at the dinette table in the kitchen and drank a few beers and smoked cigarettes and chitchatted, catching up on the time that had elapsed since they'd last been together. Around five, Johnny pulled a joint from his cigarette pack and presented it to Bobbie for approval.

"Oh yeah," Bobbie said happily, her eyes wide with delight. She'd been too broke lately to afford any pot.

Johnny lit the joint, took a long steady drag, and passed it to Bobbie, who responded in kind. By the time the joint was halfway consumed, its vapors had drifted to the back bedroom where Blossom was babysitting her little sister (half-sister, actually), Cricket.

Bobbie had given Blossom strict orders to keep Cricket entertained in the back bedroom, while she entertained her beau. But the tantalizing smell of pot smoke drew Blossom to the kitchen like a bear to honey. Blossom gave Cricket her favorite toy and told her, "You stay right here. I'll be right back."

Bobbie frowned at Blossom when she entered the kitchen. But the beer and pot and Johnny's company had put her in a good mood, and she didn't want to make a scene in front of her gentleman caller, so she didn't fuss at Blossom.

Of the two women in the room, one young and one not-so-young, Blossom was by far the more attractive. Johnny smiled hugely at Blossom, ignoring altogether her less attractive mother.

"Somethin' smells good in here," Blossom said brightly, returning Johnny's smile.

"What's up, Blossom," said Johnny, as he offered her the joint.

Blossom stepped forward, ready to grab the joint, but not without her mother's permission. She looked at her mom imploringly.

"Just a little," said Bobbie. "You're supposed to be watching your sister."

Quickly, eagerly, Blossom snatched the joint and took a long deep drag, completely filling her lungs with the sweet acrid smoke. When she finally exhaled about half a minute later, little smoke came forth; most of it had been absorbed.

"Good stuff," Blossom said as a compliment to Johnny, smiling, her eyes dreamy. She took another mighty drag on the joint.

Johnny's eyes never left Blossom for a moment. Bobbie wasn't exactly jealous; Blossom was cuter than she was, sure, but Bobbie knew who Johnny would be with that night when the lights went out. Still, she didn't want Johnny to be overly distracted.

"That's enough for you," Bobbie told her daughter, as if she were the judicious voice of moderation, and not at all concerned with Johnny's wandering eyes.

"When are we gonna eat?" asked Blossom. "I'm hungry now."

"I'll call you when supper's ready," said Bobbie. "Bye."

"Hey, how about we order up some pizza?" Johnny gallantly suggested. "I'm hungry too."

"As long as you can pay for it," Bobbie allowed. "We ain't got any money."

"Sure, no problem," said Johnny. "We'll order two—anything you want."

Blossom rushed to the phone in the adjacent living room and picked up the receiver. "I want pepperoni and mushrooms and olives and green peppers. What do you guys want?" she asked.

"I want you to go back where you were and keep an eye on your sister," Bobbie said sharply, a keen cutting edge in her voice. "I know what you want. I'll call you when the pizza's here."

Blossom hung up the phone and returned to the back bedroom. Bobbie got up and phoned in their order.

The pizzas arrived half an hour later. The four of them—Johnny Dollar, Bobbie, Blossom and Cricket—sat around the little dinette table and ate without plates or silverware. Johnny and Bobbie drank beer. Bobbie let Blossom have a beer, too, but "just one." Cricket drank Coke. Nobody spoke. The three older people were too high and hungry to say anything, and the little one, Cricket, was virtually a mute: at the age of four, she had not uttered more than a hundred words in her life.

After dinner, the foursome retired to the living room and watched a videotape, *As Good as It Gets*. Johnny and Bobbie snuggled and cuddled together on the sofa, while Blossom and Cricket sat on the floor. Cricket wasn't at all interested in the movie, so Blossom kept her entertained with toys. At times, in ways, Blossom looked as childlike as her little half-sister as they played happily on the floor.

When the movie ended, Bobbie hit the REWIND button on the remote and told Blossom it was Cricket's bedtime. Cricket, like her mom and half-sister, kept late hours, typically sleeping from four or five in the morning until one or two in the afternoon. But Blossom could take a hint; she knew her mom wanted to be alone with Johnny Dollar.

"See ya later, Johnny," said Blossom, as she gathered up her little sister. "Thanks for the pizza."

"Later," said Johnny.

Bobbie inserted into the machine another corny romance movie, *Sleepless in Seattle*, and switched off the lamp, making the TV the room's only source of illumination. Night had fallen; Bobbie was finally in her element—darkness. She rejoined Johnny on the sofa, cuddled up close, and the two started kissing. Soon their hands were grasping and caressing each other's tender parts. When Bobbie was certain Johnny had passed the point of no return, she separated herself from him ever so slightly and said, "Johnny, honey, I got a little favor to ask you."

"Huh? What...?" Johnny mumbled.

"I got a ticket a while back. If I don't pay it, well, the cops are liable to come here and serve me a warrant."

"How much?" Johnny asked bluntly, his manly passion suddenly deflated.

"Not much," said Bobbie, her voice as soft and sweet as she could make it. "A couple hundred bucks is all. I'll pay you back..."

"How much?" Johnny asked again, more bluntly than before.

"Well, I guess maybe a hundred and fifty *might* take care of it," Bobbie replied, her temper rising. She couldn't stand to be challenged in any way, shape, or form.

Johnny was silent for a moment, and rather tense. Then he suddenly relaxed and said, "I don't know if I got that much on me. Let me look." He straightened up on the sofa, extracted his wallet, opened it, and tilted it toward the TV to inspect its contents. "It looks like I got one-forty-something. Here." He handed all the wallet's bills to Bobbie.

Bobbie placed them on the end table next to the sofa. "Thanks, Johnny. I'll pay you back, really."

"Don't worry about it," said Johnny, suddenly moved by his own generosity. "If that ain't enough, I can run out to a money machine somewhere."

Bobbie briefly considered asking for more, but didn't want to press her luck. "I think I can manage with this," she said. "Thanks."

"Don't worry about it," said Johnny. "I got something else for you I think you'll *really* like." He pulled his cigarette pack from his shirt pocket and inserted his pointing finger and dug around until finally he extracted a one-inch square of folded aluminum foil. Bobbie waited anxiously while he carefully unfolded the foil.

"What is it?" Bobbie asked breathlessly.

"Acid," said Johnny. "It's good, too. Do you feel up to trippin' tonight?"

Bobbie squirmed with pure delight, but then became still. She had her daughters, and other matters, to consider. "I don't know," she demurred with uncharacteristic restraint. If only her court fine was settled already, and she didn't have that to worry about, she wouldn't have hesitated a moment. And, she would have preferred to have been at Johnny's house in Louisville, with no maternal responsibilities to get in the way of her fun.

"Blossom can take care of Cricket," Johnny coaxed. "Come on—you know you want to."

Bobbie considered, and decided Johnny was right: Blossom could, and would, take care of Cricket. And the cops weren't likely to serve a warrant at this time of night, or during the night, and definitely not tomorrow because tomorrow was Sunday and the cops rarely conducted official business on Sunday.

"Oh hell," said Bobbie. "Why not?"

"Good," said Johnny. "This is good stuff—you'll love it." He touched the tip of his finger to his tongue, and then touched his moistened fingertip to a tiny tab of acid, securing it firmly in place.

"Open up," said Johnny. He placed the hit of acid in the middle of Bobbie's tongue. Her lips closed around his finger and sucked as he withdrew it. Johnny consumed the remaining hit of acid in a similar fashion.

"Tastes like soap," said Bobbie. "What do they call this stuff, anyway? Does it have a name?"

"They call it Windowpane," said Johnny. "You're right—it does taste like soap. You want another beer?"

"Yeah, sure," said Bobbie.

Their lovemaking temporarily suspended, they sat on the sofa and sipped their beers and watched the romantic comedy on TV, waiting for the acid to take hold. After half an hour or so, the movie became for them less of a romantic comedy, and more like theater of the absurd. Johnny chuckled after almost every line of dialog. Bobbie could only smile her closemouthed smile, but inside she was laughing uproariously.

After an hour, as they neared the peak of their acid trips, the movie made no sense whatsoever. Johnny and Bobbie felt perfectly sane; it was the characters in the movie who were totally and hilariously crazy. Soon the movie was too much to bear, too great an assault on their heightened and twisted senses.

"I can't take any more of this," said Johnny.

"I know," Bobbie agreed, with the paramount empathy peculiar to trippers. "Come on—let's go to bed."

Bobbie's bedroom was located in the far end of the trailer opposite the room where Blossom was babysitting Cricket; they couldn't be more separated and still be inside the same structure. Still, even with her bedroom door securely locked, Bobbie felt her daughters' proximity and was bothered by it. Indeed, her bedroom door was closed and locked but her mental doors of perception were opening widely, providing access to the far reaches of the cosmos, if that's where she wanted to go. The mere fifty or sixty feet, and four or five walls, that separated her from her daughters were as nothing, less than nothing.

Johnny seemed to read her mind. "Don't worry about the girls," he said soothingly. "They're a million miles away. It's just you and me now."

The words struck Bobbie like a powerful hypnotic suggestion. Immediately her bothersome sense of her daughters' proximity vanished, gone. She stood by the bed and undressed in the dark, while Johnny waited for her under the covers.

With their senses heightened to an unimaginable degree, their lovemaking was nearly painful in its intensity. It seemed to last an eternity, or at least for several hours, though the digital clock on the nightstand revealed the passing of less than twenty minutes.

Their passions drained at last, they stared at the ceiling where a psychedelic fantasia played out in brilliant fluorescent colors. Kaleidoscopic patterns, constantly changing, dazzled and amazed. As their heartbeats slowed and their blood pressure dropped, the patterns were transformed into livid and psychedelic cartoon figures, not Donald and Mickey, but a host of fantastic phantasms escaped from their subconscious minds to roam freely about the ceiling and walls. Occasionally they saw, or imagined they saw—under the influence of LSD, there was no discernable distinction between perception and imagination—the same cartoon character simultaneously.

"Who's that?" asked Johnny, looking at a character which appeared, like a creation of Doctor Moreau, to be half-man and half-beast. "He looks like a cow."

"I don't know," Bobbie said, trying to see what Johnny saw. "Oh, that. That must be Woodbine, my neighbor."

"He looks like he's pissed off about something," Johnny commented with a faraway voice.

Bobbie watched with mounting horror as huge pointed horns sprung from the bovine character's forehead. Its eyes blazed luridly red like the fires of hell, and the horns grew ever longer and more pointed, aimed directly at her face.

"I don't like that guy," Bobbie said, her voice rather fearful. "Let's look at something else. Tell me about our farm."

For the past few years Johnny had been telling Bobby that when he retired from General Electric he would buy a farm somewhere—not here, or even close to here, but somewhere else, maybe in a different state—and they'd all live happily ever after. It was rather more than a pipe dream. Johnny owned outright a house in Louisville he'd inherited from his parents that was worth about a hundred and fifty thousand dollars. He was scheduled to retire from GE in a few more years, at which time he would draw a modest pension. Despite his frequent drug use, Johnny was responsible with money, and he was always kind and attentive to Bobbie's children. He never mentioned marriage, and Bobbie didn't want him to; if they were married, her eligibility for social security disability payments would be contingent upon his income and she would lose her monthly check and probably her food stamps, too. Johnny didn't know much about farming, but Bobbie had garnered a good bit of farming and agricultural knowledge during her lifetime. Her dad had been a farmer, and her neighbors were all farmers, and most of her friends were farmers; and Bobbie always had had a way with animals.

Hours passed as Johnny comforted and entertained Bobbie with his vision of their future life together on their imaginary farm. Johnny wasn't much with words; his descriptions were not elegant or eloquent. But on and on he softly droned, describing in great detail their future farmhouse, and barns, and livestock, creating a pastoral tableau that came to life in Bobbie's mind and was instantaneously displayed on the ceiling, as if by a magical, mystical overhead projector.

Sometime around two in the morning, the acid began to wear off; Johnny's voice and imagination began to give out as well. The magic pictures on the ceiling became increasingly indistinct, less colorful and dazzling—hazy, blurred. Bobbie got up, put on her bathrobe, and excused herself to use the bathroom. When she emerged from the bathroom, Johnny was fully dressed and seated at the dinette table, sipping a beer.

"Me too," he said, rising, and then hurrying off to pee. When he returned, Bobbie was seated at the dinette table nursing a beer.

"Well, was that good acid or what?" asked Johnny, reclaiming his seat and his beer.

"It's still good," Bobbie replied. The acid was gradually wearing off, but everything in her peripheral vision still melted and swirled like hot wax stirred with a stick. If she focused on something directly, though, it appeared more or less normal.

"I'm gonna finish this beer and then I'll be shoving off," said Johnny.

Making love to Bobbie was rather like the lovemaking of black widow spiders. Johnny knew it was a good idea to get gone while the getting was good.

"Don't leave yet," said Bobbie, who was not quite ready to deal with the lingering effects of the acid on her own. "How 'bout some pizza?"

"No thanks—I couldn't eat anything right now. I need to go home and get some rest. I gotta go to work tomorrow."

Bobbie didn't want him to leave, but said nothing. If he had to work, well, he had to work. Still, it angered her more than a little. Work or no work, he could stay there with her at least a few more hours if he wanted.

"Before I forget," said Johnny, reaching again into the druggy treasure trove of his cigarette pack. "Here, you can smoke it later—it'll help take the edge off." He presented her with a joint.

Bobbie grabbed it and stuck it behind her ear. "Thanks," she said. "Are you sure you don't need it?"

"Yeah, I'm sure. I got more at home. Are you sure you don't need any more money? I don't want you to get yourself locked up or anything."

Bobbie again considered asking for more money, but again she prudently refrained. "Nah—I'll be alright." Johnny had done so much for her already: for several wonderful hours she had forgotten entirely about her troubles—trouble with the law, and trouble with Woodbine. She didn't want to be greedy. Nor did she want Johnny to leave.

Johnny drained the last of his beer and said, "I'm shoving off now. You take care of yourself. First thing Monday morning, I want you to pay that fine you owe."

"Don't worry about that—I hate havin' the law breathin' down my back. I'll pay it first thing Monday morning for sure."

"Okay then—bye." Johnny stood up from the table, walked around to Bobbie, and kissed her softly on the lips.

Bobbie stared sullenly at the label on her bottle of beer while Johnny left the trailer. She couldn't bear to watch him go.

Pot Shot 10

Johnny Dollar left the trailer; the door closed behind him with a solid thump. Blossom heard the door slam shut and correctly assumed that Johnny had left. She emerged from the back bedroom with little Cricket at her knees.

"Did Johnny leave already?" Blossom asked.

"Yeah, he's gone," Bobbie replied rather angrily while she stared at her bottle of beer.

"I want a beer," said Blossom, opening the refrigerator door.

"Just one," her mother replied automatically. "While you got that open, get Cricket some pizza and milk. Then I want both of you to go to bed."

Bobbie and Blossom and Cricket sat at the dinette table, the older two sipping beer and smoking cigarettes, while little Cricket worried a slice of cold pizza with tiny teeth.

"What's the matter, Mom?" asked Blossom. "You don't look happy."

Bobbie was not happy. When Johnny left, her idyllic vision of happiness, as well as her temporary escape from reality, left with him. Her nerves were becoming increasingly jangled as the acid continued to wear off. Former worries and cares, mercifully absent during Johnny's visit and their acid trip, were returning with a vengeance, revisiting her now with the trappings of psychotic paranoia.

Bobbie shrugged off her daughter's question with a nonchalance she truly did not feel. "I'm okay. We'll be okay. Now finish your beer and go to bed."

But Bobbie did not feel okay. She dreaded her trip to the courthouse on Monday. If they wanted, they could arrest her as soon as she walked in the door for her failure to appear in court. She didn't think they would, but they could if they wanted. And even if they didn't, after paying her fine for driving without insurance she would be broke again, or almost broke. It seemed she was always broke, or almost broke. She mainly had learned to live with it, but at times the cumulative effect of many long years of poverty bore down on her all at once with a crushing weight, nearly too great to bear.

"Did Johnny talk about the farm?" asked Blossom.

More than once, Bobbie had shared with Blossom her and Johnny's dream of a better life in the future. It was as comforting and appealing to Blossom as it was to Bobbie.

"Yeah, he talked about it some," Bobbie said wearily. "But that's still a long ways off. He can't retire from his job for at least a few more years yet. Now finish your beer and go to bed, and take Cricket with you."

Blossom drained the last of her beer and dutifully complied. "G'night, Mom," she said over her shoulder.

"Goodnight," Bobbie muttered.

Bobbie pulled another beer from the fridge and carried it to the sofa in the living room. She powered up the TV and VCR—they comprised an indispensable life-support system for her, practically the only items of value she hadn't taken, and would never take, to a pawn shop—and pushed the PLAY button on the remote.

The movie, *Sleepless in Seattle*, began playing about halfway through, at the point where she and Johnny had abandoned it. It made a bit more sense now than it had earlier, but it wasn't funny or romantic or in any way entertaining. Still, Bobbie stared stupidly at the screen until the movie was over.

Sunrise showed weakly through the trailer's front windows, those with an eastern exposure. Bobbie turned off her electronics and thought about going to bed. But she was not at all sleepy.

She decided she wanted some fresh air. Not infrequently she went outside early in the morning, while darkness and night still lingered just the other side of the horizon, before the sun waxed bright and bothersome. Not infrequently she sat in her bathrobe in a lawn chair behind her trailer and smoked a little pot and gazed out upon her dad's beautiful lake, soaking up the dawning day as it brought forth hope and promise, and then carrying that hope and promise with her to bed as fodder for hopeful and promising dreams.

She opened the trailer's backdoor, then suddenly stopped. Where was that joint that Johnny had given her? She searched her cigarette pack; it wasn't in there. She searched the dinette table and ashtray; it wasn't there either. Maybe Blossom had taken it; she had pilfered drugs from her in the past.

"Blossom!" Bobbie shouted madly. "Blossom, you get your little ass in here!"

Blossom emerged from her bedroom wearing an oversized T-shirt as a nightgown, and a sleepy, addled look on her face. "What'd I do now?" Blossom asked.

"Johnny gave me a joint before he left. Did you take it?"

"No Mom—you got it. It's stuck behind your ear."

Bobbie reached up with her left hand and felt nothing.

"Your other ear," Blossom said helpfully.

Bobbie reached up with her right hand, found it, and stared accusingly first at the joint, and then at Blossom. "Why didn't you tell me earlier when we were sittin' at the table?"

"You didn't ask. Can I go back to bed now?"

"Yes. Goodnight."

Blossom shook her head and returned to her bedroom.

Feeling rather stupid, but glad she had solved that little mystery, Bobbie sat outside in her favorite lawn chair and fired up the joint. Its mildly hallucinogenic properties enhanced and fortified the lingering effects of the LSD. She began to hallucinate again. Most of the deciduous trees were topped with the new green leaves of spring. Bobbie saw the trees as giant stalks of broccoli. It struck her as a novel realization and discovery: Trees were like giant stalks of broccoli, and broccolis were like little tiny trees. She wondered idly if anybody had ever thought of that before. Maybe not, probably not, but there it was, as plain as day. How strange…

She detected movement in her peripheral vision off to her left. She turned and saw maybe thirty of Woodbine's cattle ambling towards the little creek that fed her dad's lake. Slow and placid and separated from her by a barbed-wire fence, of course the animals posed no threat whatsoever; they only wanted to drink. But Bobbie had a flashback of Woodbine as she'd seen him earlier, his eyes fiery red, and huge twisted horns sprouting from his forehead; the image was superimposed somehow on every cow and steer.

Plodding slowly towards the little creek, the cattle appeared evil and diabolical in their intent. Bobbie became fearful and angry and resentful.

Woodbine had two hundred acres on which to pasture his cattle. Why did they have to intrude on her little moment of stoned-out peace and solitude?

Woodbine, too, was watching his cattle at that moment, gazing at them through his kitchen window while he sipped at his morning coffee. As always, he took great pleasure in the mere sight of his fat, sleek animals. His pleasure, however, was soon overtaken by concern as he noticed some of his herd ambling down to the little creek to drink, close to the Johnsons' property. He hadn't seen any of the Johnsons' dogs since yesterday's attack and had no idea where they were. But he deemed it best to move his cattle away from the Johnsons' property, lest they present an irresistible temptation to the dogs.

Woodbine donned his boots and cap and went outside, intent on herding the animals away from the little creek, and towards the two half-acre cow ponds on the far side of his property where most of his cattle were watering already.

The sun had climbed fully above the horizon, glowing brightly, warmly. Bobbie found the bright light harsh and annoying. She stubbed out the roach on a leg of the lawn chair and stuck it in her cigarette pack; she'd smoke it later when she got up. She was almost, but not quite ready to go to bed.

The cattle drinking from the little creek raised their heads and turned in the direction of Woodbine's voice as he hailed them with a loud and repeated nonlinguistic huff: "Harrugghh! Harrugghh!"

Bobbie also looked in the direction of the voice, and saw Woodbine plodding towards her.

"Harrugghh! Harrugghh!" Woodbine huffed again. He always hailed his cattle that way.

Bobbie's flashback returned more vividly than ever; she stared in horror as Woodbine plodded towards her, closer, ever closer, his eyes fiery red, wicked twisted horns sprouting from his forehead, aimed straight at her, while he bellowed like a bull.

In that same instant, Woodbine first saw Bobbie. He stopped immediately and wondered what to do. His first instinct was to wave, an ordinary neighborly wave like he would give any of his neighbors. But Bobbie's demeanor gave him pause. She looked both crazy and mad. Perhaps he had better not wave. Maybe later he'd have a chance to talk to Edgar and would patch things up with the Johnsons. But right now

Bobbie appeared to be even more furious than yesterday when she'd slammed the door on him, so he withheld the wave. Further, Woodbine felt mildly embarrassed to be staring at a woman, any woman other than his wife, dressed only in a bathrobe. Blushing slightly, Woodbine looked away from Bobbie and returned his attention to his cattle, perhaps a moment or two too late.

Bobbie, maddened by her hallucination of the fiery eyes and wicked horns, rose suddenly from the lawn chair and dashed into the trailer. Something had snapped. She grabbed a single-shot .22 rifle from the gun rack high on the living-room wall and dashed back outside.

Woodbine saw her run into the trailer and figured he'd embarrassed her by catching her outside in her bathrobe. He didn't know what to think when she ran back out of the trailer with a rifle in her hands. He still didn't know what to think, or what to do, when she leveled the rifle in his direction.

The little .22 cracked sharply, but not much louder than a firecracker, really, when Bobbie pulled the trigger. She was a good shot; her dad had taught her to shoot when she was no more than seven or eight. She didn't aim directly at Woodbine, but at one of the horns sprouting from his head. Maybe she hit it; the horns disappeared immediately. Bobbie immediately ran back inside.

Woodbine both heard and felt the bullet whiz right past his ear, as the tiny projectile pushed air out and around its rapid trajectory. Woodbine didn't run exactly, but he quickly turned and trotted off towards home with the ambling gait of a steer. Inside, he stood at the kitchen sink and trembled uncontrollably; he thought he might throw up.

His wife, Gertie, was in the bathroom getting ready for church. She heard the sharp report of the .22, and figured somebody was shooting at a squirrel or a rabbit. She didn't know if either critter was in season just then (they were not), but that didn't matter; people thereabouts were always sniping at critters, or just plain shooting for fun.

But she sensed that something was amiss when she heard the back door slam shut and her husband's heavy footfalls resounding through the house as he hastened towards the kitchen. She found him there, leaning against the sink and drinking a glass of water. His complexion was pale, ashen, and she noticed he was trembling.

"What in the world is goin' on now?" she asked concernedly, irately.

"Bobbie just took a shot at me," Woodbine stated as calmly as possible.

"She what?!? Is that what I just heard?!? That tears it—I'm callin' the police right now and don't you try to stop me."

"Wait," said Woodbine. "Let me think a minute."

"I will not wait, not one more minute!" Woodbine's wife took a few quick steps to the phone on the kitchen wall and snatched up the receiver.

"Just wait a minute, Gertie," Woodbine insisted. He walked over to his wife and, after a brief and mild struggle, took the receiver out of her hand. "Let me call Flo Goody first. Maybe she'll be able to help."

"Gary Woodbine, you must be out o' your mind. That crazy pothead is out there takin' potshots at you, and you want to talk to Flo Goody? Why, she don't have no more control over those lunatics over there than you got on the moon. She can't do nothin' with 'em—she told you that yesterday. You need to call the police. If not for the grace of God you'd be layin' out there dead right now. I'm callin' the police."

She grabbed for the phone in her husband's hand. Woodbine pulled it away. "Just let me talk to Flo first," Woodbine persisted. "Bobbie knows how to shoot and she wasn't all that far away. I don't think she was aimin' to hit me."

"Gary Woodbine!—my soul to thee! I never heard such foolishness in all my born days! Go ahead, then—call Flo Goody, for all the good it's gonna do ya. I don't care what she says. As soon as you hang up I'm callin' the police. I swear to you, I swear on my mother's grave, that crazy lunatic is gonna be locked up, and locked up quick. Go ahead—call Flo Goody. Don't pay me no never mind."

"Would you bring me the church directory out of the hallway, please?" Woodbine asked.

"Why sure I will. The sooner this foolishness is over, the better."

She returned momentarily with the directory. Gary phoned Flo Goody.

"Flo?—this is Gary Woodbine."

Flo's voice was worried and tense. She suspected there'd been more trouble with the dogs. "Yes?—this is Flo."

"I'm sorry to be botherin' you again like this, but I'm afraid there's been more trouble."

"Oh?—how's that?"

"Well, I was outside a little while ago, fixin' to move a few head o' cattle away from your brother's place, and Bobbie was sittin' out back there in her bathrobe, and …"

"That don't surprise me none," Flo interjected. "That girl never did have a lick o' common decency."

"Yeah, well, next thing I know, it's like she went all crazy all of a sudden. She ran inside the trailer and came out with a gun and, next thing I know, there's a bullet whizzin' right past my ear."

"My Lord," said Flo, after a brief, shocked silence. "I knew that girl was crazy, but I didn't think she was *that* crazy. What're you gonna do about it? Have you called the police?"

"No, not yet. I wanted to talk to you about it first."

"What's there to talk about? I know that girl's got a lot o' problems and all, but ain't nobody got the right to go takin' potshots at their neighbors."

"Well, I know that. But what would you do…?"

"If it was me, Gary, I'd call the law on her in a heartbeat. Ain't nobody got the right to go shootin' at their neighbors like that."

"I don't suppose you'd want to try talkin' to her for me? She's got those kids over there—that little one can't be more than three or four years old."

"She's four, but I don't see where those children have got anything to do with it. They'd probably be better off without that sorry mess of a mother they got anyway. Maybe it's time somebody taught her a lesson once and for all."

"I see," Gary said rather disappointedly. "Well, thanks anyway."

"I'll see you in church…?" Flo asked hopefully.

"Maybe," said Gary. "I'll have to see how things work out here."

"Well, if not this morning, I'll see you next Sunday for sure."

"Sure thing. Thanks—I'm sorry to have bothered you."

"It's no bother at all. I'm sorry for all the trouble that my brother and his no-good daughter have caused you."

"Well, let's just pray that somehow it all works out for the best."

"Sure, I'll be a-prayin', Gary. I'm sorry I can't do *more* to help."

"Me too. Goodbye."

"Bye."

Woodbine's wife had listened in on the phone in the hallway. Gary had heard the click when she picked up, but figured she might as well listen in; she'd hear every word of it eventually, one way or the other.

This way, at least, he was spared the misery of her dragging it out of him.

"Are you gonna call the police now?" she asked.

"Yes," said Woodbine. "I hate to do it but I guess I've got to."

Woodbine phoned the police.

Old Edgar was inside his little camper, breakfasting on a can of sliced peaches and a few store-bought chocolate cupcakes, when he heard the sharp report of a rifle. It sounded like Bobbie's little .22, and it sounded as if it had originated near the trailer. He figured she had shot at a snapping turtle. There were many snappers in Edgar's lake, *too* many in Edgar's opinion, and he'd told Bobbie many times to shoot them on sight, and occasionally she did.

Edgar finished his cupcakes and peaches, savoring every last drop of the syrupy nectar he drained from the can. He always slept in his clothes so he didn't need to get dressed. He fixed his red Marlboro cap firmly atop his head and went outside to greet the day.

As soon as he stepped outside, he looked for Bobbie near the trailer, but Bobbie was nowhere to be seen. He stuffed a chaw of tobacco in his mouth, and then walked to the woods behind his camper and peed. With no toilet in his little camper, the woods received most of his bodily wastes. Always he was careful to distribute his wastes widely throughout his woods, where they would decompose quickly and naturally without ever accumulating into an offensive and unsanitary mess. That little business concluded, he decided to mosey over to the trailer and ask Bobbie if she'd killed a turtle, and ask her to fix him a cup of coffee.

Edgar had covered about half the distance to the trailer when the dog pack came bounding up from God-knows-where; most of the animals were opportunistic vagabonds who roamed freely for many miles around. Edgar claimed ownership and responsibility for only two of them, Tony and Blue, who sometimes roamed with the pack but more often stayed close to Edgar, especially during cold weather. He noticed the big black dog was not in the pack, but thought nothing of it.

The dogs rollicked and gamboled around Edgar as he told them, "I ain't got nothin' for you just now but maybe Bobbie's got somethin' in the trailer. Now you all settle down, ya hear me?" The dogs settled down a bit.

Edgar knocked loudly on the backdoor of the trailer. There was no response. He knocked a second time more loudly. He didn't care if he woke anybody up; in fact, he rather hoped he did. He detested Bobbie's and the girls' nocturnal behaviors. Their "ass-backwards way of sleeping," as he called it, coupled with their occasional drug use, were the main reasons why Edgar had never bothered to claim a place to sleep inside the trailer, save on the coldest of nights, say, less than twenty degrees, when he ordered them all into bed at eleven o'clock, and then slept on the sofa. Edgar always rose with the sun and went to bed before eleven, and firmly advocated those hours for Bobbie and the girls as well. But they always ignored him.

Despite her crazy drug-addled condition, Bobbie knew she had made a terrible mistake very shortly after shooting at Woodbine. She regretted having done it, but regret would serve no useful purpose, so she busied herself with more practical matters like trying to remember where she had stashed the roach, and disposing of it, and locating the marijuana seeds she'd planned to plant in a few weeks, and disposing of them. She knew the police were likely to arrive at any moment, and desperately wanted to prepare as best she could. She wanted to wake up Blossom, and prepare her for the arrival of the police as well. But what could she say to her daughter? *Get up and get dressed so you can watch the police haul me off to jail.* No, it was better to let her daughters sleep, she decided. After all her posturing as a responsible and worthwhile mother, there was no way she could face Blossom with the shamefulness of her recent misbehavior yet so fresh upon her.

Edgar pounded loudly a third time on the trailer door. He tried the knob; it was locked. "Goddamn it Bobbie!—get up and answer the door!" he hollered.

Bobbie was relieved, and not relieved, to hear her father's voice. She'd thought all his knockings were those of the police, and was just about to open the door when she heard Edgar's angry voice. What could she say to her father? She had no idea, but she had to open the door.

"Are you deaf, child?" Edgar asked hotly. "Didn't you hear me a-poundin' on your door? I've done wore my knuckles black and blue."

Bobbie stepped quickly outside, lest they wake the girls. "Daddy," she began in a small petulant voice. Her lips tried to tremble, but lacked sufficient mass to quite do so. "I've done a bad thing, a really bad thing."

Bobbie was a tough girl, as mean and tough as any girl in the county.

Edgar had never seen her looking so uncharacteristically tore-up and puny. He was immediately concerned. He extracted the chaw of tobacco from his mouth and tossed it aside so he could concentrate fully on what she had to say, and reply plainly, without the chaw getting in the way of his words.

"Well, what is it, Bobbie? I seen Johnny Dollar's car over here last night. Did you two get in a big fight or somethin'?"

"No Daddy—it's a lot worse than that."

"Speak up, girl," Edgar said firmly. "I'm a-listenin'. Just calm yourself now and tell me what's the matter."

"Well, Daddy, I kind o' took a shot at Gary Woodbine this morning with the twenty-two," Bobbie confessed at last.

"Good God in the morning!" exclaimed Edgar. "What in the world did you go and do that for?"

"I was trippin'," Bobbie stated honestly.

"Trippin'? What in the hell does that mean? Are you talkin' about some kind o' crazy goddamn drugs?"

"Yeah. I'm sorry."

"Jesus, Bobby, Jesus. Why do you all fool around with that kind o' shit in the first place? Goddamn it anyway. I've always let you drink all the beer you wanted, whiskey too when you wanted it. That's always been all I've ever needed, whiskey and beer. Why do you have to fool around with those crazy drugs like that? Seems like you would've learned somethin' from your first marriage—it was drugs what made you and Jimmy act so crazy all the time, and it was drugs what finally killed Jimmy Day. Jesus, Bobbie—Damn!"

"I know Daddy. I'm sorry."

The full realization of Bobbie's criminal action and its likely consequences suddenly caught up with old Edgar. He started pacing quickly about, this way and that, that way and this, while removing his cap and replacing it every few seconds. After a minute or two of these highly animated antics, he stopped and stared Bobbie squarely in the face.

"Was you aimin' to hit him? Tell me the truth now—was you aimin' to hit Woodbine?" asked Edgar.

"No, Daddy," Bobbie stated. "I really wasn't aimin' to hit him." Then she paused briefly as a plausible story—not quite an alibi, but a story—took shape in her mind. At least part of it was true. "Woodbine was over here yesterday claimin' he'd just shot Blackie and tellin' me to bury him. That's what pissed me off. First he shot Blackie and then he told me to bury him. That's why I shot at him. But I didn't really shoot *at* him. I shot way up into those trees over there. I swear I wasn't aimin' to hit him. I was just aimin' to let him know we didn't much appreciate him shootin' Blackie."

"Woodbine shot Blackie? That no-good son-of-a-bitch. Why didn't you tell me about it sooner? You should've come and told me about it right off. I would've taken care o' Woodbine myself, and you wouldn't be in the mess you're in. But I see now why you done what you done. Now tell me again, Bobbie—do you swear you wasn't really aimin' to hit Woodbine?—that you shot way up into the trees?"

"Yeah, I swear."

"How far up?"

"I don't know—way up, way up high in the leaves." (Way up high in the broccoli tops, she almost said.)

"I believe you, Bobbie. I know you can shoot 'cause I taught you how to shoot. If'n you was really aimin' at Woodbine, as big as he is and all, you would've hit him for sure."

For a brief moment, Bobbie reveled in her father's pride and confidence in her marksmanship. Then came the wailing of a police siren, increasing in volume as it shortened the distance to its quarry, loudening like the baying of a hound as it closes on its prey.

"There's the law," Edgar said grimly. "Well, let 'em come. You just tell 'em what you just told me, that you wasn't aimin' to hit Woodbine, that you shot way up into the trees on account o' him shootin' Blackie yesterday, and let's just see what they have to say about that. Ain't no way they can hold that again' you, not after Woodbine killed Blackie. I wanna hear what they have to say about that. Come on, let's go." Edgar grabbed Bobbie's arm and hurried her around to the front yard to confront the police as soon as they arrived. The dogs followed excitedly, still anxious for something to eat. Edgar wheeled on them and raged, "You all get out o' here now!— ever' goddamn one o' you! Go on—git!" The dogs stared for a moment at Edgar's hard, stern face, and then they all bounded off towards God-knows-where.

Edgar planted himself firmly and squarely in front of the trailer, his arms folded across his chest and a look of supreme righteousness on his face. He removed and replaced his cap one last time, and then he was ready for anything.

Bobbie was not nearly so ready. She hadn't told her dad about her traffic ticket and subsequent failure to appear in court last week; they could arrest her for that if they wanted. And despite her dad's wholehearted belief that she had been justified in shooting *way up into the trees*, she knew that wasn't exactly truthful, and if it came down to her word against Woodbine's in a court of law—in the courthouse where Gertie Woodbine worked, and where Gary Woodbine was also highly regarded—she knew she'd come out holding the short end of the stick.

Edgar stuffed a fresh chaw of tobacco in his maw as the cruiser turned onto the drive. Then he refolded his arms across his chest and waited. There were two officers in the county police cruiser. As soon as they saw Bobbie and Edgar standing there in plain sight, the siren shut off but the lights kept flashing.

The officers got out of the car. Edgar knew them both; he knew all the deputies in the sheriff's department, but from a far different perspective than the Woodbines. One of the officers was Tom Stinnett; the other was an older guy named Luther Hunt.

Edgar stared defiantly as the officers approached, the younger man limping, the other walking slowly so he wouldn't get ahead of his partner. Bobbie stared at the ground. She wanted to look at the officers, but couldn't. Edgar spat tobacco juice in their general direction when they were maybe ten or twelve feet away. The officers took another step forward, and then stopped.

"Tom, Luther," Edgar said, with a brief nod of his head. "Before anybody here goes off half-cocked..." he looked directly at Tom Stinnett, cracking smart about his mishap, but the officer didn't seem to get it. "I want you men to listen to Bobbie's side o' the story. I don't know what Woodbine's told you, but I want you to stop a minute and listen to what Bobbie has to say."

"Okay," said the older man. "We're listening."

"Bobbie," Edgar prompted. "Go ahead and tell 'em what you just told me. Tell 'em you wasn't aimin' at Woodbine, that you shot way up into the trees on account o' Woodbine killin' Blackie yesterday. Go on—tell 'em."

"Woodbine shot one of our dogs yesterday," Bobbie stated rather lamely, her eyes averted. "Then he came over here and told me to bury it."

"I saw your dog," Tom Stinnett replied harshly. "I saw the calf it killed too. That was the third calf they've lost in the past month. Mister Woodbine had every right to shoot your dog, every right in the world. Is that all you got to say?"

Bobbie was mute. She was scared out of her mind. It didn't help that she was still coming down off her acid trip and high as a kite, either.

Blossom stuck her head out the front door just then and asked loudly, "Mom? Grandpa? What's going on?"

"Get back in the trailer Blossom and keep an eye on Cricket and don't stick your nose out here again!" Edgar shouted fiercely. Blossom disappeared immediately. Edgar quickly recomposed himself somewhat and took up the defense of his daughter. "Luther, you've known me a long time now, and I've known you and your people a long time too. I used to drink with your daddy ever' now and then. He was mighty partial to my shine as I recall."

"Yeah, Edgar, I know all about you and my daddy. He's been passed away a long time now. What's that got to do with anything?"

"All I'm a-sayin' is that you know me Luther Hunt, and you know I wouldn't stand here and lie in your face, and neither would Bobbie. Now Bobbie here has told me that she wasn't aimin' to hit Woodbine—that she shot way up into the trees. Is that what Woodbine said?—or did he have somethin' different to say?"

Luther Hunt turned to his partner and said, "Tom, you took the call. What did Gary tell you?"

The younger man spoke directly to Edgar. "Mister Woodbine told me that he heard the bullet whiz right past his ear. He said Bobbie was aimin' straight at him and he heard the bullet whiz right past his ear." He turned his attention from Edgar to Bobbie as he concluded his statement, but Bobbie continued to stare at the ground.

"Then I say Woodbine is a goddamn liar," Edgar countered hotly. "If Bobbie here was aimin' straight at him, as big as he is and all, she would've hit him for sure. Bobbie's done told me that she shot way up into the trees, and…"

Luther Hunt interrupted. "Edgar, we're not here to stand as judge and jury—you know that. We're just doin' our jobs is all, and we're gonna have to take Bobbie in."

"I'll be goddamned if you will! Are you gonna stand here and tell me there's a law against shootin' way up into the trees!?! Goddamn it

Luther!—you wasn't here! She might've been shootin' at a squirrel for all you know!" And then, in a more moderate tone, "Bobbie's got them two little babies to take care of—you know that. What are them babies gonna do if their mother's in jail? Tell me that, Luther—what are them babies gonna do all alone in that trailer with no mother to look after them?"

"Edgar I'm sorry, I truly am sorry, but we got a job to do. Bobbie *will* be arrested and that's all there is to it. Don't make this any harder than it has to be."

"Don't tell me about your goddamn job," Edgar barked. Before either of the officers could respond, he grabbed Bobbie's arm and hurriedly struck off towards the area behind the trailer. The officers followed immediately. Tom Stinnett pulled his revolver from its holster and shouted, "Stop! Stop right there!" as he limped along behind them.

"Don't tell me to stop!" Edgar hollered back, even as he stopped in Bobbie's backyard. "Now Bobbie—where was you standin' at when you shot your rifle? Show us where you was standin'."

"I was there, right next to that lawn chair," Bobbie muttered.

"And where was Woodbine?" asked Edgar.

Bobbie pointed far to the left of where Woodbine actually had stood. "I don't know exactly—over there somewhere."

"And where did you shoot, Bobbie?" asked Edgar. "Point to where you shot your rifle at."

"Up there," Bobbie pointed, indicating treetops a few hundred feet to the right of the location where she had placed Woodbine.

"See? Do you see now what I've been tryin' to tell you?" Edgar asked excitedly. "She wasn't aimin' nowheres near Woodbine. You can't haul her in for shootin' a few leaves out of a tree, now can you? O' course not—o' course you can't."

Edgar appeared to have rested his case. He looked challengingly from one cop to the other, as if daring either man to rebut his brilliant defense.

"I'm not sayin' you're wrong," Luther began tactfully. "But we got another warrant to serve on Bobbie anyway for failing to appear in court last week. Right now that's all we'll charge her with. I'll personally talk to Woodbine and verify what he told Tom before we go any further with this shooting business. But right now we're placing Bobbie under arrest for failure to appear in court."

Edgar was totally and instantly ruined. He had thought he'd won. "What're you talkin' about, Luther? What failure to appear in what court?"

Luther was securing Bobbie in handcuffs; she was known throughout the force to be violent at times. "She was supposed to be in court on Wednesday for driving without insurance. Didn't she tell you about that?"

"Bobbie, Bobbie," Edgar woefully exclaimed. "Is that true?"

Bobbie faced him briefly with guilty, sorrowful eyes.

"Bobbie, Bobbie, Bobbie—why didn't you tell me? I would've given you money for your fine, if that's what you needed. I'll pay it right now. I ain't got it on me just now but I can get it. Just give me a minute to call Royce Taylor and we'll pay you what we owe."

Luther ignored Edgar completely. He informed Bobbie of her Miranda rights while he escorted her to the police cruiser.

Edgar followed closely at their heels, protesting all the while. Tom Stinnett followed closely behind Edgar, ready to grab him, or shoot him, if need be. He still had his revolver in hand.

Luther carefully placed Bobbie in the cruiser's backseat and then turned to address Edgar one last time. "Edgar, you know the deal so I'm not gonna waste time explaining it to you. Bobbie will be arraigned tomorrow morning at nine o'clock. That's all I can tell you right now. Goodbye." He climbed in the cruiser and closed his door.

Tom Stinnett continued to watch Edgar closely, prepared for any desperate last-minute move the old man might make. Edgar, too, was known to be violent occasionally. Satisfied that Edgar posed no threat, he finally holstered his revolver and opened his car door.

"Next time you take a notion to shoot yourself Tom, why don't you aim a little bit higher?" Edgar taunted, just as Tom's door slammed shut.

Bad News   11

Cold temperatures and extremely unsettled weather followed the few short days of February's false spring. It was late-March when the weather settled down enough for Joe Bass to think about fishing again. On a Friday afternoon after work, he cleaned out his tackle box, discarding hooks that had rusted and soft-plastic lures that had lost their elasticity and other tackle that was no longer serviceable, and neatly arranged his various lures and floats and hooks and sinkers in their individual compartments. He disassembled his fishing reels and cleaned their gears and inner workings with WD-40, and then lubricated them with 3-IN-ONE oil. After reassembling the reels, he stripped off and threw away all the old fishing lines, and refilled the reels with fresh new monofilament.

This cleaning and maintenance of his fishing tackle was an annual rite of spring for Joe Bass. Always it piqued his fishing fever, preparing him both mechanically and mentally for the new fishing season. He planned to go fishing the next morning and he very much looked forward to it. After a few months of gray and dreary winter, the warm blush of spring offered the glowing promise of rebirth and renewal for the natural world, and that included Joe Bass. Birds would nest, flowers would bloom, groundhogs would emerge from their winter burrows, and Joe Bass would sally forth to catch some fish.

On Saturday morning, Joe loaded his cooler and fishing poles and tackle box into his big red Ford truck and headed towards Nolin Lake. Halfway there, the OIL light flashed red on the dashboard, and a few miles later the engine stopped running.

Eventually his truck was towed to a service station where Joe learned he needed a new oil pump. For nearly a week he and his family were forced onto an early and late schedule, as Jolene drove him to and from work each day.

Trouble, the old-timers say (and the old-timers were well represented in the persons of Jolene's parents), always comes in threes. The day Joe got his truck back from the service station his son came down with a nasty cold and tenacious ear infection that lasted the better part of two weeks. As soon as the boy showed clear signs of improvement, their daughter came down with the very same things.

Joe and Jolene hoped their daughter's illness marked the third and final episode of the proverbial triple-threat traditionally posed by Trouble. But Jolene wasn't so sure. She didn't know if their children's illnesses constituted one single calamity, or two separate misfortunes. Joe pooh-poohed her superstitious misgivings, although as a fisherman, he was occasionally superstitious himself.

"You shouldn't even think like that," Joe chided. "Superstition is for old people and stupid people. Let's just be grateful that the kids are finally well and move on from here."

"What about you and your lucky fishing pole?—the one your dad gave you?" asked Jolene.

"That's different," said Joe, smiling.

"Oh yeah? How is it different?"

"Well, let's just say that it's okay to believe in good luck, but not bad luck."

"Good or bad, luck is luck," Jolene replied. "Either you believe in it or you don't."

"Wrong—I believe in good luck only, and I totally do not believe in bad luck. Now let's stop talking about it. I'm going fishing tomorrow and you're about to spoil it for me."

"How's that?" asked Jolene. "Am I giving you bad luck by talking about it? How can I give you something you don't believe in?"

"You're *not* giving me bad luck, but you're not giving me good luck either. What I need now is good luck. I want to catch some fish tomorrow, if there are any left. From what I hear, the crappie run is almost over already. I've missed it, or most of it."

"I'm sorry the kids have been sick," said Jolene. "You've been an angel, staying home and helping me take care of them."

"Well, let's just be grateful it's all over with now."

"I am," said Jolene. "Good luck with your fishing tomorrow."

"Thanks," said Joe. He kissed the top of her head for even more good luck.

The next morning, Joe fished his favorite and usually most productive area of Nolin Lake for nearly two hours and landed just one keeper crappie. When a boat and two fishermen came within shouting range, Joe called out, "You guys having any luck?"

"Not really," one of the fishermen replied. "The crappie run's just about over. They've moved down off the beds already. Somebody told me to try some deeper water but we can't find 'em out here either."

"Thanks," Joe shouted, with no real gratitude.

Joe gathered his gear and toted it back to his truck. It was not quite nine o'clock. He was not at all ready to call it quits for the day. He decided to try his luck in the river.

There he found only one vehicle in the parking lot and one fisherman fishing, which was not a good sign, especially on a warm and promising Saturday morning in May. Word spread quickly when the fish were biting, attracting throngs of eager anglers to the river below the Nolin River Dam. Conversely, when the fish weren't biting, the river was usually pretty much deserted.

Joe recognized the lone angler as Lloyd Sanders, an old river rat and catfisherman who lived about a mile and a half from the dam. Everybody who fished the river below the dam knew old Lloyd. Not only did he fish there more than any other single person, he frequently gave away his catch to anybody who wanted it, friends and strangers alike, endearing himself to one and all. Related or not, most people called him Uncle Lloyd.

"Uncle Lloyd," called Joe as he picked his way along the rocky bank.

Old Lloyd threw a hand in the air as a wave or salute.

"Where is everybody?" asked Joe. "Aren't they biting today?"

"I don't guess they are," said Lloyd. "There've been a dozen come and go while I've been here and I didn't see anybody get a bite. It might be a little too early for 'em, or a little too late—hell, I don't know. They just ain't bitin'."

"I just came from the lake and they're not doing much up there either. I caught one fish. The crappie run is just about over already," said Joe.

"I might try fishing over at Edgar Johnson's place," he added, surprising himself with the sudden declaration. He had had no prior plans to fish in Edgar's lake.

Lloyd's broad weathered face lit up with instant recognition and astonishment at the mention of Edgar's name. "Edgar J. Johnson," he stated slowly, pronouncing each and every syllable with great import. "I didn't know he was still alive. What's he up to these days?"

"Not much, I don't guess," replied Joe, who naturally had no idea what Edgar was up to. "He's got one hell of a fine fishing lake—I can tell you that much. Best damn lake I've ever fished in my life."

"Sure, I've been there," said Lloyd. He looked as if he were somewhat embarrassed by the fact. "I could tell you stories you wouldn't believe."

"Drinking…?" Joe prompted.

Lloyd nodded, and elaborated, "Drinkin' ain't exactly the right word for what we done. Sometimes we laid up drunk at Edgar's place for weeks at a time. Women would get to missin' their husbands after a while, and they'd have to send the sheriff over to Edgar's to pick 'em up and bring 'em home. It was a mess over there, I'll tell you what."

Joe wasn't too surprised to hear of the debauchery that had occurred at Edgar's place in days gone by. And he wasn't going to allow it to come between him and Edgar's lake.

"Good luck, Uncle Lloyd," Joe told the old fisherman. "I hope you catch a big one… or two."

"You be careful now," Lloyd replied.

Hope springs eternal, the poet wrote, and the axiom especially holds true for fishermen. Joe Bass had caught just three fish all year, but that could change very soon. If only he could find Edgar at home, Edgar would keep the dogs off him and he could catch another big mess of fish. It didn't seem like a lot to hope for; Edgar seemed like a person who didn't go out much, and his lake was undoubtedly still full of fish.

Joe's hopes rose even higher as he turned onto Sycamore Church Road. Prudently, though, he tempered it with caution. No way would he endure another attack from the pack of crazy dogs. He planned to drive slowly past Edgar's place and look for him from the road. If he saw Edgar, all would be well and good. If he didn't see Edgar, he'd turn around and go home.

Joe was thrilled to spot old Edgar immediately, standing in his driveway and facing the road expectantly, as if he'd been waiting for Joe to show up. Joe unconsciously held his breath as he crept along the twin ruts in the broom grass, expecting the dog pack to arrive and attack at any moment. But the dogs never showed, not even one lone animal. Joe stopped at the end of the drive, keyed off the motor, and breathed a sigh of relief that the dogs were not around before climbing out of his truck.

Edgar rushed up and pumped Joe's hand warmly, enthusiastically, as if he were a long-lost friend, or brother, and not someone he'd met only once. "Joe Bass," he started. "I am so glad you're here. I've got terrible news, just terrible. We've been hit hard, Joe. I don't know how we're gonna make it."

"What happened?" asked Joe. "Where are the dogs?"

"The dogs are part of it, Joe. We had to get rid o' the dogs. But it's Bobbie I'm worried about. They put my little Bobbie in jail."

"Bobbie?" asked Joe. He'd forgotten Edgar had a daughter named Bobbie.

"Bobbie … Roberta … we call her Bobbie. That's my daughter. Woodbine over there had her arrested. They got her down at the county jail. They sentenced her to a year, Joe—a whole year in jail."

"Who's Woodbine?" asked Joe.

Edgar indicated with a broad sweep of his hand the pastures across the road and also next door, on the far side of his lake. "Woodbine, he owns all that over there, and next door, too. I never saw it myself and I don't believe it's true, but Woodbine claimed our dogs were chasin' his cattle. Woodbine, he went out there with a shotgun and killed one of 'em, a big black dog, I don't know if you ever saw him or not. We called him Blackie, is what we called him. He was a tad bit on the wild side but I don't believe he needed killin'. Woodbine shot him dead."

"Did you report it to the police?"

"The police know all about it but that didn't do us no good. Woodbine's wife works at the courthouse, and Woodbine's a big man around here—a deacon at his church. I don't know why that fat son-of-a-bitch had to go and call the law on Bobbie in the first place. I don't have much use for the law. I think we'd all be better off if they let people work things out on their own. I'd be over there at Woodbine's right now takin' a two-by-four to his head."

"So what happened?" asked Joe. "Why is your daughter in jail?"

"Well, like I said, Woodbine shot Blackie, and that didn't sit too good with Bobbie. A few of those dogs acted pretty wild but we never saw any of 'em botherin' Woodbine's cows. Well, Woodbine went over to the trailer and told Bobbie he'd killed Blackie, and then he told her to bury it for him. Can you imagine that?"

"What did Bobbie say?"

"She didn't say a goddamn word. She slammed the door in his face is what she done. But then she gave him a little warning. She saw him out workin' his cattle the next day and she fired way up into the trees with a rifle, way up over his head, just to let him know she didn't appreciate him killin' Blackie. And Woodbine had her arrested for shootin' at him. Can you believe that? Let me tell you what, now—I taught Bobbie how to shoot, and that girl can *shoot*. I've seen her shoot the eyes out of a snappin' turtle from a hundred yards away. If she was aimin' at Woodbine she would've hit him for sure. She shot way up into the trees is what she done, but Woodbine swore in court that he heard the bullet whiz right past his ear, and now my little Bobbie's in jail, and her two babies are over there in that trailer without a mother to take care of 'em."

"I'm sorry to hear all that," said Joe. "I don't suppose there's anything I can do…"

"No, no, I'm afraid we can't help her now. I had a lawyer for her, sort of. He acted like he could've maybe done us some good if we'd had us some money. If we'd had us a big pile o' money then maybe we could've just paid a big fine to the court, and paid Woodbine for the stock he claims he lost, and Bobbie wouldn't have had to do any jail time. But we didn't have any money to speak of, so Bobbie's in jail. Do you think that's justice, Joe?—My little Bobbie's in jail just because we didn't have us a big pile of money to pay the court? Do you think that's fair?"

"I wish you would've let me know," Joe said concernedly. "I could've maybe loaned you some money."

Edgar earnestly searched Joe's face, looking for sincerity. Finding it, he said, "Bless you, Joe—God bless you. I truly believe you would've helped us. God bless you. There ain't many around who would help us these days."

"Well, I would've helped if I had known," said Joe.

"I believe you Joe. I truly do believe you. Royce Taylor, he said he would've helped us too, but I couldn't ask ol' Royce for anything. He's done too much for me already. Bobbie's boyfriend, Johnny Dollar, he said he would've helped too, but he didn't find about it till it was too late. I don't know why Bobbie waited so long to call him. I can't imagine she was ashamed of herself. It ain't the first time she's been in jail. She should've called Johnny sooner. It's too late to help her now."

Edgar seemed nearly overwhelmed with emotion, but shortly found the strength to continue. "Let me tell you what else that judge went and done. He told us we had to get rid of all our dogs. We can't have another dog here on our property for five years, not even a little bitty dog for five whole years. How can a judge do that, Joe? I'd like to see it written in a law book somewheres that a judge can tell people they can't have a dog. Do you think that's in a law book, Joe?"

"Probably not," said Joe. "I think that's what they call creative sentencing."

"What?" asked Edgar.

"Creative sentencing," Joe repeated. "I think that's what they call it."

"Well, I call it wrong, is what I call it. It's just plain wrong." Edgar winced as if suddenly racked by a sharp inner pain. "Oooohhh," he moaned loudly. "Joooe. I don't know how we're gonna make it Joooe. Woodbine has laid us looow."

"Edgar, I'm sorry," said Joe. He truly was sorry about Edgar's situation, but not about the dogs being gone. Joe was glad and relieved the dogs were out of the picture, regardless of the circumstances. Truth be told, if he'd had a gun during his last visit, he might've shot one of the beasts himself.

"So what happened to the dogs?" Joe asked.

"I had to get rid o' the dogs, Joe. They were gonna send animal control out here to kill 'em or lock 'em up somewheres, but I didn't want to give those bastards the satisfaction so I took care of it myself. I killed ever' last one of 'em, even Tony and Blue. Ol' Blue—'ceptin' for maybe Royce Taylor—Ol' Blue was just about the best friend I had. After my cabin burnt down, before I bought my little camper, I was sleepin' out here in my car at night and Ol' Blue was the only one who stuck with me. He was the only one who'd sleep out here with me in my car. Ol' Blue, he kept me from shiverin' on many a frosty night, I'll tell you what. Blackie, he was a tad bit on the wild side, but Ol' Blue wasn't nothin' like that. Ol' Blue, he was the best dog I ever owned, and I've had quite a few dogs in my time."

"I really am sorry," Joe said. Then he wondered aloud, "Why didn't you sleep over there in the trailer after your cabin burnt down?"

"That's Bobbie's place," Edgar replied gruffly, looking down at the ground. "I stay down here at my lake."

"Well, I'm sorry about your dogs," Joe stated as sincerely as possible.

He was glad they were gone, but nevertheless allowed that maybe a few of the dogs didn't deserve to be put down.

"Thank you, Joe," Edgar stated with paramount sincerity as he again pumped Joe's hand. "Thank you. Thanks for comin' out to see me today. I was hopin' you'd come back to see me, and here you are. You and Royce Taylor, you're the only two friends I got left, now that Ol' Blue's gone."

"Yeah, well…" Joe was very sympathetic towards Edgar's troubles, but he was somewhat bothered and disturbed by the inappropriate familiarity Edgar displayed toward him. Joe felt as if he was guilty of something—he wasn't sure what—if only by association. Even with the dogs gone, he wasn't very comfortable and wanted to leave.

"Did you bring your fishing pole, Joe?" asked Edgar. "Sure you did. That's fine. If you want to fish you just make yourself at home. Don't let me bother you none."

"You're not bothering me," Joe stated emphatically, though it was not entirely true. "But maybe I should come back some other day. This doesn't seem like a good time for you. I know you're worried about your daughter and all."

"Yeah, sure I am. But you came here to fish and I want you to fish. This lake is just about all I have in the world and I'm happy to share it with you. You just make yourself at home now and catch you some fish."

"Well, okay," Joe agreed. "If you're sure…" The moment he grabbed his poles every dram of hesitance vanished without a trace. He was ready to catch some fish.

"Right here is good," said Edgar, indicating the lake directly in front of them. "It's all good, really."

"Great," said Joe. "I'll give it a try." He followed Edgar along a narrow footpath down and around to the lakefront. He caught a very nice crappie on his first cast.

"That's a good one, ain't it?" asked Edgar. "What do you think it weighs?—about a pound, maybe?"

"Yep, about a pound I'd say," Joe agreed as he tossed it into his cooler. "It's a good crappie, nice and thick."

"You won't catch any little fish out o' my lake," said Edgar, his voice ringing with pride. Joe liked it better than the whiny, bitter indignation he'd been hearing thus far.

"You might be right about that," Joe said pleasantly enough. "Leastways, I don't think I've caught a little fish out of here so far." Just then Joe hooked another fish, a great big buster bluegill, truly a very nice specimen.

"That's a good bluegill, ain't it?" said Edgar. "All my fish are good. That's why Woodbine wants my lake. He's tried to buy it off o' me twice already. He's greedy, is what he is. He ain't satisfied that he's already got most o' my farm; he wants ever' last bit of it. But we're not gonna let him have it, are we Joe?"

Joe was trying to tune out Edgar to the extent that he could focus on his fishing, but still he listened with one ear. "What? What did you say about Woodbine?"

"Woodbine wants my lake, Joe. He doesn't want it for himself; Woodbine doesn't fish. He wants it for his daddy—his old daddy likes to fish. But I'm not gonna let him have it. Somehow I'm gonna find me a way to hang onto it. Don't ask me how. He's got us crippled now with Bobbie in jail. But I'm gonna hang onto it somehow. I've got to, Joe. This is all I've got left."

"Bobbie's kids—you said she has two babies? How old are they?"

"The oldest girl, Blossom, she's sixteen or seventeen I guess. The little one, Cricket, she's four."

"Are you staying over there at the trailer now to take care of them?"

"No, I'm still sleeping over here in my little camper. My sister Flo stops by and checks on the girls. Matter o' fact, she ought to show up here anytime now to check on 'em, and then we're goin' over to the jailhouse to visit Bobbie."

"How many brothers and sisters do you have?" asked Joe.

"Just the one—Florence, we call her Flo. She's a few years older than me."

"And Bobbie?—she's your only child?"

Edgar hesitated a moment before replying. Finally, he said simply, "Yeah."

Joe caught another good crappie. He now felt certain that another big mess of fish was right there for the taking, just waiting to be transferred from the lake to his cooler. Too bad he'd found Edgar laboring under such difficult circumstances. Otherwise they might've enjoyed a sunny and pleasant May morning together.

On the other side of the lake a car pulled into the more clearly defined gravel drive leading to the trailer. "There's Flo come to check on the girls," said Edgar. "Flo and her husband Pete."

"If you need to go talk to her, you go right ahead," said Joe. "You don't have to stay here with me."

"No—she'll be over here directly. Right now she's just checkin' up on the girls is all. She had to promise the court she'd check on 'em every day when they made her legal guardian. Ya see, somebody had to be their legal guardian or they were gonna put them babies in foster care. They wouldn't let me be legal guardian 'cause I'm a man, and Blossom and Cricket are both girls. Does that seem fair to you Joe? I don't think it's fair. But the court named Flo legal guardian till Bobbie's out of jail so she comes over here to check on the girls every day."

Joe was catching fish and wasn't much interested in Flo. But he took a moment anyway to look across the lake and watch a white-haired woman get out of the car and enter the trailer. He was too far away to see her clearly, but she appeared decently dressed and of an average size; she wasn't a tiny person like Edgar, nor was she slovenly and unkempt. Joe couldn't see the car's driver. After no more than a few minutes, the woman came out of the trailer and climbed back in the car, which immediately backed around and started for the road.

"Did Bobbie work anywhere?" asked Joe, while he reeled in another fish.

"No, no—she's got a lot of problems from her divorce so they put her on disability. She's supposed to draw a check every month, but the law says a person can't draw a disability check if they're in jail so now they're not givin' it to her. Does that seem fair to you, Joe? If a person is disabled it don't matter if they're in jail or not—they're still disabled, right? And if they got babies to take care of, they still need that check to buy food and pay bills, don't they? I don't know how we're gonna make it, Joe. Woodbine has laid us low."

The car containing Flo and her husband shortly drove down Edgar's meager dirt drive and parked behind Joe's big red truck. Flo got out; her husband did not. Edgar pulled his head down between his shoulders and his jacket collar up around his ears as if he wanted to hide from his sister, or defend himself from imminent attack. Apparently he wasn't going to make the least little effort to meet or greet her. She was going to have to come to him.

Flo came quickly and nimbly down the little footpath. Joe ceased fishing momentarily and watched her approach. Like many elderly people thereabouts, her posture and body language evinced a youthful person, while her face displayed the deep wrinkles and wear of many long decades.

Edgar remained hunkered down inside his jacket collar, staring straight ahead at his lake. Joe felt obliged to introduce himself when Flo stopped nearby. "Hi, I'm Joe Bass."

Flo nodded curtly, and then said to Edgar in a clear plain voice, "Those girls need food in that trailer, Edgar."

"Well, why don't you buy it for 'em, Flo? You're their legal guardian now, ain't you?" Edgar's voice was unpleasant, if not downright mean.

Flo looked at Joe Bass and smiled slightly, conspiratorially, as if to let him know she didn't take Edgar or his gruffness seriously.

"It's only the middle o' the month," Flo told her brother. "Don't tell me you're broke already in the middle o' the month."

"No, Flo—I ain't broke," Edgar growled. "I'll buy 'em some more food as soon as we get to town, if that'll make you happy."

"If you don't, and that woman from social services comes over and finds there's no food in that trailer, they'll put those girls in foster care for sure," Flo cautioned.

"I said I'd buy 'em some food when we get to town," Edgar repeated, still not looking at his sister. "I'll do it right now if you're ready to go."

"Not right now," said Flo. "I got a few cakes in the car I need to run over to the church's bake sale right quick. We'll be back to pick you up in a little bit."

"Don't you get to yakkin' all day with them old biddies at your church," snapped Edgar. "Visitin' hours is over at noon and it's a quarter to ten already."

Flo ignored Edgar's comments entirely as she stepped right up to Joe Bass and smiled in his face. "It was nice to meet you. I'm Flo—Edgar's sister." She smiled a beautiful smile, very much like the one Edgar had displayed during his and Joe's first meeting.

Joe returned the smile and felt kindly toward the old woman. "Joe Bass," he told her again. "It was nice to meet you too."

Quickly and nimbly Flo returned along the little footpath, climbed in the car, and was gone.

"Your sister seems very nice," Joe commented as he resumed

fishing.

"You don't know her the way I do," Edgar countered.

"Well, she *seemed* nice, anyway," said Joe.

"She's alright ever' once in a while," said Edgar. "But sometimes she goes too far."

"What do you mean?—she goes too far."

"I mean, she goes too far sometimes, that's all. Like when the court was talkin' about puttin' those babies in foster care. Flo said it would be the best thing that ever happened to 'em. Can you believe that? I told her right then and there, I told her, 'Flo, sometimes you go too far.'"

"Well, it's nice of her to come and check on the girls every day, don't you think?"

"In a way it is, sort of. It's just that, well, I had to beg her to sign the papers makin' her legal guardian, and now she acts like I don't count for much around here."

Joe tossed another fine crappie into his cooler. Already he had seven or eight fish, enough for a good fish fry. He was torn between catching a really big mess of fish, say, about thirty or so, and extricating himself from a sticky situation.

"You need to get ready to go visit your daughter," said Joe, testing the waters. "I've got enough fish for a good fish fry already. Maybe I'll come back again next weekend if the weather holds out."

Edgar turned and looked at Joe as if he were his only salvation. "There's no need for you to go rushin' off now, Joe. Why don't you stay and catch you some more fish?"

"Well, I could stay a little while longer," Joe allowed.

"I kind o' wish you would," Edgar said in a small humble voice. "I ain't had much company out here since the trouble started. Flo and her husband are just about the only people I see and we don't get along too good. My ol' buddy Royce Taylor, he don't care to get out much till it's warmed up real good—Royce likes it hot. I wouldn't mind if you stayed and talked awhile longer. You can catch all the fish you want."

Just then Joe hooked what proved to be a very nice four-pound bass, removing all doubt if he should stay or go. "I appreciate your hospitality, Edgar," said Joe. "Sure, I'll stay awhile longer and we can talk all you want."

Edgar's story   12

Joe Bass placed the four-pound largemouth inside his cooler and breathed a deep sigh of satisfaction. He looked to Edgar for some congratulatory remark and noticed for the first time something different about the old man: Edgar's one-lens glasses were not on his face.

"Did you lose your glasses?" asked Joe.

"No—I just had the one lens and I busted that out a few weeks ago."

"Those glasses with the one lens, they reminded me of a joke," said Joe.

Edgar adopted an attentive attitude that indicated he was listening. So Joe went on with his joke: "A guy from Indiana picks up a hitchhiker in rural Kentucky who only has one shoe. 'What happened?' the driver asks. 'Did you lose a shoe?' 'No,' says the hitchhiker. 'I found one.'"

Edgar nodded curtly at the end of the punch line, but nothing in his face made the smallest step toward laughter.

Joe hoped he hadn't offended the old man; he had intended to maybe cheer him up a little. "I'm not very good at telling jokes," he stated apologetically.

"You told it just fine," said Edgar. "I just don't feel much like laughin' here lately."

"I understand," Joe said sincerely. Just then he felt very sympathetic toward the old man. "It's none of my business, really, but if you need a little money to buy groceries for your granddaughters, I could probably help you out a little bit."

"Thank you Joe. I really do appreciate that. There ain't many around who'd help me here lately. But I still got me a little money left from my check this month. I think we're okay for now."

"What about new glasses?" asked Joe. "Do you need money for glasses?"

"No, no, I get my glasses from the VA. They give me new glasses for free."

"Well, you just let me know if there's ever anything I can do for you, okay? I really appreciate you letting me fish in your lake like this. So you just let me know, okay?"

"This ain't no pay lake," Edgar stated bluntly. "You don't owe me nothin'. I let people fish here 'cause they're my friends, not 'cause I want somethin' from 'em."

"I didn't mean it like that," said Joe, somewhat taken aback. "I meant it as one friend to another."

"That's fine, then," said Edgar, mollified. "I'm glad you think of me as your friend."

Joe caught another fish. He now had maybe a dozen or so good fish and planned to stay long enough to catch at least twice that many. And, now that the dogs were out of the picture, he planned to return to Edgar's lake frequently in the future. He even ventured so far ahead in time as to rue the day five years hence when Edgar might begin to accumulate another pack of dogs. But of course that distant possibility was not an immediate concern.

Joe's immediate concern was Edgar. Certainly the old man seemed to have a checkered if not notorious past, with most of his problems related to alcohol. But he didn't strike Joe as an evil man or a dangerous man or even a boozy man. Joe figured Edgar didn't deserve entirely the terrible reputation foisted on him by abstentious Baptists and other holier-than-thou Christians. Edgar's main faults were being poor to the point of being impoverished, and undereducated to the point of lacking many fundamental life skills. But these few shortcomings definitely were not criminal, Joe noted, or half the county would be incarcerated.

Joe tended to view the poor and undereducated folk thereabouts with pity and compassion, not as stupid trashy people to be feared and reviled. Further, he respected and admired Edgar's generosity. Joe was honest enough to admit to himself that, if he owned a fantastic fishing lake like Edgar's, he wouldn't invite a total stranger to fish there. At least in the area of generosity, Joe recognized Edgar as his moral superior. And maybe that held true in the area of friendliness as well. Hadn't it been Edgar who had spoken first when they met by the spillway?

Thus far Edgar had related the details of his past in random and disconnected dribs and drabs, most of which Joe had forgotten during the months that had passed since their last conversation. Further, Joe wanted to see the big picture, partially because he truly was interested in his newfound friend, and also because he thought he needed as much information as possible if he was to help Edgar and his family through their difficult circumstances. Joe knew that most elderly people liked to relate their personal history, and in that regard Edgar was quite typical.

"Now that we're friends," Joe began. "Why don't you tell me about yourself? You grew up right here on the farm, is that right? Tell me about that. Was it hard growing up around here?"

"It was and it wasn't," Edgar replied. "It was a lot o' hard work, that's for sure, but we never really lacked for much. We raised cows and hogs and chickens and a great big vegetable garden. My dad taught me how to trap and hunt. There were great big catfish in the creek here where I built this lake. I wouldn't say it was hard, but I wouldn't say it was easy, either."

"What kind of animals did you trap and hunt?"

"All kinds, everything. We hunted deer and rabbits and squirrels and such to eat, but some animals, all we wanted was their skins. There used to be good money in skins. Late fall, early winter, that was the best time to trap and hunt for skins. Some years we'd have us a hundred dollars cash money by Christmastime. That was a whole lot o' money back then. We'd have us a big ol' Christmas."

"When you were a kid, did you all have a house, or a log cabin, or what?"

"We had us a shack, I guess you'd call it. One big room. Boards runnin' up and down on the outside—it wasn't none too tight. A woodstove. No electricity. No plumbin'—we fetched our water from the spring. Coal-oil lamps for light. It was a shack…"

"There were four of you there? Your parents, you, and Flo?"

"Yep—just the four of us."

"Where'd you go to school?"

"It wasn't too far—a couple miles south o' here. I can't say I ever cared much for school."

"How far did you go in school? Did you go to high school?"

"Yeah, I had almost two years of high school. Then they kicked me out."

"Really? What happened?"

"I was a baseball player, a catcher, and this other boy, Danny Duvall, he was the pitcher. We'd played together—him pitchin' and me catchin'—since we were little kids, and we were awful good, me and

Danny. We were *awful* good. Our second year in high school, it looked like our team was goin' all the way to the state championship, but then we lost a game right there at the end and they blamed it on me and Danny, and they kicked me out o' school."

Joe rather ruefully recalled when he had been suspended from high school for something that was not his fault, and felt sympathetically toward old Edgar.

"They kicked you out of high school for losing a baseball game?" Joe asked incredulously, indignantly. "That doesn't seem right…"

"It *wasn't* right," Edgar agreed emphatically. "But schools were different back in those days. They didn't treat kids all nice the way they do nowadays. They used to be mean, real mean. Why, I remember in the first or second grade I must've done somethin' wrong, and the teacher drew a little circle on the blackboard way up high, and I had to stand on my tiptoes and stick my nose in that little circle, right up against the blackboard, and stand there like that for an hour. I can still smell that chalky blackboard to this day…"

"That's rough," said Joe. "And they kicked you out of high school for losing a baseball game?"

"Yep. We had us a big lead about halfway through the game, so Danny and me— Danny was the pitcher—when it was our turn to bat, we had us a jar o' shine tucked away there behind the dugout, and we took us a little drink or two. Then after we lost, the coach smelled it on us and he told the principal that Danny and me was drunk, and the principal kicked me out o' school."

"But not Danny?"

"No, they let Danny stay. That wasn't fair, was it Joe?"

"No, I wouldn't think so."

Joe noticed a pattern emerging in Edgar's revelations: Always he was the innocent or mainly innocent victim unfairly treated by authority figures. Amazingly, perhaps, Joe scarcely considered the possibility that Edgar was not as innocent as he wanted to be perceived. Instead Joe gained an increasingly unfavorable opinion of the local school system and local judicial system, past and present. Indeed, as Joe warmed to the old man's personal history, he felt unkindly toward anybody and everybody who ever had mistreated or maligned old Edgar, and doubted not his innocence and inherent goodness.

"So, what did you do after you left high school?" Joe prompted.

"Not a whole lot, I don't guess—more farm work probably. The war was still goin' on and I wanted to join the Marines, but my folks wouldn't let me, said I was too young. After the war was over they finally let me go. It was nineteen forty-six. I was sixteen years old."

"You joined the Marines when you were sixteen? I thought you told me you were in the Army?"

"I *was* in the Army, but that was later. I started out in the Marines. I had to lie about my age to get in—lots o' guys did that. I went to boot camp at Parris Island and let me tell you what, it was rough. Most of the cadre had just fought in the war, and they weren't foolin' around none, not one tiny bit. There I was, just a skinny little kid, really, and it was plenty rough. But I made it through okay. They thought I was okay 'cause I never was afraid to fight, and on account o' how good I could shoot. My dad taught me how to shoot, just like I taught Bobbie, and I always could hit what I was aimin' at."

Joe continued to relocate fish from the lake to his cooler. He was becoming accustomed to doing two things at the same time: fishing, and urging Edgar forward with his story. Indeed, the two activities were beginning to complement each other. Edgar's revelations enhanced somewhat Joe's fishing experience, imparting a sense of historical significance and intrinsic meaning—a piquant provenance—to an otherwise simple and relatively meaningless pastime.

"How long were you in the Marines?" asked Joe.

"Three years. When they let me out I came back home."

"And then what happened?"

Edgar looked as if he was momentarily stymied by Joe's question, and unable to respond. He stuffed a chaw of tobacco in his maw and worked it around with careful deliberation, as if it might provide an answer to Joe's question if he chewed it just right.

Finally he said, "I stayed here awhile but I had trouble adjusting to civilian life, so then I joined the Army." A moment later he repeated the phrase, "I had trouble adjusting to civilian life," as if it were worth repeating.

"And you were in the Army for how long?"

"Eleven years. California, Germany, Korea—I seen about all of it there was to see."

"Three years in the Marines, eleven in the Army—you were getting fairly close to your twenty-year retirement. Why'd you get out?"

Again Edgar was slow to respond. Furiously he worked the chaw of tobacco in his maw until it finally exuded an answer. "Well, the Army was lettin' a lot of people go just then. They were givin' everybody an intelligence test of some kind, to see how good you could read and write and so forth, and if you didn't get a high enough score then they kicked you out. I done okay on that test but a lot of my buddies didn't, and they got kicked out. I didn't think that was fair. I thought: The hell with it. I didn't want to stay in the Army no more after they kicked my buddies out like that. So I went ahead and got out too. I came back here and went back to farmin'."

"Is that when you got married?"

"Yeah, it was right along in there somewheres I guess."

"And you all had the one child—Roberta?—Bobbie?"

Edgar looked away, watched a car that happened to be passing by on the road just then. "Yeah," he said.

"What kind of crops did you raise?"

"Different things—a whole lot o' tobacco, some cucumber pickles. For a few years there strawberries were bringin' in a real good price, so I grew strawberries for a while. Three years in a row I had to hire ten men to help me harvest my berries. Then everybody started growing strawberries and they flooded the market—berries weren't worth a dime that year. So I took me about fifty pounds of berries and made me some strawberry whiskey. Best damn whiskey I ever made, tasted just like strawberries."

"That sounds good. How'd you make it?"

"Same way I always made my whiskey—spring water, sugar, and yeast. But instead of usin' corn meal I mashed up about fifty pounds o' strawberries for flavoring. You can make whiskey out of anything. All you need is sugar and water and yeast and you can make sugar whiskey. Anything else you add to that is just for flavoring."

"Did you ever make sugar whiskey?"

"Sure, I made sugar whiskey in Korea. One day the company commander called me into his office and said, 'Johnson, I hear you're from Kentucky.' And I told him, 'Yes sir.' He said, 'I hear you Kentucky boys know how to make whiskey.' I told him, 'Well, some do and some don't. It just so happens that I do.' Liquor was hard to come by in Korea, and the captain was a-wantin' him a drink. He told me to just let him know what I needed to cook up a batch o' whiskey and he'd get it for me."

"You made moonshine in Korea, then?"

"I made sugar whiskey. The cook had plenty o' sugar but he couldn't get hold o' no corn meal, so I made sugar whiskey."

"Did the company commander drink any of it?"

"Oh yeah, the company commander got drunk, just about everybody in the whole damn company got drunk. Even the battalion commander, a full-bird colonel, he drank some of my sugar whiskey and he got drunk, but he tried real hard to act like he wasn't."

"That's funny," said Joe, smiling. "I bet you were a real popular guy."

Edgar found nothing humorous in the recollection. "Yeah, *too* popular," he stated, a distinct complaint.

"Tell me about your wife," Joe urged. "It's none of my business, but..."

"She died," Edgar stated with real iron in his voice. "She died when Bobbie was four years old. She had a brain tumor and she died."

"I'm sorry," said Joe. "How long were you married?"

"Ten years," said Edgar. His facial features, as well as his voice, had the qualities of iron.

"What was her name?"

"Frankie. Her name was Frances but we called her Frankie." The iron seemed to bend under the strain as Edgar pronounced his wife's name.

Joe figured Edgar had enough problems to deal with just then—his daughter in jail, and his granddaughters dangerously close to foster care—without dredging up more painful memories. He chose not to ask Edgar about the year he'd served in a federal penitentiary for making moonshine.

"When did you build this fantastic lake?" Joe asked brightly.

"About thirty years ago. Royce Taylor—do you know him? It was pretty much his idea."

"No, I don't think I've heard of him," said Joe.

"Royce and me go way back. It was Royce who sold me that little camper I sleep in. He comes out here and fishes ever' once in a while. You'll probably see him out here one o' these days."

"Don't you ever fish?" asked Joe. "Man, if this was *my* lake..."

"No, I ain't never been keen on fishin'. I used to pull a few catfish out o' the creek when I was young, but I ain't never even tried to catch a fish out o' this lake. I didn't build it for me. I built it for my friends."

"That was a very nice thing for you to do for your friends," said Joe.

"Yeah, well, most of my friends are dead now. Ol' Royce still comes around once in a while. And now, you. But that's about it."

Joe regretted hearing the sadness in Edgar's voice when he talked about most of his friends being dead. On the other hand, Joe was glad to hear that quite possibly he was one of only two people to enjoy fishing privileges at Edgar's lake. He was very glad indeed.

"Tell me about your log cabin," Joe coaxed. "When did you build that?"

"About ten years ago. I only had it about two years before it burnt down. I wasn't even finished workin' on it, really."

"Do you know how it caught fire?"

"No, not really. A little voice woke me up in the middle o' the night and told me to get out o' there. Seasoned oak, it went up pretty quick. The next day I asked the Lord why He let my cabin burn down like that. He told me, 'Edgar, what are you complainin' about? I saved your life, didn't I?' So I never thought another thing about it. My cabin was gone but I was still alive, and I had to be grateful for that. Are you a believer, Joe?"

"I was raised Catholic," Joe replied. "But I don't go to church anymore."

"I didn't ask you if you went to church. I don't go to church none myself. What I was askin' is, are you a *believer*? Do you believe in God? It's okay with me if you don't. My buddy Royce don't believe in God and he's the best friend I got. It's okay with me either way."

"I believe in *some* things," Joe stated vaguely, noncommittally. "I don't believe everything that's in the Bible, that's for sure."

"Do you believe in God the creator?" asked Edgar.

Despite Edgar's avowal of tolerance, Joe was afraid of displeasing him with an unsatisfactory answer. "Well, something like that," he stated carefully. "Man has always applied the word GOD to things he doesn't understand, and that definitely includes the creation of the universe. Scientists nowadays talk about the Big Bang theory, but that's just a theory, really. Nobody knows for sure how everything got started. You might as well call it GOD if you want. It's as good a word as any."

"Is that what you think God is? You think God is just a word?"

Edgar asked incredulously.

"No, more like a concept, really—an abstract idea."

"I don't understand what you mean by all that, Joe. Me, all I gotta do is watch the sun come up in the morning and go down at night, and look at all the birds and the fishes and the frogs and the turtles, and I *know* it was His hand that created it all. What about a seed, Joe? Have you ever planted a seed and watched it grow? There has to be a divine power behind that…"

"Seeds are easy," Joe stated matter-of-factly. "Scientists understand exactly how seeds grow. They don't understand exactly the origin of the universe but they can tell you exactly how seeds grow."

"Then tell me this, Joe. Where did the first seed come from?"

"I don't think anybody knows exactly where the first seed came from," Joe stated patiently, as if he were talking to one of his kids. "I don't think the scientists have figured that out yet. You might be right about that one. Maybe it *was* God who made the first seed."

"Sure it was God," Edgar stated forcefully. "It *had* to have been God. Who else could have done it?"

"I'm sure you're right," Joe said agreeably, but not convincingly.

"Yeah, and I'll tell you another thing, something Woodbine is gonna find out here one o' these days: 'Vengeance is mine saith the Lord.' The Lord won't stand for Woodbine puttin' my little girl in jail. What kind of a man could do such a thing, Joe? What kind of a man could put a little girl like Bobbie in jail?"

"I don't know," Joe replied softly. Edgar was becoming increasingly riled. As old as he was, and as little as he was, he didn't look exactly dangerous. Still it was not a pleasant sight.

"And he calls himself a Christian," Edgar snarled. "He thinks he's a big shot 'cause his wife works at the courthouse and he's a deacon in his church. He don't know the half of it, Joe. I've read the Bible, I read ever' last word of it when I was in prison. I know what it says, and I'll tell you what it says: 'Vengeance is mine saith the Lord.' Vengeance is mine. One o' these days, Woodbine over there is gonna find that out the hard way."

"I hope you're not gonna do anything that'll get *you* in trouble," Joe said levelly.

Edgar sort of shrugged as if to indicate maybe he would and maybe he wouldn't. "The Lord's gonna take care of Woodbine one o' these days—that's all I know. I just hope I live long enough to see it."

Joe tossed another crappie in his cooler and said, "I *hope* you leave it up to the Lord. I hope *you* don't do anything foolish now."

Joe and Edgar heard and then saw a car on the road. It was Flo and her husband returning to pick up Edgar for their visit to the jail. Joe decided it was time to say goodbye.

"Edgar, I need to go home and clean these fish and you need to go visit your daughter. I've had a great time fishing here this morning. I'll come back real soon and we'll talk some more, okay?"

"Will you Joe?" Edgar asked plaintively. "Are you sure you'll come back and see me again?"

"Of course I will," Joe replied loudly, expansively. "Wild horses couldn't keep me away."

Edgar smiled, or almost smiled, for the first time that morning. "I'm awful glad to hear you say that, Joe. But you don't need to go rushin' off now just because I'm leavin'. You're welcome to stay as long as you want and catch all the fish you want. You're always welcome here. You come on back whenever it suits ya, and if I'm not here, you just make yourself at home. "

"Thanks, Edgar. I really do appreciate it. I guess maybe I'll stay and catch a few more fish. You take care of yourself now, and take care of those girls, too. I'll see you again before too long, maybe next weekend."

"Sounds good," said Edgar. "But I gotta go now." He glanced at his watch. "Good God, it's almost eleven o'clock already. Flo's been yakkin' up a storm all mornin' with them old biddies at her church—after I told her not to. See what I mean about Flo? Now we ain't got much time to visit with Bobbie. See ya later, Joe."

"I'll see you later, Edgar."

Cleaning Fish   13

Cleaning fish was always a mixed bag. On the positive side were pride and accomplishment and acquisition and provision. On the negative side were gore and stink and tediousness and repetition. Early in the year when he was hungry for fish and there were no fish in the freezer, Joe leaned toward the positive and felt mostly good about cleaning fish. Later in the year, after cleaning a few hundred fish, he leaned toward the negative and didn't like it much at all. This was Joe's first significant catch of the season; he was happy to clean fish.

Joe had a nice setup for cleaning fish in his garage. He kept a section of workbench permanently vacant to receive the two-foot-square piece of plywood that served as a cleaning board. There was water nearby in an outside spigot. An aluminum pan was always on hand to receive the freshly cleaned fillets. Offal was tossed in a five-gallon bucket and later carried to the far back of the yard where it would be scavenged by critters and crows and cats.

He started by sorting and counting his catch, mainly so he could brag with authority and precision to the guys at work on Monday. There were four bass, four bluegill, and twenty-two crappie—an even thirty fish. As he finished counting the last crappie, Jolene entered the garage.

"Hi," she said gaily, smiling. "When did you get home?"

"Just a few minutes ago," he replied, also smiling, happy to see his wife. "What do you think of my fish?" He stepped back from the workbench lest he impede her view of his impressive catch. Clearly, he expected praise or a compliment.

Jolene's eyes opened wide with amazement and pleasure and she started to say something nice. Then her eyes narrowed and her mouth closed and she looked away from the fish. She fixed her gaze on her husband and asked pointedly, if not meanly, "Where did you catch them?"

Joe's smile fell nearly to the floor. "What difference does that make?" he asked defensively. "Is that a nice mess of fish or what?"

"Yeah, sure Joe. Nice fish." Her voice was flat as a pool table and cold as January.

"If you don't want me to keep them, I can toss them out back for the critters," Joe threatened indignantly.

"Don't be ridiculous," Jolene said. "All I asked was, 'Where did you catch them?'"

"I caught them at Edgar's," Joe replied forthrightly, a tad defiantly.

"Well, okay. That's fine, then," Jolene said, obviously displeased.

"You say it's okay, but you sure as hell don't act like it's okay," Joe complained.

"Well, I just don't see why you have to go *there* to fish. What happened to the lake and the river? Aren't there any fish left in the lake and the river?"

"I missed the crappie run in the lake this year because the kids were sick, and the river is always hit-or-miss," Joe replied calmly, authoritatively, a fisherman talking to a non-fisherman. He thought he was gaining the upper hand.

"Well, we don't need all those fish anyway," Jolene jabbed, casting a furtive and mildly contemptuous glance toward the workbench.

"Who says we don't?" Joe countered. "I catch 'em, I clean 'em, I even cook 'em. I don't see what you've got to bitch about."

"Oh, so now I'm a bitch, am I? You're calling me a bitch…?"

"I did not call you a bitch," Joe corrected, struggling to keep his voice level, hoping to maintain whatever small advantage he imagined he had. "And I don't want to fight and argue. It's been a fairly nice Saturday so far. Why can't we enjoy what's left of it?"

"It's been nice for you, maybe. I cleaned the bathroom first thing this morning and now I'm doing laundry."

"Well, I'll tell you what—I'll trade you. I'll do laundry and you can clean fish. How does that sound?"

"No, no—I wouldn't want to take you away from your precious fish," Jolene declined sarcastically.

Joe's fine mess of fish had seemed precious indeed just a few minutes ago. Now that they served as the focal point of contention with his wife, they seemed more a burden and a bother. He resented the change wrought by his wife's comments and attitude.

"I am forty-four years old," Joe stated severely. "I've been around the block a time or two—I can take care of myself. I don't see what you and your parents are so worried about. There's nothing wrong with Edgar that isn't wrong with half the county—he's just poor and undereducated is all. I'm not saying he's a saint, not be any means, but he's not such a bad person, really. He's nice enough to let me fish in his lake, told me come back anytime and make myself at home. That counts for a lot in my book. I don't see how you can hate him so much. You've never even met him."

"I didn't say I hate him," Jolene corrected. "I just wish you wouldn't go over there. And I hope I never do meet him, ever."

"Why don't you grow up Jolene? You're forty-one years old. Why do you let your mommy and your daddy tell you what to think? I bet your parents haven't even seen Edgar in twenty or thirty years. What do they know? I just saw him today. Doesn't my opinion count for anything?"

"It does," replied Jolene. "It really does. Maybe he's not as bad as my folks let on, not now, anyway. But I still don't understand why you can't fish in the lake or the river."

"I tried the lake and the river. They weren't biting. Maybe in another week or so—"

"So," Jolene interrupted. "In another week or so you'll start fishing in the lake and the river and you won't go near that old man's lake ever again, is that right?"

Joe resented both the interruption and the declaration. "No Jolene, that's not right. As a matter of fact, I told him today I'd go back and visit him again real soon. He's having a pretty rough time right now."

"Oh really? What's his problem?"

Joe saw no way to sidestep the truth, even though he knew how it would sound to his wife. "His daughter's in jail, and that leaves him with two granddaughters to take care of."

"Why is his daughter in jail?"

"One of their neighbors claimed she shot at him with a rifle, but—"

"How lovely," Jolene quipped smartly. Then she quickly left the garage, left Joe alone with his fish.

Joe grabbed the largest bass, the big four-pounder, slapped it down on the cleaning board, and sliced viciously with his filleting knife just behind its gills.

He hated cleaning fish.

Hot Summer   14

Perhaps intentionally, perhaps coincidentally, Jolene kept her husband busy the following weekend. On Saturday, Joe raked the old dead leaves that had served as winter mulch out from under the bushes, cleaned the gutters, washed and waxed his truck and her SUV, and mowed the lawn. On Sunday morning, he straightened up and swept out the garage, and thought that was finally the end of his weekend chores. But before he could even think about fishing at Edgar's or anywhere else, Jolene announced they were going shopping in Elizabethtown that afternoon. Joe quietly complied. But as he trudged along behind his wife and kids down countless aisles in various stores, he firmly decided to go fishing the following Saturday.

Friday evening, as soon as the kids had left the supper table, Joe made the announcement to his wife. "I'm going fishing tomorrow," he proclaimed grandly, as if issuing a royal decree. He didn't look directly at Jolene when he said it. Even though she sat directly across the table from him, he somehow managed to look over and around her, as if addressing the many lords and ladies that comprised the royal court.

Jolene was too tired to argue. She had labored mightily spring-cleaning the inside of the house the previous weekend while Joe performed the outside chores. And she had had an unusually demanding week at work, publicizing and promoting the opening of the new bypass in Leitchfield. She planned to rest as much as possible over the weekend and didn't really care if Joe went fishing, or where he went fishing, as long as she got her rest.

"That's fine," she said. "Good luck."

"Thanks," said Joe. The phone on the kitchen wall rang just then, precluding further comment. Joe got up and answered it.

He was pleased to hear the voice of John Garner, a fellow fisherman he knew from work, calling to invite him to go fishing with him tomorrow.

"Upshaw was supposed to go with me but his wife decided she had other plans for him," Garner explained.

"Yeah, I know how that goes," said Joe.

"Well, I know it's short notice and all, but I'd be glad to have you go with me if you want," said Garner.

"Yeah, sure, I'd love to go. I was planning to go fishing tomorrow anyway. Do you want to slide by here and pick me up, or...?

The logistics of their trip finally concluded, Joe hung up the phone and told his wife, "That was John Garner from work. We're going fishing at Nolin tomorrow."

"That's fine," said Jolene, as she stacked dishes in the dishwasher. "Good luck."

Joe was excited about the morrow. John Garner owned a big new bass boat, and Joe liked fishing from a boat more than fishing from the bank; a boat afforded a far greater variety of fishing strategies and techniques, and Joe simply enjoyed being out on the water. Further, as an "outsider" from Louisville, Joe had failed to connect with any of the locals to any meaningful extent; he had lots of buddies, but had made no real friends. Joe liked John Garner, and hoped their fishing trip might initiate a real friendship.

The fishing was good but not great. They fished exclusively for largemouth bass and caught about twenty, but due to the fifteen-inch size limit at Nolin, they were allowed to keep just four fish. During a lull in the action, Joe vaguely remembered telling Edgar that he'd try to visit him again real soon. He dismissed it at once; he hadn't really promised the old man anything and, well, Edgar would just have to get over it.

Joe and John Garner hit it off fairly well. As it happened, Garner's parents owned recreational property in Wisconsin. Around two that afternoon, as the two men were preparing to call it a day, Garner invited Joe and his family to vacation in Wisconsin with him and his family when school let out in June.

Joe had been talking to Jolene about a suitable destination for their summer vacation. Usually they went to a theme park: Kentucky Kingdom in Louisville, or Holiday World in Indiana, or King's Island in Cincinnati, or Dollywood in Tennessee. But both Jolene and their daughter suffered mildly from motion sickness and were not keen on thrill rides, so Joe and his wife had been trying to come up with something different. The trip to Wisconsin sounded ideal.

"That sounds great," Joe stated effusively. "I'll talk to Jolene about it and I'll let you know something Monday at work."

Joe talked it over with Jolene, and they decided to accept.

It proved to be one of the best, if not *the* best, vacation they'd ever had. The Garner property in Wisconsin was absolutely beautiful—a huge A-frame cabin designed to accommodate guests, situated on scenic Deer Run Lake. The Garners had two children a few years younger than the Bass kids, yet they all got along splendidly despite their slight age differences. Jolene embraced Garner's wife as the sister she never had; they too got along marvelously. Joe Bass and John Garner fished frequently and with much success, catching bass occasionally, but more often, feisty yellow perch. Joe never had caught yellow perch and quickly declared them his favorite fish species. They were plentiful and easy to catch and incredibly sweet, sweeter even than bluegill.

Joe loved the weather up in Wisconsin, consistently cool enough for a campfire at night and a flannel shirt in the morning, and warm enough to swim in the afternoon. Unlike the fickle weather in south-central Kentucky, which all too often was too hot or too cold or too windy or too rainy or too something, the Wisconsin weather was invariably pleasant, at least while they were there.

Mostly, though, Joe enjoyed the company of his coworker and newfound friend, John Garner, especially while fishing. Fishing was much more fun with a friend. A lighthearted, good-natured competition between them sharpened their fishing skills. And there was always somebody nearby to show off to when one or the other caught an especially good fish. Jolene gave not the slightest indication of disapproval when Joe drank a few beers with John by the campfire at night, Joe's first taste of beer in years.

At the end of nine blissful days, the two families caravanned home to Kentucky refreshed and renewed to the bottom of their souls. Joe and John both transported home in coolers several packages of yellow perch fillets. As soon as they got home, Joe stacked them up in his freezer like cordwood.

With a huge cache of fish in his freezer, and having recently satisfied his fishing bug to a degree previously unimaginable, Joe never gave a thought to fishing at Edgar's place during the remainder of June. And then it got hot, blazing hot—mid-nineties by two in the afternoon day after day after day, and rarely dipping below seventy-five at night. Occasionally a little thunderstorm popped up, dumping just enough rain to make the grass grow, but never providing any real relief from the heat.

It was always difficult to pry the Bass kids away from their videogames during the summer months, but now they refused to venture out of the house entirely, even to go swimming in Nolin River Lake on Saturday mornings, as was their custom in summers past. Joe too became housebound and dreaded the times he had to spend outside, mowing the grass or whatever. During all of July it remained blazing hot, and August was even hotter.

By the end of August the entire Bass family suffered from cabin fever, as surely as if they'd been trapped indoors by a blizzard for the past two months. The Bass kids were actually glad to return to school. Joe savored his memories of their Wisconsin vacation until they became as flavorless as old chewing gum, then started talking to Jolene about moving to Wisconsin. He knew she wouldn't move a hundred miles from her parents, much less all the way to Wisconsin, but merely talking about the prospect of escaping from the interminable heat and humidity provided some small degree of relief.

The last Saturday in August dawned hot and muggy, as had the first Saturday in August, and the first Saturday in July. Joe couldn't stand it any longer. He tossed his fishing tackle in the back of his truck and drove to Edgar's place. He didn't care if he caught fish or not. He didn't care if Edgar was there or not. He simply wanted to get out of the house and do something, anything, to alleviate his cabin fever.

There was no sign of Edgar. Joe figured he was visiting his daughter at the jail. He grabbed his tackle and walked down to the lake to fish. He noticed small handmade wooden benches, a total of four, each about four feet long, positioned around the lake at ideal fishing spots. He also noticed that the lake was about two feet low, undoubtedly due to the hot dry weather, and the water looked greener than usual, somewhat stagnant. The broom grass and other various weeds and grasses had grown thicker and taller during his absence. Otherwise, the place looked pretty much the same.

Joe placed his tackle box on one of the wooden benches and made his first cast, a rather lazy and halfhearted effort. He found himself thinking that he really didn't want to be there, but wished instead that he was up in Wisconsin fishing for yellow perch. But at least it was not yet blazing hot. Overhead the sky was thick with clouds. Probably they'd burn off by ten o'clock or so, and then it would be blazing hot, again. How he wished he was up in Wisconsin...

Joe detected motion out of the corner of his eye. He turned and saw Edgar making his way slowly, haltingly, across the earthen dam. He took eight or ten steps and stopped. Another eight or ten steps and stopped. His posture was stooped as he walked, and each time he paused he stooped even more. When he raised himself up to continue walking, it seemed to require a mighty effort, and he never straightened up completely.

Even from a distance, Joe saw something was clearly wrong. He called loudly, questioningly, "Edgar!?!" He dropped his pole and started in the old man's direction. But Edgar waved him off, waved him back. Whatever the problem, the old man still showed plenty of gumption and spunk.

About twenty feet from Joe, the old man stopped again. From that distance Joe could see his face plainly, and he saw old Edgar close his eyes and wince with pain. Joe hastened to his side. "Edgar, are you all right? What's wrong, buddy? Come over here and sit down." He tried to grab Edgar's arm and help him over to the bench, but the old man shook him off. He looked like he wanted to be mad at Joe, but lacked the strength to be mad at Joe or anybody else. All his effort was being spent just staying on his feet.

"Oh, I'll be okay, Joe," Edgar gasped as he collapsed on the bench. "I just need to sit a spell."

"What's wrong?" asked Joe, truly concerned. "You look like you're in pain."

"I *am* in pain," Edgar said grimly. "It's back here, in my back, and around through here in my kidneys." He traced with his right hand a line from the small of his back around his waist to the spot just above his front pants pocket.

"Well, what is it? What's wrong with you? Have you seen a doctor?"

"I can't say for sure exactly what it is. It started out I got all colicky—I couldn't stop crappin' to save my soul. Then it spread from my bowels around here to my back. Now it feels like it's spread all the way around through here." Again he traced the imaginary line around his waist.

"Have you seen a doctor?" Joe asked again.

"No, not yet. Flo's been tryin' to get me to go, but I hate to ask her to take me. She does enough takin' me out to see Bobbie and takin' care of the babies."

"Well, why don't you get your friend Royce to take you?"

"Royce don't see good enough to drive very far. But he brought me out these benches for us to sit on. What do you think of these benches Royce brought me?"

"They're very nice benches," said Joe. "But I think you ought to let somebody take you to the doctor. Why don't you let me take you? We can go right now. I have plenty of time this morning."

"Would you do that for me, Joe?" asked Edgar, a weak smile on his face. "I thought you'd given up on me. I thought you weren't ever comin' out here to see me again."

"It's been too hot to fish," Joe hastened to explain. "It's been too hot to do most anything. I couldn't even get my kids to go swimming this summer, it's been so hot. The only reason I'm here is because I had to get out of the house."

"Yeah, it's been plenty hot," Edgar agreed. "I wonder if maybe this heat has got me down somehow, maybe poisoned my blood, but hot weather never bothered me none before. I don't know exactly what's wrong with me here lately."

"Well, I wish you'd let me take you to the doctor."

"Thanks, Joe, but not today. I think I'll be okay." Edgar stood, raised himself fully upright, and smiled at Joe a bit more convincingly. It was not the beautiful womanly smile Joe had seen in the past, but it was a definite improvement. "Maybe I'm just gettin' old," Edgar stated philosophically as he slowly sat down again.

Joe became somewhat less concerned. Maybe an immediate trip to the doctor was not necessary after all. "How's Bobbie doing?" he asked. "I thought you'd be visiting her this morning."

"Flo came by to take me like she always does but I just didn't feel up to it this morning. I told her to go ahead on by herself and tell Bobbie I couldn't make it, that I was sick. Bobbie's doin' okay. They've been talkin' about lettin' her out early for good behavior. I'm gettin' tired of hearin' 'em talk about it. If they're gonna let 'er out, I wish they'd just go on and do it instead of just talkin' about it all the time. Sometimes I think they do it just to be mean—they know she's worried about her babies and all, and just dyin' to come home."

"How long has she been in jail now?"

"It's been about four months. Another few months and she'll have served half her sentence. Maybe they'll let her out then. I hope they will."

"I hope so too," said Joe. "I don't think it's helping you any, worrying about her and her kids all the time. I know it must be hard on you."

"Oh, I think I'll make it, Joe. Somehow I'll make it. Me, Bobbie, and the kids, we're all gonna make it somehow."

"That's the ticket. I know you're a tough old bird. You hang in there. If anybody can make it, it's you."

Edgar looked strengthened by Joe's exhortations. He didn't look well, but he looked less sick. "Say, why ain't you fishin', Joe? Don't let me bother you none. You go right ahead and fish. Have you caught anything yet?"

"No, I was just getting started when you came. But I'm not worried about fishing just now."

"Well, don't you worry about me none. I got these here pills Flo brought me this morning." He pulled a container of pain medication out of his pocket, removed the lid, tossed several caplets into his mouth and gulped them down.

"Whoa there," said Joe. "Hold on a minute. How many of those have you taken?"

"Oh, I don't know. I've had quite a few I guess. They help some—not a lot, but some."

"I wouldn't take any more of those just now," Joe said admonishingly. "You're probably not supposed to take more than eight a day."

"Okay," Edgar said complacently as he replaced the pills in his pocket. "They're startin' to leave a bad taste in my mouth anyway. Go ahead and fish, Joe. I want to see you catch a fish. It ain't right, you comin' all the way out here and not catchin' any fish."

"Well, okay," said Joe. "But I'm really not worried about fishing just now. We can just sit here and talk if you want."

"No, no, I want you to fish. That's what I built this lake for, so my friends could come out here and fish. Don't worry about me none. I'm fine."

Edgar didn't look exactly fine, but Joe went ahead and made a cast. He hooked and caught a smallish bluegill, barely a keeper. When he looked again at Edgar, his eyes were closed and his mouth was formed in a small tight grimace.

Joe tossed the small bluegill back into the lake and asked, "Edgar?

Are you okay?"

Edgar opened his eyes at once and exclaimed, "I'm okay Joe, really. Did you catch one just now? I wasn't payin' attention. Go ahead and catch you another one."

"I'm really not worried about fishing today. I wish you'd let me take you to the doctor."

"No, no doctor, not today. But I'll tell you what, Joe. These pills here ain't gettin' the job done. I'll tell you what would set me straight, is some whiskey."

"Whiskey?" Joe asked incredulously. "I don't think you need any whiskey just now. I don't see how that would help you if your stomach's bothering you."

"I believe a little whiskey is *exactly* what I need," Edgar firmly insisted. "Not much, not a whole lot, just a few little drinks would set me straight. How about we take us a little drive down to Bowling Green?"

"I don't know," Joe demurred. "Whiskey? It's kind of early in the day for whiskey, don't you think? And hot? This heat's enough to make a man sick. Whiskey…?"

"If you don't want to take me that's fine." Edgar said, petulant and disappointed. "You just go right ahead with your fishin' and don't mind me none."

"I'd be glad to take you if I really thought it would help," said Joe. "But…"

"Then let's go," said Edgar. He bounded off the bench with a vitality Joe wouldn't have believed possible just ten minutes earlier. "You can leave your fishin' tackle here. Nobody will bother it while we're gone."

"If you're sure," Joe said to Edgar's back. Edgar had struck off for Joe's truck already with quick, mincing steps. By the time Joe reached his truck, Edgar was in the passenger's seat and had his seatbelt fastened.

Whiskey Run   15

Edgar sat compactly with his legs crossed above the knee and his arms folded tightly across his chest. He wore battered old combat boots, filthy blue jeans cuffed at least six inches, a raggedy black T-shirt with an American eagle emblazoned across the chest, and his ubiquitous red Marlboro cap. He looked even smaller than he actually was as he gazed steadily out the window to his right, rigid and unmoving.

"Are you sure you want to do this?" Joe asked before firing the ignition.

"Sure I'm sure," Edgar replied firmly, still gazing out the window. "Let's go."

They drove to the end of Sycamore Church Road in silence. Heading south on the main highway, the sky ahead was very dark and reached all the way down to the ground.

"It looks like bad weather up ahead," said Joe.

Edgar continued to gaze out the window to his right, but nevertheless agreed, "Yeah."

"Do you mind if we listen to the radio?" Joe asked.

"Nope."

"Is there anything in particular you like to listen to? Country? Rock? What kind of music do you like?"

"It don't matter to me Joe. You listen to whatever you want."

Joe turned on the radio. It was tuned to a variety station that played "hits from the 60s, 70s, 80s, 90s and today." The song playing just then was "Magic Carpet Ride," by Steppenwolf. Somehow it seemed both very appropriate and very inappropriate. Joe left it on, but turned it down.

Halfway to Bowling Green the sky turned pitch black, closed in around them like a shroud, and let loose a torrential rain. The rain hammered fiercely, loudly on the truck; lightning flashed and thunder boomed relentlessly. Joe flipped on his lights, turned his windshield wipers on HI, turned off the radio which they couldn't hear anyway, and slowed down from fifty-five to forty-five. During the very worst of it, he hazarded a quick sideways glance at Edgar to see how he was weathering the storm. Edgar continued to gaze out the window to his right, as rigid and silent as stone.

They drove out of the storm just as they reached Bowling Green. Rainwater ran in fast-moving streams along both sides of the highway. Steam rose from the road in a thick gray cloud that swirled like angry ghosts when vehicles sliced through it. They pulled into the parking lot of a big modern liquor store just on the edge of town.

Edgar hadn't moved a muscle throughout the entire trip. But now in a flash he unhooked his safety belt, popped open the truck door, and leapt out onto the steaming asphalt. Joe hastened to follow.

Edgar paused just inside the door and cast his head around this way and that. He looked as if he were trying to catch a scent, and not locate with his eyes. Just as Joe caught up with him, Edgar struck off toward the whiskey aisle.

Joe made one last attempt to switch Edgar to a milder poison. "Hey Edgar. How about we get us some beer instead? Beer is better when it's hot anyway, don't you think?" Truth be told, Joe Bass had been hankering for a beer since downing a few up in Wisconsin.

"No, Joe. I'm afraid beer wouldn't get the job done. I need me some whiskey. It don't have to be nothin' fancy—just some plain ol' whiskey."

Joe noticed the occasional customer and store employee staring at old Edgar. Joe was glad that, despite Edgar's pervasive filthiness, the old man never really smelled bad. Joe didn't understand it. As far as he could tell Edgar bathed infrequently at best, but somehow he never stank. Rather, he exuded an earthy outdoorsy odor of trees and rocks and plants and dirt and chewing tobacco. But the old man really was a sight. Joe wasn't exactly embarrassed, but he nonetheless wanted to get out of the store as quickly as possible. He deemed it best to take charge of the situation.

"Okay then—what kind of whiskey do you want?" Joe asked. "I'm buying."

"It don't matter to me, Joe. Whatever you want. Store-bought whiskey is pretty much all the same to me."

Joe opted for a fifth of Old Fitzgerald, a good reputable whiskey, he recalled from his drinking days, but not as pricey as most of the premium brands. "How about some Old Fitz?" he asked, as he snatched the bottle off the shelf.

"Whatever you say Joe. It's all the same to me."

Joe grabbed a six-pack of Coke on the way to the checkout counter.

"What's that for?" asked Edgar.

"Bourbon and Coke," Joe replied. "You like bourbon and Coke, don't you?"

"I don't need me no soda pop with my whiskey, but you get whatever you want."

Joe shrugged and proceeded to the checkout counter. He paid with a credit card and they left.

Inside the truck, Joe placed the sack of Cokes and whiskey on the seat between them, then fired the engine and carefully backed out of the parking space. By the time he had the truck pointed in the right direction, Edgar had uncapped the whiskey and had drawn the bottle to his lips. He poured a huge slug of whiskey into his mouth before Joe could begin to protest.

"Hold on there, Edgar. Hold on a minute. What in the world do you think you're doing?" They were stopped at the edge of the parking lot just where it met the road.

Edgar swallowed slowly, purposefully, and then struggled mightily against the inevitable burn. After it passed, he turned to Joe with watery eyes and a look of supreme satisfaction on his face. Silently he offered the bottle to Joe.

"No, no—it's against the law to drink in a moving vehicle," Joe protested. "Can't you wait till we get back to your place?"

"I ain't drivin', and I don't see no cops around, do you?" Edgar's voice was lower, deeper than usual.

"That doesn't matter. There's an open-container law in this state. It's against the law to have any kind of alcoholic beverage open in a moving vehicle."

"That's a stupid law. If I ain't drivin', what difference does it make?"

"It would make a lot of difference if we got pulled over. Can't you wait till I get you home?"

"I'll keep it down, Joe. Don't worry about me. You just drive."

"Well, I really wish you'd wait till I get you home."

"I'll keep it down, and I'll keep an eye out for cops. Don't worry so much. You just drive."

Edgar replaced the cap on the bottle and held it perched on his right leg. He looked straight ahead through the windshield and not out the window to his right. The highway narrowed from four lanes to two as they drove out of the city limits. Edgar decided it was time for another drink. It was another huge gulp, three or four ounces at least. Again he braced against the inevitable burn. After it passed, it was as if a powerful spring uncoiled inside him. His entire body relaxed, and seemed to spread out, to grow larger. His face glowed bright red, and looked calm, serene, its focus inward.

Edgar evinced not the slightest sign of his former discomfort and pain. Joe wondered if that had been a devious ruse purposefully designed to dupe him into making the whiskey run.

There was little traffic here on the two-lane. Joe still wasn't happy about Edgar drinking in his truck but reasoned there was little danger of being pulled over. Another twenty or twenty-five minutes and he'd have Edgar home. Edgar downed another big slug of whiskey as they began the steep climb up Chalybeate Knob.

"You're gonna be drunk by the time I get you home," Joe stated matter-of-factly.

Edgar ignored the comment completely. "Joe, Joe, Joe," Edgar began, his voice deep and thick with sentiment. "How did I ever find you, Joe? Tell me that, Joe, tell me that one thing—how did I ever find you?"

"We met at the dam, remember? You invited me out to your place to fish."

"There's got to be a reason for it, Joe. They say there's a reason for everything. Do you believe that, Joe?—that there's a reason for everything? There's got to be a reason why we met." Edgar's voice and words plainly revealed his drunkenness. Joe didn't care. Another twenty minutes or so and he'd have him home.

"Oh, I don't know. Sure, I guess so. We met so we could be friends," Joe said agreeably.

"We *are* friends, ain't we Joe? *Good* friends. A man needs to have good friends. Me, I got old Royce. Royce, he… Royce…" Edgar couldn't find the words he wanted. "Royce is my friend, and now you're my friend too."

"Sure we're friends," Joe agreed pleasantly. "Good friends."

"A man needs to have good friends, Joe, especially when times are tough. That's when you find out who your friends really are, when times are tough. You kind o' caught me at a bad time, Joe, what with Bobbie in jail and all." Edgar's temperament took a turn for the worse as he talked about his daughter. He darkened and frowned, then rallied and brightened a bit. "But you're still with me, ain't you Joe? You ain't the kind of man who'd give up on his friends, are you Joe?"

"No, I'm not. I'll be your friend as long as you want me to be your friend."

"Joe, Joe, Joe. How did I ever find you? You're just the kind o' friend I need right now. Tell me again—how did we meet? I know you just told me, but…"

"We met at the dam. You invited me to your place to fish."

"That's right, I remember now. You told me your wife was sick, and was wantin' her a mess o' fish to eat to make her feel better. And I told you that you could come over to my place and catch you some fish for your sick wife."

Joe didn't respond. He had no idea where Edgar dredged up the business about his "sick wife." Probably he had him confused with someone else. Joe didn't care much that it was pure hogwash. Another ten minutes and he'd have Edgar home. Actually, Joe felt rather kindly toward old Edgar just then. All that talk about friendship was so much drunken nonsense in a way, but in another way Joe felt it to be true. He really was friends with the old man, drunken old rascal though he was.

Edgar took another drink and was silent. Soon they turned left onto Sycamore Church Road, and then down Edgar's drive. The recent storm had turned Edgar's scant dirt driveway into a veritable quagmire. Joe felt his tires slipping and sliding in the muddy rain-filled ruts and potholes. The truck bounced along jarringly as Joe kept his speed up enough to prevent getting stuck. At the end of the drive he was careful to park on a grassy hillock from which he could manage to turn around and drive back out eventually. But first he had to tend to Edgar.

"We're here," Joe announced gaily, glad that the whiskey run had been accomplished without serious incident.

Edgar shifted the whiskey bottle to his left hand, opened the door with his right, and tumbled heavily out of his seat onto the thick wet grass. Joe exited his own door more conventionally, and hurried around to Edgar.

Edgar lay sprawled out on his back, his arms and legs akimbo, his eyes closed, a huge beatific smile on his face. His left hand clutched the whiskey bottle with unmistakable ownership and purpose.

Joe stooped down to help him. "Edgar? Are you alright? Did you hurt yourself?"

Edgar's beatific smile broadened even further. His eyes remained closed. "It's good to be home, ain't it, Joe?"

"Here, let me help you up. Come on now—damn, you're all wet, Edgar. Come on, let me help you up. You're soaking wet."

Edgar opened his eyes, and provided some small assistance as Joe helped him to his feet. It felt to Joe as if few of Edgar's body parts were connected. The only firm and fully functional parts were the arm and hand that clutched the whiskey bottle.

"Do you have dry clothes in your camper?" Joe asked. "You need to go put on some dry clothes."

"I don't need dry clothes. Just wait awhile and I'll dry out. Help me down to the lake. I want to show you the benches that Royce brought me. You haven't seen the benches Royce brought me, have you?"

Joe did not respond. Dutifully, rather reluctantly, he kept a solid grip on Edgar's good arm, the one with the hand clutching the whiskey bottle, and ushered him down to the nearest bench, the one where he'd left his fishing tackle. Joe sat him down squarely in the middle of the bench, where Edgar swayed unsteadily. Joe stood close by, prepared to grab Edgar should he start to fall.

"I'll be alright here in a minute, Joe. Just let me rest a spell. That truck o' yours sits way high up off the ground, don't it Joe? I ain't used to sittin' so high up like that. It's made me kind o' dizzy."

"I think it's the whiskey that's made you dizzy," Joe stated the obvious.

"Yeah, well, maybe a little," Edgar allowed. "But I'll tell you what now—this here whiskey is a-settin' me straight. This is good stuff you bought me, Joe. Here, let me pay you for it. You don't have to buy my whiskey for me, Joe. I can buy my own whiskey."

"No, no, it's on me. As nice as you've been to me, letting me fish in your lake and all, the least I can do is buy you a bottle of whiskey."

"This ain't no pay lake," Edgar said firmly. "I let people fish here 'cause they're my friends, not 'cause I want somethin' from 'em. I thought I told you that already."

"You did, and I appreciate it. But I don't want any money for the whiskey."

"Suit yourself then, Joe. But I'll tell you what—next time it's my treat. Beer, whiskey, whatever you want—next time I'm buyin'."

Joe definitely, desperately hoped there wouldn't be a next time. But he said, "Okay."

"Why ain't you fishin', Joe? Grab your pole and catch you a nice mess. They ought to be bitin' real good after this rain. I'll just sit here and watch, maybe have me another little drink."

"It's getting close to lunchtime," said Joe. "I'll be leaving to go home for lunch pretty soon. Aren't you getting hungry, Edgar? Do you have any food in your camper? Maybe you should eat a little something before you think about drinking any more whiskey."

"Canned peaches and chocolate cupcakes is all I care to eat these days. Here lately that's all I've had a taste for—canned peaches and chocolate cupcakes."

"Well, how about I go up to the camper and get you some? I bet you didn't eat any breakfast this morning. How about I bring you a little food?"

"No thanks, Joe. Not now. I'll tell you what. How about you and me have us just one more good drink and then maybe we'll think about lunch. You'll have a little drink with me, won't you Joe? I know you have a college education and all, but you don't think you're too good to have a little drink with me, do you Joe?"

"No, not at all. But it's too early in the day for me."

"It ain't never too early to take a little drink, Joe. Come on, just one little drink. You'll take a little drink with me. Sure, I know you will."

Truth be told, Joe rather wanted a drink just then. It had been a trying morning, and the sweet smell of bourbon had brought back a few warm memories.

"Well, okay—just one. You'll have one and I'll have one and then we'll get you some lunch."

"Now you're talkin', Joe. That's what I want to hear." He offered Joe the bottle.

"Let me go up to my truck and grab a Coke," said Joe. "I can't drink it straight out of the bottle like that."

"Suit yourself then, Joe. I'll wait right here till you get back."

Joe took his fishing tackle up to his truck and grabbed the Cokes from the cab. When he returned, Edgar made a little room for him on the bench. Joe took a seat and popped open the Coke, poured out about half of it, and poured in about two ounces of whiskey.

"Come on now, Joe," Edgar complained. "That ain't no kind of a drink for a man to be takin'. All you got there is soda pop."

Joe grudgingly added maybe one more ounce. Edgar wasn't satisfied but Joe didn't care. The Coke was not cold, but cool from being in the store's, and then the truck's, air conditioning. The cocktail was syrupy sweet and made a big warm place in Joe's middle.

Edgar was absolutely delighted to see Joe drink. It was very important to him that they drink together, the ultimate bonding act between two men. Edgar drank straight from the bottle, and afterwards seemed stronger, steadier than before. His turquoise-blue eyes sparkled with a fair amount of their former glory, but the sparkling was partially screened by a rheumy wetness that covered his eyes like a watery film.

"I'll tell you what we ought to do now, Joe," Edgar declared loudly, forcefully. "We ought to jump in that truck o' yours, drive over to that jailhouse, and bust Bobbie out o' there right now. Let's go do 'er, Joe. You and me, we can do 'er. Let's go bust her out o' that goddamn jailhouse before she rots in there."

"Now, Edgar. That's foolish talk and you know it. We're not gonna bust anybody out of jail. You shouldn't even think about such things. Besides, I thought you told me they're maybe gonna let her out early in another month or two."

"The lyin' bastards, there ain't no tellin' what they're gonna do. Sometimes I think they talk about lettin' her out just to be mean. That's a Ford truck you got, ain't it? Bonnie and Clyde used to drive a big Ford coupe, that's how come the law couldn't catch 'em. And Jesse James, he always had fast horses. I know a lot about outlaws, Joe. That's what I am, really, Joe—I'm an outlaw, an old outlaw. You probably didn't know you were drinkin' with an old outlaw, did you Joe?"

"I know you've had your problems," Joe said levelly. "But I don't see why you want to talk about yourself that way. I don't think you're a bad person, not at all."

"Joe, Joe, Joe," Edgar said, softening. "How did I ever find you, Joe? You tell me that—how did I ever find you?"

Joe refused to answer that question again. He took another drink from his can and said nothing.

Maybe Edgar was offended by Joe's silence. He stared hard at Joe and bristled once more. "Okay then, I'll tell you what else we can do. Let's you and me walk over there next door and knock the tar out o' Woodbine. You and me, Joe—let's do 'er. I'll tell you what—all you have to do is knock on the door and get him to come outside and I'll knock the tar out of him myself. He's big but it's mostly fat. I ain't afraid o' no fat man, are you Joe? Woodbine, he's the one what started all the problems around here in the first place. You and me, Joe—how 'bout it? Let's go knock the tar out o' that fat bastard Woodbine."

Joe shook his head woefully from side to side. "I hate to hear you talk like that, Edgar. I really do. I thought you told me you were a believer?—a Christian? That's no way for a Christian to talk."

"Oh, I know the Bible," Edgar declared loudly, hotly. "Vengeance is mine saith the Lord. Vengeance is mine!"

Edgar sprang up from the bench, immediately lost his balance (if he had any balance to lose), and fell backwards and to one side, the side toward the lake. Before Joe could respond, Edgar tumbled down the bank seven or eight feet, his legs flying every which way, and landed facedown with his head and most of his upper body underwater. His legs didn't move; nothing moved.

Joe bounded down to the water's edge, slipped a bit on the muddy bank, quickly regained his footing, and grabbed Edgar by his leather belt and the collar of his shirt, barely visible beneath the dark green water. With a mighty heave he pulled Edgar up and out of the lake, and mainly carried him up onto the footpath and safety.

"Damn it, Edgar! Jesus! Look at you—you're a mess. Are you okay? Talk to me, Edgar! Talk to me now! Let me hear you say something!"

"I'm okay," Edgar finally muttered, his voice weak and small.

"That is *definitely* a matter of opinion. Are you sure you're okay? Did you swallow any water or anything? Are you sure you're okay?"

"I'm okay," Edgar repeated. He looked like a drowned rat, a very naughty and guilty drowned rat. He stared at the ground and nowhere else. "I think I need some dry clothes now. Help me up to my camper."

"Good. Fine. You need to put on some dry clothes, eat some lunch, and go to sleep. I want you to promise me that's what you'll do." Joe started Edgar moving in the direction of his camper.

"Wait," said Edgar, shaking free from Joe's grasp. He quickly searched the area where he'd fallen in the lake, and found the capped and intact bottle of Old Fitzgerald, its content depleted by two-thirds. Somehow he'd managed to toss it to safety before taking his plunge.

"And promise me you won't drink any more of that stuff," Joe added.

Edgar said nothing. Joe held him firmly with an arm around his back and half-carried, half-escorted him up to the camper.

"You saved my life, Joe," Edgar gushed. "That's what you did—you saved my life."

Certainly Edgar made the statement sincerely, but to Joe it sounded rife with histrionics, theatrics. Joe had no more patience for the old man's drunken sentiments.

"Yeah yeah yeah. Now listen—I want you to put on some dry clothes, eat some lunch, and then go to sleep. And no more whiskey," Joe commanded harshly.

"Okay Joe—whatever you say," Edgar sheepishly replied.

"That's better," said Joe, finally managing to compose himself somewhat. The morning storm had done little to alleviate the heat, but Joe was trembling like a leaf in a brisk breeze.

Edgar's fall and subsequent plunge into the lake had upset Joe a lot more than Edgar. Edgar was mainly sorry that their little drinking party had ended so abruptly, and that he'd embarrassed himself in front of his young friend. Joe was furious with himself for agreeing to make the whiskey run in the first place. He blamed himself for everything—Edgar's drunkenness, his fall, everything.

Joe couldn't stand it there a moment longer. "I have to go now," he stated bluntly. "Goodbye."

"Goodbye Joe. You come on back anytime now, ya hear? You're always welcome. If I ain't here, you just make yourself at home."

Joe silently, angrily, quickly climbed into his truck, fired the engine and took off. At the end of the muddy, slippery drive he turned sharply onto Sycamore Church Road without looking for traffic. Fortunately there were no oncoming vehicles. But his muddy and mud-filled tires initially failed to find traction. He skidded sideways as he turned sharply onto the road and nearly found the deep drainage ditch on its far side.

His shivers returned, nearly uncontrollably now. He couldn't feel the steering wheel in his hands or the pedals at his feet. He forced himself to think about his wife and kids—he would see them soon—and to turn his back on Edgar and all the long morning's mistakes and mishaps. At the end of Sycamore Church Road he stopped and waited while his breathing and heart rate slowed, waited until a car finally pulled up behind him.

Then he turned left onto the main highway and drove home.

Royce Taylor   16

Royce Taylor was tall for an old man, six-foot-one, and lean as a rail. In his prime he'd stood six-foot-three, but he was eighty-six now, and growing shorter and leaner with each passing day. Still, his long lanky frame spanned the entire length of the sofa on which he slept. Nearby his television glowed warmly in the dark, its volume turned down low, as the soft pleasant voices of CNN newscasters kept him company throughout the long dark night. He might've been more comfortable in his bed, but lately he'd taken to sleeping on the sofa with the TV on to keep him from feeling so alone.

Daybreak filtered in through the lightly curtained windows, and Royce came awake. Fully twenty minutes passed before he mustered the strength and desire to get up off the sofa. In the bathroom he peed and brushed his teeth and washed his face, and at some time during his ablutions decided to go fishing at Edgar's that morning.

Royce had been born and raised in the country, the third of eleven children. About all he could remember of his distant childhood was interminable work on the farm, and rarely having decent clothes to wear, or even enough to eat. In 1939 he was seventeen years old. As World War II loomed grimly on the horizon, he left the farm and enlisted in the U. S. Navy.

He was trained as an anti-aircraft gunner and stationed aboard the U. S. S. Houston, a Northampton-class heavy cruiser assigned to the Asiatic Fleet based at Pearl Harbor. The Houston was out on patrol in the China Sea during the infamous attack, but it proved a short reprieve. On March 1st, 1942, less than three months after the attack on Pearl, the Houston was sunk off the coast of Java during one of the first major naval battles against the Japanese; the last surviving ship of the Asiatic Fleet survived no longer.

Of the original crew of one thousand and sixty-one officers and sailors, only three hundred and sixty-eight survived the sinking of the Houston. Royce Taylor was plucked from the sea and taken prisoner by the Japanese. For the next forty-two months, three and a half years, he was shunted about various prison camps in south Asia, enduring horrific conditions of cruelty, privation, starvation, and disease. Much of his time in captivity was spent building the infamous Burma-Thailand Railroad, soon to be known as the Death Railroad (and later featured in the fantasy film, *The Bridge on the River Kwai*; there was no River Kwai but French author Pierre Boulle thought it sounded good). About a hundred of his shipmates who had survived the sinking of the Houston died as prisoners of the Japanese.

Finally liberated by U. S. troops, Royce was shipped back home and processed out of the Navy. He was awarded about twenty-seven hundred dollars in back pay and separation pay—little compensation for the horrors he'd endured, but a real fortune for a poor country boy who'd never seen more than a hundred dollars in his life. For the next few years Royce lived high on the hog—eating rich foods, womanizing, staying drunk most of the time, eventually marrying, all in a desperate attempt to make up for lost time and forget the horrors of war.

When the money ran out, Royce found himself in a bad way. His wife divorced him; he was mainly alcoholic and unable to work, and possessed no meaningful job skills had he been able to work. He received disability benefits through the Veterans Administration, a few hundred dollars a month, which was enough for a simple country boy to at least survive.

He married again, and was divorced again, married again, and was divorced again. But each wife helped him both financially and emotionally, and eventually he managed to make some sort of life for himself. He was what the old country people called a "horse trader." Cars, trucks, tractors, farm equipment, and later, boats, he bought for a pittance from people down on their luck or desperate for drinking money, and he always sold them at a substantial profit. He was never rich by any means but his disability benefits, coupled with an occasional windfall from the sale of something, enabled him to buy a modest house and property, to never want for food or drink, and to attract a seemingly endless procession of women, a few of whom he married, most of whom simply lived with him awhile.

As the crow flies, Royce's property was about two miles from Edgar's place, twice that far when traveled by roads. When Edgar left the Army in 1960 and returned home, little time elapsed before the two men found each other. Royce and Edgar had at least a few things in common: Both were country boys with a deep love and appreciation for the land, both were military veterans, and most important, both men loved to drink. It wasn't long before they were the best of friends.

Royce traveled by roads the four miles to Edgar's place. He drove slowly because his eyesight and reflexes were not good, and because he knew Edgar probably was visiting his daughter in jail and wouldn't return home for another hour or so. He parked behind Joe Bass's big red Ford truck and got out of his car. His poor eyesight observed the blurry shape of a man fishing on the far side of the lake. He wasn't sure, but it looked like the man was reeling in a fish.

Edgar had told Royce about a "young hotshot" who'd fished at his lake a few times. "Best fisherman I've ever seen," Edgar had told him. "Not a bad guy—a little too citified, maybe." Royce wanted to meet this young hotshot. For years he'd enjoyed nearly exclusive fishing rights at Edgar's place, and even though he didn't fish much these days, he mildly resented Joe Bass's presence. For many years he'd been Edgar's best, and virtually his only, friend. Royce was just a little bit jealous, and a little bit concerned. Edgar's friendly and generous nature had led him to invite more than a few strangers to fish in his lake in the past, sometimes with dreadful results. Some people had left big messes of beer cans and garbage; some had set out gillnets and pulled hundreds of fish from the lake; one sorry drunk drove his car into the lake, nearly drowned, and decimated the fish stock when the car's antifreeze and oil and gas leaked out. Edgar had assured his old friend Royce that Joe Bass was on the up-and-up, a good guy, but Royce wanted to see for himself.

Royce was a bit tottery in his old age, but he comported himself with an erect military bearing at all times. He carried in his hands a fishing pole, tackle box, live net, and a small container of worms. He crossed the little wooden footbridge and the broad earthen dam, and walked to a bench nearest the spot where Joe Bass was fishing.

Joe was slightly disconcerted by the old man's arrival. All week he had wrestled with the guilt that resulted from the whiskey run and Edgar's drunkenness and subsequent fall in the lake. At times he'd told himself that he'd never visit Edgar or his lake again. But he truly was concerned about old Edgar, and wanted to see how he was faring after last week's drunken debacle.

While waiting for Edgar to show, Joe had caught maybe seventeen or eighteen fish. Primarily, though, he was there to check on Edgar, and square up whatever matters needed squaring. He hoped the new arrival wouldn't prevent him and Edgar from tidying up last week's mess, if and when Edgar arrived.

Royce Taylor ignored Joe completely as he placed his tackle box and worms and live net on one end of the wooden bench, and readied his fishing pole. Although it was quite warm, about eighty degrees, Royce was dressed in long pants and a flannel shirt buttoned all the way up to the neck. Atop his head he sported a red Marlboro cap exactly like Edgar's. Joe felt obliged to speak first.

"Good morning," Joe called, presenting Royce with a cautious smile.

"Mornin'," Royce replied. "You havin' any luck?"

"Why sure," Joe stated rather proudly. "I always catch fish in this lake. Best damn fishing lake I've ever seen in my life."

Just then Joe hooked and reeled in another large crappie. Royce walked over to where his tired old eyes could get a better look at Joe's catch. When Joe opened the lid of his cooler, Royce peered anxiously inside. "Good God," Royce exclaimed. "How many mouths you got to feed? You got enough fish in there for an army."

"There are four of us," Joe stated rather sheepishly. "Edgar's always told me to keep all the fish I want. This lake is chockfull of fish."

Royce frowned disapprovingly. "Yeah, well, Edgar always has been too generous for his own good. Me, I never keep more than four or five fish myself," he stated modestly, yet proudly.

Royce returned to the bench and continued to ready his pole. "You don't mind if I fish a little bit, do you?" he asked, his voice tinged with sarcasm.

"Of course not," said Joe. "I'm Joe Bass. You must be... I can't remember the name... the guy who sold Edgar his little camper."

"I'm Royce Taylor," the old man stated grudgingly, as if Joe was not quite entitled to the benefit of his name. And then, somewhat accusingly, "Edgar has told me about you."

"Nothing bad I hope," Joe said lightly, good-naturedly.

"No, I reckon not," Royce allowed at last.

"I guess you and Edgar go way back," Joe stated, trying to be agreeable.

"*Way* back," Royce agreed. "Forty-five years or more. How long have you known Edgar?"

"Maybe seven or eight months now," Joe replied. "We met last December, I guess it was."

A slight, nearly imperceptible snort of disgust or contempt escaped from Royce. He looked as if he might've said something derisive, had he not been focused entirely on the task of threading a worm onto his hook. By the time he was finally rigged up and fishing, Joe Bass had caught two more crappie.

"Is that what you're fishin' for?—crappie?" Royce asked.

"Anything that bites," Joe replied. "But yeah—crappie mostly, I guess."

"I'm fishin' for bluegill," said Royce. "That's all I ever fish for. I think they're sweeter than crappie."

"I can't argue with that," said Joe. "They *are* sweeter than crappie."

Royce's fluorescent red bobber went under and stayed under. Royce didn't seem to notice.

"I think you're getting a bite," Joe stated helpfully.

Royce started turning the crank on his fishing reel and shortly pulled in a huge male bluegill, darkly purple, nearly black. "My eyes ain't what they used to be," said Royce. "Sometimes I don't see 'em when they bite, but I feel 'em when they pull."

"Hey, whatever works," said Joe. "That's a mighty fine bluegill."

Laboriously old Royce unhooked the fish, placed it in his live net, tossed the live net into the lake, and threaded another worm on his hook. A full ten minutes passed before Royce was fishing again, during which time Joe caught another crappie and a bass.

Joe had more than twenty fish in his cooler, enough for at least a few good fish fries. Already old Royce had accused him of hoggishness. Joe knew the lake had plenty of fish to spare, but he didn't want to rile or displease old Royce. Joe continued to fish, but just barely; he made short ineffectual casts and paused for several long moments between casts, as he tried to strike up a conversation with Edgar's old friend.

"Edgar's a good old guy, isn't he?" Joe asked rather stupidly.

"He's good to his friends," said Royce. "But you don't want to get on his bad side."

"I guess not," Joe said vaguely, lamely. "Hey, didn't Edgar tell me something about you putting him up to building this lake? Was this your idea?"

"Yep," Royce answered. "It probably was."

"I know Edgar doesn't fish. What?—you thought it'd be nice if he had a lake for his friends to fish in?"

"There's a bit more to it than that. Has Edgar told you about his wife, Frankie?"

"Well, yes. He told me she had a brain tumor and she died."

Royce paused, as if uncertain how much he wanted to reveal to Joe Bass. Finally he continued. "One night Edgar and his wife were over at my place drinkin'. We used to drink a lot back then. I guess you know about that."

"I've heard a little bit about it," said Joe.

"Well, Edgar and his wife left my place about two in the morning. Edgar was drunk but he didn't have far to drive home, a couple miles is all. He'd gone home drunk from my place a hundred times before. They made it about halfway home and drove head on into a tree. His wife's head went through the windshield; it hurt her pretty bad. About the time her head healed up the doctor said she had a brain tumor. She didn't live too long after that."

"That's really sad," Joe said sincerely. "I hate to hear that."

"Yeah. The doctor told Edgar it was all his fault, on account o' her head goin' through the windshield. Edgar took it real hard, thinkin' it was his fault and all. He always liked to drink, but after that he stayed drunk mornin', noon, and night. There wasn't nobody who could do a damn thing with him, neither."

"That's terrible," said Joe. "I don't know how a doctor could tell him such a thing. If his wife had a tumor, a cancerous tumor, well, cancer is a virus, and I've never heard of cancer being caused by physical trauma. Cancer is a virus, and she might've gotten cancer without the car crash. Who knows? She might've had cancer before the car crash. I can't believe a doctor would tell him that."

"Well he did, and Edgar blamed himself. A couple years there he wasn't worth spit—wouldn't work, couldn't work, just stayed drunk all the time, *bad* drunk."

"That's really a shame," said Joe.

"Yeah, well, Edgar drove a bulldozer off and on for years, mostly during the winters when there weren't any crops to fool with. I told him that if'n he had himself a bulldozer, he could build us a nice big lake right here."

"And that's when he bought his dozer?"

"Edgar didn't have enough money to buy a dead cat. He never did have no money. He never was no good with money, but I have a little knack for it sometimes."

"So, you bought him the dozer?"

"I found him a good used dozer to buy and I loaned him the money to buy it. He never would take money as a gift; I always had to loan it to him. That little camper he sleeps in? I tried to give that to him but he wouldn't take it. He made me set a price on it, four hundred dollars, before he'd take it."

"I don't guess he's ever paid you back for anything."

"Nary a dime, but that's okay. Edgar's been a good friend to me for many long years. I'd do more for him if I could, but he's a proud man."

"So, did that help? He got the dozer and started building this lake. Did that help him?"

"It probably saved his life," said Royce. "He never did quit drinkin', of course. He kept a bottle o' whiskey with him on the dozer the whole time he worked. But it gave him somethin' to do, somethin' to look forward to. By the time he got this lake finished he was a whole lot better."

"Does Edgar drink much these days?" Joe asked cautiously. "Do you guys still get drunk together?" Joe rather hoped the answer would be Yes. He didn't want to think that he was responsible for Edgar falling off the wagon.

"No, Edgar don't drink much at all these days. He's too old for it now. I bring him a couple beers once in a while. He does alright with a few beers now and then. But you don't ever want to get him drinkin' no whiskey. He ain't strong enough for whiskey no more."

Joe colored darkly with embarrassment and shame.

"What about you?" asked Joe. "Do you still drink?"

"Nary a drop. I gave it up about ten years ago, cigarettes too. The last woman I had, I had her take me to the clinic in Bowling Green and they dried me out. I'm too old for it now. What about you? Do you drink?"

"No," said Joe. "I used to drink some when I was in the Army, and when I was in college, but nowadays I can't say I drink much at all."

"You got a family?"

"Yeah, I got a wife and two kids."

"You got a job?"

"Yes sir, I got a pretty good job. My wife works too. We do alright for ourselves."

"That's good," said Royce. "If a man's got a good family and a good job to help take care of 'em, well, you can't ask for much more than that."

"I guess not," said Joe.

"Me, I've been on disability most all my life. The Japanese held me as a prisoner-of-war for forty-two months. Then I got on the booze real heavy, and I never was much count after that. I make a little money now and then. Say, you wouldn't be interested in buying a pontoon boat, would you? I've got 'er fixed up real nice. I'll make you a good deal on it..."

"No, no, not right now. I appreciate the offer, though."

"Maybe some other time then," said Royce, ever the horse trader.

"So tell me—what do you think of Edgar?" Royce asked, taking a different tack.

"Well, I know he's got a few problems but I think he's a good guy," Joe replied. "He's always been good to me. I really appreciate him letting me fish here."

"That's good," said Royce. "Edgar speaks mighty highly of you. It wouldn't be right for you not to like him."

"I like him just fine," said Joe, happy to hear that Edgar spoke highly of him.

"That's good," said Royce again. "Edgar's always had problems with his drinkin' and all, but he's always had a good heart. People around here talk awful bad about Edgar, *awful* bad, but he don't deserve most of it. He's always had a good heart. And you talk about a workin' devil? He wasn't much count when he was drinkin' real heavy, but you should've seen him out here a-buildin' this lake. Every day, rain or shine, he went flat out from sunup till sundown till he got 'er done. You see these paths he carved around this lake? Take a *good* look—that's solid sandstone. He carved out these paths with an axe and a pick and a shovel. I never seen a white man who could do hand work like Edgar. I've seen a few Chinamen who maybe could keep up with him, but never a white man."

A car pulled into Edgar's drive, old Edgar got out, and then the car left. Royce peered myopically in the direction of the activity. "Is that Edgar?" he asked.

"Yeah, that's him. He's heading this way."

"He's just now gettin' back from visitin' his daughter," Royce stated knowingly. "I guess you've heard about his daughter bein' in jail."

"Yeah, I've heard."

"I'll tell you somethin' else about Edgar before he gets here: Whatever you do, don't ever say anything bad about his daughter Bobbie. She's just about all he's got left in this world, and he's awful touchy about that girl—her, and the grandkids too. You best mind what you say about Bobbie and those kids, you hear?"

"I've never met her or the kids," said Joe. "But thanks. I'll be careful."

Edgar slowly walked up and joined them. More exactly, he walked up and joined his old friend Royce. He virtually ignored Joe Bass altogether. "Royce, it's good to see you," he gushed, smiling. "Have you caught any fish?"

"I've got two or three I reckon. It's this feller here who's catchin' all the fish."

"Yeah, I know he's a fisherman," Edgar said without looking at Joe. "Have you been here long?"

"Maybe half an hour or so," said Royce. "How's Bobbie gettin' along?"

"Well, she's a-makin' it. It's awful hard on her bein' away from her kids like she is, but she's a-makin' it, I guess. They say that if she keeps up like she's been doin', they might let her out early. She might not have to serve the whole year."

"That's good," said Royce. "Next time you see her, you tell her that old Royce says to hang in there."

"I'll do it," said Edgar.

Finally, Edgar saw fit to acknowledge Joe's presence, at least indirectly. "I guess you two have met already," he said to Royce.

"Yeah, we've been talkin' a spell," said Royce.

Edgar turned and spoke directly to Joe. "Royce Taylor here, you don't know what a good man he is. They just don't come no better than Royce Taylor, I can tell you that much for sure."

"He seems like a very nice man," said Joe. "I've enjoyed talking to him."

"You'll be lucky if you grow up to be half the man Royce is," Edgar continued. "They just don't come no better than Royce Taylor."

"I'm sure you're right," said Joe. At first he'd felt slighted by Edgar's comparative lack of recognition. But now he saw more rightly that Edgar was merely acknowledging his greater friendship and admiration for his old buddy Royce, putting matters in their proper perspective, and not trying to slight or insult him personally. Joe Bass was not exactly jealous of the deep bond between the two old men, but recognized it as something rare and fine and touching.

Joe was relieved that Edgar appeared to have recovered from last week's drunken debacle. Edgar looked somewhat healthier than he had last Saturday. His color was not good, and he was still stooped over a bit, but he didn't look all that bad. Maybe he'd had nothing more than a bad stomach flu and was mainly over it now.

"Well, I'm sure you two guys have a lot of catching up to do," said Joe, preparing to leave. "Mister Taylor, it was very nice to meet you, sir."

"I'm Royce, just plain Royce," the old man corrected. "It was nice to meet you too. I'll probably see you out here again one o' these days."

"You probably will," Joe agreed. "Edgar, thanks for letting me fish. I've really enjoyed it."

"Come back anytime," Edgar replied, with much less than his customary enthusiasm.

When Joe was out of earshot, Edgar asked his friend, "What do you think of that guy?"

"I reckon he's alright for a city boy," said Royce. "He's maybe a bit too full of himself, but he's young yet. I guess he's alright."

"Yeah, that's what I think too."

Flo Goody   17

Flo Goody made biscuits the same way her mother used to make them, with flour, lard, and buttermilk if she had it, sweet milk if she didn't. She did not roll out the dough with a rolling pin and cut neat circles with a cutter. Rather, she shaped the dough with her hands into disks roughly three inches wide and half an inch thick. She didn't need or want perfectly uniform biscuits that could be sliced neatly in half to receive butter and jelly. These biscuits would be broken to bits and smothered with gravy. She arranged them on a baking sheet and popped them in the oven. She began the gravy with a simple roux of lard and flour. When her roux was the color of dark honey or light molasses, she added sweet milk, salt, and pepper, and stirred the mixture till it was thick and bubbly.

"Pete," she called. "Come eat some biscuits and gravy."

Flo's husband Pete sat at the kitchen table, sipped cautiously from a cup of steaming hot coffee, and then went to work on the plateful of biscuits and gravy.

Flo did not eat with her husband. She stood at the kitchen counter and made two more platefuls of biscuits and gravy, one for herself, and one for her brother, Edgar. She covered the plates with aluminum foil and placed them on top of the hot oven. The plateful for Edgar she would deliver personally as soon as her husband finished eating. The plateful for herself she would eat when they got back home. She was an old country girl, steeped in country customs and traditions, and would not eat until after all the men folk had eaten.

Flo and her husband Pete drove the few short miles to Edgar's place, the foil-covered plate of biscuits and gravy on the front seat between them, and parked near the little camper. There was no sign of Edgar. Flo got out and hollered for him, but still there was no Edgar. She got back in the car and told her husband, "I can't raise him. He might be over to the flea market with Royce Taylor. I reckon we'll wait awhile."

A big red truck pulled into the drive and parked behind them.

Royce's presence had prevented Joe from squaring matters with Edgar two Saturdays ago. Edgar hadn't given him the impression there was anything to square, but Joe still felt mildly guilty about the whiskey run, and he wanted to make sure their relationship remained viable and healthy. He'd brought along his fishing gear and hoped to catch some fish as well.

Joe recognized the car and its occupants and got out of his truck to greet them. He stepped up to the driver's open window and said, "Good morning."

Flo's husband Pete nodded, and then turned to stare straight ahead through the windshield. Flo smiled brightly and said, "Good morning."

"I don't know if you remember me—I'm Joe Bass. And you're Flo, right?"

"That's right. Of course I remember you, Joe. This is my husband, Pete. I don't think you've met him."

"It's nice to meet you, Pete." Joe was ready to shake hands if Pete wanted to shake. But he didn't even look Joe's way. He stared straight ahead through the windshield.

"Have you seen Edgar?" asked Joe.

"Not today," Flo replied. "I don't know where he is. Maybe he went somewhere with Royce. Have you met Royce Taylor?"

"Yes ma'am. I met him here two weeks ago."

"Sometimes Royce and Edgar go to the flea market on Saturday mornings," said Flo.

"What about his daughter, Bobbie? I thought you all were visiting her on Saturday mornings?"

Flo started to say something, and then stopped. It was awkward carrying on a conversation from the passenger's side, around and through her husband. She got out of the vehicle and walked around to meet Joe at the front of the car.

"You've never met Bobbie, have you?" she asked.

"No, never."

"Well, you ain't missin' much. She's twice as stubborn as Edgar is, and ten times as mean."

"Have they released her from jail? I know they were talking about letting her out early."

"No, she's still locked up and mad as blazes. She was callin' her girls collect every night—they have to call collect from the jailhouse—

and she run up a huge phone bill that Edgar couldn't pay so they turned off the phone in the trailer. She's actin' all stubborn now, says she don't want to see nobody till she's walkin' free. It don't surprise me none that she don't want to see me. We don't much get along. But Edgar?—it surprises me that she won't even see her daddy. It's a-killin' poor Edgar is what it's a-doin'—it's tearin' the heart right out of him. Edgar's in a bad way just now. When was the last time you seen him?"

"I saw him two weeks ago," replied Joe.

"How was he when you saw him?"

"I thought he looked okay. He'd been complaining earlier about his stomach bothering him, but I thought he looked better the last time I saw him."

"Yes, he's had a terrible misery in his stomach. I gave him some pills but he's still in terrible pain. We keep tryin' to take him to the doctor but he won't go. Poor Edgar—I think the life he's led is finally catchin' up with him. He never eats right. He doesn't take care of himself. He sleeps in that little old camper like some kind o' wild animal— no heat, no water, no electricity, nothin'. We have a nice big house about two miles from here and we've asked him to come stay with us I don't know how many times. But he won't do it. He says he has to stay here and keep an eye on things."

"I know he doesn't eat right. He told me that all he eats are peaches and cupcakes."

"That sounds like Edgar. He never did take care of himself. We bring him over some food every so often. I brought him some biscuits and gravy this morning. He loves my biscuits and gravy. I wish he was here to eat 'em. They're probably cold by now."

Joe tried to think of something nice to say about biscuits and gravy, but couldn't. He'd never tried biscuits and gravy until he moved to the country. His wife Jolene was crazy about her mother's biscuits and gravy, but Joe thought they were way too starchy—a thick glutinous mess.

"Maybe Edgar and Royce will be back soon," Joe said.

"Maybe, but there's no tellin' with those two. We'll wait awhile longer I guess."

Joe couldn't decide if he wanted to wait or not. His residual guilt was all but gone now that he'd taken the time and effort to check up on old Edgar. It wasn't his fault that Edgar wasn't home. Joe still wanted to fish, but Flo acted like she wanted to talk, and Joe didn't want to stand there and listen to her yak all morning.

Apparently Flo sensed the possibility of Joe leaving, and appeared to want him to stay. She took a small step closer to Joe and said, "You know, Edgar just thinks the world of you. You ought to hear the way he talks about Joe Bass. He claims you're the best fisherman that's ever fished in his lake. You ought to hear the way he carries on…"

"Well, anybody could catch fish out of this lake. It's not hard, really." Despite his explanation, Joe was nevertheless flattered.

"I think it's good of you to be a friend to Edgar. He needs friends right now. Royce, him and Edgar go way back, but Royce is old, he's eighty-six years old now. Me and Pete are both eighty. We all do what we can to help Edgar but we're all old now, and Edgar can be so stubborn at times."

"Yeah, I can believe that."

Flo smiled conspiratorially, as if they shared a secret knowledge, then her face suddenly fell like a stone. "Poor, poor Edgar. He's been through so much in his life. I guess he's told you about his wife…"

"Yes, and Royce told me about it too. That was a terrible tragedy."

"Oh, I know it was, and it wasn't the first time something like that happened to him. Did Edgar ever tell you about him joinin' the Marines?"

"Yes."

"And when he got out?"

"He told me he came back home, but he couldn't adjust to civilian life, so then he joined the Army."

"Is that all he told you?"

"Yes."

"Well, I don't know if you've noticed it or not, but Edgar doesn't always tell the whole truth about things."

"Yeah, I've noticed that."

"And sometimes he's a big fibber."

"Yeah, I've noticed that too. The first day we met he told me a big cock-and-bull story about three hundred thousand dollars in a long-lost bank account."

Flo shook her head woefully from side to side, clucking her tongue on the roof of her mouth, and then continued, "Well, Edgar came home from the Marines and all he did was drink. He wasn't but nineteen years old but he drank enough whiskey for ten grown men. Edgar always did have a taste for whiskey."

"Yes ma'am."

"Please, just call me Flo. Well, Edgar was out drinkin' somewheres one night, and he was comin' home on the highway out there when he run head on into another car. The old man drivin' the other car, he was killed, but Edgar wasn't hurt a bit. Anyway, the old man was known to take a drink ever' once in a while, and the way the cars were piled up on the road it wasn't real clear whose fault it was. Edgar couldn't remember how it happened. He never denied bein' drunk, so they hauled him off to jail. They had a little trial, and that old judge acted like it had to be somebody's fault, and since Edgar was the only one still alive the judge laid the blame on him. That old judge told Edgar he could serve two years in jail or go back in the service. Edgar went back in the service."

"Yeah, the Army. Why didn't he go back in the Marines?"

"I honestly don't know. We all hated to see him leave again so soon. He hadn't been home but a month or so. But he had to go."

"Edgar told me he was in the Army for eleven years." Joe now felt it necessary to confirm points of fact.

"Yeah, I guess it was about that long. You know why he got out of the Army, don't you?"

"He told me something about his buddies being forced out because of some kind of intelligence test, so he decided to quit."

"That's nonsense. They kicked him out o' the Army for makin' moonshine and bein' drunk all the time, that's what they done. Edgar swears to this day that it wasn't his fault, that one of his captains put him up to makin' the shine, but I don't know. That's somethin' else about Edgar that maybe you've noticed—nothin's ever his fault; it's always somebody else's fault."

"Yeah, okay."

"He done pretty good for a while when he first got home from the Army. He still drank, he always drank, but he worked hard and he found himself a lovely wife. Things were pretty good there for a while, till he had the wreck with his wife. After she died all he kept saying was, 'I've done it again. God help me I've done it again. And now I've killed my little Frankie.' Nobody could do a thing with him. And drunk…? I don't know how any man could drink the way he did without it killin' him. You've never seen anybody so tore up as he was after his wife passed away. Poor Edgar…"

Joe felt somewhat less than sympathetic toward Edgar just then. Previously he'd defended Edgar in the matter of his wife's death, arguing that she might've had already the fatal brain tumor at the time of the accident. But now he wasn't so sure. Possibly, probably, two people dead as a result of Edgar's drunk driving?—that was a bit too much to swallow. Also, he resented the fact that Edgar had been decidedly less than honest when talking about his past. Joe had based his affection and friendship on faulty and false information. Now that he knew the truth, he wasn't entirely sure if he still liked Edgar, or if he still wanted to claim him as a friend.

"That's when he lost the farm," Flo continued. "We had a beautiful farm here, two hundred and twenty acres, good land, most of it, some of the best farmland in the county." She turned and indicated with a broad sweep of her hand the breadth of their erstwhile farm. "Our parents left it to both of us you know, me and Edgar both. Pete never was much on farmin'—he worked a little job in town—so we let Edgar have the full run o' the place. We just used a tiny little bit where we have our house, that's all.

"Well, after Frankie passed away Edgar quit workin' altogether. He stayed drunk all the time and he was in jail a lot. I still don't know how he managed as long as he did unless Royce was giving him money. Then one day Edgar told me he wanted me to sign some mortgage papers; he wanted to mortgage the farm. Pete was dead set against it, said the way Edgar was actin' he'd never be able to make any mortgage payments. But Edgar said he had it all worked out, said he was gonna lease the tobacco acreage to a man he knew and use that money from the tobacco to make the payments. Pete still wouldn't go for it, said I was givin' the farm away for nothin', just givin' it away so Edgar could stay drunk another year or two. Turns out he was right. That man with the tobacco lease, he got sugar and died, and Edgar never did make but maybe one or two payments on the mortgage. Pete's never spoke a word to Edgar since."

"Edgar told me something about a tobacco lease and a man who had diabetes and died. He never said anything about a mortgage."

"I'm not surprised. He's got a real knack for twistin' and turnin' things around. He'd have you believin' the sky is green if you gave him half a chance. Here lately he acts like he believes his own stories. I don't know if he's even capable of tellin' the truth anymore. He always was a big fibber, but here lately he acts like he doesn't know what the truth really is."

"What about Woodbine? How did Woodbine come to own the farm? Edgar acts like Woodbine…"

"Oh, I know how Edgar acts. Let me tell you about Gary Woodbine. He's one of the finest men you'd ever hope to meet in your life. We go to church with Gary Woodbine. We're churchgoin' people, me and Pete."

Flo looked expectantly at Joe, hoping to share a moment of mutual faith. Joe shook his head to indicate No, he didn't go to church.

Flo shrugged slightly and continued. "I've known Gary Woodbine since he was a baby. He's a wonderful man, has a lovely family—he's a deacon in our church. After the bank foreclosed on the mortgage Gary made 'em a good offer on the place and they sold it to him. I hated to see it go but I was glad that Gary was the one who bought it. They don't come no better than Gary Woodbine. Shame on Edgar for talkin' and actin' the way he does. He's hated Gary ever since he moved out here and he's let Gary know it, too. If Gary wasn't such a good Christian man he wouldn't have put up with half of it."

"What about Bobbie shooting at Gary Woodbine? What's up with that?"

"Edgar's poisoned her mind against Gary and he don't deserve it not one tiny bit. Those dogs they had out here—did you ever see those dogs? Why, I was afraid to get out o' the car when those dogs were around and I ain't afraid o' dogs. They killed three o' Gary's newborn calves, killed 'em and ate 'em. Gary tried to be nice about it. He tried talkin' to Bobbie, told her he didn't want to make trouble, but he didn't want those dogs killin' any more o' his cattle. Bobbie cussed him out, told him to get off her blankety-blank property. Edgar and Bobbie, they're both mean as snakes, and Bobbie's even worse than he is. When I think of the way that poor girl was raised, never hardly knew her mother, Edgar drunk all the time, it's no wonder she's as mean as she is. At least Edgar had a mother. We had us a good mother."

"I see," said Joe. Indeed, Joe now saw a horrible picture of a mean and hateful drunk that obliterated completely his previous image of a harmless and rascally old sot.

"Gary called me on the phone after Bobbie shot at him. He didn't want to call the police on her. He wanted me to go over there and talk to her, try to make peace somehow. But there ain't no makin' peace with

Bobbie. She's like Edgar—once she takes a notion in her head she won't let loose of it. Me and Bobbie don't get along much anyway. Bobbie blames me for…"

Flo stopped, evidently deciding not to say what she had intended to say. She backtracked a short step and continued, "Well, like I was sayin', Gary didn't want to call the police on Bobbie, he really didn't. But he felt like he had to do somethin'. When Gary killed that big ugly black dog the whole pack of 'em had just killed another one of his little calves, the third one this year. Gary never did call the police when his calves got killed and that cost him good money. His insurance company wouldn't make good on his claims without a police report, but he didn't want trouble with Edgar and Bobbie. It was Gary's wife who called the law when they seen that third calf gettin' killed. Gary's wife, she ain't quite so nice and forgivin' as what Gary is. Even after Bobbie took a shot at him, Gary still didn't want to call the law. He called me on the phone and asked me what I thought he should do."

"And what did you tell him?"

"I told him to call the police and report it. I don't care who it is, ain't nobody got the right to go shootin' at people like that. I told him that if'n it was me, I'd call the police in a heartbeat. Edgar don't know I told Gary that. You're not gonna tell him, are you? He'd be awful mad if he knew I told Gary to call the law on Bobbie. He'd never speak to me again."

"No, I won't tell him."

Joe hated becoming entangled in their awful family affairs, hated being privy to their mean secrets. He wanted to leave, if and when Flo ever stopped talking.

"Gary tried to get 'em to go easy on Bobbie. His wife works at the courthouse and both of 'em are very well thought of around here. Gary called me on the phone after the trial. I wanted to go to the trial but Pete wouldn't drive me and I don't drive a car so I couldn't go, but Gary told me all about it. He said Bobbie told the judge that she shot way up into the trees nowheres close to Gary, not even close. Then Gary told the judge that he heard the bullet whiz right past his ear. Gary told me on the phone he hated to have to say that in court, but it was the truth, and he'd been sworn to tell the truth, so that's what he done. I told him I'd have done the exact same thing. Once you swear on the Bible you have to tell the truth. Gary tried to get the judge to go easy on her but Bobbie's been in trouble lots o' times before so the judge said to lock her up. She probably would've had a bigger sentence if Gary hadn't talked to the judge."

Joe looked conspicuously at his watch and shifted his feet a bit.

"Did Edgar tell you they're talkin' about lettin' Bobbie out early?" Flo asked.

"Yes."

"That's because o' Gary. I've been tellin' him when I see him at church how hard this is on Bobbie's two girls. I've been doin' what I can but those girls, I hate to say it, but those girls need their mother even if she ain't the best thing in the world. Gary's been tryin' to pull some strings down at the courthouse. If they let Bobbie out early it'll be on account o' Gary."

"He sounds like a fine Christian man," Joe commented with a mild sarcasm that flew just below Flo's radar, just as he intended.

"Oh, he is. They don't come no better than Gary Woodbine."

Joe was anxious to leave, but as long as Flo was giving him the real story about Edgar he wanted to clear up a few things. "Was Edgar really kicked out of high school? He told me he was kicked out of high school for drinking moonshine during a baseball game."

"That was one of the sorriest days of my life," Flo said. "They had them a really good team that year. Danny Duvall, he was a great pitcher, and Edgar done real good catchin' for 'im. We had us a lot o' good players that year. Half the county turned out for that game. If they won, they were goin' all the way to the state championship."

"Wow," said Joe.

"Oh yeah," said Flo. "It was mighty big doin's around here. We had us a pretty good little lead, I don't recall the score exactly, but we were winnin' about halfway through. Everybody thought we would win for sure. But then, by the end of the game, Danny couldn't pitch and Edgar couldn't catch—they were drunk as monkeys, both of 'em. That other team beat us pretty bad."

"Edgar told me that they kicked him out of school, but not Danny Duvall."

"That's right. They asked who brought the shine to the game, and sure enough it was Edgar, so it was Edgar they kicked out."

"What about his cabin burning down? He *did* have a cabin, a log cabin, didn't he?"

"Yes, he *did* have a cabin. It was a right smart piece o' work, really.

Edgar always could do most anything he put his mind to. The trouble was he mostly put his mind to drinkin' and stayin' drunk all the time."

"Do you know what caused the fire?"

"No, not exactly, and Edgar don't know nothin' about it neither 'cause he was drunk as a monkey when his cabin burnt down. It's a miracle he got out o' there alive. He claims he heard God or some kind o' spirit a-tellin' him to get out o' there, but I don't know. I don't think God talks to drunks, but maybe He does. Edgar really was lucky to get out o' there alive, as drunk as he was that night."

"Edgar told me that he started helping his dad and his granddad make moonshine, and he had his first drink of moonshine, when he was three or four. He said he drank it out of a two-quart jar. Is that true?"

"I can't say for sure, I wasn't standin' right there to see it, but it probably is. Our daddy, he… well, we had a good mother. We had us a really good mother."

"I see. Well, I really have to be going now. Maybe I'll see you again sometime."

"I surely hope so. And I hope you'll keep coming out here to visit Edgar. He thinks the world of you, you know, and Edgar needs friends just now."

"Yes, well…"

"Oh please keep coming here to see him. You're the nicest friend he's had in a good long while and Edgar needs friends just now. Do you really have to rush off? Edgar might be back any minute now. Did you bring your fishing pole? Why don't you stay and fish awhile?"

Joe rather wanted to stay and catch some fish, but he was afraid Flo would follow him down to the lake and yak his ear off. More, in light of recent revelations, he wasn't sure he wanted to see Edgar just then, or ever again.

"I really have to be going," said Joe. "If you see Edgar, tell him I stopped by."

"He'll be so sorry he missed you. Please come back and visit again real soon, will you?"

"Okay," Joe said unconvincingly. "Goodbye."

"Goodbye. It was nice talkin' to ya."

Nice was not a word that Joe would apply to any part of that morning's conversation.

More Trouble   18

Joe Bass spent the rest of the weekend trying to digest the disturbing truths revealed by Edgar's sister Flo. They sat heavily in his gut like bad meat: toxic, indigestible, and vile. He wished there was someone with whom he could share his miserable sense of betrayal and disillusionment, but there wasn't. If he tried to talk to Jolene about it, she would probably respond with so many I-told-you-sos. His best friend was John Garner at work, but their friendship was relatively new and still somewhat superficial, and he didn't want to jeopardize or belabor it with the onerous and offensive details of his relationship with Edgar.

He was glad to return to work on Monday. His company was preparing to expand and hire sixty new employees, good news for the local community, and Joe was glad to write and distribute a press release proclaiming the good news. It helped transport him back into the world of honest people, industrious people, civic-minded people, and away from Edgar's sordid world of lies, crime, and drunken hatefulness.

On Wednesday morning, John Garner told him during their coffee break he'd heard the bass were biting in Nolin River Lake and proposed a fishing trip for the upcoming weekend. Joe readily, happily accepted. He'd have to check Jolene's calendar, but they tentatively planned the trip for early Saturday morning.

On Wednesday evening Jolene called her husband to the phone. She didn't know who it was; it sounded like a young woman. It was not a young woman. It was Flo.

"Joe, this is Flo Goody. I hope you don't mind me calling you like this. I found your number in the phone book."

"Okay."

Joe's heart fell to his feet. He'd been watching a good movie he hadn't seen before, a riveting action-packed thriller that claimed the better part of his attention. His mind had rarely strayed from the intense drama, and when it had done so, it was always in the direction of his upcoming fishing trip with John Garner at Nolin River Lake. Finally,

finally he had managed to put Edgar and his sorry affairs completely out of his mind. And now Flo was on the phone.

"Have you seen Edgar lately?"

"No."

"Oh, my—he looks just awful. I saw him today and it broke my heart. I've never seen Edgar in such a bad way before. I don't know what to do."

"You should take him to see a doctor."

"We've been tryin', but he won't go. There's somethin' bad wrong with him, Joe—I don't know what it is. He's all doubled over, can't hardly walk, won't eat a thing. He's laid up in his little camper morning, noon and night. He gets up to use the bathroom once in a while but that's about it. I just don't know what to do."

"If he's really that bad, maybe you should call an ambulance and have them take him to the emergency room."

"We thought about that, but Edgar says he won't go to no hospital unless it's the VA hospital and he ain't ready to go there just yet."

"Have you talked to Royce? Maybe Royce can get him to go see a doctor."

"Yes, I did. He won't listen to Royce neither."

"Well, what do you expect me to do?" Joe asked, exasperated. "If he won't listen to Royce I don't know why he'd listen to me."

"Oh, but Edgar just thinks the world of you Joe. I told him you were out to see him Saturday and you should've seen the way he lit up—first time I've seen anything like a smile on his face in I don't know how long."

Something sparked in Joe's chest. He didn't like it, but there it was—a small but undeniable spark of humanitarian concern.

"Could you please go out there and talk to him, Joe? I think maybe he'd listen to you. Pete and me would be glad to drive him to the doctor's if you can just get him to go."

"I guess I can try."

"Oh, would you? Thank you. I knew you'd want to help. Thank you, Joe. When do you think you'll be going out there to see him?"

"Sunday, maybe?"

There was a silence on the other end that somehow suggested disappointment. It was confirmed in Flo's voice when she spoke. "Oh, I was hoping… well, okay. But he's really in a bad way just now. Can't you get out there any sooner?"

"I guess I could stop by there early tomorrow morning before I go to work. If you really think it's necessary…"

"Oh, God bless you Joe. God bless you. Thank you *so* much."

"You're welcome."

"Let me give you my phone number. If it's not too much trouble give me a call and let me know how it turns out."

"Okay."

Flo gave him their number, thanked him again, and hung up.

The next morning dawned cool and very foggy. Joe left the house at six-thirty, an hour earlier than usual, explaining to Jolene he'd fallen behind in his work and needed an early start. Proceeding slowly through the thick fog, he wished he'd left at six. At this rate, even if he spent no more than fifteen or twenty minutes with Edgar, he'd still be late for work.

The fog thickened as he neared Edgar's place; it drew substance, moisture from the lake. Joe slowed to a crawl and peered wide-eyed through the fog, looking for the meager opening in the broom grass that marked the beginning of Edgar's drive. Just where he thought he should find it, a county sheriff's cruiser was pulling out onto Sycamore Church Road.

Joe stopped dead on the road, his turn signal flashing uselessly, and tried to see if Edgar was in the police car. Peering intently, he made out the vague silhouette of the driver behind the clean swath of the cruiser's windshield wipers. The rest of the car's glass was fogged over. Maybe Edgar was in the backseat; there was no way to know for sure. There could've been three of four people in the backseat and Joe wouldn't have known. The police cruiser passed him and drove on.

Joe drove to the end of Edgar's drive, parked, and got out. He noticed that Edgar's car was not in its usual space, now revealed as a car-sized bald spot in the broom grass. He called loudly, "Edgar?" There was no response. He knocked loudly on the door of the camper. No response. He opened the door and looked inside. It was a dark morning made darker still by the dense fog, and the camper's tiny dirty windows allowed scant light to penetrate its gloomy interior. "Edgar?" he called again. No response.

He stepped inside and looked around, seeing little at first until his eyes adjusted to the darkness. It was fuggy and musty inside the camper, like the den of a burrowing creature. Eventually he was able to discern individual items amongst the jumbled mess: various and numerous articles of clothing, assorted boxes, a chain saw, a rifle, a stack of red Marlboro caps, at least eight or ten tucked neatly one within another, but no clue as to Edgar's whereabouts.

He saw at the rear end of the camper a sleeping berth containing a big lump of clothing and a sleeping bag that might've contained Edgar. Panic jabbed his heart like a sword as he thought that might be Edgar, dead. He stepped gingerly forward and said loudly, "Edgar?" No response. Reluctantly he disassembled the lump of clothing and sleeping bag, and was immensely relieved to find nothing else.

He turned to leave the fuggy musty camper and nearly fell when he stepped down on something hard and cylindrical that rolled beneath his foot. It was the fifth of Old Fitzgerald he'd purchased for Edgar, and it was completely empty. Feeling guilty and discouraged, Joe stepped down out of the little camper.

Outside, a pair of oncoming headlights poked weakly through the fog, aimed straight in Joe's direction. Joe froze like an escaping prisoner caught in the guard tower's searchlight. More cops? He had to assure himself that he'd done nothing wrong. That wasn't "breaking and entering." He was merely looking for Edgar.

Finally he recognized the car and face that belonged to Royce Taylor. He rushed to Royce's car and walked alongside the driver's window as the car decelerated and stopped.

Royce powered down his window. "What are you doin' out here so early of a mornin'?" he asked. There was suspicion and caution in his face and voice.

"Flo called me last night and asked me to come see Edgar, but I'm afraid he might be in trouble."

"What kind of trouble?"

"I don't know for sure. I just got here maybe ten minutes ago and there was a police cruiser pulling out of the drive."

"Was Edgar in it?"

"I don't know. I couldn't see. It's too foggy."

"You got a cell phone?"

"No, I have one but I don't keep it with me. I used to, but it made my life busier and more complicated than it has to be so I…"

While Joe explained his aversion to cell phones, Royce rummaged around inside his jacket and produced one. "Here. You dial. I have trouble workin' the numbers."

"Who do you want me to call?"

"Who was it you saw drivin' out o' here?"

"It was a county sheriff's cruiser, I'm sure."

"Then call the sheriff's office."

Joe looked down at the phone, and then quickly looked up again. "Do you know the number?

"Nope."

"Well, how can I find it?"

"I don't know. You can't get information on that thing. It ain't set up for that. Why don't you call home to your wife and get her to look it up for you?"

Joe desperately tried to think of someone to call other than Jolene. John Garner was the only other person he could think of, but he was probably on his way to work. He thought about driving off to find a phone book somewhere, but the situation seemed to require more prompt and immediate action. So he called home to his wife and told Jolene what he wanted, but not why he wanted it.

"No there hasn't been an accident and I'm not in any kind of trouble. Please, Jolene, just give me the damn number. I'll explain when I get home. There's nothing to worry about, I swear. I'll explain it all to you later."

Joe poked at the tiny number buttons on the phone and then placed it to his ear.

"Is it ringin'?" asked Royce.

"Yes."

"Then give it here." Royce grabbed the phone away and listened for what seemed an inordinate length of time. Finally he said, "Yeah, this is Royce Taylor. Yes, that's right, Royce Taylor, you all know me down there. Listen, I'm callin' to see what I can find out about my buddy Edgar Johnson. That's right, Edgar J. Johnson. Did you all pick him up this morning? You did. Well, what'd he do? He did? Well, when are you lettin' him out? Is that right? Well, you tell him to call me if I can help out, okay? Thank *you*. Yeah, I'll try. Okay. Goodbye."

Royce snapped shut the phone and said, "They got him."

"So I gathered."

"They said he was over to Tina's restaurant this morning, drunk.

Somebody called the law on him I guess, unless they was already in there and seen him drunk." Royce sounded almost bored, as if this were business as usual, just another dark and foggy morning, nothing to get riled up about.

"What's he charged with?" Joe asked.

"They got him on drunk drivin' is all. His registration is expired and he don't have no insurance but they ain't gonna lay that on him just now. They know he don't have no money." Royce looked and acted as if he were thinking about going back home to bed.

"So what do we do now?" asked Joe. "I need to get to work."

"I reckon there ain't much we *can* do just now. They'll send somebody from the prosecutor's office over to the jail to talk to him this afternoon."

"What about bail? Won't it cost money to get him out? Are you gonna post bail for him?"

"I will if it comes to that. But they know he don't have no money. They'll probably let him out on his signature. What I can't figure out is how he got himself drunk. I ain't brought him no beer or nothin' since he's been real sick here lately."

Joe felt guilty but said nothing.

"I'll tell you somethin' else what's puzzlin' me is how he got up outta that trailer and drove all the way to Tina's. It ain't but a couple o' miles, but when I left here yesterday evenin' he didn't have strength enough to fart. He told me honest-to-God he didn't think he'd make it through the night. He told me that and I believed him. I've seen men before when they…"

Royce paused, closed his eyes a moment, seemed to break free of something, opened his eyes and continued. "That's why I'm here so early of a mornin'. To tell you the truth, I didn't know if he'd still be alive or not. He's been awful poorly here lately."

"Yeah I know. He needs to go see a doctor."

"I *know* he does, but Edgar never will do nothin' till he's damn good and ready."

"Yeah, well, listen—I really gotta go to work now. Good luck. Oh, you might want to give his sister Flo a call and let her know what's happened. She's been awfully worried about him lately. That's why *I'm* here."

"You can call her if you want but I ain't a-goin' to. I've known

Edgar and his bunch a lot o' years and I've learned it's best to stay out o' their business. Once you get into it, it's hard to get back out again. There ain't none of 'em get along very good 'ceptin' maybe Edgar and Bobbie."

"Yeah, well, whatever. I need to get to work. Bye."

"See ya later, sport."

Joe didn't like the way Royce called him "sport," but that was the least of his concerns. He was going to be at least a half hour late for work, and he had to explain things to Jolene when he got home. More bothersome still was the nagging sense of guilt and responsibility he felt when he thought of the empty whiskey bottle in Edgar's camper. Given Edgar's proclivity for liquor, he found it hard to imagine him not drinking what they'd left in the bottle a few weeks past until just last night or this morning. Repeatedly his sense of guilt poked at him like a sharp stick. Repeatedly he told himself he was not, could not be responsible; Edgar must have gotten his liquor from somewhere else.

Distracted and disturbed, Joe muddled his way through his workday. It was impossible to concentrate on his work. Hours dragged by like days but finally, mercifully, it ended.

He mentally composed a dozen different explanations for Jolene on his way home from work. None of them seemed suitable or worthwhile. As he pulled in his drive he decided to tell her the truth.

When he stepped through the door there was Jolene, waiting with phone in hand. Her face was dark and scowling. "It's for you," she said crossly. "It's somebody calling from the jail."

Joe winced, took the phone from his wife, and said, "Hello." He expected to hear Edgar's voice in reply, but heard instead a lady jailer. She had a very pleasant voice which set Joe a bit more at ease. Edgar was being released on his signature and he'd given them Joe's name as the person to call to come and pick him up. Joe told her he'd be there in twenty minutes.

"I gotta go take Edgar home from jail. I'm sorry. I'll explain when I get back. I'll be home as soon as I can."

Jolene said nothing, but scowled furiously. Joe rushed off to his truck, and then to the jail.

The lady jailer had directed him to DOOR EIGHTEEN at the rear of the jail complex. Joe stood outside the designated door, looked up at the security camera, and managed a small, rather goofy smile. "Yes?" a gruff metallic voice inquired through an outside speaker.

"I'm Joe Bass. I'm here to pick up Edgar Johnson."

The lock on the door buzzed and then clicked loudly. Joe pulled open the door and entered into the harshest, starkest waiting area he'd ever seen—concrete floor and walls, and a steel bench about eight feet long. On his left a thick sheet of Plexiglas, maybe four feet tall and eight feet wide, provided a view of the jail's interior, to include its front desk. A pleasant-looking woman behind the desk was talking on a phone, maybe the same woman who'd called him. A few other jailers behind the desk were busy with papers and paperwork. Inmates were escorted hither and yon by uniformed jailers. A solitary inmate swabbed the linoleum floor with a mop.

"Yes?" asked the same gruff metallic voice.

"I'm Joe Bass. I'm here to pick up Edgar Johnson."

"Wait," the voice commanded imperiously. Joe was looking all the while at the people behind the front desk, trying to identify the speaker. But no one's face matched the words. Joe imagined somebody behind a curtain somewhere, like the Wizard of Oz. Indeed, everything about the jail seemed dreamlike, surreal, belonging to another dimension. It was his first visit inside a jail, and it struck him as something considerably less, and considerably more, than the jails he'd seen on TV.

Reality descended like a ton of bricks when first he saw old Edgar. Clad in a bright orange jumpsuit and cloth slippers, he was stooped over halfway to the ground, his arms and elbows cocked behind him like the wings on a little bantam rooster. He shuffled slowly to the front desk and tried to raise himself up to address the jailer, but he couldn't straighten up. So he twisted, turned his torso and head sideways, and awkwardly managed a few small words. The jailer handed him down a fishnet bag containing his filthy old clothes and boots. Edgar looked like walking death—gaunt, pale, totally defeated. Shocked out of his usual and meaningful mental processes, Joe had only one thought: 'He needs his cap. He'd be alright if he only had his cap.' Edgar shuffled away from the front desk to a room opposite the front desk and disappeared inside. Several long minutes later he emerged half-dressed—his flannel shirt unbuttoned, his blue jean pants unzipped, his belt unbuckled, and his feet bare. He trudged to the front desk and again twisted his upper body and managed a few small words. The jailer said something to the inmate with the mop. The guy stopped mopping and ushered Edgar back into the room. Ten minutes later Edgar emerged fully and properly clothed. Joe was glad to see him wearing his red Marlboro cap.

Again Edgar managed a few words with the jailer at the front desk, and then dragged himself to the door separating the inside of the jail from the waiting area. The door buzzed and clicked. Edgar pushed but lacked the strength to open it. Joe pulled it open from his side. Edgar craned around awkwardly and said, "Hi Joe."

"Hello Edgar. Are you ready to get outta here?"

"I reckon I am."

The door to the outside world buzzed and clicked open and they left.

Edgar was silent until they were off municipal property. Then he said softly, "I'm sorry, Joe. I'm sorry to put you through all this. I wanted to have them call Royce but I couldn't think of his last name. Can you imagine that? I've known Royce for forty-five years or more and I still can't think of it. What *is* his last name, Joe?"

"Taylor. It's Royce Taylor."

"Sure it is—Royce Taylor. I remembered your name because of the fish—bass, Joe Bass. But I couldn't think o' Royce's name for nothin'. I don't know what's wrong with me, Joe. I think I might be dyin'."

"Oh hell, Edgar. You shouldn't talk like that. You're not dying."

"I believe I might be, Joe. I truly believe this might be it."

"Well, if you really feel that bad, why don't you go see a doctor? I'll tell you what—we can stop at a doctor's office or the hospital right now and have somebody check you out. You really need to see a doctor."

"Not now, Joe, not today. I just want to go home. Take me home, Joe." His voice, weak and pitiful, trailed off into nothingness.

"I really think you should see a doctor. I think we should do that today, right now," Joe said firmly, commandingly.

"No, not today, Joe. I might go to the VA hospital before too long but I ain't a-goin' today. I just want to go home now."

Joe decided not to press it any further just then. "Well, have you eaten anything? We can stop anywhere you want here in town and get you something to eat."

"Not right now, Joe. I just want to go home."

"Just tell me what you want, Edgar. Chicken, a hamburger, fish?"

"No, I couldn't eat a bite right now, Joe. Just take me on home."

"How about something to drink then?—water, Coke, coffee?"

"Well, I *am* awful dry. I could maybe drink a little Coke."

Joe ordered a cheeseburger, fries, and a large Coke at a McDonald's drive-thru window. Edgar sipped mightily through the straw in his Coke but adamantly refused to touch a bite of solid food. The Coke seemed to refresh him a little.

"I sure do wish you'd eat something," Joe persisted.

"I can't eat, Joe, not now. I was hungry this morning. That's what got me in trouble."

"Tell me what happened. The sheriff's office said you were at Tina's…?"

"You remember that whiskey you bought me a while back, Joe?"

"Yes."

"Well, after you and me got drunk that day, you remember? You pulled me out o' the lake that day. You saved my life."

"Yeah, I remember."

"Well, after that I got to feelin' so poorly I didn't even want no more o' that whiskey what was left in the bottle. Every once in a while I'd have me a little sip, just one tiny little sip is all. Then yesterday when I really needed it there wasn't but two or three little sips of it left. I never felt so bad in my whole life, Joe, as what I did yesterday and last night. Royce come out to see me and stayed till dark. I told Royce I thought I was dyin'. After he left I tried to go to sleep but I couldn't. I just laid there a-thinkin', 'This is it. This is the end o' the road. This is as far as I go.'"

Edgar spoke softly and laboriously, his voice raspy and croaky. Talking seemed to wear him out. He took another sip of Coke and continued.

"Somewhere 'long about five or six in the morning I thought, 'Well, if I'm a-dyin', I might as well drink me that last little bit of whiskey before I go.' It wasn't but two or three little sips is all, not even one good swallow, really. But Joe I'll tell you what—that good whiskey you bought me really set me straight. I drank it down all in one swallow and then I was hungry, *real* hungry. Maybe I shouldn't have been drivin' Joe but I was hungry and I wanted me some biscuits and gravy. You ever eat biscuits and gravy, Joe?"

"Sometimes."

"I love biscuits and gravy, especially Flo's—she makes 'em like our mother used to make 'em. But I couldn't just sit around and wait to see if

Flo would bring me some, so I drove over to Tina's restaurant. You ever ate at Tina's, Joe?"

"No."

"They got good biscuits and gravy. They're not as good as Flo's but they're pretty good. It's them people what work there, Joe—they ain't good people. You'd never know it from eatin' their biscuits and gravy but those people what work there ain't no count at all. I'll tell you what they done to me. I ordered me up some biscuits and gravy at the counter, see? And that woman back there turned up her nose somethin' awful. I guess maybe I still smelled a little bit like whiskey. Well, a feller I know name of Jim Jenkins... Do you know Jim?"

"No."

"Well, Jim Jenkins called me over to his table and we started talkin' is all. I kept waitin' for 'em to tell me to come and get my biscuits and gravy, but they never did. They was stallin' me, Joe, stallin' me till the law could get there. That woman back there what smelled the whiskey on me—she called the law on me, Joe, I know she did."

"Maybe."

"Ain't no maybe to it. And I'll tell you what else they done. That sheriff's deputy they sent didn't come in there to get me, no sir. He waited, parked out back behind the restaurant and waited till I took off down the road. Then he come a-chasin' out after me so they could charge me with drunk drivin'. That ain't right, is it Joe? If they thought I was such a menace, why didn't they just come on in the restaurant and grab me before I got out on the road?"

"I don't know. Tell me—how'd you get your car home? I saw it there this morning."

"You were out to see me this morning?"

"Yes. I saw the cop car pulling out just as I was about to pull in. I couldn't tell if you were in it or not. It was too foggy to see. Royce was out there, too."

"Royce and you? You and Royce both? God bless you, Joe. God bless you and Royce both. Does Royce know they locked me up?"

"Yes. We called the sheriff's office on his cell phone this morning. He was all ready to go bail you out if you needed to make bail."

Edgar looked like he was about to cry. "Royce... Royce Taylor. You too, Joe. I don't know where I'd be if I didn't have you two guys to be my friends."

"Yeah, well—how'd you get your car home?"

"Well I'll tell you what—that was easy enough. I seen those lights a-flashin' behind me, but I didn't stop, didn't even slow down, I just drove on home. It made that cop mad as hell, too. 'Why didn't you stop?' he asked me. 'Didn't you see my lights?' You know what I told him, Joe? I told him I thought it was a school bus behind me."

Edgar smiled a little mischievous grin at the recollection. It was weak and puny but it was there.

They turned off the highway onto Sycamore Church Road. "Almost home," said Joe. "I'm sorry, but I won't be able to stay and visit. My wife's mad enough already."

Edgar nearly fell out of his seat. "Oh no, I hope she ain't mad on account o' me puttin' you out like this. I'm sorry, Joe, I truly am sorry."

"I'm just sorry you feel so bad, Edgar. I can deal with my wife okay. I just wish you'd go and see a doctor."

"Soon, Joe. Maybe soon."

"Do you want me to call Flo and tell her you're okay? She's been awfully worried about you."

"No, no, no—don't tell Flo nothin'. If she finds out I've been in jail there ain't no tellin' what she'll do. You can call Royce and tell him that you sprung me out o' jail. I don't want old Royce to worry about me."

"Okay, I'll call Royce. Do you want me to walk you over to your camper?"

"No, no, Joe. You've done too much for me already. I can manage. You tell your wife I'm sorry to cause you all so much trouble, you hear?"

"Don't you worry about my wife. You just worry about Edgar."

"Whatever you say, Joe. Whatever you say. You come on back and fish anytime you want. I might hang on another few days yet, or maybe even a week."

"Don't talk like that. You're too mean and ornery to die. I'll see you again real soon."

"Maybe you will, I don't know. Goodbye Joe."

"Goodbye Edgar. You take care of yourself."

Edgar exited the truck in something like a controlled fall, or skid, and trudged off slowly toward his little camper.

Joe turned his truck around and left.

Nashville Bound   19

Joe spent the following evening with his family at the high school where his daughter's chorus group was putting on a concert. Already he'd smoothed things over with Jolene, more or less. Her ire had diminished considerably when he'd explained how terribly sick Edgar had appeared. Her compassion and sympathy, however, did not stretch too far. If Edgar was really that sick then he needed a doctor, not Joe. And if his sister and his old friend Royce Taylor couldn't compel him to see a doctor, there was no reason whatsoever why Joe should assume that responsibility, either.

Mainly Joe was not worried about Edgar just then. He snapped pictures with his digital camera of his daughter performing onstage and listened with pride and appreciation to the concert, a medley of songs that originated in colonial America. When his mind occasionally wandered, it drifted forward to the next morning when he was going fishing with his friend John Garner. Only rarely and briefly did he think about old Edgar. Somehow, without good reason to do so, he had decided Edgar probably had kidney stones. Joe's dad had suffered from kidney stones and the symptoms seemed somewhat congruous with Edgar's problems. So whenever he thought about Edgar and his health problems he immediately thought *kidney stones* and let it go at that.

When they returned home after the concert their phone was ringing as they entered the door. "I'll get it," Joe said quickly. He rather expected it to be John Garner calling to iron out the last few details of their fishing trip.

It was Flo. "Did you hear about Edgar?" she asked hurriedly, excitedly.

"Yes," Joe shortly replied. He thought she was referring to Edgar's arrest and incarceration.

"I'm still in shock," said Flo. "I just can't believe it. I didn't know what in the world was wrong with Edgar but I didn't think it was cancer."

"What?"

Flo was slightly confused, but continued. "Yes—he's got cancer of the colon. He finally let us drive him to the clinic in Bowling Green this morning and then an ambulance took him to the VA hospital in Nashville. They can't operate on him. It's spread out too far already."

"I'm really sorry," said Joe, shocked. Why was he thinking kidney stones?

"I am too," said Flo. "They'll be runnin' tests the next few days but right now it don't look too good."

"I guess they'll try chemotherapy treatments eventually."

"Yes, but not for a while. They say they'll have to get him a whole lot stronger before he can have any chemo. He's awful weak. He's dehydrated and about half-starved. He never did eat right."

"I know."

"I wish he was somewheres closer where me and Pete could go see him. Pete can drive to Bowling Green okay but I don't think he could make it all the way down to Nashville. He's eighty years old, same as me, and I never did learn how to drive a car."

Joe was silent. He wasn't going to volunteer for anything.

"Let me give you the phone number for Edgar's room in the hospital," said Flo. "I know he'd love to hear from you."

Joe said, "Okay." Flo gave him the number.

"I wouldn't call for a few days," said Flo. "They're busy givin' him tests right now."

"Okay."

"Did you see him yesterday?" asked Flo. "You said you were goin' out there first thing in the morning but I never heard back from you."

"I saw him."

"How was he when you saw him?"

"Not good."

"Yeah, well, I guess the main thing now is that he's finally in a hospital where people can take care of him."

"Yes, that's the main thing."

"Maybe you can go visit him sometime," said Flo. "Maybe you and Royce could drive down there together. Edgar told me today to make sure you and Royce know he's in the hospital. I done called Royce already."

"We'll see," said Joe.

"Oh, you don't need to rush down there right away. I think he'll be in the hospital for at least a couple weeks."

"Okay."

Flo's voice registered some disappointment at Joe's terse unresponsiveness. "Well, at least I hope you'll call him sometime. You can do that much at least, can't you?"

"Absolutely."

"Well, I hope so. I hope I haven't *bothered* you…"

"No, no bother at all. I really am sorry to hear about Edgar. I just don't know what to say right now."

Flo sounded somewhat mollified. "Yes I know. It really is a shock, isn't it? Well, I'll let you go now. You keep in touch, Joe, okay?"

Joe said he'd keep in touch, and he said goodbye.

Jolene had been listening in on Joe's half of the conversation from a polite distance. Her interest had been piqued at the word "chemotherapy." She figured somebody had cancer, probably Edgar, and wanted confirmation.

"Who was that?" she asked lightly.

"That was Edgar's sister, Flo. Edgar has colon cancer. He's at the VA hospital in Nashville."

"That's too bad," Jolene stated flatly. "You're still going fishing tomorrow, aren't you?"

"Yes."

"Good," Jolene said. She turned and hurried off.

The following morning was cool, dark, and gloomy. Not summer, not fall, it was what Joe's dad called the "in-between time" of fishing, and it was not a good time to fish. Joe and John caught a few small bass, a few small crappie, and a smattering of small bluegill. All totaled it was barely enough to stink up a skillet. They quit around eleven and dumped their meager catch back into the lake. John noticed his buddy Joe was not in a good mood, but attributed it to the gloomy weather and poor fishing. John wasn't exactly chipper that morning, either.

"That's fishing," John said as they drove away from the lake. "Sometimes you catch 'em and sometimes you don't."

"Maybe next time," Joe replied, forcing into his voice some small optimism that he truly did not feel.

"Yeah," said John. "Maybe next time."

But neither man felt sufficiently confident to set even a tentative date for their next outing. The dark and gloomy weather was not only oppressive, but ominous as well. It felt like a good day to have a flat tire or catch a cold or break a window or a mirror. Both men were glad to be safely home by noon.

Joe was not obsessed with thoughts about Edgar, but neither could he get him out of his mind. Cancer—the Big C. It was both a shock and a surprise but it was not a shock or a surprise. He knew Edgar was very sick. Why shouldn't it be cancer? Lots of people came down with cancer. Why not Edgar?

On the other hand: Why Edgar? Joe did not believe in God except in a figurative sense, as an abstract concept. He certainly did not believe in Him as an omniscient and all-powerful Being who rewarded the faithful and punished the sinful. But even if he had believed all that, he didn't think poor old Edgar deserved to have cancer. He was a liar and a drunkard and meaner than he should be, but he was an old man who probably didn't have a lot of years to look forward to anyway. Joe didn't think it was fair. He knew cancer was a virus totally incapable of determining fairness, but still it didn't seem fair.

The dark oppressive weather persisted for the next few days. Around nine o'clock on Wednesday morning the clouds finally disintegrated and the sun came out. Joe's mood brightened as well. He decided to call Edgar during his coffee break.

"Hello?" Edgar answered. His voice was weak and small.

"Edgar, it's me—Joe Bass."

"Joe Bass, how are you doin' Joe?" The voice was much stronger and livelier. Joe could almost see him smiling his beautiful womanly smile.

"I'm okay, Edgar. How are *you*?"

"Oh, I don't know, Joe. They're takin' pretty good care of me here but I don't know if I'll make it or not."

"You'll make it."

"Well, Joe, I can't say for sure if I will or not. You know I have cancer…"

"Yes."

"Well, it ain't good, Joe. They tell me the cancer has spread all through my bowels already; they can't operate on it."

"Yeah, well, maybe they can cure it with chemotherapy."

"They're gonna try me on that chemo stuff as soon as I get strong enough to take it. I talked to Royce the other day. He said one o' his brothers had colon cancer and they whipped it with those chemo treatments. Have you talked to Royce lately?"

"No, not lately."

"Well, Royce is wantin' to come down here and see me, good ol' Royce. But he ain't fit to drive this far. I told him maybe you could pick him up and the two of you could drive down here together."

"Maybe. I'll have to see."

"I hope your wife ain't still mad at you. She ain't still mad about you fetchin' me out o' jail, is she?"

"No, she's not mad."

"Good. Then maybe you and Royce could come down here and visit sometime." Edgar's voice was rife with hopefulness and longing. "I sure would like to see ol' Royce again. You too, Joe. I'd like to see you too."

"Okay," said Joe, touched by the emotion in Edgar's voice. "How about we try to make it down there on Saturday? Do you think you'll still be there this Saturday?"

"Sure I will be. It's gonna take 'em at least a couple weeks to get me strong enough for that chemo. I'll be here."

"Okay then. I'll talk to Royce and we'll try to get down there Saturday."

"God bless you, Joe. God bless you. I surely would like to see ol' Royce again. And you, too."

They said their goodbyes and hung up. Joe called across town and talked to Jolene at work. No, she didn't mind if Joe drove to Nashville Saturday. Joe called Royce at home and asked if he'd like to visit Edgar on Saturday. Royce said Yes. Joe obtained directions to Royce's house and said he'd pick him up at eight.

Royce lived in a little one-story white frame house, just two miles from Edgar's place as the crow flies. There were three or four cars parked here and there in the yard, along with a few trucks, one old tractor, and a few boats. Royce was sitting in a chair on his front porch, waiting for Joe's arrival. He was ready to go.

Royce opened the door to Joe's big red Ford truck, and balked. "Ain't no way I can get up in there unless you want to pick me up and set me in."

"I guess I can pick you up," Joe said helpfully.

Joe walked around his truck and prepared to boost Royce inside. But Royce quailed when Joe reached to grab him. "I got a better idea," said Royce. "How about we take my car? I know I can get in and out o' there easy enough, and I filled 'er up with gas yesterday. You wouldn't mind drivin' my car, would you?"

"No, I guess not. Give me the keys."

A few minutes later they were out of the yard and driving down the road in Royce's late-model Toyota. "I'm surprised you'd own a Toyota," Joe commented.

"Why's that?"

"It's a Japanese car, isn't it? Didn't you tell me you were a prisoner of the Japanese for what…? Thirty-two months?"

"*Forty*-two months. I don't much think about that no more," said Royce.

"I've seen some shows on the History channel about the Japanese prison camps," said Joe. "Were they really that bad?"

"Worse, probably. But I don't never care to watch it on the television so I don't know what you seen."

"Well, it was bad. The Japanese officers chopped off people's heads with their samurai swords just to show off how sharp they were."

"Sometimes, maybe. I never seen it. I heard they done that sometimes."

"And they beat the hell out of prisoners for no reason at all."

"Yeah, there was a lot o' that."

"The prisoners all looked like they were starved to death. They were lucky if they got one bowl of rice a day. A lot of them ate bugs and mice and lizards and anything else they could get their hands on."

"Yeah, they didn't feed us much, that's for sure. It was the only time in my life I was ever glad I grew up the way I did—poor and hungry all the time. I was kind o' used to it I guess. It was the fat city boys, guys who were used to eatin' three meals a day, they were the first to go. But I reckon I was kind o' used to it already." He cast a sideways and appraising and somewhat reproachful glance at Joe's middle-aged paunch which seemed to indicate that Joe would've been one of the fat city boys who were the first to go.

Royce spoke without rancor or sorrow, but a certain dullness in his voice suggested he didn't like talking about his years as a prisoner-of-war. Joe took a slightly different tack.

"Were you in the Army, Navy, what?"

"Navy. I was an anti-aircraft gunner on the U.S.S. Houston, a heavy cruiser. It went down in the Battle of the Java Sea a few months after the Japs attacked Pearl Harbor."

"Was it hard being an anti-aircraft gunner? Was it hard to hit the enemy planes?"

"It was a lot harder than you'd think. They moved pretty damn fast—you had to lead 'em a mile."

"Did you ever hit any?"

"I maybe hit one or two I guess."

"Was it loud, the anti-aircraft gun? I bet it was loud."

"Yeah it was loud. All they gave us was cotton balls to stick in our ears. It didn't help much."

"I fired an M-60 machinegun when I was in the Army and it was loud as hell. Every round felt like somebody clapping their hands on my ears."

"You were a machine-gunner?" asked Royce, mildly interested.

"No, I was a company clerk. But I fired a machinegun once."

"Oh," said Royce, not interested at all.

It wasn't the first time Joe's stint in the peacetime Army had failed to impress a war veteran. He decided not to talk about the military anymore. They drove in silence until they were somewhere between Bowling Green and the Tennessee state line.

"I talked to Flo a while back," Joe broke the silence.

Royce sort of shrugged: So what?

"She told me things about Edgar that, well, they weren't the same as what Edgar told me."

Again Royce indicated utter indifference.

"I think Edgar sometimes fudges the truth a little," Joe said carefully. He didn't want to come right out and call Edgar a liar.

"Not with me he don't," Royce replied defensively. "Edgar's always straight with me; Edgar always has been straight with me."

Now it was Joe who shrugged to indicate indifference.

"If Edgar's told you things that ain't exactly true, it's because he likes you," Royce explained. "Edgar's done some things he ain't exactly proud of, and if'n he told you things that wasn't exactly true he only done it 'cause he likes you and he didn't want you to think bad about him."

"I see."

"You ought to hear the way Edgar talks about you. Edgar thinks the world of Joe Bass, especially since you sprung him out o' jail." Royce sounded as if he didn't share Edgar's high opinion of Joe Bass; he pronounced Joe's name as if it were something he scraped off his shoe.

"I see," Joe repeated. "But I was wondering… you told me Edgar never had enough money to buy a dead cat. But Flo told me he mortgaged the farm; that's how they lost it. What did he do with the money he got from mortgaging the farm?"

"Edgar always was a generous man, *too* generous, 'specially when he was drinkin'—that's a lot of his problem. That money didn't last much more than a year. If there was anybody needin' a few dollars, Edgar gave 'em a twenty. And so long as he had money he kept half the county drunk. Wasn't nobody ever lacked for a drink when Edgar had money. If he had a million dollars I reckon he'd keep half the state of Kentucky drunk for as long as the money held out. He always was generous like that."

When they crossed the state line into Tennessee, Joe honked the car horn.

"What'd you toot the horn for?" asked Royce.

"I don't know. I always honk when I cross a state line."

Royce thought city people sure could be stupid at times. He looked curiously at Joe and wondered how a man with a college education could be so God-almighty stupid. "Well, I reckon they know we're here now. You don't need to toot the horn no more."

"I won't," Joe said reassuringly, smiling. "Don't worry—I won't wear out your horn."

They made the rest of the trip in silence.

Hospital Visit   20

Joe led the way through the hospital corridors, pausing briefly at the information desk, then proceeding up to Edgar's room on the third floor. Joe walked very slowly but still he needed to stop every so often and let old Royce catch up.

"I usually ain't so slow," Royce explained. "But I got all stiff a-sittin' in that car so long. You go on ahead without me. I'll find my own way there."

"No, no," said Joe. "We'll go up there together. Then I'm gonna leave you guys alone for a while. I know you two have a lot to talk about."

Royce brightened a bit at the prospect of Joe leaving him alone for a while. Somehow he found the wherewithal to quicken his pace slightly.

Joe found the right door and knocked. "Come in," Edgar called from inside.

Joe stepped aside and let Royce enter first. It was a single-occupant room, very small.

"Royce!" Edgar happily exclaimed. "It's good to see you!"

Joe entered the room and was similarly greeted. "Joe! It sure is good to see you guys! It's awful good of you to drive all the way down here to see me. It's a long ways, ain't it?"

Royce, exhausted, plopped down on the room's only chair. Joe tarried by the door. "It's not that far," said Joe, who had noted the odometer's readings. "It's exactly one hundred miles from Royce's place to the Nashville city limits."

"One hundred miles," Edgar stated expansively. "You guys drove one hundred miles to see me."

Edgar was dressed in a light blue hospital gown and white paper slippers. He stood by his bed mainly erect, not stooped over like he had been for the past several weeks. His eyes sparkled and he smiled happily. His skin was absolutely radiant—it glowed bright pink—and his face and figure were filled out considerably.

Joe was enormously relieved. He had expected to find Edgar very sick and weak. But old Edgar was the very picture of radiant good health.

"You're looking good, Edgar," Joe stated honestly. "What've they been feeding you here?"

"I still can't eat much," Edgar replied. "But I've been drinkin' a lot o' this stuff." Edgar motioned to a large wicker fruit basket on the table next to his bed that contained a bountiful supply of a canned nutritional drink, flavored with vanilla, chocolate and strawberry.

"Well, I'm glad to see you looking so good," said Joe. "Listen—I'm gonna get out of here and let you two guys talk awhile. I'll be back soon."

"Where are you goin'?" asked Edgar, concerned. "Don't rush off. Stay and visit with me a spell."

"I'll be back in about forty-five minutes or so. I know you guys have a lot to talk about, and besides, there's only one chair in here."

Edgar reached for a white cable with a Call button. "Wait. I'll fetch us a nurse and have her bring in another chair," he said.

But Joe was already halfway out the door. "I'll be back in a little while," he insisted. "You guys have fun."

Joe returned to a lobby area they'd passed earlier by the third-floor elevators. He looked at his watch; it was a few minutes past ten. He found a few magazines and read for nearly an hour. At eleven o'clock he returned to Edgar's little room.

The old men seemed much calmer, more quiet and relaxed, than when he'd left them. It was apparent that whatever they'd had to say to each other had been said already, and they were now simply enjoying each other's company.

"Joe—you didn't need to rush off like that," Edgar said softly, soberly. "We're all friends here, ain't we?"

"Of course we are," said Joe, smiling. He looked to Royce for confirmation; Royce looked him squarely in the face and nodded reassuringly.

"You and Royce are both my friends," Edgar added. "You're the only good friends I got."

"Yep, we're all friends," Joe agreed.

A nurse entered the room and unhappily surveyed the little gathering. "Are you still here?" she said to Royce in a professional, impersonal way. Then she looked at Joe and said, "Mister Johnson needs his rest."

"These are my friends," Edgar stated grandly, proudly. "They drove a hundred miles to see me."

The nurse, a middle-aged black woman, was unimpressed by the disclosure. "You still need your rest, Mister Johnson. Ten more minutes and that's all."

The nurse left the room. Edgar said, "I don't know why she's actin' like that. She's usually a lot more friendly."

"How friendly is she?" Royce asked, teasing. "You been gettin' you a little chocolate, Edgar?" He turned to Joe and teased, "Edgar always did like a little chocolate now and then."

Edgar's bright pink color darkened to a scarlet red. "We ain't *that* friendly," he said. "But she's been takin' good care o' me. All of 'em here have been takin' real good care o' me."

"That's good," Joe said encouragingly.

"I hate for her to make you rush off," said Edgar. "There's some favors I need to ask of you before you go."

Joe and Royce listened.

"Royce, I'd like you to call down to the courthouse and tell 'em I'm stuck here in the hospital. I'm supposed to be in court next week but it don't look like I'll be able to make it. You tell 'em that for me, will you, Royce?"

"Sure, I'll tell 'em."

Edgar nodded gravely at Royce, and then turned to Joe. "Joe, what kind of weed-eater do you got?"

"What? I don't know. It's just a plain gasoline weed-eater I guess."

"Well, I was wonderin' if you'd knock down some of the weeds what's grown up around my camper and all. I was so sick all summer I couldn't manage by myself. Just clear me a path around my camper and down to the lake is all. I hope to be goin' home in another week or so and I don't think I'll be able to fight my way through those weeds."

"I can do that," said Joe. "No problem."

"If you guys can do me those two little favors I'd surely appreciate it," said Edgar.

"Not a problem," said Joe.

"I'll call the courthouse first thing Monday morning," said Royce.

The nurse re-entered the room scowling, wordlessly insisting that visiting hours were over, and then left quickly, immediately, as if to set an example for Royce and Joe. Royce slowly rose to his feet and shook hands with his old friend. Joe stepped forward and also shook Edgar's hand.

"Thanks for comin' all this way to see me," Edgar stated sincerely, his voice dripping with emotion. "I don't know where I'd be without you guys."

Joe and Royce said their goodbyes to Edgar and left.

Joe and Royce were heading north now on I-65. After ten or twelve miles Joe felt comfortable driving again. "I thought Edgar looked real good," Joe commented optimistically.

Royce did not share his optimism. "They've been givin' him IVs so he's got some fluids back in him, but he's still in real bad shape. That cancer he's got is way far along already. I don't know if they can do anything with it or not. Edgar doesn't think so."

"Why'd he wait so long to go to the hospital?"

"That's just Edgar. He's just stubborn I guess."

"They're still gonna try him on chemo, aren't they?"

"If they can get him strong enough to take it they will. Right now his blood ain't no good. They can't give him chemo till his blood gets better."

"What's wrong with his blood?"

"I don't know how to explain it. It's somethin' about his blood count bein' too low or too high or somethin'."

"Well, if they can raise his blood count or whatever, and start him on the chemo, he still might make it, right?"

"I don't know. Edgar's old; that's one thing against him. He claims he thinks he could whip that cancer if'n he was younger and stronger. Edgar used to think he could whip anything or anybody, but not now. The only reason he's tryin' to hang on is 'cause those girls of his need his disability check. Now that Bobbie's in jail, that's all they got to go on is his disability check. About seven hundred dollars a month, that's all they got, and they're already way behind on everything."

"Disability check? I thought Edgar was drawing retirement benefits from Social Security."

"Who told you that?"

"I don't know. Nobody, I guess. I guess I just assumed it."

"Edgar don't draw a dime from Social Security," Royce explained. "He never paid enough into it to be eligible. He draws a disability check from the military every month, same as me."

"What's his disability?" asked Joe. "He never told me anything about a disability."

"It's pretty much the same as me," said Royce. "After his wife died he was real heavy on the booze for a few years and couldn't work. I drove him down here to the VA hospital and they allowed him to claim a disability."

"For what?" asked Joe. "For being drunk all the time and not working?"

"I guess you could put it that way. It used to be that if'n a feller was real heavy on the booze they'd give him a disability for it. I don't think they do that no more."

"I don't think they do either," said Joe.

Again Joe was amazed and bothered by the sudden realization of how little he actually knew about Edgar. Eventually he decided it didn't really matter. Retirement benefits or military disability—what difference did it make? Still he was somewhat bothered. It seemed like whenever he thought he finally knew the truth about Edgar, some new revelation popped up.

Joe honked the horn when they crossed the state line into Kentucky. Royce shook his head, annoyed. "I don't understand why you do that," he complained.

"I don't know—it's something my dad always did. I don't understand why it bothers you so much."

Royce shrugged, and turned to stare out the window. They drove in silence until they were on the other side of Bowling Green.

"You got you a good weed-eater?" Royce asked.

"I guess it's okay," Joe replied.

"Are you gonna knock down those weeds out at Edgar's place like he asked you to?"

"Of course I am. I told him I would."

"If'n yours ain't up to the job, I got me a great big heavy-duty machine that I'd let you borrow."

"Thanks," said Joe. "I'll keep that in mind."

More silence ensued until they were back at Royce's place. Joe parked Royce's car in his yard and handed him the keys.

"I appreciate you drivin' me down there," said Royce. "I don't mind you tootin' the horn. We ever drive down there again you can toot the horn all you want, okay?"

"Okay," said Joe. "Thanks."

"You keep in touch now, ya hear? If I ever find out anything about Edgar I'll give you a call. And if you ever hear anything then you call me, okay?"

"Okay," said Joe. The two men shook hands.

Joe still had the feeling that old Royce wasn't overly fond of him. But clearly they shared a common bond in their concern over Edgar. Joe felt quite fondly toward old Royce just then.

Joe climbed in his truck and drove home. He was very hungry for lunch.

Christian Virtue   21

The following morning, Sunday, Joe felt better than he had since his vacation in Wisconsin. Perhaps his lack of faith, or more precisely, his lack of church attendance caused some small guilt on a subconscious level that usually made him feel less good on Sunday mornings than he might have felt had he not been raised as a churchgoing Catholic. But Joe felt good this Sunday morning, good clear down to his heart and his soul. Christian or no, he felt good that he'd taken the time to drive Royce down to Nashville to visit Edgar. He felt equally good that he now had a useful service to perform for his old friend.

He loaded his weed-eater and a can of gas in his truck and said goodbye to his kids and Jolene. He'd already squared it with his wife. She wasn't happy about it but she wasn't unhappy either. No way would she try to prevent Joe from fulfilling his promise to a sick old man.

Joe parked near the end of Edgar's drive, got out of his truck, and gazed longingly at Edgar's lake. Now that Edgar was safely in the hospital, Joe foresaw no immediate problems that would prevent him from fishing here in the future. His prior feelings of betrayal and disillusionment were mainly forgotten. Yes, Edgar had been less than truthful with him in the past, but that was only because Edgar greatly valued his friendship and didn't want him to think badly of him. And yes, Edgar had a checkered past, to say the least. But Joe could not and did not harbor any resentments or ill feelings toward a poor and sick old man fighting for his life against cancer. On the contrary, Joe felt nothing but goodwill towards him.

The air was cool and crisp, around sixty degrees. The sky was a brilliant bluebird blue. A light breeze stirred small ripples on the lake, ideal for fishing. But Joe was there to work, not fish. Reluctantly he pulled his thoughts away from the lake and fishing, filled the weed-eater with gas, and fired it up.

Joe made good progress with the assorted weeds and grasses down around the lake. But the thick broom grass around Edgar's camper and drive defied his small machine. Repeatedly it bogged down and quit, bogged down and quit, half a dozen times or more. Each time it was more difficult to restart, until finally it gave off a nasty burnt odor, the smell of a scalded engine, and would start no more.

Joe's joyful sense of Christian virtue waned considerably as he considered the cost of a new weed-eater. Cursing mildly, he tossed his useless weed-eater in the back of his truck and, remembering Royce's offer of a heavy-duty machine, drove off to borrow it.

He found Royce sitting on his front porch, nursing a cup of hot coffee. Royce didn't look surprised to see him. "I bet you want my weed-eater," Royce said knowingly.

"I'm afraid so," said Joe. "I think mine's had it."

"Let's see what you got," said Royce, walking to the rear of Joe's truck. He screwed up his face disdainfully at the sight of Joe's little weed-eater. "Hell's bells, I could o' told you that little bitty thing wouldn't cut it. That broom grass is tough as nails. It smells like you done fried 'er good."

"It might be okay after it's cooled down," said Joe.

"No it won't. You done fried 'er up good. The engine's scalded; I can smell it from here."

"Well hell, Royce—you don't need to rub it in. Just let me borrow your good one. I still got a lot of work to do."

"You should've come here in the first place," Royce chided as he headed toward his garage. "I could o' told you that little bitty thing wouldn't cut it. Now you're gonna have to buy a new machine."

"Yeah, well, what's done is done."

Royce came out of his garage with a big heavy-duty industrial-type weed-eater. "This here is what you need," he stated proudly. "You got gas for it?"

"Yes, I have plenty of gas."

"Well, take it easy now, ya hear? If it smells like it's gettin' too hot, turn it off and let it cool down a spell."

"Okay, I will."

"When will you have it back here?"

"I don't know. Two or three hours, maybe."

"I'll be here," said Royce. He returned to his porch and his coffee.

Joe returned to Edgar's place. Royce's big weed-eater had a powerful engine and two heavy cutting lines. Still it balked at the wiry broom grass if Joe went at it too quickly. Soon, however, he found the proper speed and rhythm, back and forth, back and forth; the broom grass fell in sheaves.

Lunchtime came and went. Time and again Joe refilled the gas tank of the big weed-eater and renewed his efforts. Probably he cut more than was necessary, more than Edgar would require for easy access to his camper and lake. But as long as Joe had a suitable and efficient machine, he wanted to make good use of it.

For the umpteenth time he ran out of gas and headed back to the place where he'd left the gas can. He had been cutting along the road out front, whacking down the grass that grew in the drainage ditch alongside the road, and between the ditch and the road. As he walked in the space between the ditch and the road he saw someone, a woman, walking toward him. She walked almost in the middle of the road, just a little to one side. She looked straight at Joe as she walked.

From a distance of about a hundred feet she appeared to be an attractive woman— small, nearly petite, and shapely. From a distance of fifty feet Joe noticed something that caused him to doubt his earlier appraisal; he didn't know what. The woman wore plastic flip-flops, tiny cutoff blue-jean, or Daisy Mae, shorts, and a bright red tank top. Tattooed wreaths of barbed wire encircled her left biceps and right ankle. But it wasn't the scanty clothing, too meager for the cool temperature, and too risqué for a woman who appeared to be around forty, that gave him pause. Nor was it the tattoos that disagreed with him. It was something else; he didn't know what. By the time they finally met face-to-face near the entrance to the drive, Joe had a creepy uneasy feeling that bordered on fear.

The woman screwed her face into a sneering smile. It was not a pleasant sight. She was missing at least a few teeth on the bottom and one up top. The smile, such as it was, disappeared when she saw the apprehension in Joe's face. "Who are you?" she inquired challengingly.

"I'm Joe Bass," Joe stated formally. "I'm a friend of Edgar's, the owner here. Do you know Edgar Johnson?"

"I guess I ought to know him," the woman snarled. "He's my dad. I'm his daughter, Bobbie."

"Oh, I see," Joe said lamely, surprised. "Well, it's nice to meet you. I visited your dad in the hospital yesterday and he asked me to knock down some of these weeds."

"It's nice to meet you too," Bobbie replied uncertainly. She acted as if she wanted to be polite and civil but didn't quite know how. Her voice was the worst thing about her, nasal and off-key and brutally raw. Joe wondered if she always had talked like that, or if it was a voice she'd adopted in jail to ward off potential threats and enemies. It certainly made Joe wish he was a safe distance, and not just a few feet, away.

"How's my dad doing?" Bobbie asked.

"I thought he looked pretty good," said Joe. "I took Royce with me, Royce Taylor. Do you know Royce?"

"Only since I was born," Bobbie replied sarcastically. "Did my dad say he was gonna pay you for this?"

"No, not at all. Your dad has been letting me fish here and I…"

"Good, 'cause we ain't got any money. I guess you know I've been in jail."

Joe was afraid to say anything. Bobbie had the demeanor of a sleeping dragon; her eyes peered at him suspiciously from beneath heavily drooping eyelids. At the slightest provocation she might suddenly roar into life and burn him to a cinder with her fiery breath. Joe simply nodded affirmatively, he knew.

"They let me out Friday," Bobbie said. "They let me come home on account of my dad being sick and all."

"That's good," said Joe. He wasn't at all sure if it was good or not. Previously he had thought it would be very good if Bobbie was released from jail. Edgar wouldn't worry so much about her and her kids, and maybe she'd be able to help with his medical care. But now Joe wasn't sure at all.

"I hate for my dad to be sick but I'm glad to be out of jail," said Bobbie.

"Yeah, well, I can understand that."

"They were gonna let me out soon anyway."

Joe simply nodded at her again.

"I'll be on probation till my original sentence is over with, but I ain't worried about that. Probation ain't nothin'—I'm just glad to be out o' jail."

Again Joe nodded.

"We're gonna try to get down there and visit him one day this week," said Bobbie. "He doesn't know I'm out of jail and I want to surprise him."

"I'm sure he'll be glad to see you."

"I'm trying to find somebody to take us down there, me and my girls. My car wasn't running too good when I went to jail and now it won't run at all. When were you gonna go see him again?"

"I'm not sure," said Joe. Edgar was tentatively scheduled to be released in a week or so, and Joe actually had no plans to visit him again in Nashville.

"We were really wantin' to go down there this afternoon," Bobbie stated pointedly, expectantly. She was fishing for a ride.

"I can't go today," Joe told her firmly. "I was just down there yesterday, and I promised your dad I'd get these weeds knocked down for him."

Bobbie stared at Joe with abject disdain, as if she could compel him into driving her to Nashville with her mean and scornful looks. Eventually she shrugged and said, "Well, next time you go down there make sure you let me know. We don't have a phone right now so you'll have to knock on the trailer."

"Okay," said Joe.

"Just make sure you don't come around before noon," Bobbie added. "We like to sleep late."

"Okay."

Bobbie turned abruptly and headed back toward her trailer. After a few steps she stopped and turned toward Joe again. "Thanks for knockin' down the weeds," she muttered perfunctorily, dutifully, like a child being forced to mind its manners.

"You're welcome," said Joe.

Bobbie went back to her trailer and Joe went back to work. He decided to burn up one more tank of gas in the weed-eater and call it quits. Already he'd cut more than was necessary, and his conversation with Bobbie had made him long for home.

Joe whacked weeds for about ten more minutes. Then he noticed movement out of the corner of his eye. At first it looked like Bobbie returning to talk some more, maybe to harangue him some more about a drive to Nashville that afternoon. But this woman was different. Not a woman at all, he noticed as she approached, but a girl, a teenaged girl.

She wore plastic flip-flops, Daisy Mae cutoff shorts, and a light red tank top. She was smaller than Bobbie, very petite. She carried in her hand a plastic bottle of spring water. She smiled radiantly as she drew near, a beautiful smile, Edgar's old smile. And her eyes sparkled with the same soft turquoise blue.

Joe turned off the weed-eater and set it aside and waited.

"Hi," the girl said gaily, smiling. "I'm Blossom—Edgar's granddaughter. We thought you might be thirsty." She offered the bottle of water.

"Thanks," said Joe, eagerly accepting the bottled water. "I'm Joe Bass. I'm a friend of your grandfather's. And I *am* very thirsty."

Joe uncapped the bottle and drank. He was indeed parched.

Blossom watched him drink, smiling approvingly, graciously. When the bottle was half empty she said, "My mom told me you saw Grandpa yesterday. How is he?"

"I thought he looked pretty good," Joe replied. "A lot better than the last time I'd seen him."

"Was that when you brought him home from jail?" asked Blossom. Her smile did not diminish but it took on a different nature, as if she were amused.

Joe was taking another drink of water, and nearly choked. "Yes," he replied, shocked. "How did you know about that?"

"I know a lady who works at Tina's. She told me about Grandpa getting arrested. Then I saw you bring him home in your truck. That's your big red truck, ain't it?"

"Yes," said Joe, surprised. During all the times he'd fished here and visited Edgar here he never had caught so much as a glimpse of Blossom or Bobbie's other daughter, Cricket. Nor had he ever detected the slightest sign of life—no lights, no movement, no curtains being opened or closed, nothing. It seemed strange and amazing to actually and finally meet one of the girls, and doubly strange and amazing to find her as pretty as this.

"Grandpa doesn't know my mom's out of jail. We're trying to find a ride down to the hospital this afternoon so she can surprise him." Blossom smiled ever so sweetly and batted her beautiful eyelids a few times. They were shaded blue and complemented her eyes perfectly.

Joe forced himself to look away, although it was a captivating sight. "I can't go back down there today," Joe said, his eyes lowered, averted. When he finally found the courage to look at her directly again, she smiled more sweetly still and batted her eyelids a few more times. "Not today," Joe insisted.

"Okay," said Blossom, still smiling. "Maybe we can find someone else to take us."

Unreasonably, Joe became mildly jealous of whoever that someone might be. He reconsidered briefly: Why not call it quits with the weed-eater right now and drive them down to Nashville? He could be back in four or five hours. Jolene wouldn't have to know about it if he didn't want to tell her.

Apparently, Blossom sensed his indecision. She stepped up closer to Joe and postured in a way that suggested familiarity, intimacy, if not downright desire. "Oh come on—why not take us? We could be back in a couple hours," she purred persuasively.

Joe wavered for a very brief moment, and then took a step backwards, shaking his head. "No, I really can't do it today. I'm sorry but I can't. I have to finish up here with the weed-eater real quick and then I have to go home. Sorry."

"Okay," said Blossom, still smiling, but somewhat less sweetly now. She looked at Joe's empty water bottle and asked, "Are you finished with that?"

"Yes, I am."

"Here—I'll throw it away for you." She reached and grabbed the bottle.

"Thanks," said Joe.

"Oh no—thank *you*. I really appreciate all you've been doing for my grandpa. It was very nice of you to get him out of jail and to visit him in the hospital. And we really appreciate you choppin' down these weeds."

"You're welcome. I'm glad I can help."

"Oh, I can see that. I just wish we had a ride down to Nashville to see Grandpa today," Blossom persisted, again pouring on the charm.

But Joe had become rather inured to it by now. He stared her straight in the eyes and returned her friendly smile. "Not today. I have to finish up here and go home. My wife and my kids are waiting for me." He hoped the mention of his wife and kids would put more distance between them, would make her realize that as a married family man he was resistant to her charms. Maybe it worked; maybe not.

"Okay then," said Blossom, still smiling. "See ya." She turned and sauntered back toward the trailer, her slender hips swaying from side to side, working it, working it.

Joe stood mutely and watched her go, drinking in the sight of her sensuous motions. Finally he shook his head to dislodge the shapely image, and then took up the weed-eater again. "Trouble, and *more* trouble," he mumbled to himself, his words drowned out by the roar of the machine. Bobbie, she was one kind of trouble—the kind that led to a black eye or a bloody nose or even a bullet. And Blossom, she was a different kind of trouble—the kind that led to an angry wife or a paternity test or an arrest for statutory rape.

"Trouble, and more trouble," he repeated to himself. He resolved to maintain strictly formal relations with both mother and daughter. He was Edgar's friend, not theirs. He would treat them decently and respectfully, as Edgar would want him to treat them, but he would not become personally involved with either mother or daughter. Helping his old buddy Edgar was one thing, but those two were something else entirely. He would try to minimize his relations with those two because he thought both of them were nothing but trouble.

His thoughts of trouble were interrupted by the sound of heavy machinery bearing down on him. He was at least four or five feet away from the road but at the sound of the heavy machinery he reflexively jumped away from the road another four or five feet.

A massive tractor pulling a brush-hog mower veered off the road and stopped in the field nearby. The tractor's motor became suddenly silent and a big burly man climbed heavily down from its seat. Two young men who had been trailing the tractor afoot, each carrying a heavy-duty weed-eater, stepped up and stood alongside the man who had driven the tractor.

Joe turned off his weed-eater and stepped forward to find out who they were and what they were about.

"I'm Gary Woodbine," said the big ruddy man who'd driven the tractor. "These are my sons, Andy and Scott."

"I'm Joe Bass." Joe took another step forward and they all shook hands. "I'm a friend of Edgar Johnson."

Woodbine nodded sharply. "Yeah, I've seen you out here fishing a time or two. I saw you out here with the weed-eater today and I thought you could use some help."

"Sure," said Joe. "That'd be great."

"I would've been here sooner but I was waiting for my sons to come and help me. It looks like we're not too late. I'm glad of that." He turned from Joe and addressed his sons. "You boys go ahead and get started. I'll be with you in a minute." The two young men immediately fired their weed-eaters and walked off to get started.

"Edgar's sister Flo has told me about you," Joe said. "She told me that you go to her church."

"That's right—I do."

"She also told me about the trouble you've had with Bobbie. Did you know she's home now?—that she's out of jail? She was just over here a little while ago."

"Yeah, sure—I know all about Bobbie. My wife works at the courthouse."

"Well, I'm glad you're here to help and all, but do you think it's okay? What if Bobbie sees you over here?"

"I'm not worried about Bobbie. I don't think she'll cause any more trouble around here for a while. I guess you know about Edgar. Flo told me he's awful sick with cancer."

"Yeah. I went and visited him yesterday. I took Royce Taylor with me. Do you know Royce?"

"Sure I do. He's a good ol' boy, Royce Taylor. It's terrible what he went through during the war. How was Edgar?"

"He looked pretty good to me," said Joe. "A lot better than the last time I'd seen him."

"Was that when you got him out of jail?" asked Woodbine.

Joe was surprised and not surprised. Joe knew that the people thereabouts usually kept tabs on everybody else's business. And he knew that Woodbine's wife worked at the courthouse.

"Yes," Joe replied. "Does Flo know that Edgar was arrested?"

"Yes. She knew about it before I did. She has a friend who works at Tina's restaurant."

Joe wondered if *everybody* had a friend who worked at Tina's restaurant. "Edgar doesn't think she knows," he said. "He acted like he'd hate for her to find out."

"Well, okay—I'll tell her that. But I don't think she was gonna fuss at him about it or anything. She's really worried about Edgar. She's worried about those girls, too— Bobbie and Blossom and Cricket. We'd all like to help 'em if we could, all of us over at our church would like to help. I've always tried to help Edgar and his family but he's always turned me away. He's never had much use for me since I bought my property here, but I've always tried to help 'em anyway."

"Yeah, well, that's mighty nice of you I'm sure."

"It's nice of *you* to be out here doing what you've been doing," said Woodbine. "What church do *you* go to?"

"I don't," Joe shortly replied, mildly resentful. Until that question Joe had been forming a favorable impression of Woodbine. Why did he have to spoil it by assuming that Joe's *niceness* automatically implied church attendance?

"That's okay," Woodbine said quickly. "The only true church is here," he stated, thumping his thick chest with a heavy fist. "The only true church is in your heart."

"I'll go along with that," said Joe.

"Good to meet you," Woodbine said dismissively. "I'd better get to it. I can't let my boys do all the work."

"It was nice to meet you too," said Joe.

Joe watched as Woodbine hauled his heavy frame up into the tractor's seat, started the engine, and began dragging the big mower around the field. Already Woodbine's two sons were nearly finished whacking down everything that could be whacked with a weed-eater; Joe had knocked down most of it earlier. He carried Royce's weed-eater and the gas can back to his truck and idly watched Woodbine mow Edgar's small field. The brush-hog cleared a swath about five feet wide. In less than fifteen minutes the mowing was completed.

Woodbine stopped with his tractor pointed in the direction of his house and honked the tractor's horn. His sons, mainly finished with their labors, turned off their machines and walked quickly toward their father and his tractor. When they rejoined him, Woodbine tossed a hearty wave at Joe and headed off down the road.

Joe rather regretted Woodbine leaving without them chatting some more. He seemed a good man, Woodbine. Not for the first time, Joe considered the apparent fact that there were many good people who attended church regularly, who *believed*. They weren't all self-righteous control freaks who wanted to cram religion down everybody's throats, posting the Ten Commandments in municipal buildings, forcing children to pray in public schools, and so on.

Then again, maybe Woodbine was just that sort of guy. They hadn't discussed any of the numerous religious issues which unfortunately had been politicized in recent years. No, Joe decided, not Gary Woodbine.

Judging from what Flo had told him and what he'd just seen, Woodbine was not that kind of guy, definitely not.

Joe remembered Woodbine saying 'the only true church is in your heart.' And his last lingering doubts about Woodbine vanished into thin air. He looked around at the neatly mowed field and the neatly trimmed ditches and the banks along the lake, and he felt mighty good about his efforts. He was glad and grateful for the Woodbines' help as well. Why couldn't all Christians be like Woodbine? If they were, then maybe, just maybe, Joe might consider taking his family to church.

But then again, maybe not. *Probably* not, Joe thought, as he fired the engine in his big red Ford. Behaving like a Christian was one thing, but *believing* like a Christian was something else entirely.

Still, Joe felt mighty good as he drove toward Royce's place to return the weed-eater. He thumped his chest with his closed right fist and felt his heart respond with a fullness and warmth he had not known in a very long time.

In-laws Revisited   22

As was their custom, Joe and Jolene took their kids to Jolene's parents for Sunday dinner. Joe had eaten no more than a bologna sandwich since returning home from working at Edgar's, purposefully saving his appetite for his mother-in-law's cooking. It was always good. She had identified through the years the few specific food items that Joe did not like—pickled beets, sauerkraut, raw onions, fatback in green beans or anything else—and never served them at Sunday dinner. This evening's fare consisted of roast beef, mashed potatoes and gravy, broccoli and cheese sauce, a tossed salad, and dinner rolls. Joe was ravenously hungry. He ate silently, steadily, not slowing down until he was halfway through his second plate of food. Jolene and her parents chitchatted idly throughout the meal. Joe spoke not a word until his father-in-law, Jasper, finally spoke to him.

"I hear you've been out working over at Edgar Johnson's place," he stated casually.

"Yeah, I ran a weed-eater out there today," Joe replied. He hoped Jasper wouldn't start another lecture on the evils of Edgar J. Johnson. He still felt really good about helping out the poor old man.

"I hear he's awful sick. What is it?—cancer?"

"Yeah, cancer of the colon. It's too far along already for them to operate on it."

"That's too bad," Jasper stated sincerely.

"Why do you say that?" Joe asked rather smartly. "I thought you didn't like the man?"

"Like or dislike has nothing to do with it. Something like that is always a tragedy. Jolene told us you visited him in the hospital yesterday," Jasper said.

"Yeah. I took Royce Taylor down to Nashville with me to see him. Edgar and Royce go way back, *way* back."

"I know they do," said Jasper. "How's Royce doing these days?"

"He's okay I guess."

"How was Edgar?"

"I thought he looked pretty good but Royce wasn't so sure. Edgar is old—that's one thing against him."

"How old is Edgar now?"

"He's seventy-eight now, I think."

"Seventy-eight," Jasper repeated rather needlessly. "He has two children, doesn't he? A boy and a girl? Of course they're grown by now..."

"No, he only has a daughter, Bobbie." Joe judiciously refrained from mentioning Bobbie's recent release from jail.

Jasper looked perplexed. "I could've sworn he had a boy. Gladys, didn't Edgar Johnson have a son? I can't recall for sure."

Jolene's mother, Gladys, said simply, "I don't know if he did or not."

Had Joe been paying more attention, he would have recognized Gladys' lack of knowledge as the first and only time she had ever admitted to not knowing something, anything, about one of her neighbors, with neighbors defined as anyone who resided within a twenty-mile radius of her home. But Joe was busy helping himself to more roast beef.

Jasper, however, recognized the novelty of the occasion. "Are you telling me, Gladys, that there's something you don't know about one of our neighbors?" he asked, half in wonder, half in jest.

Gladys did not respond vocally. Instead she made a quick and furtive negative motion with her head, a sign or signal that Jasper had learned long ago as meaning: Let It Drop. Don't Say Another Word About It.

Jasper presented his wife with an acknowledging look that signified: Okay, We'll Talk About It Later. Then he turned to Joe and asked, "What about chemotherapy? Are they gonna try him on chemotherapy?"

"Yes, if he ever gets strong enough to take it. His blood count's too low or too high or too something right now."

"If they can start him on chemo he'll at least have a chance," said Jasper. "I'll pray for him, Joe, I truly will. And Gladys will pray for him too, won't you Gladys?"

"Yes," said Gladys. "Of course I will."

"Thanks," Joe said warmly, sincerely.

On a different day Joe might have pooh-poohed or rejected altogether the very mention of prayer. But this day was somehow different. This was a Sunday like Sundays were meant to be. Only one more thing was necessary to make it absolutely perfect.

"What's for dessert?" Joe asked.

Nashville Revisited   23

Joe was busier than usual at work the following week, preparing for the official groundbreaking ceremony to mark the commencement of the construction of his company's new production facility. The groundbreaking ceremony was slated to begin at one o'clock Friday. Joe had arranged for all the local newspapers to send reporters; WBKO-TV in Bowling Green was sending a camera crew as well. Joe had prepared forty press packets, at least five or six times as many as necessary, for distribution to the media. At twelve o'clock noon he ordered a dozen pizzas and a few gallons of soda pop in case any of the media representatives had missed lunch.

The construction project was not earth-shattering news, even by local standards. The media people were mostly bored, and anxious for the ceremony to be finished. It was the last assignment of the workweek for most of them. As soon as it was over they would rush back to their offices, submit their film for processing, or upload their digital images, hammer out the requisite two or three paragraphs describing the event, and then they would be free to start their weekends.

Joe, however, took the event quite seriously, mainly because that was his job. He bustled about among the various news people, chatting them up, schmoozing them, answering occasional questions, and making sure everybody ate some pizza. By two o'clock most of the news people had left. Still Joe played the gracious host, and would continue to do so until the very last newsperson was gone.

Around quarter after two, Joe was corralled by the boss's personal secretary. She handed Joe a cell phone and said, "It's for you. They said it's urgent."

"Hello, this is Joe Bass. How can I help you?"

There was a pregnant pause, and then a terrible whiny voice replied, "You can go pick up my dad at the hospital. He's ready to come home now."

"Who is this?" Joe asked, although he knew who it was.

"This is Bobbie, Edgar's daughter. I just talked to your wife. She gave me your work number."

Every sentence, even the one proclaiming her to be Edgar's daughter, sounded like a huge and bitter complaint. Joe wondered briefly if she always had talked like that, or if it was something she'd picked up in jail—the voice of perpetual complaint: *This coffee is cold, this toilet is stopped up, these slippers don't fit, this bread is stale, etc.*

"Yeah, well, I'm very busy at work right now. Is there somebody else who can go get him? I'm very busy…"

"No, there ain't nobody else. If you don't want to do it then just say so; I'll call him and tell him you don't want to do it. Maybe he can hitchhike home or somethin'."

"I can maybe break free here in another hour or so," Joe said levelly, trying to control his mounting ire. "Maybe I can get down there around five."

"We went down there Wednesday and saw him. I had to pay my neighbor forty dollars for gas and now we ain't got any money." It was yet another huge and bitter complaint.

"Yeah, well, I should be able to get down there around five."

"He's ready to go right now," Bobbie complained.

"I can't be down there right now, and I can't leave right now either. I'll try to get down there around five."

"Okay," said Bobbie, as if she'd been terribly insulted. Then she hung up.

Joe returned the phone to the boss's secretary. "Problems?" the woman asked.

"No. I need to drive down to Nashville this afternoon and pick somebody up from the hospital. But I'll stay here till all the news people have gone."

"A family member?" the secretary asked, concerned.

"No," Joe simply replied.

The secretary shrugged and went away.

Joe left for Nashville at three-thirty. Already he'd called Jolene. She wasn't happy about the impromptu trip, and was even less happy about receiving the phone call from Bobbie. "What's her problem, anyway?" Jolene had asked. Joe had declined to even begin an explanation.

He pushed hard down I-65, driving seventy-five miles an hour with his radio turned up loud. It wasn't so much that he was worried about being a few minutes late; it was a simmering resentment that pushed him hurriedly down the road.

He dashed through the hospital's corridors, scarcely bothering with politeness as he made his way around people in wheelchairs, people on crutches, lame and infirm people of all sorts, and some people who were just plain slow. He rapped quickly on the door to Edgar's room and entered quickly without waiting for a response.

Edgar sat on the edge of his bed, dressed and ready to go. Gone was the image of radiant good health. He looked tiny and sick and puny.

"Hi Joe," he said, casting a furtive glance at Joe Bass, and then quickly looking away.

The simmering resentment Joe had felt driving down to Nashville disappeared instantly. "Hi Edgar. How're you doing? Are you ready to go?"

"Yeah, I want to go home now. They've done all they can for me here. They can't start me on the chemo just yet so I want to go home."

"Well, let's go then."

Edgar handed Joe some prescription slips and said, "I'm supposed to get some medicine to take home with me. I guess we need to stop at the pharmacy first. Do you know where it is?"

"No, but we'll find it."

Joe carefully ushered Edgar out of the room and down the hallway. The old man was very weak and feeble. Half a dozen wheelchairs were on hand near the nurse's station, but Edgar refused to use one. "I can walk, Joe. I can't walk too fast now but I can walk."

"Suit yourself," said Joe.

Edgar's medicines—antibiotics and pain pills and something to control high blood pressure—were prepared and waiting at the pharmacy. Edgar signed for them and Joe gathered them up and they left.

In the parking garage they found Joe's big red truck. Joe laboriously boosted Edgar up and into the cab.

"I'm sorry, Joe. I'm sorry to be like this," Edgar apologized. "I'm sorry you have to help me so much. I truly am sorry."

"You don't need to apologize," said Joe.

Neither man spoke until they were safely on the expressway. Then Edgar said, "Bobbie came and saw me Wednesday."

"Yeah, that's what she told me."

"I'm glad she's out o' jail and all, but she's in a bad way, Joe. It really hurt her to be away from her babies for so long like she was. Now she's in a bad way and there ain't nobody wants to help her. She had a neighbor lady drive her and the girls down here to see me, and that woman charged her forty dollars for gas. Forty dollars…"

"Yeah, well, gas *is* high right now."

Edgar had a sudden idea. "Do you want money for gas, Joe? I can't pay you now but I'll pay you as soon as I get my check. You just tell me what I owe you…"

"You don't owe me anything, Edgar. Do you remember telling me about your lake, that 'this ain't no pay lake'? Well, this here ain't no taxi cab and it ain't no Greyhound bus. I'm doing this because we're friends."

"God bless you, Joe. God bless you. There ain't many around like you no more. It seems like nobody wants to help people nowadays, especially poor people."

"Yeah, well, maybe you're right."

"These churches they got nowadays, they ain't much count," Edgar continued. "I know churches that got all kinds of money but they won't spend a dime to help the poor. You know what they do with it? The preacher goes out and buys a fancy new car so he can look like a big shot. Or else they build themselves a great big fancy church buildin' just to be showin' off. I ain't got nothin' against churches, Joe. But I think they should do more to help those what need helpin'. A lot of these churches they got nowadays, I don't think they know what religion really is."

"I guess you're right," said Joe.

"There was a friend of mine, a guy named Russell Hughes who died a while back. His family went to that big ol' church what Flo goes to and asked 'em for a little money so they could bury ol' Russ. Ya know what they done? They turned 'em down cold. I *know* that church has got all kinds of money—you ought to see the big fancy car what their preacher drives—but they turned 'em down cold. That ain't right, is it Joe? And they call themselves Christians…"

"Was your friend a member of that church?" asked Joe.

"No, I don't reckon he was. But that shouldn't make any difference, should it Joe? They was a-needin' them a little money to put ol' Russ in the ground, and I know that church has got all kinds o' money, but they turned 'em down cold. That ain't right, Joe. Churches nowadays act like they don't know what religion really is. It just ain't right."

"I guess not," Joe halfheartedly agreed.

They drove in silence until they reached the Kentucky state line. Joe honked his horn when they crossed it.

"What was that for?" asked Edgar, startled.

"Nothing in particular," Joe replied. "I always honk when I cross a state line."

"I thought maybe you saw a real pretty girl," said Edgar. "I always used to honk my horn at girls if'n they was really pretty."

"I bet you did," said Joe.

Neither man spoke until they were almost to Bowling Green. Then Edgar said, "Joe, I asked the doctors if I could have me a little beer now and then."

"Oh yeah? What'd they say?"

"They said I could have me a little beer now and then, just to help give me an appetite. I still can't hardly eat nothin', but maybe a beer would help give me an appetite. The doctors said it would be okay."

"Are you sure they said that? You're not fibbin' me, are you?"

"No, Joe—that's the God's honest truth. They said I could have a little beer to help give me an appetite."

"I guess one beer wouldn't hurt you. We'll stop somewhere and I'll buy you a beer. Just one, okay?"

"Whatever you say, Joe. You'll have one with me, won't you, Joe? Just one little beer…?"

"Sure, why not. I'll have one with you. But just one."

They drove through a drive-thru liquor outlet and Joe bought two cold beers. He placed the bag on the seat between them.

"We'll wait and drink 'em when we get to my place," Edgar said judiciously.

"Good idea," said Joe.

Soon they were crossing the Green River Bridge in Brownsville. Edgar peered out his window to his right and said, "That's a long ways down, ain't it, Joe?"

It was too dark to see much just then, but Joe had seen it many times in the past. "Yes it is," he agreed.

"I had me a moonshinin' buddy once, his name was Joe too—Joe Baker. One night the law was a-chasin' him, so he parked his car right here atop the bridge and he jumped. They never did catch ol' Joe. He got plumb away."

"So what happened to him? Did you ever see him again?"

"No, there wasn't nobody ever seen him again. He got plumb away."

Edgar seemed delighted with the recollection. Joe wanted to ask how he knew the man wasn't killed when he jumped from the very tall bridge, but didn't.

"Ol' Joe Baker," Edgar repeated, draining every last drop of pleasure from the memory. "They never did catch ol' Joe. They ain't never gonna catch me neither. Royce said they've dropped the charges against me down at the courthouse. I'll never see the inside of a jailhouse again, that's for sure."

"That's good," said Joe. "I'm glad."

Edgar's mood brightened further when they turned onto Sycamore Church Road. "We're almost home now, ain't we Joe? I'm glad to be out o' that hospital. I don't think I could've stood it in there another day, not one more day."

"Do you want me to take you to Bobbie's trailer? Or do you want to go to your camper?"

"Take me to my camper, Joe. I want to see my lake. You wouldn't believe how I've missed my lake."

Joe parked near Edgar's camper, and then hurried around to help him down out of the cab. It was early fall, fairly warm, with a huge harvest moon shining brightly overhead. Edgar gazed with rapt appreciation at the neatly mowed field and the neatly trimmed ditches and paths around the lake.

"You really knocked 'er down good, didn't you Joe? You knocked down every last bit of it, didn't you?"

"Well, I had some help," Joe carefully replied.

"Woodbine," Edgar spat the name. "I heard Woodbine was out here with his mower. And I'll tell you why he done it, Joe. He knows he was wrong—that's why he done it. He knows it was wrong of him to have my little Bobbie locked up like he done, so he come out here with his mower thinkin' that'd make up for it. He knows he was wrong or he wouldn't have come out here with his mower."

Joe was silent.

"He knows he was wrong or he wouldn't have come out here," Edgar repeated, looking to Joe for confirmation.

But Joe was silent.

"Grab those beers and let's go sit down by the lake," said Edgar.

Joe grabbed the beers and ushered Edgar down to the bench where they'd drank the Old Fitzgerald.

"No, not here," Edgar protested. "Let's go sit on that bench over there."

Joe watched Edgar slowly lower himself onto the bench. Then he pulled their bottled beers from the bag. He uncapped one of the bottles and handed it to Edgar. Surprisingly, perhaps, Edgar took just one small sip of beer, seemingly disinterested. He acted like he wanted to talk more than anything else.

"Do you go to church, Joe?" Edgar asked.

Joe was certain he'd told Edgar previously that he did not. But the old man's memory seemed increasingly spotty lately, so he replied simply, "No."

"This here is my church, Joe—the lake, the woods, everything. This is where I feel the presence of the Lord. One time I even found the words for it, Joe, and I wrote me a little poem about it. But the next day I couldn't remember it. I had it in my head but I forgot it."

"That's too bad. I bet it was good."

"It was beautiful, Joe. It really was beautiful. I wish I could've remembered it."

"You're a Celt," said Joe. "Most of the people around here have Celtic ancestors and the Celts didn't believe in writing stuff down."

"Oh, I don't know about all that, Joe. But I wish I could've remembered it. I bet you don't think I could write a beautiful poem, but I did."

"I believe you," said Joe.

"I'm thinkin' here lately I'd like to go to a real church, a good church. Not some fancy church like Woodbine's, but a good church. Only thing is, it'd have to be somewheres that people don't know me."

"Why's that?"

Edgar was momentarily silent. He took another tiny sip of beer and said, "Well, I've made a lot mistakes in my life, Joe. I don't think the Lord holds them against me none but a lot of these people around here still do."

Joe finished his beer and noticed the moon seemed a bit brighter. "If you want to go to church, I'm sure there are lots of churches that'd be glad to have you. I wouldn't worry so much about what other people think."

"It'd have to be somewheres far away, Joe. I couldn't go to a church anywheres around here where people know me."

"Why do you think you want to go to church now?" asked Joe.

Edgar took another sip of beer and said, "My faith ain't quite what it used to be— maybe a good church could help. I used to believe that nothin' was impossible for a man with faith. The Bible says that if a man has faith no bigger than a little tiny mustard seed, then he can move a mountain if he wants to. All he's got to do is tell the mountain to move and it will move. But you know what, Joe? I spent more than a month havin' faith that the Lord would send me three hundred thousand dollars, and do you know what He sent me? Nary a dime, Joe—not one thin dime. I never thought He'd give me the whole three hundred thousand—I would've been happy with a whole lot less. But He didn't give me nothin', not even a dollar."

"Yeah, well, maybe you were rewarded spiritually," Joe said comfortingly.

"Maybe, Joe, maybe you're right. But I sure could've used a few thousand dollars at least. Look at all what Woodbine's got, and look what I got. I guess it's true what they say, that the Lord works in mysterious ways."

"I guess it is," said Joe.

"If I had more faith I'd probably be able to whip this cancer, but I doubt I'll be able to whip it now. It seems like the Lord don't want to help me out none here lately."

"I wouldn't say that," said Joe. "I can't imagine the Lord not wanting to help you."

Edgar shrugged to indicate his uncertainty, and asked, "You want another beer, Joe? We could walk up to the trailer and see if Bobbie has any beer. She probably does."

"No thanks," said Joe. "One's my limit. I have to be going home now. Do you want me to help you up to your camper?—or up to Bobbie's trailer?"

"No, Joe, thanks. I'm gonna sit here a spell and listen for ol' Sam. I ain't heard ol' Sam out here yet tonight."

"Who is Sam?" asked Joe. He hoped it wasn't a dog.

"Sam's my pet bullfrog. He'll probably be along here directly."

"Yeah, well, okay. I gotta be going now. Is there anything else I can do for you before I leave?"

"No, no thank you, Joe. You've done too much for me already. I'd hate to ask you to do anything else for me. You've done too much already."

"I'm glad to help," said Joe. "If there's ever anything I can do, don't hesitate to ask."

"Well, there is maybe one little thing, Joe. But I hate to ask. You've done too much for me already."

"Go ahead and ask," Joe urged.

"Well, I'm supposed to go back to that hospital again ten days from now. They're gonna check my blood again and see if they can start me on that chemo."

"What day is that?" asked Joe.

"It's October thirteenth, a Monday. I hate to ask, Joe, but I don't know who else there is to take me."

"I guess I can take off from work that day," said Joe. "I don't see why not."

"God bless you, Joe. God bless you. But maybe you won't have to make the trip after all. I might not be here in ten days. I don't know if I've got ten days left in me or not."

"You'll be here," said Joe. "What time are you supposed to be at the hospital?"

"Eight o'clock," said Edgar. "We'll have to leave awful early to make it."

"I'll be here at five-thirty," said Joe. "Will you be at your camper, or over at Bobbie's trailer?"

"You'd better pick me up at the trailer, Joe. I'll be over at Bobbie's trailer."

The deep booming voice of a bullfrog croaked nearby.

"Sam!" Edgar joyously exclaimed. "There's Sam! I told you he'd be along directly. Good ol' Sam! How are you, Sam? Did you miss me while I was gone?"

The bullfrog croaked loudly again. Edgar seemed to understand every word of it. He was still communing with his amphibious friend while Joe walked up to his truck.

Dirty Jokes   24

Joe Bass turned carefully down Bobbie's driveway and drove slowly to the trailer, turning this way and that to avoid gaping potholes. The first suggestion of daylight dawned dimly in the eastern sky. No lights were visible inside the trailer. Joe walked up to the front door and knocked. The door stood about three feet above ground level and there were no steps or stairs except for a solitary concrete block. No one answered the door so Joe knocked again, louder. After at least three or four minutes, a light came on inside the trailer and the door swung open and Joe stared directly at a woman's bare legs. Raising his head he saw a white terrycloth bathrobe above the knees and Bobbie's scowling face above the top of the robe.

"You're awful early, ain't you?" It was not really a question; it was a huge and bitter complaint.

"No, I think I'm right on time. I said I'd be here at five-thirty."

Bobbie glared down at him malevolently; she didn't like being contradicted. "It's awful early," she complained. She acted as if she might tell Joe to come back later. But finally she said, "I guess you can come in if you want."

"Okay," said Joe. He stepped onto the concrete block, took a firm hold on the door frame, and hauled himself up into the trailer.

"Dad's ready to go but Blossom's not up yet. She's going with you. You'll have to wait," Bobbie said crossly.

Before Joe could inquire about Blossom, Bobbie stomped off to a back bedroom, her heels pounding angrily on the floor.

"Hello Joe," said Edgar. Joe peered into the gloom and saw old Edgar sitting patiently on a sofa in the living room. Joe walked over to greet him.

"Good morning Edgar," said Joe. "How do you feel this morning?"

"I don't know, Joe. I'm still here—that's about all I can say for sure. I've been a-worryin' about this chemo. I don't know if I'll be strong enough to take it. I still can't eat nothin'. Even if I can take it I don't know if it'll do me any good."

"We'll have to wait and see what the doctors say," Joe calmly replied.

Blossom emerged from a back bedroom wearing an oversized T-shirt and, as far as Joe could tell, absolutely nothing else. Joe didn't stare exactly, but he *did* look. As she passed on her way to the bathroom she smiled and said, "Hello."

Before Joe could respond, Bobbie stomped back into the living room and turned on a lamp. "What time do you think you'll be back?" she asked irately, as if her patience was already exhausted.

"I don't know," Joe replied. "I guess we'll have to wait and see how it goes at the hospital."

"Make sure you get more medicine for him," Bobbie commanded. "He needs a lot more medicine."

"I'll be sure to pick up his prescriptions," said Joe. "Now about Blossom—I didn't know she was coming. I guess she can come if she really wants to, but I don't think it's necessary. I think I can manage on my own."

"Blossom's going with you," Bobbie stated imperiously. "I already decided that. If you don't want to take her I guess I'll have to find somebody else."

Joe's temper ratcheted up a notch or two. It was his truck; he was driving. Didn't he have a voice in determining who rode in his truck and who did not?

"It'll be alright if Blossom rides along, won't it Joe?" Edgar asked imploringly.

Joe was still angry, but said, "I guess, if she really wants to."

"How about some coffee, Joe?" asked Edgar. "I could have Bobbie fix you a cup of coffee."

Bobbie immediately stomped out of the room; she wasn't going to make coffee for Joe or anybody else. Edgar seemed somewhat embarrassed.

"No thanks," said Joe. "I've had two cups already. That's my limit."

Joe looked at his watch. It showed 5:45. As long as they left by six they'd be on time for Edgar's appointment. He sighed, and tried to relax. No sense getting worn out by negative emotions this early in the morning when it looked like a long day ahead of them.

Joe looked about the trailer and noticed it was neat and clean. The carpet was totally worn out, and the furniture and furnishings were old and inexpensive and mainly worn out. But it was neat and clean and it didn't smell bad.

"This looks like a nice little trailer," Joe said politely.

"Oh, yeah, Bobbie keeps a nice place," Edgar agreed. He seemed delighted to have something nice to say about his daughter.

Blossom bounced into the living room wearing essentially the same outfit as when Joe first met her—plastic flip-flops, tiny Daisy Mae cutoffs, and a tank top. "How do I look, Grandpa?" she asked gaily. But she looked directly at Joe while she spoke.

"You look fine, Blossom," Edgar said proudly. "She looks just fine, don't she Joe?"

"Yes, you have a very pretty granddaughter," Joe stated formally. "Now then, if everybody's ready, we need to get this show on the road."

"I'm ready," said Blossom.

"Let's go," said Edgar.

Bobbie stomped into the room once more and nearly shouted, "Don't forget his medicine. He needs a lot more medicine." Then she stomped back out again.

Joe was the first person out the door. He offered a helping hand to Blossom but she nimbly leapt down on her own. Edgar accepted Joe's helping hand. He accepted it yet again when Joe boosted him up and into the cab of his truck.

Blossom sat between the two men. As soon as they turned onto Sycamore Church Road she announced, "I need some coffee. Would you mind stopping at the Quick Stop so I can buy a cappuccino?"

"No, I guess not," said Joe.

"It's right up here on the right," said Blossom.

"I know where it is," said Joe. A few minutes later he parked in the parking lot but didn't turn off the motor.

"Grandpa, can you give me some money for coffee?" Blossom asked.

"I guess I can," said Edgar. He pulled a thin sheaf of folded bills from his pocket and peeled off a twenty.

Blossom snatched it from his hand. Joe climbed out of the truck to let her pass. She pranced into the Quick Stop, and shortly returned with a Styrofoam cup of cappuccino. Joe got out again so she could climb inside. He noticed she didn't give her grandpa any change from the twenty.

Five minutes later they were four miles down the road. "Oh, shoot," said Blossom. "I forgot to buy cigarettes. Can you stop and let me buy some cigarettes, please? There's another store right up here on the right."

"I guess," Joe wearily acquiesced. "But I'd appreciate it if you didn't smoke in my truck."

"Oh, I won't," said Blossom.

A few minutes later Joe parked in yet another convenience-store parking lot.

"Grandpa, I need money for cigarettes," said Blossom.

Edgar again pulled out a thin sheaf of folded bills and peeled off a twenty. Blossom snatched it from his hand. Joe glared at her accusingly as he got out and let her pass. She smiled sweetly in return.

A few minutes later she returned with her cigarettes, complaining, "They carded me in there. Can you believe that? They carded me for cigarettes."

"How old are you?" asked Joe, as he backed out of the lot.

"I'm eighteen. I turned eighteen last month, didn't I, Grandpa?"

"Yes, Blossom, you had your birthday last month."

"I can't believe they carded me," Blossom repeated indignantly.

Joe couldn't believe the little shakedown operation she'd pulled on her old and sick grandpa: A twenty for a cup of coffee, and no change; a twenty for a pack of smokes, and no change. Already she'd pocketed maybe thirty-five or thirty-six dollars of the old man's money. And Joe got the distinct impression it was pretty much business as usual. He thought about reminding her to give Edgar his change, but didn't.

"No more stops now, okay?" he said instead.

"Okay," Blossom said, smiling. "I'm fine now, thanks."

Edgar didn't look talkative; in fact he looked rather glum. Joe didn't care if his little con-artist granddaughter had anything to say or not. He turned on the radio and speeded up a bit. They drove in silence through Bowling Green and down to the Tennessee state line. Joe honked his horn.

Blossom reached out and turned off the radio. "Why did you honk the horn?" she asked.

Joe replied, "I don't know. I always honk when I cross a state line." He turned the radio back on.

A few miles and minutes down the road Blossom reached out and turned off the radio again. "Oh, look," she said, pointing to a billboard. "There's a sign for Graceland. I wanna go to Graceland someday. I just *love* Elvis Presley."

Joe didn't comment and he didn't turn the radio back on. His knuckles turned white on the steering wheel.

"Don't you just love Elvis Presley?" she asked excitedly. "I think Elvis was the greatest. Don't you love Elvis?"

Edgar remained glumly silent. Joe stated soberly, "I think he had a wonderful singing voice, a truly remarkable talent. But I think he was one sick individual."

"Elvis?" Blossom asked incredulously. "Sick? What are you talking about?"

"I think he was sick," Joe explained. "I think he was a pathetic drug addict."

"Oh, that," said Blossom. "Elvis was just keepin' it real. You gotta keep it real, you know."

No, Joe didn't know. He didn't comment. He turned the radio back on. Nobody spoke until they were stopped in the hospital's parking garage.

"We're here," said Joe. He walked around and helped Edgar down out of the truck.

Edgar stood there uncertainly. He took a tentative step forward, and then stopped. "I think I could maybe use a wheelchair this morning," he said. "All that sittin' has made me weak in the legs."

"I'll get it," Blossom said helpfully. "I know where they are." She dashed off to the hospital's entrance and quickly returned with a wheelchair.

Edgar eased his way down onto its nylon seat. Blossom wheeled him away at once. "This is fun," she called back over her shoulder to Joe. "I just love pushing him around like this." Blossom beamed radiantly at everyone they passed; she looked like a kid with a new toy, like a child pushing a baby doll in a baby carriage.

Joe managed a weak smile. Maybe the girl would prove to be at least a little bit helpful after all.

Their first stop was the chemotherapy clinic. A nurse there told them

Edgar needed to have his blood drawn and tested. Their second stop was the blood lab. At 8:15 it was already packed with patients. They took a number from a number-tab machine. It was 69. The number 32 was displayed on an electronic display above the blood lab's door. Blossom said she was going outside to smoke, and left.

Blossom returned about fifteen minutes later, not nearly as gay as she had been. "Some creep out there was tryin' to hit on me," she whispered to Joe. "He looked like he was homeless or somethin'."

"Maybe he was," Joe replied.

At nine o'clock the number 69 flashed above the blood lab's door.

"That's us, ain't it?" asked Blossom.

"Yes," said Joe. He asked Edgar, "Do you want me to go in there with you, or…?"

"No, I think Blossom can manage okay."

"Good," said Joe. "I'll wait here for you." The blood lab looked crowded, and he wanted Blossom to "earn" the money she'd pilfered from her grandpa. He was happy to let her deal with it on her own.

Their next stop was the chemotherapy clinic, again. The nurse there directed them to a check-in station where a nurse weighed and measured Edgar, and checked his temperature and blood pressure. She told them a doctor would talk to Edgar after checking his blood work, probably in an hour or two.

Blossom wheeled Edgar to a nearby lobby. Edgar abandoned the wheelchair in favor of a more comfortably upholstered chair. Still he looked glum and forlorn.

"Did you have anything to eat this morning?" asked Joe. "How about I go get you something to eat? The cafeteria is right down the hall."

"No, Joe, no thank you. I couldn't eat a bite I don't think. I'm too worried about how my blood is gonna turn out. I don't think it's gonna be good. Did you hear how much I weighed? One twenty-five. I weighed one-thirty when they weighed me here ten days ago. It can't be good, me losin' weight like that. But thanks anyway, Joe."

"I'm gonna go see what they have in the cafeteria," Joe persisted. "If anything looks good I'll bring it back here for you. If you're losing weight then you need to eat."

Then Joe asked Blossom, "Do you want anything to eat?"

"No," she said. "I'm fine."

About ten minutes later Joe returned with biscuits and gravy and two cartons of milk. Edgar brightened a bit at the sight of biscuits and gravy. He ate one of the biscuits and drank one carton of milk and then he seemed less glum and forlorn.

"You needed that food," Joe said knowingly.

"Maybe I was a mite hungry," said Edgar. "Thanks, Joe. Those are good biscuits and gravy. Not as good as Flo's, but they're good."

To Joe's surprise, Edgar picked up a nearby magazine and started flipping through the pages. Joe never imagined the old man had any appreciation for any sort of literature, not even a magazine. But Edgar appeared to be interested and entertained.

"I wanna go outside and smoke a cigarette," said Blossom.

"That's fine," said Joe. "I'll wait here with your grandpa."

"I want you to come with me," said Blossom. "There are too many creeps hangin' around out there. Grandpa will be okay for a little while, won't you Grandpa?"

"Sure Blossom, I'll be fine. You two go on ahead. You ought to go get you some o' those biscuits and gravy."

"Maybe later," said Blossom. Then she hurried down the hall. Joe caught up with her outside the rear of the building, near the emergency and ambulance entrances. She already had lit a cigarette. "Thanks for buying my grandpa those biscuits and gravy," she said, exhaling blue-gray smoke.

"You don't need to thank me," Joe replied rather sternly.

"Why not?" asked Blossom. "I really do appreciate it."

"I hope you don't take this the wrong way," said Joe. "But I'm doing this for Edgar. I'm not doing this for you and I'm not doing it for your mother. I'm doing this for Edgar."

"My mother is a real bitch, ain't she." It was not a question. "I'm sorry about the way she treated you this morning. She treats almost everybody like that. She can't help it. My mom has a lot of problems. She's even worse since she got out o' jail."

"Well, I hope I don't sound mean or rude or anything, but I really don't care about your mother's problems. I'm here to help Edgar, that's all. I'm not doing this for your mother."

"Oh, I can understand you not liking my mother," said Blossom. "But you like me, don't you?" She struck a little pose and batted her eyelids a few times.

Joe gave her the sideways smile of an amused uncle. "It really doesn't matter if I like you or not. I'm doing this for Edgar, not you."

"But you do like me, don't you?" Blossom persisted immodestly.

"I really don't know you that well, now do I?" Joe sidestepped the question.

"Well, no—I guess not. But you *have* to think I'm nicer than my mother. Don't you think I'm nicer than my mother?"

"Okay," Joe allowed. "You're nicer than your mother."

"God, I hope so—my mom's a real bitch. She calls me a bitch all the time, but one time I called her a bitch and she gave me a black eye."

Joe was silent. Blossom stabbed her butt into the sand in a pedestal ashtray and immediately lit another smoke. She put on an air that vaguely suggested maturity. "She married my dad when she was fifteen," Blossom began. "He was thirty, and a terrible drug addict. He used to beat her up somethin' awful. Did you notice how many teeth she's missing? Some people think that's 'cause of all the cocaine she did, but it's not. My dad knocked her teeth out. And that's not the worst thing he did. One time he ran over her with his car and smashed her arm all to pieces. After that they got divorced, and then he died of a drug overdose. I was only two years old. I don't remember anything about him, really."

Goodbye and good riddance, thought Joe. "Maybe that was for the best," he said.

"Maybe," said Blossom. "But sometimes I still think I'd like to meet him. I've seen pictures of him. He doesn't look so bad. He kind o' looks like Elvis."

Joe couldn't think of a single word with which to respond to her pathetic disclosures. He wished he hadn't heard any of it. It was sordid and depressing, and his main concern, his *only* concern, was Edgar. Not Bobbie, not Blossom—Edgar.

"We'd better go back in and check on your grandpa now," Joe said firmly.

"What's the hurry? That nurse said it's gonna be at least an hour or two. Let's stay out here and talk some more. I like talking to you. You're real nice to talk to."

Jesus, thought Joe. *This is gonna be a long day.*

He didn't really want to stand there and chat with Blossom. Patients and visitors, mostly men, loitering nearby in the designated smoking area, ogled her with unabashed lust and desire as they furiously puffed on their cigarettes. The few female smokers outside eyed her with ill-concealed contempt, or jealousy. Mid-October, the morning was quite cool; it was late in the year for her skimpy little shorts and tank top. Arguably, her scanty outfit was inappropriate for a hospital visit at any time of the year.

"Do you know any good jokes?" asked Blossom, her face illuminated with humor, as if she had just heard, or was thinking about, a really funny joke.

"No, not really," Joe demurred.

"Well, I got one for you. What's the difference between a dumb blonde and a rooster?"

"I give up," said Joe.

"A rooster says 'Cock-a-doodle-do.' A blonde says 'Any cock'll do.'"

Again Joe gave her the sideways smile of an amused uncle, as he struggled to subdue his initial inclination to laugh. The joke itself wasn't all that funny, but it seemed very funny indeed coming from Blossom, who struck Joe as the quintessential dumb blonde, if ever there was one. His self-control failed him after a moment or two, and he let loose with a hearty chuckle.

Encouraged by his response, Blossom smiled hugely at Joe, her beautiful turquoise eyes sparkling in the radiant morning sun. Try as he might, and Joe *did* try, he couldn't help being captivated by her beautiful sparkling eyes.

"What's the difference between a blonde and a bowling ball?" asked Blossom.

"I don't know—what?"

"You can only stick three fingers in a bowling ball."

Joe felt his body temperature vault a few degrees. Tiny beads of perspiration popped out along his hairline, and his face blushed suddenly crimson.

"You're blushing," Blossom teased, enormously pleased.

"Yeah, well…"

"What's a blonde's favorite nursery rhyme?" asked Blossom.

"I give."

"Hump-me Dump-me."

Joe's smile was transformed into a tight rictus which denoted more sexual tension than humor. Blossom seemed to find the situation eminently entertaining, and she too displayed signs of titillation, if not outright arousal.

"It's your turn now," Blossom prompted mirthfully, excitedly.

Without even thinking about it, Joe blurted out a joke he'd heard at work recently. "What did the dentist say to the blonde?" he asked.

"I give—what?"

"You have the whitest teeth I've ever come across."

Somehow during the joke-telling, the meager distance between Joe and Blossom had narrowed to nothing. She stood now directly in front of Joe, poking his chest with her perky little nipples, and smiling up at him in a way that perfectly displayed her perfectly white teeth. She laughed lightly, musically, sensually at Joe's suggestive joke.

Joe's hinterlands felt as if they had been invaded by a school of electric eels. For an extremely intense moment or two, his burgeoning lust wrestled mightily with his mounting guilt. And then the contest was over; Joe's guilt quickly won out, and he keenly regretted having told her that joke.

"We need to go check on your grandpa now," he said in a curiously deep voice, as he took a small step backwards. He forced himself to present her with the serious and authoritative face of a responsible, and very much married, adult.

"Grandpa's okay," Blossom countered. "We've only been out here fifteen or twenty minutes. Let's go sit in your truck awhile. I have something to give you—I know you'll like it. The parking garage is this way..." She grabbed Joe's forearm with both hands and tried to lead him away. But Joe stood firmly rooted in his tracks.

"No," Joe stated soberly, his voice now normal again. "We need to go check on your Grandpa." He shrugged free from her grasp and headed for the doors.

Blossom danced up alongside him and linked her arm with his, as if Joe was her escort on prom night. Joe didn't exactly reject the linkage, but he nonetheless made it clear he wasn't comfortable or pleased with the physical contact. Blossom soon relinquished his arm.

"Let's go in here a minute," Blossom suggested, as they neared the entrance to a little shop that sold gifts and flowers and over-the-counter medications and various pharmaceutical sundries. "I might buy something for Grandpa."

"Just for a minute," Joe wearily acquiesced.

He followed Blossom around the shop at a respectful distance while she browsed its many and varied items. She didn't seem really interested in buying anything, and Joe definitely wasn't interested in buying anything. He simply wanted to get back to Edgar.

Eventually Blossom ceased her casual browsing, and appeared fixated on something displayed on the wall before her. She looked at Joe and smiled, and beckoned him to join her with a slight toss of her head.

Reluctantly he complied with her silent summons. Hopefully, she had settled upon some little gift for Edgar. Whatever it was, Joe resolved he would approve of it at once; he would be only too glad to pay for it as well. And then they would finally return to Edgar.

Joe stepped up beside her and was immediately shocked, or at least, very surprised. Blossom was staring studiously at a rather large assortment of condoms.

She turned to Joe with what she thought was a grown-up air and attitude. "I'm eighteen now so I can buy these," she stated matter-of-factly, a bit braggingly.

"That's fine," said Joe, adamantly determined to steer well clear of her trap. "You buy whatever you want. I'm gonna go check on your grandpa now. I'll see you later."

Before Joe could quite turn away, Blossom asked, "What's the big hurry?"

"I'm gonna go check on your grandpa now," Joe repeated quickly.

"I don't see why you're actin' so embarrassed. What's the big deal?"

"The big deal is that I'm married and I plan to stay married. Marriage…? Perhaps you've heard of it…?"

"Oh sure, I've heard of it. I just don't believe in it," replied Blossom, a devilish little grin on her face.

"Yeah?—well I do."

"Well goody-goody for you," Blossom quipped smartly. Her devilish little grin had morphed into a smirking sneer. She looked a little bit like Elvis.

Again Joe keenly regretted having told her the dirty joke. Feeling somewhat responsible for the situation, he was no longer capable of simply turning his back and walking away. But he was increasingly uncomfortable with the little scene they were creating there in front of the condom display. The cashier behind the nearby cash register, a portly middle-aged black woman, was staring at them curiously.

"I guess I'm just old-fashioned, okay?" He looked questioningly at Blossom to see if it *was* okay.

"You're more than old-fashioned," said Blossom. "You're a regular dinosaur. But what makes you think I was gonna buy these for you, anyway?"

"What…? Listen—we really need to get back to your grandpa now. If you want to buy something, then go ahead and *buy something*, please, so we can get out of here."

"I guess I don't need anything right now," Blossom relented at last.

Joe escorted her out of the gift shop and down the hallway towards the lobby where they'd left old Edgar. Halfway down the hallway, Blossom said without looking up at him, "I still don't understand. What about that joke you told me?"

"That was just a joke and I'm sorry I told it to you. That was my bad—I'm sorry."

"What're you sorry about? We were just jokin' around, right?"

"Yeah, well—maybe when you get a little older you'll understand that love is a lot more than a dirty joke."

"Who said anything about love?" asked Blossom, rather miffed. "I thought we were just jokin' around, is all. Nothing wrong with jokin' around once in a while, is there?"

"No, I guess not."

"But not with you, right?"

"Well, yes—that's right. Look—I'm only here to help out with your grandpa, okay? He's a very sick man and he needs all the help he can get right now. Can't we just leave it at that, please?"

"Okay," Blossom said sharply. She sidled sharply away from Joe, and then nearly shouted across the distance she'd created between them, "My mom's gonna love that joke about the dentist. She'll get a great big laugh out o' that—you just wait and see!"

There was unmistakable hostility in Blossom's declaration, and it struck Joe as some kind of a threat. Why? What? Blossom had initiated the joke-telling, and she'd told three or four jokes to his one. No way could she have been offended by his joke; her jokes had been at least as vulgar as his. And hadn't she just admitted that they had been "just jokin' around"? Joe figured that, like her mother, Blossom had a lot of problems.

Joe very much wished he had stood up to Bobbie and refused to allow Blossom's accompaniment. *Jesus*, thought Joe, not for the first time. *This is gonna be a long day.*

As they neared the lobby, Blossom darted ahead and reached old Edgar well before Joe. He deemed it childish and inappropriate for her to run in the hospital, but he was glad and relieved her attention was now directed towards her grandpa, and not him.

Elvis Lives   25

Edgar was slumped down in his chair, half asleep, a closed magazine in his lap, when Blossom rejoined him. "How ya doin', Grandpa?" Blossom asked brightly.

"I reckon I'm still here," Edgar replied miserably. "Did you all get some o' those biscuits and gravy?"

"No, not yet—maybe later."

"Where's Joe?" Edgar asked, struggling to sit more fully upright, and looking worriedly around him, as Blossom plopped down in the chair to his right.

Joe stepped up just then and said, "I'm right here Edgar. Are you doing okay?"

"I'm still here I reckon," Edgar replied a bit less miserably. "I wish they'd hurry up and tell me somethin' about my blood. If I'm gonna take that chemo, I wish they'd go ahead and get me started on it."

"I know, but it looks like we're gonna be here awhile," said Joe. The lobby was just about filled to capacity, and the hallways were similarly crowded. "I saw on the news that all the VA hospitals are real busy now because of the wars in Afghanistan and Iraq. I guess there's nothing we can do but wait."

"I seen somethin' about them wars too. But look around in here, Joe. I don't see any young soldiers in here, do you? It's all a bunch o' old guys like me."

Joe looked around, and agreed, "Yeah, you're right about that."

"It's gonna be a long day, ain't it Joe?" asked Edgar.

"Yeah, you're right about that too," said Joe. "Can I get you anything, Edgar? You want to try to eat some more of your biscuits and gravy?"

"No, Joe—I'm okay. I just wish they'd tell me somethin' about my blood."

"Yeah, well—if you need anything I'll be right over there."

Joe found and claimed in the rear of the lobby a vacant seat which faced Edgar and Blossom. He flipped through a magazine until an interesting article caught his eye, and then he read, grateful for the distraction.

Blossom sat next to Edgar and stared stonily at a TV mounted high on an architectural column.

Nearly two hours later, a doctor called, "Edgar Johnson? Edgar J. Johnson?"

Joe immediately jumped up and hurried to meet him.

The doctor said, "Mister Johnson, I've been looking at your blood work and it looks like—"

"No," Joe interrupted. "Edgar Johnson is over there. I'm just a friend of his."

Joe noticed that Edgar was dozing as he escorted the doctor to meet him.

"Mister Johnson?" the doctor called loudly, right in Edgar's face. "Mister Edgar Johnson?"

Edgar slowly opened his eyes.

"How are you today, Mister Johnson?"

"I'm still here, I guess." He peered around cautiously as if unsure of where "here" was.

"I'm Doctor Shah. I've been looking at your blood work and it looks like we'll be able to start you on your chemotherapy today." He sounded as if it were wonderful good news.

Edgar was still dazed and speechless.

The doctor turned to Joe and said, "Take him across the hall to the chemotherapy clinic. They're waiting for him now. I'll be over there in a few minutes to tell him more about his treatments."

"Okay," said Joe. "Thanks."

Blossom, not Joe, managed Edgar into his wheelchair and across the hall. Inside the chemotherapy clinic were eight chairs that resembled hi-tech, space-age recliners. Each was flanked by IV equipment on one side, and monitoring equipment on the other. Cancer patients, men ranging in age from about thirty to seventy, all hooked up to IVs and monitors, reposed in seven of the eight chairs. Edgar was placed in the empty chair at the far end of the room.

A nurse attached an IV syringe to the inside of Edgar's left wrist. "We're gonna start you off on some Benadryl, Mister Johnson, just to make you drowsy. They'll have your chemo ready for you in a few minutes."

Doctor Shah, a young and handsome Hindustani man, walked briskly through the clinic, smiling this way and that at the various patients. He stepped up to Edgar and said, "We're going to start you on CHOP, Mister Johnson. Actually it's CHOP-R, that's what we call the chemo."

"Is that an acronym?" asked Joe.

"Yes, it is. It stands for..."

The doctor rattled off a string of scientific-medical words that made Joe sorry he'd asked. Then the doctor asked Edgar a series of questions about his health, most of them pertaining to his diet and bowel movements. Meanwhile the nurse attached a few monitoring devices and hung the bag of chemo.

Finally the doctor left, and the nurse was nearly finished as well. "There now, Mister Johnson. You're all set. Are you comfortable?"

"I'm cold," said Edgar, suddenly shivering. "I'm freezin' to death in here."

Edgar was dressed in blue jeans and a heavy flannel shirt. Joe saw no reason for him to be cold. But the nurse said, "I'll get you a nice warm blanket, Mister Johnson. I'll be right back."

She returned with a hospital blanket and draped it over Edgar's reclined body. She then turned to Joe and said, "The Benadryl will probably put him to sleep. The chemo will take about three or four hours. You and your daughter might be more comfortable out in the lobby."

"This is Edgar's granddaughter, Blossom. I'm just a friend," said Joe.

"Okay," said the nurse. "But this is gonna take a while."

"We'll wait in the lobby," Joe told her. And then to Edgar, "Edgar, we're gonna go wait in the lobby. We'll be back to check on you a little later."

Edgar's eyes were nearly closed already. "Thank you Joe. God bless you Joe. I'll be alright. You two go and get you some o' those biscuits and gravy."

"We'll be back in a little while," Joe said. He and Blossom left.

In the hallway, Blossom immediately announced, "I'm hungry. I want something to eat."

It was almost noon. Joe had finished his breakfast at five that morning, nearly seven hours earlier. He was hungry, too. He didn't relish the idea of dining with Blossom, but thought it would be rude not to take her to lunch.

In the cafeteria, Joe and Blossom selected cheeseburgers, fries, and Cokes. Joe paid for both meals. Blossom led the way to a booth near the rear of the cafeteria. On the wall above the booth hung a large framed poster of Elvis clad in a black leather outfit and leaning against a huge Harley-Davidson motorcycle. Elvis smiled his enigmatic Mona Lisa smile at Joe as he placed his tray on the table.

"Look," said Blossom. "Elvis."

"Yeah," said Joe. He didn't believe in ghosts per se but it seemed as though he were being haunted by Elvis today. He couldn't get away from Elvis. Of course, Joe reasoned, he wasn't *really* being haunted. He *was* in Nashville, the "music capital of the world," a place where Elvis would live forever, in much the same way as Jesus lives on in Rome.

They ate in silence until their cheeseburgers were gone. Then they nibbled at the last of their fries.

"Have you met my Aunt Flo?" Blossom asked.

"Yes."

"What did you think of her?"

"I think she's a nice lady."

"I think she's a bitch," said Blossom. "My mom really hates her. She didn't take good care of us while my mom was in jail."

"Well, maybe your mom will stay out of jail in the future."

"She never would give me money for cigarettes or anything. Not even a dollar."

"I don't think your aunt has much money. But she always made sure you had food, didn't she?"

"Yes."

"Well, maybe you should be grateful for that."

"I'm not. We hate her. Me and my mom both hate her. We don't even think of her as part of the family."

"That's too bad. It's a shame you all can't get along better."

"Aunt Flo broke up our family when my mom was little. That's why we hate her. When my grandma died, you know, Grandpa's wife?—Frankie? When she died Grandpa started drinkin' real bad and he was in jail a lot. They were gonna put my mom and her brother in foster care but Aunt Flo said she'd take care of them so they went to live with her and my Uncle Pete."

"Your mom has a brother?" asked Joe.

"She *had* a brother, my Uncle Mike. He was about four years older than my mom. Aunt Flo stole him."

"What do you mean?—she stole him."

"Grandpa got better after a few years and they said it was okay for my mom and my Uncle Mike to live with Grandpa again, but Uncle Mike stayed with Aunt Flo. He never did live with my mom and Grandpa again. He took off after he got out of high school and nobody's seen him since. Aunt Flo got a letter from him once. He was in California."

Joe shook his head miserably. Would there never be an end to it all?

"Aunt Flo wanted me and Cricket to go live with her when my mom went to jail, but Grandpa told her 'No Way.' My mom told her that too. They didn't want her to break up the family again."

"I see," said Joe. Not for the first time he felt betrayed by Edgar's lack of honesty and disclosure. He had no more appetite and picked up his tray to leave.

"I'm finished too," said Blossom. "Let's go outside where I can smoke. I always smoke after I eat."

"You go on ahead," said Joe, balking as he recalled their previous trip to the smoking area. "I'm sure you'll be okay."

"You got to come with me, please? I don't want to be alone out there."

"Okay," said Joe. It couldn't get any worse.

Outside, Blossom lit up a smoke and started to say something.

Joe cut her off. "Why aren't you in school? You should be... what?—a senior now?"

"I *should* be a senior. But I quit."

"That wasn't smart. When did you quit?"

"I graduated from middle school. Then I went a little bit in the ninth grade."

"You have an eighth-grade education, and that's it?"

"It wasn't my fault. I've got a nervous condition. I can't sleep at night and my stomach hurts a lot. Now that I'm eighteen I'll probably go on disability pretty soon— because of my nervous condition."

"How old was your mom when she went on disability?"

"I don't know. I think she went on it after she got divorced. But I'm not getting divorced because I'm never getting married."

"You're awfully young to be making a decision like that, aren't you?"

"No, I don't think so. I've had a lot of boyfriends, a *lot* of boyfriends." She smiled at Joe, and then opened her mouth in a way that displayed a silvery tongue stud he hadn't noticed previously. She waggled her tongue slightly, suggestively, and smiled again. "I always get bored with my boyfriends after a month or two. There was one guy I dated for almost five months but then he got boring too. I could never stand to be married."

"Marriage isn't about having someone to keep you entertained all the time. It's about having someone you can trust, someone you can depend on, forever—a life partner."

"Yeah, right," Blossom replied rather disgustedly. She stabbed her butt in the nearby ashtray and fired a fresh cigarette.

"You're young," Joe continued. "You have your whole life ahead of you. You can still go back to school, or at least find some kind of a job. Have you ever worked anywhere?"

"No, and I don't want to work because I don't like people. People either piss me off or they bore me."

"Your grandpa is on disability, and your mom's on disability, and now you want to go on disability. Do you see any kind of a pattern there?"

"No, not really. Some people are smart enough that they don't have to work, I guess."

"You think it's smart to go on disability, and stupid for people to work? Do you think I'm stupid?"

"No, I didn't say that. But would you still want to work if you didn't have to? If you won the lottery or something, would you still want to work?"

"I don't know. I *do* know that I'd try to do something meaningful with my life. Are you gonna try to do something meaningful with your life?"

"Hey man, I'm just keepin' it real. You gotta keep it real, you know." She stabbed her cigarette into the pedestal ashtray and looked at Joe as if he didn't know a thing about keeping it real. It was not a pleasant look. "I wanna go check on my grandpa now," she said sharply.

Joe followed Blossom to the chemotherapy clinic. Previously she had acted very chummy with Joe, almost as if they were out on a date. But now she was cold and aloof and acted like Joe was a total stranger.

Edgar was asleep in the fancy recliner. His face was gray and his mouth was open and he looked like he very well might be dead.

"I'm here to check on Mister Johnson," Joe told the nurse on duty. "Is he okay?"

"He's fine," the nurse replied. "It'll be a few more hours until he's finished with his chemo. There's a lounge right outside."

"Yeah, I know. Thanks."

Joe found a seat in the rear of the lobby close to where he'd sat earlier. Blossom sat as far away as possible, on the opposite side of the lobby, and stared at the elevated TV.

Joe read a magazine from cover to cover while an hour dragged slowly by. He and Blossom ignored each other until she finally walked up and said, "I'm going outside to smoke. You can stay here if you want."

"Thanks, I will."

Blossom returned about fifteen minutes later and reclaimed her seat and stared at the TV again. Joe read magazines for another hour or so.

Then the nurse from the chemotherapy clinic approached Joe and said, "Mister Johnson is finished with his chemo. He needs a unit of blood before he can go home. You need to take him up to the third floor and check in with the people at Same-Day Procedures. They'll know what to do."

Blossom had hurried over and was standing nearby. "He's *my* grandpa," she stated importantly. "I'll take him."

Joe was irritated at first, but quickly got over it. He was glad to see Blossom take responsibility for something, or someone. Maybe she would learn something from it.

It was nearly four o'clock when Edgar was situated in a bed on the third floor in the area designated Same-Day Procedures. Edgar was awake now but still rather dazed and confused. Blossom sat on a chair next to his bed and held his right hand and stroked his forearm. Joe stood just inside the door.

Doctor Shah came in and checked on Edgar. After a brief examination and a few perfunctory questions he turned to Joe and said, "Mister Johnson appears to be doing very well with his chemo. We'll try him on more chemo in four weeks. Let us know if there are any problems before then—excessive diarrhea, blood in his urine or stool, or if he starts running a fever."

Joe nodded. Blossom got out of her chair, stepped up to the doctor, and flashed her prettiest smile. "I'm Blossom. I'm his granddaughter." She glanced disdainfully in Joe's direction and said, "He's just a man who gave us a ride down here."

"Well, that's fine," said the doctor.

"Grandpa needs more medicine," said Blossom. "My mom said to make sure he gets more medicine. He's had a lot of pain."

"I've already taken care of his prescriptions," the doctor said. "You can pick them up anytime. The pharmacy is open until six."

"Thank you, doctor," Blossom said, smiling sweetly and posturing and batting her eyelids.

The doctor left and a nurse came in with a bag of blood.

"Hi," said Blossom. "Is that for my grandpa?"

"Is your grandpa named Edgar J. Johnson?"

"That's him," said Blossom.

"Then this is his blood. Or at least it will be after we get it in him. It'll take a few hours or so."

"It looks like you have everything under control here," Joe said to Blossom. "I'm going down to the pharmacy and pick up his prescriptions. That way we'll be ready to go as soon as he has his blood."

"Bye," said Blossom.

Joe took the elevator down to the first floor. There was plenty of time to pick up the prescriptions. He decided he was hungry again. The cafeteria officially closed at four, and it was now a few minutes past four, but there was still a little food left and a few people eating. He picked up a barbecue sandwich and a Coke and paid for them and settled in a booth far away from Elvis and his smirking little smile.

Joe was feeling a little sorry for himself. What had he gotten himself into? What was it that Royce had said? *It's best to stay out of their business. Once you get into it, it's hard to get back out again. There ain't none of 'em get along very good 'ceptin' maybe Edgar and Bobbie.*

He had started the day with the best of intentions but it seemed to be getting worse with each passing moment. Or was it? The doctor had said that Edgar was doing very well with his chemo, and that was a good thing. That was the *only* thing, really. If Blossom was pissed off at him, that was really too bad. The little ingrate—third generation welfare, and it showed. She didn't go to school, didn't work, didn't want to work; she had always had a free ride and expected she always would have a free ride, and that included a free ride from him.

Still, Joe couldn't help but pity her in a way, or ways. She never really had a father, and her mother was atrocious. Joe tried to imagine having a mother like Bobbie and shuddered. Ultimately, though, Bobbie was someone to be pitied as well. No mother, a terribly alcoholic father—what chance had she ever had in life? Edgar, too—what chance had he had?—learning to drink moonshine at the age of four. What chance had any of them had? They were who they were because *that's who they were*; that's how life had shaped them. Probably there was little or nothing Joe could do to change them, even if he tried.

Joe thought about his own family—his wife and his son and his daughter. By comparison theirs seemed the most wonderful little family imaginable. His heart ached sweetly as he looked forward to rejoining them that night. He hoped his kids would still be awake. If not, at least he'd be able to see Jolene. How he looked forward to seeing his own family again...

A custodian was clearing and wiping off tables nearby. He looked at Joe as if he was interfering with his work, as if he should leave. Joe left.

Joe went to pick up Edgar's prescriptions at the pharmacy window. He was first required to show a picture ID, and then sign for the medications. "You have to sign for a controlled substance," the pharmacist said.

"What controlled substance?" asked Joe.

"The pain medication contains codeine," the pharmacist explained. "It's a controlled substance. That's why you have to sign."

Joe signed and carried the large sack of medications back to Edgar's room.

Edgar's eyes were closed. Joe couldn't tell if he was sleeping or not. Joe looked inquiringly at Blossom, who sat next to Edgar's bed. Blossom's eyes were fixed firmly on the sack of medications in Joe's hand.

"Is that Grandpa's medicine?" she asked.

"Yes."

Blossom got up quickly and took the sack from Joe and immediately rifled through its contents. In a very few seconds she found what she wanted, a sizable jar of pain pills.

"Is that you, Joe?" Edgar asked as he tried to focus his sleepy half-open eyes.

"Yeah, Edgar—it's me," Joe replied. "How are you doing?" He had one eye on Edgar and his other eye on Blossom as he spoke.

"I guess I'm still here, Joe. I feel pretty weak right now but I'm still here."

Blossom noticed Joe watching her. She placed the pain pills back in the sack and placed the sack on top of an adjustable food-tray stand.

"The doctor said you're doing very well with the chemo," said Joe. "That's good news, isn't it?"

"I heard what he said but I don't know, Joe. I feel pretty rough right now."

"Yeah, well, that's to be expected. Chemo is some pretty rough stuff. It has to be rough to kill the cancer."

"I hope it works, Joe. But I can't tell if it's killin' the cancer or if it's killin' me."

"You'll be alright," said Joe. "You'll feel better in a day or two I'm sure."

An orderly came in with a tray of food and placed it on the adjustable food-tray stand. It looked like turkey and mashed potatoes and carrots and peas.

"They've brought you some supper, Grandpa," Blossom exclaimed as she appraised the food. "It looks good. There's turkey here. How 'bout some turkey?"

"No, no, Blossom. I couldn't eat a bite right now. Maybe I'll eat somethin' when I get back home. You and Joe eat it. I don't want it."

Blossom looked at Joe and asked, "Do you want it?"

"No, I just ate."

"You ate without me?" she asked indignantly.

"Yes."

Blossom looked at him as if he were the rudest man in the world and said, "Then I'll eat it. I'm hungry."

Blossom liberated a white plastic fork from its cellophane wrapper and picked at the turkey and mashed potatoes. She didn't look very hungry.

Joe stepped closer to Edgar's bed and said, "We'll have you home before long, Edgar. It'll be good to be back home, won't it? I bet Sam will be waiting up for you."

"Sam?" asked Edgar, perplexed. "Oh yeah, Sam—good ol' Sam, my bullfrog. Yeah, he'll still be there I reckon."

Out of the corner of his eye, Joe saw Blossom make a quick motion with her hand. He turned quickly to see exactly what she was doing, and saw her screwing the cap back on the large jar of pain pills.

"Are you eating your grandpa's pain pills?" Joe asked crossly, accusingly.

"Just a few." She made a pouting little face and said, "I had to. My stomach's hurting me."

"Is your mom eating them too? Is that why she was so worried about Edgar's medications?"

"Just a few. Her arm still hurts sometimes from when it was run over by a car."

"Your grandfather has cancer. Do you get it?—*cancer*. How do you think that feels? Has he been getting any of his pain medication or have you and your mother been eating it all?"

"We've just snitched a few, that's all. Grandpa takes them when he needs to."

"Joe? What's wrong, Joe?" asked Edgar. Apparently, he hadn't picked up the details of Joe's dispute with Blossom, but he had sensed something amiss.

"Nothing, Edgar—nothing's wrong. You just relax now, okay?"

"It sounded like somebody was fussin' about somethin'. What?—ain't that food any good?"

"The food's fine, Edgar. Blossom's eating it. Listen—I need to stretch my legs. I'll be back in a little while, okay?"

"Okay Joe. We'll be here."

Joe stormed out of the room without so much as a glance at Blossom. How lowdown can some people get? Perhaps, probably, that was why Bobbie had insisted that Blossom tag along. She knew Blossom would be sure to lay hands on the pain pills. It was simply inconceivable that they could deprive a cancer-stricken man, any man, of badly needed medication. How could Bobbie do that to her father? How could Blossom do that to her grandfather? It was simply inconceivable. He took the elevator down to the first floor; he didn't want to be on the same level with such a person, literally or figuratively.

Joe wandered aimlessly through the hospital corridors, steaming mad, until he came upon a phone bank near the main lobby. He phoned home, collect. Jolene answered and accepted the call.

"What's wrong, Joe? You sound upset. Is the old man okay? Was he able to take the chemo?"

"Yeah, he took the chemo okay. They're giving him a unit of blood right now and then I'll be heading home."

"You sound upset," Jolene repeated.

Joe didn't want to go into it. "I'm just tired. It's been a long day. Are the kids okay?"

"Yeah, they're fine. They're playing videogames as usual."

"Tell them that I love them, okay? Will you tell them that for me please?"

"Of course I'll tell them. What time do you think you'll be home?"

"I don't know. It'll be nine-thirty or ten I guess."

"Joe, are you okay? You don't sound okay."

"I'm fine, really. I'm just tired."

"Well, you take care of yourself. I don't think you need to be doing all this, really. Isn't there anybody else who can drive him down there? He's going to need more chemo treatments, right?"

"Yeah, he's supposed to take another one in four weeks. I don't know. I'll see if I can think of something. You're right. I don't need to be doing this."

"Good. We'll talk about it when you get home."

"I love you Jolene."

"I love you too, Joe. You take care of yourself. I'll see you when you get here. Bye."

"Bye."

Joe felt better after talking to Jolene. He didn't feel good but he felt better. He sat awhile in the main lobby and looked at a magazine without really reading it. The hospital was mainly deserted now, much quieter, much less hustle and bustle, and eventually he managed to compose himself somewhat. Around seven o'clock he headed back to the third floor.

He walked right past Edgar's room without so much as a sideways glance, straightway to the nurse's station where he asked the nurse who had attended Edgar how much longer it would be. Just then a buzzer buzzed on a counter in the nurse's station, and the nurse said, "That's all of it right there. Give me a few minutes to get him unhooked and you all will be free to go."

Joe followed the nurse to Edgar's room and stopped just outside the door. He made sure that Blossom saw him, but adamantly remained just outside the door.

About ten minutes later Blossom wheeled Edgar out of the room. Her pupils were dilated and she had a dreamy, boozy look on her face.

"Can you manage that wheelchair okay?" Joe asked.

"Sure I can. I can still drive. I'm a good driver. You wanna see my license, officer?" She looked at Joe and smiled. Her teeth were still white and her lips were still red but there was something wrong with the smile.

Blossom was feeling no pain.

Party Time   26

Joe couldn't remember when he was ever so happy to see his big red Ford truck. He boosted Edgar up and in while Blossom returned the wheelchair. When Blossom was seated inside, Joe climbed in beside her and fired the engine; it was a wonderfully reassuring sound.

"Music," said Blossom. "I wanna hear some music." She reached out and turned on the radio and cranked it up too loud.

Joe turned it down and said, "We can listen to the radio but not too loud."

"Yes sir, mister officer, sir." Blossom said. Then she laughed at her own cuteness.

"How are you doing over there, Edgar?" Joe asked. The old man looked as if he might fall over had he not been pinned between Blossom and the door.

"I'm fine, Joe. We're headin' home now, ain't we? That's good, Joe. I'm ready to go home now."

"I'm ready to go home too," said Joe. "It won't be that much longer."

An hour later they crossed the state line. Joe didn't honk the horn; he was in no mood for frivolity of any kind. Amazingly, perhaps, Blossom picked up on it. "Hey, that was the state line. Why didn't you honk your horn?"

Joe tapped his horn and said nothing.

"Oh, you're no fun," Blossom said. "You're just like my boyfriends—you're fun at first but then you're boring."

"I don't care if you think I'm boring. Just be quiet, will you? I'm tired."

"Tired? You're tired? I know just what you need. I wanted to give it to you this morning but you were too stupid to take it." Blossom rummaged around in her purse and pulled out a white and slender cylindrical object. Even in the dim glow of the dashboard lights, Joe readily recognized it as a joint. She stuck it directly under Joe's nose and said, "Smell this. Do you know what this is?"

Joe pushed her hand away and said, "Yeah, I know what it is. Put it away. Put it away now."

"Don't worry about Grandpa. He's out of it. He wouldn't even notice if we smoked it. Besides, he wouldn't care none. You've seen me and Mom smoke pot lots of times, haven't you Grandpa?"

Edgar was silent. Joe didn't know if he was following the conversation, or if he was even awake.

"I don't care what your grandpa has seen," said Joe. "This is *my* truck. Put it away. Put it away now."

"You're mean," said Blossom. "You're *real* mean."

"I don't care if you think I'm mean. Put it away now."

"Yes sir, mister officer, sir." Blossom stashed the joint in her purse.

Joe sped up to seventy-five miles an hour. As the big powerful Ford carried them quickly forward, Joe's thoughts drifted backwards to that morning when Blossom had tried to drag him to his truck. What exactly had she said? Joe thought he remembered her saying she had something to give him. He had assumed, wrongly perhaps, that she had wanted to present him with her sexual favors. Maybe she had only wanted to offer him the joint.

But then again, there was no mistaking her sexual intentions when she'd teased and taunted him in front of the condom display. Or was there? Joe had been married, faithfully married for so many years he no longer trusted his instincts and perceptions in such matters. It was like a foreign language he'd studied in school but had mostly forgotten. Or a card game or board game he'd played in his youth, the rules and strategies of which had mainly escaped him with the passing of time. *Parlez-vous* Pinochle? *Sprechen sie* Yahtzee? No not much—

Guiltily, Joe considered the disturbing possibility that he had misread Blossom's intentions. He recalled from his bachelor days the undeniable fact that many girls simply liked to tease. They liked to prove to themselves that they could have a man if they wanted, even if they didn't really *want* him. Joe had always figured it was mainly some sort of ego trip, or power trip. But then again, Blossom seemed too young and stupid and naïve for such games. But then again, was any female of the species ever too young or too anything else for such shenanigans? No not really—

Joe recalled his first encounter with Blossom, and how she had tried to cajole him into driving her and her mom down to Nashville. Her design had been quite plain that day; she had wanted a ride to Nashville, and had flirted shamelessly in the hope of getting it. But why had she flirted with him at the hospital? The only reason Joe could imagine was that she had wanted to form a closer bond with him, a close and personal bond that would ensure Joe's continued loyalty and service to her Grandpa. But Joe thought he had made it abundantly clear that he was perfectly willing to help old Edgar, regardless of his feelings towards Blossom and her mother.

Trouble, and more trouble, that had been Joe's initial appraisal of Blossom and her mother, and it seemed truer now than then. He keenly regretted having allowed Blossom to tease him as she had; he was forty-four years old and he should have known better. Definitely, he never should have told her that dirty joke.

Joe's Catholic feelings and sentiments, like so many aspects of his youth, had long since atrophied due to neglect and disuse. Still he retained a vestigial inclination to sometimes feel responsible for people for whom he wasn't really responsible, and to feel guilty when he was in fact innocent, or nearly innocent. He reminded himself that it had been Blossom who had started telling dirty jokes, and Blossom who had urged him to tell one of his own. And just look at the way she was dressed; every guy in and around the hospital had helped himself to an eyeful of Blossom. Nevertheless he felt guiltily responsible for having told her that joke, and for whatever sort of little game they'd played afterwards. *Mea culpa, mea culpa, mea mea culpa—*

"Where are we, Joe?" asked Edgar. "Are we in Bowling Green yet?"

"Almost," said Joe. "We'll be there soon."

"Do me a little favor, Joe. Let's stop in Bowling Green and get me a little beer. Just one little beer."

"I don't think you need a beer, not after chemotherapy and everything else you've been through today. Maybe this weekend I'll bring you a beer, after you've had a chance to recuperate."

"Just one little beer, Joe. That's all I want. It'll be my last one, Joe. I promise you that. It'll be my very last beer, ever. I promise I'll never ask you again."

"I want beer," Blossom chimed in. "I want beer." She sounded like a little kid begging for candy. Joe was struck by how childish she sounded;

it made him feel guiltier still, as if he were, or had acted like, an old lecher—damn near a pedophile.

"Edgar, are you sure?" asked Joe.

"I'm sure. It'll be my very last beer, I promise."

"Okay," said Joe. "Just one."

"God bless you Joe," said Edgar. "God bless you."

In Bowling Green, Joe pulled up to the window of a drive-thru liquor outlet and ordered one cold bottle of Budweiser. Blossom leant past him and hollered, "Make that a case of Bud Light. We want a case of cold Bud Light in bottles."

The clerk was naturally confused. Joe quickly asserted, "No, not a case—Just one cold bottle of Budweiser please."

"Make that a case of cold Bud Light in bottles please," Blossom hollered around him again.

Joe turned to confront her. She confronted him right back. "I've got money. I've got my own money. I'll pay for it. Why are you being such a dick?"

"Yeah, I saw how you got your money this morning. Listen—do you want to walk home?"

"Let 'er have the beer, Joe," Edgar said calmly, patiently. "I'll pay for it. Let 'er have what she wants. It's better that a-way. Just this one last time, Joe. I promise I'll never ask you again."

Joe turned to the clerk and said, "Make that a case of cold Bud Light in bottles." He snatched a twenty-dollar bill from Blossom and paid for the beer and placed it on the floor at Edgar's feet. "You are *not* drinking any of that in my truck," Joe told Blossom directly.

"Oh, that's fine. I'm okay now."

Oh I bet you are, thought Joe. *A case of beer, a big jar of pain pills, some marijuana—yippee, it's party time.*

He drove very quickly, almost recklessly, from Bowling Green to Bobbie's trailer. He parked his truck and left the motor running and climbed out of the cab.

Bobbie came running out to meet them with little Cricket at her knees. "How's my dad doing?" she asked Joe. "Did you get his medicine?"

Joe simply stared at her, mute, angry.

"We got his medicine," Blossom answered gaily. "And look what else we got—we got us a case o' beer!"

"Do I owe you anything?" Bobbie asked Joe.

"No."

"That's good, 'cause we ain't got any money."

Blossom was already at the trailer with the case of Bud Light, her purse and the large sack containing Edgar's medicines perched atop it. She turned and called to her mother, "Come on, Mom. I got a real funny joke to tell you. You won't believe how much fun we had at the hospital. We had *lots* of fun at the hospital today, didn't we Joe?"

Blossom's tone of voice, taunting and somehow threatening, scraped at Joe's sensibilities like a dull and rusty razor. He stared at Blossom angrily, while Bobbie stared at him. Blossom returned Joe's stare with the falsest smile he'd ever seen; then she quickly turned and clambered up into the trailer with the beer and drugs.

Bobbie continued to stare at Joe. "What've you been up to?" she asked meanly, suspiciously. A light next to the trailer's front door was in Joe's face, more a hindrance than a help. Still he saw Bobbie's eyes narrow and her muscles tense.

"Nothing," Joe replied with as much force as he could muster, which wasn't much.

"Well, I guess we'll just see about that," snapped Bobbie. She fired one last baleful look at Joe, then gathered little Cricket in her arms and dashed off into the trailer.

Edgar was still in the truck, unable to climb down without help. Joe helped him down. Edgar's right hand retained its firm grip on Joe's right hand, and shook it firmly. "God bless you, Joe. I'll never forget you, Joe. I appreciate all you've done for me. I appreciate it more than you'll ever know. I'll never forget you and what all you've done to help me."

"I'm glad I was able to help," said Joe.

"Little Blossom—I hope she wasn't too much of a bother for you, Joe. She wasn't too much of a bother for you, was she?"

"No," Joe said weakly, nearly inaudibly.

"Blossom's a good little girl—she really is, Joe. It ain't her fault she acts the way she does; it ain't Bobbie's fault neither. Blossom never had her a daddy, and Bobbie never had her a mother to raise her up right. It all comes back on me, Joe. It's all my fault things have turned out the way they have."

"We all make mistakes," Joe said consolingly. "You shouldn't worry about all that right now. You just worry about getting better, okay?"

"I guess I'll try to get better, Joe, but I can tell it ain't gonna do me no good. That chemo ain't helpin' me none. I'd know it if it was. All it's a-doin' is a-poisonin' my blood."

"Everybody feels bad after chemotherapy," Joe said reassuringly. "You'll feel better in a day or two. You just hang in there, okay? You'll feel better real soon, I'm sure. Just give it a day or two, okay? I'm sure you'll feel better real soon."

"God bless you, Joe. God bless you for sayin' all that and for all what you've done to help me. There ain't many around like you no more. Nowadays ain't nobody wants to help nobody, not if there ain't somethin' in it for them."

"Yeah, well..." Joe said noncommittally. He was very tired and very much wanted to go home. Edgar had thanked him enough and Joe wanted to leave.

"I reckon you're anxious to get home to your family now," Edgar stated. "I don't blame you a bit. That's all a man's got in this world really, Joe, is his family. It's all he's really got and it's all he'll leave behind him when he goes. I learned that a mite too late, I'm afraid. I learned a lot o' things a mite too late."

"Don't worry about it," said Joe. "You just worry about getting better, okay?"

"I'll try Joe. I reckon I'll try. But I can tell already it ain't gonna do me no good."

"Give it a chance," said Joe. "That was only your first treatment."

"Yeah, I know—and it'll probably be my last. I don't think I'll last another four weeks, Joe."

"Now, Edgar—you shouldn't even talk like that. The doctor said..."

"I heard what he said, Joe, but I ain't got much faith in doctors. Besides, he don't really know how I feel. I doubt I'll last another four weeks."

It had been a long and trying day, and Joe hated to volunteer his future services. Still he felt he needed to give old Edgar something to look forward to, even if it was only another trip to the hospital.

"I think you'll make it," said Joe. "I'll plan on picking you up again four weeks from today, same time, okay?"

"Whatever you say, Joe. I doubt I'll be here four weeks from now, but thanks for the offer. I'll never forget what all you've done to help me."

"Come on," said Joe. "Let me help you up in the trailer." He escorted Edgar to the trailer door and boosted him up and in. "Goodnight, Edgar. And good luck."

"Goodnight, Joe. God bless you."

Extortion Attempt 27

Joe Bass got home around nine-thirty. His kids were brushing their teeth and preparing for bed. Joe gave them huge hugs and told them how very much he loved them and how very proud he was of them. The kids, slightly embarrassed by his grandiose and nearly desperate outpouring of affection, returned the hugs and the avowals of love and then went to bed. Jolene hugged him, too.

Joe showered. Usually he showered only once a day, in the morning, but tonight he felt like he needed another shower. Then he brushed his teeth and went to bed. Jolene was propped up on pillows and reading a book. She marked her place with a bookmark and placed the book next to the phone on the nightstand. Then she flipped back the covers, and Joe climbed into bed.

"You poor thing," said Jolene. "You look exhausted. Do you want to talk about it, or do you want to go to sleep now?"

"I think we should talk," said Joe.

Joe spent the better part of an hour relating the day's events. He judiciously declined to tell her about the dirty jokes and his brief flirtation, or whatever it had been, with Blossom. Occasionally Jolene issued some small comment or asked a question, but mostly she listened in silence.

When Joe concluded his little narrative, Jolene asked, "It's kind of like a soap opera, isn't it?"

"I guess," said Joe. "A hillbilly soap opera."

"We're not hillbillies," said Jolene, and for the umpteenth time she explained to Joe that hillbillies lived in the Appalachian and Ozark Mountains—hillbillies lived in the "hills."

"Okay then," said Joe. "A hick soap opera."

"We're not hicks, either," said Jolene.

"Okay," said Joe. "You're not hicks."

"I wish you hadn't told the old man that you'd drive him back down there again," said Jolene. "You used up most of your off-days back in the

Shine

spring when the kids were both sick. What about Bobbie's car? What's wrong with her car? It seems like she could drive him to the hospital if her car was running."

"I don't know what's wrong with it. I guess I could ask her."

"If it's nothing major, maybe we could pay to have it fixed," said Jolene. "I know we'd never see the money again but it'd be cheaper and better than you taking off work and driving him down to Nashville all the time."

"I guess I could ask her," Joe repeated, though he dreaded the notion of talking to Bobbie for any reason whatsoever.

"And what about the aunt—Flo? I know you said that she and her husband are both eighty, but if they can drive to Bowling Green they ought to be able to drive to Nashville, don't you think? It's only about twice as far to Nashville as it is to Bowling Green."

"It's more like three times as far, but you're right. I think they probably could make the drive," said Joe. "The problem is that Bobbie and Blossom both hate their Aunt Flo, and Pete still hates Edgar for losing the farm way back when."

"I don't care who hates whom," said Jolene. "That's their problem, not ours. They need to get over all that. It seems like with the old man sick, they should put aside their family squabbles for a while and try to help out."

"I agree, but they're awfully stubborn people."

"Stubborn and mean," Jolene amended.

"Yeah," said Joe. "That too."

"I think I'll call the VA tomorrow," said Jolene. "It seems like they should have some kind of transportation service for invalid patients. It wouldn't hurt to ask."

"Good idea," Joe said passively. He was nearly all talked out. He didn't feel exactly sleepy yet, but he was tired of talking.

"One way or another, we need to find somebody else to drive him down there, don't you agree?" Jolene asked.

"Okay," said Joe. "It's still four weeks away. I'm ready to go to sleep now. Goodnight." He reached over to the lamp on the nightstand and switched it off.

"Goodnight," said Jolene.

Several long minutes later, Joe muttered, "Damn."

"What is it?" asked Jolene.

"It's those girls. I wish I'd never met those girls. I was glad to help old Edgar. I really was. It gave me a good feeling inside, almost like I was a Christian or something, the way that Christians are supposed to feel. It's those girls—damn, they're impossible. Old Edgar might very well be dying, and all they care about is snitching his pain pills."

"I know, honey," Jolene said soothingly. "But let's not worry about it any more tonight, okay? Tomorrow's another day."

"Okay," said Joe. But it was not okay. Fretful, difficult hours passed before he finally fell asleep.

He had just begun to sleep soundly, dreamlessly, forgetfully, when the phone rang. Joe, closest to the nightstand, glanced at the alarm clock as he reached for the phone. It showed 3:17. "Hello," he muttered, his voice thick with sleep.

"Hello yourself," said a terribly nasal, whiny voice. It was Bobbie.

"Hello," Joe repeated a bit more clearly, as he struggled to wake more fully.

"This is Bobbie."

"Yeah—what do you want? Why are you calling so late? Is your dad okay?"

Bobbie ignored the latter question. "Blossom told me what you told her at the hospital today—you dirty old bastard you." Her speech was slurred by drink and drugs; still it related unmistakable malice and viciousness.

"Who is it?" asked Jolene. "What's wrong?"

Joe shushed his wife and then said into the receiver, "Nothing happened—do you hear me? Absolutely nothing happened. I don't know what Blossom told you, but—"

"That ain't the way I heard it," Bobbie interrupted. "I heard there was a whole lot goin' on with you and her at the hospital."

"Well you heard wrong. Listen—it's too late for you to be calling here. I have to go to work in a few hours, my wife too. Why don't you—"

"Yeah, okay—why don't you let me talk to your wife? I bet she'd like to hear all about you and Blossom today."

"You're drunk and you're talking nonsense," Joe replied hotly. He felt panic and anger, mostly anger. "I'm hanging up now."

"Okay—hang up. I'll call back some other time and talk to your wife."

Joe resisted the urge to scream "Go to hell!" and slam down the receiver. Instead he asked as levelly as possible, "Why are you doing this? I've tried my damnedest to help your dad—I took off from work and spent my time and my gas money driving him down to Nashville. All I've tried to do is help, and now you—"

"I know what you tried to do, you son-of-a-bitch. Blossom's done told me all about it. And I thought I could trust you with her—hah! You men are all alike! And you say you were just tryin' to help my dad—yeah, right. Tryin' to get in Blossom's pants is what you were doin'."

"That's not true," Joe stated emphatically. "I'm hanging up now."

"No you're not. Listen—you've done showed me I can't trust you no more. Next time, I'm gonna have to take my dad to the hospital myself—'cause I can't trust you."

"That's fine. You take him then. He's your father. He's your responsibility, not mine. Goodbye."

"Yeah, well—we need a new car. Not a brand new car or nothin', but somethin' better than what I got now. You need to loan us some money for a car. You need to loan us a couple thousand dollars for a car."

Amazingly, perhaps, Joe actually considered loaning her the money. He and Jolene had discussed giving her some money to have her car fixed. A couple thousand dollars—it'd almost be worth it to be rid of Bobbie and Blossom and the whole sordid mess once and for all.

Just then Joe heard Blossom clamoring in the background: "Tell him we want five thousand! He's got it, Mom, I know he does! Tell him we want five thousand!"

Joe immediately resolved a loan would not be forthcoming. "No, Bobbie—No. I'm not going to loan you any money."

"Then let me talk to your wife."

Again Joe felt like shouting obscenities and slamming down the receiver. Then suddenly he recalled an important, but previously forgotten, fact.

"Aren't you on probation, Bobbie? How about I talk to your probation officer?— tell her about you and Blossom getting high on Edgar's pain pills? I can tell her about that joint Blossom had, too. While I'm at it, I can tell her about you trying to extort money from me and my wife. I'll call the probation office first thing this morning…"

There was a brief silence. When Bobbie rejoined the conversation, her voice was markedly subdued and conciliatory.

"Hey, man—ain't nobody tryin' to extort nobody. I was just askin' for a little loan. You're such a *good friend* of the family and all, I thought maybe…"

"You thought wrong, and the answer is No. Now let me tell you something else," Joe began, vibrant with victory. "From now on, you're on your own. I am *not* driving Edgar to the hospital next month or ever again. He's your father and your responsibility, so *you* deal with it. I have my own family to take care of. And don't you ever call me or my wife again or I'll talk to your probation officer—you got that?"

"Hey, man—you don't need to be so radical. I know he's my dad and I want to take care of him, it's just… how 'bout a thousand dollars so I can get my car fixed? If you don't want to loan it to me, you can loan it to my dad and he can…"

"Not one thin dime," Joe stated forcefully. "You're on your own now. I've done all I can do, all I'm going to do, and that's all there is to it. Have a nice life."

Joe listened a moment or two for a response, but there was none. So he returned the receiver to its cradle.

Bobbie continued to sit at the little dinette table with the receiver held to her ear, staring stonily at nothing, initially unable to accept the finality and severity of Joe's rejection. Apparently she had some vague and mistaken hope that Joe might come back on the line and finally offer her money.

Blossom, seated to her right, chirped loudly, "So how much are we gettin', Mom? How much are we gettin'?"

Bobbie returned at once from the netherworld of misbegotten hopes and dreams. She slammed down the phone receiver, and then lashed out at Blossom with a quick right jab that landed squarely on her left cheekbone. Blossom's head snapped back so sharply that her neck would hurt for nearly as long as she'd sport her purplish-blue black eye.

"We ain't getting' nothin' thanks to you, you stupid little bitch," Bobbie shrieked. "He was all ready to give us a couple thousand and then *you* had to get greedy! You had to start hollerin' about five thousand dollars! You done fucked everything up—I hope you're proud o' yourself."

Blossom dashed from the table and took shelter in the bathroom, locking the door behind her. She gingerly daubed at the swelling under her eye with a cold damp washcloth, and watched in the mirror as the first blush of blue began to darken and spread.

Bobbie pounded angrily on the bathroom door and shouted, "Open this door! I ain't through with you yet! Open this door or I'll bust it down!"

"I'm sorry, Mom," Blossom called as plaintively as possible. Bobbie was perfectly capable of breaking down the door and giving her daughter a matching shiner. "I'm really sorry, okay? Please, Mom—you already busted me good."

Bobbie continued to rant and rage, and Blossom continued to plead for mercy, while about ten miles distant, Joe tried to settle his wife.

"I think that's the last we'll hear from her," Joe said. "Goodbye and good riddance. Now let's try to get some sleep. We have to get up in a few hours."

"Why would she think you'd loan her so much money?" asked Jolene. "A couple thousand dollars? I'd be reluctant to ask my folks for that kind of money."

Joe still hadn't told his wife about the dirty jokes, and he never would. "She's crazy, Jolene—just plain crazy, and she was drunk and probably high on Edgar's pain pills. If she was in her right mind she wouldn't have called here in the middle of the night to ask for a loan or anything else. She's just plain crazy—that's all."

"If she's that messed up, do you think she'll be able to get her dad to the hospital next month? I don't like her any more than you do, but I hate to think about the old man missing one of his chemo treatments. I want to call the VA tomorrow—later today, and see if they have some kind of ambulance service for invalid patients."

"That's fine," Joe said wearily. "But we need to get some sleep now."

"Okay Joe. Goodnight."

"Goodnight."

Last Words   28

Joe was not a happy camper at work. He'd claimed little more than an hour of sleep after talking to Bobbie, which brought his nightly total to maybe three hours. His eyes felt grainy, as if they were covered with a dusting of fine sand, and his mouth felt dry and nasty after drinking five cups of coffee, three more than his usual daily limit. He was supposed to be writing a product description of his company's latest and greatest addition to their fine line of air compressors, but after a few hours of unfocused effort he was still bogged down on the very first sentence: *Small and lightweight, the HAC-350 packs pound for pound more pressurized punch than many of its larger and heavier cousins.*

He didn't like the word *small*; it smacked of diminutiveness and inferiority, so he changed it to *compact* which, to his mind, sounded sturdy and respectable. *Compact and lightweight*—that didn't sound quite right; he didn't know why. He inverted the adjectives—*Lightweight and compact*... Better?—he wasn't sure. Nor was he satisfied with the word *cousins*. Perhaps, probably, it was too metaphorical, too poetic for a commercial product description. He changed it to *predecessors*, and wasn't satisfied. He tried *contemporaries*, and was even less satisfied. Enough with the personifications—he was describing a machine, damn it, a machine. *Lightweight and compact, the HAC-350 packs pound for pound*—no, make that *pound per pound*; more alliterative and mathematical, as if their engineers had figured it out precisely—*more pressurized punch than many larger and heavier machines.* But why call it simply and merely a machine when it was in fact an air compressor? And, by comparing the lightweight and compact new product to larger and heavier models, wasn't he making the latter sound comparatively cumbersome and clunky and outmoded?

Joe was persistently and pervasively distracted from the task at hand by the recollection of his phone conversation with Bobbie. Joe had never claimed to be the noblest or more virtuous man on the planet. But he considered himself to be, at the very least, a man of his word. And he'd told Edgar in no uncertain terms that he'd drive him to Nashville for his next chemo treatment, one day less than four weeks hence.

It wasn't his fault, Joe told himself repeatedly; it was Bobbie's fault that he no longer intended to honor his word. Still, he found little solace in his rightful assignment of blame and culpability. Further, he recalled having told Edgar during the homeward leg of their whiskey run that he'd be Edgar's friend as long as Edgar wanted him to be his friend. And Joe felt he was essentially abandoning Edgar in his time of greatest need. What kind of friend was that?

Joe was relieved, and not relieved, when Jolene called him at work that afternoon. "I have good news," she announced brightly. "I just talked to the VA, and they have a shuttle service that runs from the VA outpatient clinic in Bowling Green to the hospital in Nashville. We know that Flo and her husband can drive to Bowling Green, so that solves the problem, right?"

"Yeah, okay," said Joe. It was feasible enough, but it seemed cold and impersonal for poor, sick old Edgar to be shuttled back and forth by strangers.

"At least we don't have to worry about *that* anymore, right?" asked Jolene.

"Right," said Joe. "Thanks."

"I can call Flo and tell her if you want. I know you're pretty fed up with the situation. It's Flo Goody, right? Yeah, here it is in the phone book—Pete and Flo Goody…"

"No—no need to call her just now. Maybe I'll call her later."

"Okay then—I'll see you later, honey. I love you."

"I love you too. Goodbye."

It didn't seem an ideal solution to the transportation problem, but an ideal solution was not immediately necessary; Edgar's next chemo treatment was still nearly four weeks away. Maybe a better solution would present itself before then. Maybe Bobbie would get her car fixed, or something like that. Joe decided not to worry about it just then. He would worry about it later, maybe.

Joe returned to his mighty labors: *Lightweight and compact, the HAC-350 packs a powerful pressurized punch. Guaranteed to meet the everyday demands of homeowners and professionals alike…* No—he needn't *guarantee* anything; all new compressors were sold fully warranted. *Designed to meet the everyday…* No—*everyday* smacked of ordinariness; and he shouldn't infer that homeowners and contractors were demanding; nor should he imply alikeness between homeowners and professionals. *Designed to meet the needs of homeowners and professionals, this tiny titan...* No—it was compact, not *tiny*.

Joe called it quits a few minutes after eleven and took an early lunch.

Flo Goody called Joe at home that evening right after supper. "Thank you so much for taking Edgar down to Nashville yesterday. I talked to him this morning. You wouldn't believe how much he appreciates everything you've done for him. We all really appreciate it."

"You're welcome," said Joe. Immediately he began searching for a way to broach the topic of future transportation, but nothing immediately came to mind.

"You know he's supposed to take more chemo in four weeks, right?" Flo asked.

"Yes."

"Well, me and Pete have talked it over and we think we can drive him down to Nashville next time. We drive down to Bowling Green all the time, and Nashville isn't that much farther, really. It'll be like drivin' down to Bowling Green twice is all."

"Well, it's a little farther than that, but that's a good way of looking at it," said Joe.

"I hear Blossom went with you yesterday," said Flo. "What do you think of Blossom?"

"I'd rather not say."

"Oh, I know," Flo stated confidentially. "She's not as bad as her mother but she's headed down the very same road. I wish I could get them straightened out somehow but they don't want to have anything to do with me."

"Blossom told me about Edgar's son," said Joe.

"Mike? She told you about Mike, did she? I don't know what she told you but Mike was a really good boy, a wonderful boy. He was a good student and he went to church with us every Sunday and he never wanted to have anything to do with alcohol. We took him and Bobbie both after Edgar's wife died and he was drinkin' real bad and in jail most o' the time. We had a son of our own you know, and we always treated Mike and Bobbie the same as we treated our own, but Bobbie never did like neither one of us. She didn't like me and Pete both. But Mike was a really good boy. He begged us— Mike *begged* me and Pete not to make him go live with Edgar again when Edgar got out o' jail. Edgar was so mean to that poor child. He always made Mike do all the chores around the place so he could just lay around drunk and not worry about nothin'. Mike said he'd run away somewheres if he had to go live with Edgar again, so we kept him home with us. He was a really good boy. He went to church and he graduated from high school, Mike did."

"Whatever happened to him?" asked Joe.

"We don't rightly know. He took off after he graduated from high school. We got a letter from him maybe ten or twelve years ago. He was livin' in California somewheres, he didn't say where, but the postmark said San Francisco. There wasn't no return address so we couldn't write him back. I wish I knew how to get a-hold of him. I think he should know about Edgar bein' so sick and all."

Joe didn't respond.

Flo continued, "I wanted to tell you about Mike, but I was afraid you might say somethin' to Edgar about him and that wouldn't be good. Edgar's touchy about a whole lot o' things, but he's awful, *awful* touchy about Mike. Whatever you do, don't ever say anything about Mike, okay?"

"Okay."

"Well, I guess I'll let you go now. I just wanted to tell you that me and Pete think we'll be able to take Edgar down to Nashville the next time he has to go."

"Thanks," said Joe. "I'm very glad you called."

They said their goodbyes and hung up.

Joe told Jolene about Flo's offer to drive Edgar down to Nashville for his next chemo treatment.

"That's great," said Jolene. "Now you don't have to worry about it anymore."

"Right," said Joe.

But it wasn't right. Whenever Joe tried to picture or imagine Pete and Flo driving Edgar down to Nashville, his mind went blank. It wasn't that he doubted Pete's ability to drive that far. Perhaps he anticipated Bobbie causing trouble; he knew she hated her Aunt Flo. But surely Bobbie wouldn't be so mean and lowdown as to prevent her aunt and uncle from driving Edgar to a potentially lifesaving medical treatment. Nobody could be that mean and lowdown. Still, he wasn't satisfied that the matter of Edgar's transportation was resolved.

The weekend came and went. Sometimes Joe was able to ignore his concerns about Edgar's situation, and sometimes not. He slept poorly at nights, and he jumped whenever the phone rang. He stayed as busy as possible at work, but still he was plagued by doubts and worries, some nameable and some not.

On Tuesday afternoon, Flo phoned him at work. Her voice was very somber and serious and unnaturally formal. "I'm sorry to bother you at work, Mister Bass, but your wife said it would be okay."

"It's not a problem. Please, call me Joe."

"Joe, have you seen Edgar lately?"

"No, not since last week when I took him to the hospital."

"He's in a really bad way, Joe. He's *really* bad. He hasn't eaten a bite since he took that chemo. He won't even eat my biscuits and gravy. Me and Pete have been tryin' to get him to go to the hospital for the past three days but he says he won't go. He's a-layin' out on a blanket in the field by his trailer and he's just about too weak to walk. I don't know what to do. I thought it might help if you'd go talk to him."

"What do you want me to say?"

"Well, just tell him that he needs to let me and Pete take him to the hospital. He really needs to go. I'm sure he really needs to go."

"Is Bobbie causing trouble?" asked Joe. "Is she the reason Edgar won't let you take him to the hospital?"

"I don't know—maybe. Edgar ain't sayin' much to nobody. He's just a-layin' out there on a blanket and he won't talk and he won't eat and he won't go to the hospital."

"I think I should be able to get out there in maybe another hour or so," said Joe. "I'll see what I can do."

"Oh, thank you, Joe. Thank you so much. Maybe I'll see you over there. We were gonna go check on him again in a little while. If I don't see you there, call me and let me know what's going on, okay?"

"Sure," said Joe. "Goodbye."

Enough was enough. Joe didn't care if Bobbie had a gun or if she had a tank. Enough was enough. She needed to get over her problems with Flo and let her and Pete take Edgar to the hospital. Joe left his office and got in his truck and drove quickly to Bobbie's trailer. He rapped loudly on the door, and then he rapped some more.

Finally the front door swung inward. At three in the afternoon, Bobbie was dressed in her white terrycloth bathrobe. Her eyes were glazed and unfocused. She tried to focus them as she peered down at Joe. She also tried to smile; it was not a pleasant sight.

"Oh, it's you. I'm glad you're here," said Bobbie. "You need to take my dad to the hospital."

"I just talked to your Aunt Flo. She said she's been trying to take him for the past three days."

"I hate that bitch!" Bobbie screamed, her face contorting hideously. "She's not even a part of this goddamn family! My dad needs to go to the hospital, but if you don't want to take him why don't you go tell him that?!? He's layin' on a blanket over there in the field! Why don't you go tell him you won't take him to the hospital?!?"

"I didn't say I wouldn't take him. All I said was—"

"I heard what you said! I want you off my property *now*, goddamn it, and don't you ever come back! You're not welcome here no more!"

Bobbie slammed the door so hard every window in the trailer bulged out and its entire metal skin boomed like a big cheap drum. Joe got back in his truck and drove over to see Edgar.

Edgar was stretched out on an old army blanket, flat on his back, staring at the sky. He didn't move as Joe parked nearby, turned off the engine, and closed the door to his truck.

"Edgar?" Joe hailed as he drew near.

Edgar turned his head toward Joe and asked, "Joe? Is that you, Joe?"

"Yes, Edgar. It's me. I thought I'd come see you this afternoon. I hear you're not feeling too good." Joe intentionally kept his voice light and sweet, although he was still steaming from his confrontation with Bobbie.

"Right here is where we'll build 'er, Joe. Right here is where we'll build me a new log cabin. We'll build 'er up good and strong, Joe. We'll build 'er out o' solid oak. And once she's done we'll cook us up a good big batch o' shine to celebrate. That's one thing I know about, Joe, is makin' good shine. We'll cook it just right, Joe, not too fast and not too slow and then we'll double it down to make it smooth and clear."

Edgar's voice was weak and raspy and somehow impersonal, as if he wasn't talking directly or exclusively to Joe, but addressing a larger and unseen audience. Joe sat down cross-legged, Indian-style, directly in Edgar's field of vision.

"That sounds good to me, Edgar. But first we need to get you well.

We'll get you all finished up with your chemo treatments and then we'll build your cabin."

"I want me a big front porch on my new cabin, Joe. I didn't have me a porch on my old cabin, but we'll build us a nice big front porch facin' out over the lake and we'll sit up there in rockin' chairs and we'll drink us some shine."

"That sounds good, Edgar. It really does sound good. We'll do that just as soon as you finish up with your chemo."

"No, Joe—no more chemo. I'm afraid that ain't gonna help me none."

"Well, that's for the doctors to decide. I'm not a doctor and neither are you. We need to let them decide what's best."

"No, Joe—no more doctors. Flo's been tryin' to get me to go to the hospital but I ain't a-goin'. No more chemo, no more doctors—"

"How about I drive you down there, Edgar? We can go right now. You'll let *me* drive you to the hospital, won't you?"

"No, Joe—no thank you. But I appreciate all you've done for me Joe. I really do. I talked to Bobbie and Blossom both, and I told them that you're always welcome to fish here in my lake. It don't matter if I'm here or not. I told the girls that Joe Bass can fish in my lake anytime he wants. You and your son both—you're always welcome to fish in my lake. You have a son, don't you Joe?"

"Yes."

"He's always welcome here too, Joe. You be sure and bring your son along too. You and your son are always welcome here. I done already told Bobbie and Blossom that you and your son can fish here anytime you want."

"Thanks," said Joe.

"Flo thinks I'm mad at her but I'm not," said Edgar. "I just don't want to go to the hospital, that's all."

"Flo doesn't think you're mad at her," said Joe. "She just wishes you'd let her and Pete drive you to the hospital."

"Somethin' bad happened, Joe, and I'll tell you what it was. You remember when we was sittin' down by the lake one night and I was talkin' to ol' Sam?"

"Sam? Oh yeah, Sam—your pet bullfrog."

"Well, I was talkin' to Sam the other night and all of a sudden there was a big ol' splash and Sam let out a terrible scream and then he was gone. Somethin' got him, Joe. A big bass or a big catfish or maybe a big ol' snappin' turtle—somethin' got ol' Sam the other night and I ain't been the same since."

"That's too bad," said Joe. "But maybe you need to get over that and worry about taking care of yourself now. You look awfully weak, Edgar. Can you walk?"

"Yeah, Joe, I can still walk a little I guess. The girls have been helpin' me into my camper at night and I've been draggin' myself out in the mornings. But I ain't been the same since I lost ol' Sam. It's been awful quiet out here at night without him. I keep listenin' for him but he's gone, Joe. Somethin' got ol' Sam."

"What about you, Edgar? It's you that I'm worried about. Have you been taking your medications?"

"The girls are bringin' me a few pills ever' now and then, Joe. They've been bringin' me food too but I can't eat a bite. They're good girls, Joe. They really are. I know you don't think they are, but they are. They're doin' all they can to help me. They're doin' all what they know how to do."

"Yeah, okay, but they're not doctors, and you need to see a doctor."

"No, Joe—no more doctors. I'm just a little tired is all. I'll be alright after I rest up a spell. I'm just a little tired right now is all."

"Please let me take you to the hospital, please? Please, do it as a favor to me, okay? I've done favors for you, right? Now it's your turn to do a favor for me. Please, *please* let me take you to the hospital. You'll do that for me, won't you?"

"No, Joe—not today. Maybe we'll go down there one day next week, but I don't quite feel up to it today. Maybe we'll go one day next week."

Edgar turned his head away from Joe and closed his eyes. He was incredibly gaunt; his face looked like a skull with gray parchment stretched across it. His arms were folded neatly across his middle as if he were laid out in a coffin already.

Joe was choked with emotion. He was almost glad Edgar had discontinued their conversation because he didn't trust his voice not to crack and break. He felt very helpless. He wanted to help old Edgar but it seemed there was nothing he could do.

Joe didn't want to leave just then. He rose to his feet, stood a silent vigil over Edgar for about ten minutes, and then walked down to the lake. His legs, like his voice, had all but abandoned him. His legs were rubbery and weak.

Joe wearily, dejectedly, lowered himself onto a wooden bench. A large solitary cloud passed between him and the sun. It was close to seventy degrees outside, not at all cold, but Joe shivered in the sudden gloom.

A large green grasshopper landed on the tip of a slender blade of grass just at the water's edge. After a moment's hesitation it bounded off toward a different blade of grass. Its spindly arms and legs failed to find purchase and it fell onto the surface of the lake. Distressed and disoriented, it immediately kicked its powerful hind legs and scuttled not toward the bank, but away from it. Maybe the insect realized its mistake or maybe it was randomness; some seven or eight feet from shore the grasshopper turned in a big sweeping arc and headed in toward land and safety. Just when Joe was starting to think it would make it, a big bass rolled up beneath the bug and gulped it down.

On an ordinary day Joe would've been stricken with desire at the sight of a feeding fish, especially a large bass. He would've grabbed a fishing pole and hunted some grasshoppers to use as bait. But this was not an ordinary day. Joe gazed at the lake's darkness and its sloping banks and it looked like nothing but a giant pit filled with water—a giant trap. Insects and reptiles and amphibians and mammals and birds were all inexorably drawn to the water; they all needed water to live. But if they made one little misstep, as the grasshopper had made, it usually meant their death. Joe too had been drawn to the lake, like so many other animals. Sitting on the bench by the edge of the lake he felt a dark and mysterious and malevolent force trying to pull him in, trying to pull him down into the jaws of the trap, trying to claim him completely.

The cloud that earlier had blocked the sun moved off to the east and the sun came back out. Again Joe shivered. The shiver passed quickly and then Joe felt stronger, strong enough finally to escape from the trap. He stood up on steady legs and said aloud, "Goodbye, lake." Then he walked up the hill to say goodbye to Edgar.

"Are you awake, Edgar?" Joe asked softly.

"Joe? Is that you, Joe?" Edgar's eyes opened and his head turned slowly, ever so slowly. "I thought you were gone already."

"No—you know I wouldn't leave without saying goodbye. But I think I will be leaving now. Goodbye, Edgar."

"Goodbye, Joe. God bless you, Joe. You come back and fish anytime you want. You and your son both. It don't matter if I'm here or not. I already told the girls…"

"Thanks, Edgar. I appreciate that."

"I'll never forget you, Joe."

"I'll never forget you either, Edgar. Goodbye."

"Goodbye, Joe." Again Edgar closed his eyes.

Joe climbed in his big red Ford truck and fired the engine and started down the drive. He didn't look back at Edgar or the lake. When he was about thirty feet from Sycamore Church Road, a car turned into the drive in front of him. Both vehicles stopped immediately. It was Flo and her husband, Pete.

Flo leapt from her car and raced to Joe's open window. "Have you talked to him?" she asked excitedly, concernedly. "Will he let us take him to the hospital now?"

"No, I don't think so."

"Well, I hate to ask, but do you think you could take him? He's in a really bad way…"

"I know. I tried every way I could think of to talk him into it but he won't let me take him either."

Flo looked suddenly deflated. "He really needs to be in a hospital. I don't know what to do."

"The only other thing I can think of is to call an ambulance and have them pick him up and take him to the emergency room."

"We thought about that too," said Flo. "But Edgar says he's not goin' anywhere in anything, not to the hospital or anywhere else."

"Well, what if you called them anyway? He's too weak to fight. I don't see why they couldn't just pick him up and drive him off to the hospital."

"Well, no—I couldn't do that. When Edgar says No, then that means No. I couldn't do somethin' like that without Edgar sayin' it's okay."

"I couldn't either," said Joe.

"I just feel so *helpless*," said Flo. "I wish there was somethin' we could do."

"I know just how you feel," said Joe. "I'm sorry. But maybe there's nothing we *can* do for him now."

"There *has* to be somethin'," Flo said, frustrated, desperate.

"Maybe, but I don't know what it is. I'm sorry."

"I'm sorry too. I've brought him a little chopped-up turkey meat. I keep telling him he needs to eat somethin', even if it's just a few bites.

He really needs to eat somethin'…"

"Good luck," said Joe. "Call me if I can help."

Flo got back in her car. Joe backed into the neatly mowed field and let them pass and then he drove home.

Joe felt somber and subdued and respectful the rest of the week; he felt and acted as if he was in church. On Saturday morning, as he quietly finished his breakfast of ham and eggs and toast, the phone rang. He did not jump; he was not startled. A part of him had been expecting the phone to ring.

It was Royce Taylor. "I guess you heard about Edgar," said Royce.

"No."

"Well, Edgar died yesterday."

"Okay."

"It was real peaceful-like, they tell me. He was in the trailer with Bobbie and the girls and he died real peaceful with the girls holding his hands."

"I'm glad he died peacefully," said Joe.

"Yeah, me too. Well, I just thought I'd call and let you know. Edgar thought a lot of you and he really appreciated you tryin' to help and all."

"Thanks."

"Maybe I'll see you fishin' over there sometime," said Royce. "You're still gonna go fishin' there, ain't you?"

"Honestly, Royce, I don't think I will. It wouldn't be the same without Edgar there."

"You know, that's the way I feel about it too. I doubt I'll fish there either. I can't imagine fishin' there without ol' Edgar. It just wouldn't be the same, would it?"

"No," said Joe. "It wouldn't."

"Well, maybe I'll see you around then. You take care now. Goodbye."

Joe said goodbye and hung up the phone. Jolene was standing nearby. She already knew what had happened from Joe's half of the conversation with Royce, but she wanted to hear it from Joe.

"Edgar died yesterday," said Joe.

"I'm sorry," said Jolene. "I really am sorry."

"I know. Thanks."

Joe was walking out of the kitchen when the phone rang again. It was Flo.

"Have you heard about Edgar?" she asked.

"Yes. Royce Taylor just called me."

"I can't believe it," said Flo. "I always thought he'd make it somehow. I just can't believe he's gone."

"I'm sorry," said Joe. "Edgar was a remarkable man. They don't make 'em like that anymore."

"No they don't, do they?"

Joe did not respond. Flo continued.

"We're at the mortuary in Bowling Green. Edgar said he wanted to be cremated and he wanted his ashes scattered on his lake. There's not gonna be a funeral or nothin' but you can come here to visit if you want."

"I said goodbye to him the other day," said Joe. "I don't feel like I need to say goodbye again."

"Okay," said Flo. "I guess I can understand that. Do you want me to let you know when we scatter his ashes? It won't be nothin' fancy. Our minister is gonna say a prayer or two is all, and maybe we'll sing a little hymn."

"No," said Joe. "I already said goodbye. I don't think I… we already said our goodbyes."

"Well, okay. I guess I'll let you go then. I just wanted to make sure you'd heard about Edgar. He thought the world of you, Joe. Edgar really thought the world of Joe Bass."

"I thought a lot of him too."

"He was really a good man deep down in his heart," said Flo. "He had a lot of problems with his drinkin' and all but he always had a good heart."

"I know he did," said Joe.

Flo did not speak, but Joe heard little sniffling noises.

"Thanks a lot for calling," said Joe.

"Thank you," said Flo. "I know you really cared about him. Goodbye."

Joe said goodbye and hung up. To Jolene he said simply, "That was Flo." Jolene nodded respectfully.

Joe went out to the garage and putted around for a few hours. Thoughts of Edgar were foremost in his mind and he did nothing to push them away. Eventually he recalled his first encounter with Edgar at the dam. He saw the little old man with his red MARLBORO cap and his pointy white beard and his one-lens glasses and his sparkling turquoise-blue eyes and his beautiful, almost womanly smile.

And Joe smiled. Then suddenly his smile turned upside-down and he started to cry. It took him totally by surprise; he hadn't cried out loud in many, many years. But there he was, alone in his garage, and he was crying. It was very painful. It truly hurt Joe to cry. Whoever said that crying made a person feel better was totally wrong. It hurt to cry. It hurt a lot.

Joe cried for the better part of ten minutes and then he stopped. Immediately he felt much better. Crying did not make a person feel better, not at all, but he did feel much better after he stopped. Joe dried his eyes on his flannel shirt and took a few minutes to gather his composure and then he went back in the house.

His kids were on the sofa in the living room watching a Jim Carrey movie. Joe claimed a seat between them on the sofa and gathered them up next to him with his arms wrapped snuggly around them. Usually Joe thought Jim Carrey movies were silly and stupid. But Joe laughed out loud and then he laughed some more and he continued to laugh until the movie was over. Jolene came in the room a time or two and looked at him curiously, but said nothing.

When the movie was over, the kids left to play videogames. Joe went to the kitchen and picked up the phone and called his buddy, John Garner.

"Yeah, Joe. What's up?"

"Not much, John. I was wondering—do you have any plans for tonight?"

"No, not really. Were you thinking about going fishing, or…?"

"No—no fishing. I was thinking we might drive down to Bowling Green tonight and maybe drink a few beers."

"That sounds good to me, buddy. Do you want to drive, or…?"

"How about you drive? I might have more than a few."

John laughed and said, "That sounds good. What time do you want me to pick you up?"

Photo: Logan Heinz

Mark Heinz lives and works near Nolin Lake in Kentucky. This is his first novel.